The Dream Engine

Sean Platt
Johnny B. Truant

The Dream Engine

by Sean Platt &
Johnny B. Truant

The authors greatly appreciate you taking the time to read our work. Please consider leaving a review wherever you bought the book, or telling your friends about it, to help us spread the word.

Thank you for supporting our work.

Dedication

To our Fiction Unboxed backers, we couldn't have done this without you, and wouldn't have wanted to even if we could have. This has truly been an amazing experience. Thank you for everything you do to keep our creative lives so vibrant.

Welcome to Realm & Sands

We make reading fun. To get an early alert for the next book in *The Dream Engine* series, free books, and exclusive stories that you can't get anywhere else, visit the links at the end of this book.

THANK YOU FOR READING!

Sean Platt & Johnny B. Truant

The Dream Engine

Sean Platt
Johnny B. Truant

Chapter One
A Psychic at Solstice

TOWARD THE END OF THE midway, past the game barkers with their black top hats culling the crowd for pigeons, past the tents of oddities and unlicensed innovations, stood a great machine that had been unfolded from the backs of three flatcars on an east-west locomotive. Eila and Cora, who lived in the Rose Belt — walking distance from the empty field that bloomed into festival grounds at the solstice — had been watching it progress from parts to behemoth for days, in dribs and drabs as Eila's time off from the Ministry permitted.

Before its birth, the machine was nothing but struts and girders, pistons and clockwork. Then it was assembled, slowly taking shape, shifting into a new vision with every visit. Today, as the girls stood before its final form, the machine seemed like something terrible Eila might have Built at the Ministry as it came to her from the Aether … or from one of her troublesome visions. The behemoth stood a hundred feet tall, with giant gears and mechanisms swinging wide from a coil, side to side, up and down. On each cycle, a cloud of steam vented from a central boiler with a great hiss, as those strapped into it screamed for mercy.

"No." Cora looked upward. Her face was paler than usual, managing to make even her long, blonder-than-blonde hair seem dark by comparison.

"Yes," Eila said.

"Absolutely not. It looks like an instrument of torture."

Eila grabbed her friend's arm and pulled her forward as one of the machine's cogs seemed to slip out of groove. The coil dipped closer to the ground than it should have. But the machine had been

Built by someone and assembled by professional festival staff, which meant the slip was intentional: an awkward cog to give riders a thrill. If the design had a fault, the machine would never have been Built. As Rabbit Brampton always blabbed on about in the media, the Ministry of Manifestation didn't Build mistakes.

"That's the idea, Cora. It's *supposed* to be like torture. You're supposed to feel like you might die when you ride it. If you're not scared, it's not worth the rittern we paid to be here."

Eila kept tugging, but Cora stayed rooted. She was only fifteen, thin enough to tip in a breeze … but for Eila, the same age and only slightly larger, dragging her still wasn't simple.

"No way, Eila. You ride it. There's no way I'm going to."

"You rode the coaster!" Eila protested.

"The coaster is a coaster. Up, down. No big deal. But this thing?" Cora looked upward, her face like someone staring a demon in its eyes. Despite Eila's grip, her arms had moved up and shifted her sketch bag aside, crossing tightly across her chest, as if hugging herself to stay warm.

"We've been talking about riding it since we saw it unloaded. I said, 'I've never seen anything like it. Can you imagine riding it at the festival?' and you said the same thing."

"Yes, Eila. I said the same thing. Like this: 'Oh Crown, I've never *seen* anything like it! Can you imagine *riding it at the festival?*'" Cora shivered to prove her repulsion.

"You promised you'd ride with me."

"I did not!"

"You're being a baby."

"If you want to ride, go ahead! I won't stop you. But I'm not riding with you."

"It's safe!" Eila insisted. "How could it have been Built otherwise?" Eila's body language salted her indignation with scorn. The comment wouldn't have the same effect on Cora as it would on another Builder (Cora worked as an aide when she bothered to work at all), but Cora had seen just as much Ministry propaganda as anyone else with a viewbox in their living rooms. Even without being a Builder, she should know better.

"The festival staff could have put it together wrong."

Eila managed not to roll her eyes. "It's been running all day. Has it fallen apart?"

"That doesn't mean it won't fall apart later. Even if it doesn't, just look at it! What makes you think I want even a 'safe' ride on it?"

Eila couldn't win this argument. Cora's tone had shifted. She'd played along with Eila's good-natured goading, but the Shuttle Shaker terrified her for some reason and she wouldn't ride it no matter how much Eila pestered. In a way, Eila could sympathize. Over the past two weeks, she'd learned better than most what it felt like being frightened to the core.

Eila closed her eyes and sighed. In the blink of darkness, she saw a long-fingered hand, its fingers gnarled bark come to life. She saw a boy, his smile full of mischief, his hair a nest of messy black, calling and waving her closer. She saw yellow eyes, their pupils like horizontal bars rounded at the edges, like the capsules of Crumble in the vial on her nightstand.

Eila's eyes snapped open. She didn't want to think about that. Not in the bright light of the year's longest day. Or, ideally, ever again.

"Okay." She let go of Cora. "We can play a game. Or see a show. You choose."

"Games." Cora half sneered. "Festival games just make you feel stupid. And that's just the *legitimate* ones. Half of the gamesmen have pickpockets for partners; they'll steal you blind while you play."

Eila looked down at Cora's dress. It was nearly long enough to brush the ground — a dirty, dappled brown that made her hair and skin seem almost snow white. Her waist was tiny enough that Eila thought she'd probably worn her corset as if headed to a ball. The clockwork coaster couldn't have been comfortable, riding with a circle of bones shoving her waist toward her middle.

"You don't even *have* any pockets," said Eila, who was wearing a much more summery, much more casual dress. Eila's came to just below her knees and had an open neckline. Cora's neck was almost throttled by her own dress — tight like the leather-and-buckles chokers worn by some of the showier gameswomen.

"I have a bag, don't I?" said Cora, patting the satchel she seemed to always carry, her sketchbook and pencils hidden safely inside.

She put a hand on one hip and looked back across the midway. The festival had been set up in a field on the outskirts of Waldron's Gate, but scarce rain had turned dirt into shriveled clods, the usually lush grass flattened by tromping feet. The sides of the field were lined with tents, teeming with games and shows. Cora's gaze turned toward one side, toward the performers showcasing their wares.

"Oh, I guess we could go see the psychic," Cora sighed. "If you *must*."

Eila stifled her smile. Cora wanted to see the psychic almost as much as she did — but for Cora, their tickets to a session with Palpatine Malvern meant mere entertainment as they would for anyone other than Eila. Cora's protests were bogus: resisting to recover her dignity after backing away from the Shuttle Shaker.

"If you'll *allow* me," said Eila, still holding the smile down, "that would be great."

"Sure. But you know it's stupid."

"Of course."

"And a waste of money."

Eila shoved Cora as they turned toward the entertainer tents. She'd protested enough. Eila would get over her disappointment; the Shaker would be there next season, if not something better. They could stop vying for each other's festival time and get back to just being friends. And *as* friends, they knew a visit to Malvern could never be a waste of money. With his ample fame, the girls were lucky the psychic had even set up at the festival. Even though the song and dance they'd both seen him do during stage shows for the Gate's wealthiest women cost thirty ritterns, Cora would see it as money well-spent just to be near the city's most charming entertainer.

Eila, on the other hand, had watched Malvern's biggest predictions and believed he had at least some genuine abilities — a secret hope she hadn't admitted to Cora lest she seem stupid. Maybe he could help her with the visions that had been plaguing her. Or, at least, tell her whether she was losing her mind.

"Oh, it's only thirty ritterns."

Cora said, "That's more than I make in a week."

Eila rolled her eyes, no longer able to help it. She gave Cora another shove, slightly harder than the first. She didn't need to say what she was thinking, because they both knew it. Cora's family, despite having less prestige than Eila's household of Builders, was actually one of the wealthiest on the Row. Her job existed mostly to keep her occupied. Her employer was one of her mother's phenomenally wealthy society friends, and Cora came and went as she wanted. Whatever tasks she didn't want to do (or wasn't present for) were handled by the woman's servants. Thirty ritterns may have been more than a week's salary for *most* hardworking aides, but Cora wasn't one of them. She was a rich girl who sometimes did odd jobs because her parents wanted her out of the house and wanted to try to teach her some appreciation for rittern. Cora would never know what it meant to work in a fabrication mill or own a small dry goods store, earning a few hundred ritterns a year and budgeting every bit for food and home.

"He's a sham, you know," said Cora. She was smiling, because it was part of the game. She'd just suggested heading to the psychic, but it was Eila who'd birthed the idea in the first place. Eila didn't normally believe in psychics more than any reasonable person — and especially not showy ones like Malvern — but after having seven frightening visions in two weeks (each of which she'd shamefully recorded in her journal, buried like treasure), she'd been ready to grasp at straws. Besides, seven was a lucky number — even if it counted visions that might mean you were losing your mind.

She'd booked and paid for an appointment with the psychic as soon as she'd heard he was coming to the festival. At this point, *not* going would be a waste of money.

"Let it go, Cora. It'll be fun."

Eila looked over at her friend as they walked, trying to decide if Cora knew about Eila's hope that Malvern's abilities would end up being real. But Cora's profile, looking forward, told her nothing.

They found Malvern's tent easily. It was the largest and showiest — more like a circus tent than a vendor's. It was brightly colored, parapets jutting from the top like a city building with walks and balconies. The tent stood proud but sagging on a square of land three times larger than those occupied by the other psychics. Eila was certain, looking at it and thinking of Malvern as he appeared in broadcasts and photos, that he hadn't paid one rittern more than anyone else for his spot. He'd either charmed his way into a better plot or demanded it. If The Great Palpatine Malvern were to grace the Waldron's Gate Solstice Festival, he would receive the royal treatment — or he wouldn't come at all.

There was a line outside the tent, but a man in barker's attire shooed their arrival, trying to get them to leave.

"I'm sorry, girls," said the man as Cora and Eila approached. "Private readings only. His Omniscience is sold out — the folks inside with foresight to book their appointments paid a premium for their privacy."

Eila pulled two slips of paper from her bag. "We have appointments."

The man looked at the slips, tested the seals' authenticity using a device with multicolored lenses on the table at his side, then looked up with something like embarrassment.

"I'm so sorry, I thought you were … I mean … oh, well, you know how it is here. And you're so young."

"Lots of our friends are going to see psychics today," said Cora.

"Well, yes, maybe the hucksters. But for a genuine reading from Mr. Malvern … most people serious enough about their futures to pay the fee are older."

Cora rolled her eyes so that only Eila could see. What they'd booked with Malvern was no more "serious about their futures" than what other girls were doing with unknown psychics in smaller huts. They were at Malvern's at Eila's insistence, and because they could afford it. Cora probably assumed Eila had wanted a premium experience (the kind of entertainment Malvern was known for), but in truth, Eila had insisted on "His Omniscience" for a different reason. She believed that most — not all — psychics were fakes. But if *some* psychics were real, Malvern might very well be one of them.

Cora shrugged, choosing not to volunteer the sources of their income. If Malvern's assistant wanted to know, he could ask the psychic.

With a nod, the man vanished. The girls found themselves alone, listening to the nearby sounds of walkers outside the tent, the distant riding of rides, and a far-off motor somewhere above, probably a skyship.

After a few moments spent in the tent's anteroom, a man with salt-and-pepper hair and a modest, mostly white beard parted the flaps to the inner chamber. Thankfully, he wasn't in full show garb. He was wearing a simple suit, a small and somewhat flat-top hat, and black gloves that made his hands almost invisible in the dimly lit tent. Eila had seen him wear a cape in broadcasts, but he spared them one now.

"Ah, Cora," said Malvern, looking mystically into Cora's eyes. "I've been expecting you."

"Of course you have," she said, with a sarcastic glance to Eila.

"And you, Eela."

Cora scoffed. Malvern gave her a look.

"It's pronounced 'eye-lah,'" Eila corrected.

"Of course." Malvern smiled. *"Eila."*

Again Cora snorted, and again Malvern shot her a look. The greeter must have handed the tickets to the psychic behind the curtain, but he'd pronounced the name wrong in his attempt to dazzle them with his mind-reading. Malvern probably thought he'd bagged a pair of pigeons, and now had feathers in his face.

"Who would like to go first?" Malvern asked.

"You tell us," said Cora.

Malvern's voice was curt. "I always demur to the in-the-moment whims of my subjects."

"You go first, Cora."

Eila was eager for her own reading, but she was also nervous. Her true reason for being here suddenly felt raw and blistering: She'd spent time in a world that existed solely inside her mind, and wanted to know why even though she was terrified to find out. Maybe the psychic, if he was *truly* psychic, would be able to tell her how to rebuild whatever dam had shattered inside her. Or maybe he'd tell her that she was losing her mind and should book herself into Joffrey Columns with the rest of the insane before the decision was forced upon her.

"You too, then," said Cora.

"I'll go after."

"I meant, you sit in on my reading." She looked at Eila, her eyes pleading. This was all in fun, but like the Shuttle Shaker ride not taken, the experience of a phony psychic reading was (in Cora's mind, anyway) better when shared. And although she didn't want to say it, she didn't want to be alone in a room — even if it was a room in a tent — with Palpatine Malvern.

"Okay, but you can't sit in on mine," said Eila.

"Are you afraid he'll declare your crush on Victor?" Cora scoffed. "I don't need a psychic to know that."

Cora laughed as Eila raised her eyebrows, giving her the look she'd practiced in the mirror just that morning. Eila had serious brown eyes lined with long, dark lashes. Her stare told Cora the deal: she could take it or leave it, all jokes aside.

"Okay, fine," said Cora, deflated.

Malvern held the tent's drape back, and the girls entered under his arm. Inside the inner room, they found no outlandish props, which made Eila immediately hopeful. No crystal balls, wands, or showy clockwork kaleidoscopes promising truth — just a simple table in the middle of the large chamber, surrounded by three unimpressive, cheap-looking chairs. Apparently, either Malvern or his assistant had been psychic enough to guess that they'd want to do at least one of their readings together.

Malvern held out chairs for each girl in turn, then sat on the other side. He removed his gloves, put his hands on the table, and turned them palms up toward Cora, inviting her to take them with her own. She did.

"You're a skeptic," he said.

Cora gave a tiny laugh. To Eila's surprise, Malvern's mouth made a smile. Small, but not without humor.

"You could say that."

"And you don't mind admitting it to me?"

"I don't like keeping things to myself."

"How do you think I'm going to deceive you?"

"We had to make reservations. You've known our names for weeks. You could have researched us."

"What else?"

"You have our rittern, probably in an account rather than here. You know that even if we don't like the reading, we almost certainly won't demand it back, because it would require time and paperwork.

You'd need to send pneumatics back and forth with your bank to make it happen."

Malvern chuckled.

"This is funny to you?" It was all in good fun, but Cora couldn't stand condescension. He could insult her if he wanted, but it was below the belt to act superior.

"A little. Tell me: what might I have learned in this research?"

"Where we live. Who we know. That I'm an aide and that Eila is a Builder."

"Third-generation Builder, I believe," said Malvern. "At least, that's what my research would have told me."

"But not, apparently, how to pronounce Eila's name."

"Contact is always different. Sometimes I see things. Sometimes I hear. I did not *hear* Eila's name. Which, by the way, is lovely."

Cora narrowed her eyes. "Isn't this *my* reading?"

"Your name is mundane," Malvern said. "As is your skepticism."

Cora started to rise.

Malvern kept hold of her hand. "But wait. I haven't had a chance to tell you what you want to hear."

Cora pulled harder, but Malvern held fast.

"Because that's what I do, isn't it? I tell women what they want to hear. I'm glitz and glam, not a molecule more. That's what you've told Eila over and over and over, including that time you talked her into taking an unscheduled break, ducking out of the Ministry when Mr. Brampton had his back turned because someone had broken a lens on one of the collectors. Doesn't it seem bit risky — taking a girl brand new to her job, with but a week's tenure, away from her station, no matter *who* her father might be? You don't know how the machine works, do you, Cora? What if you had severed her from the array during Pianoforte, when the—?"

"Let go of my hand!" Cora cried out.

Sitting stiff in her chair, Eila said, "Sit down, Cora." Her voice was smooth but barely calm.

Cora obeyed, silent in her chair, looking bewildered at Eila.

Nobody outside the Ministry of Manifestation knew of Pianoforte. *Nobody.* Eila was afraid to acknowledge that Malvern had struck a nerve — not in Cora, but in her — for fear of what it might mean.

"Shall we continue?" Malvern asked.

"You won't let go of my hand anyway," Cora said.

"But do you believe me? Because if you don't believe me, I'm wasting my time."

Cora gave a small, angry shake of her head. Looking over, Eila saw wet eyes. Cora was willing herself not to cry because the psychic, being a man, might think she was scared or beaten instead of angry.

"No."

"Let her go," said Eila. Cora might be out of sorts, but Eila had learned what she needed to know. "Give her rittern back."

"But the pneumatics," said Malvern in an almost singsong tone, clearly enjoying his victory. "The bank."

Cora snatched her hand back. "I could report you."

"You wouldn't be the first," he said. "But you were wrong about me in another way. Before I do a reading, I take the fee out of a safe and keep it close. I *want* to refund those who aren't happy, you see? It happens so seldom that I have more money than I'll ever need. It's worth it to have convinced a nonbeliever."

He reached into his jacket and removed a pale yellow envelope. The flap was sealed with wax, stamped with what looked like a map of Alterra surrounded by stars and planets. He laid it on the table, then pushed it toward Cora.

Cora broke the seal and opened the envelope. Inside were six five-rittern bronze coins.

"This is only thirty," said Cora. "We paid sixty."

Instead of answering, Malvern's eyes moved toward Eila. Seeing them, Cora's eyes followed until they were both focused on her, waiting for Eila to speak.

"I still want my reading," she explained.

"After *that?*"

"I need to be alone, though. Can you wait outside?"

"Eila, are you crazy?"

I sure hope not, she thought.

"Just a few minutes, okay?"

"I can't leave you in here with him. He'll rip you off. He'll take advantage of you."

"He already has my money and just gave you yours." She turned her eyes from Malvern to Cora. "And if your concerns lie elsewhere, I'm fast and good with my fists." It was true. From birth, Eila's family had known she had the mental talent to be a Builder, but her father was unwilling to let Eila settle into a life of high-paid luxury. The family, thanks to both of her parents' enviable positions, had everything they wanted, but they'd made Eila work menial jobs to teach her one set of life's lessons… and taught her to defend herself in order to school her in another.

"Eila … "

Eila's eyes flicked toward Malvern, who was patiently waiting for the friends to decide.

"Please, Cora."

She began to retort, then met Eila's gaze. Her shoulders drooped. Her eyes rolled up, and she shook her head slowly, sighing.

"Your funeral. I'll be outside."

"Meet me at the Carnival of Curiosities." Eila didn't want Cora right outside. They were in a tent, not a building, and sound traveled.

Cora nodded. Then, after another moment's hesitation, she walked out.

When Cora was gone, Malvern extended his arms and again laid his hands on the table, palms up. They'd snapped into business as usual, as if nothing strange had just happened. She was the client of a psychic … but at least now she knew he was legitimate.

Eila reached out and laid her hands in his. They were surprisingly smooth, as if lotioned, powdered, and ignorant of toil.

"You're hiding something," he said.

Eila wasn't sure about that. She'd lied to Cora about her visions, but mostly she'd said nothing either way. "A little."

"It's curious. It's as if you've raised a wall. Let it down. Let me in."

Eila tried, but there was nothing to release within herself. "I can't."

"It's like there's a diverging road inside you," he said, apparently able to proceed without entry. "Tell me: where do you live?"

"Here, in Waldron's Gate."

"Among the roses, I see. And what is the machine room to you?"

"I work in the Ministry of Manifestation." But Malvern knew

that already, along with the untellable things he'd mentioned to Cora not five minutes earlier.

"This isn't the Ministry I see. It's … "

In front of Eila, Malvern froze. His mouth was open mid-word, as if he'd realized something. Or had been shocked into silence.

"There's a door," he said. "Open the door."

"What door?"

"In your mind."

"You said it was a wall."

"You're a Builder, yes?" Then, without waiting for a reply: "You Build ideas that are served to you by the Ministry's engine. But you — you *know* where those ideas come from, don't you?"

Eila shrugged. "From the Aether."

"I sense more. I *see* more. There is a doorway."

"I don't know what you're talking about," said Eila.

Malvern was barely listening. He seemed to be asking Eila questions while talking to himself.

"You live in the house. You work in the Ministry. That is one place. But it's like you live somewhere else. Like one of those photos in the curiosity tents, where a trickster has laid one image over another, to convince festivalgoers that it is a single thing: a strongman with an alligator tail. A woman with a snake's head in place of her own. It's like you live in both places at the same time." With his eyes closed, the psychic scrunched his brow into a knot. "What *is* this other place? And how are you able to live in both?"

"I don't understand what you're asking," she said.

But although she didn't understand Malvern's questions, he was describing exactly what she *felt*. Most of the time she was Eila Doyle, living in Waldron's Gate with her family, attending her new job at the Ministry. She walked clean streets under blue skies peppered with Parliament's protective flying machines, took her Crumble pills every few hours the same as anyone, and stayed far away from the Fog that surrounded Alterra. But sometimes she woke not to her room and bed … but instead to another reality. She would see a boy with black hair beckoning her closer, his face and hands smeared with soot and grease. A reality where up was sometimes down, where you could run from a beast and feel as if your feet were in sap, where creatures of legends fled lore for reality, where scenes unhinged like loose carpentry and terrifying fires burned unabated. The black-haired boy, watching her. Searching. Calling in whispers. *His* thoughts somehow inside her as creatures of fantasy, alive for real, gnashed their claws and tried to grab her.

Malvern's deep green eyes opened.

"Tell me of this other place. I see it plainly, but I can't tell how or when you have visited." He shivered as he added, "Or why you ever would."

Eila looked at him for a long time. She'd come for answers. Malvern might not have them, but holding back fenced in his chances.

"I came to you because … "

"I know why you *came*," he said, sounding almost annoyed. "You came because you are terrified. But I cannot say why you are terrified. You have memories … of your past? It is hard to say. They cannot hurt you now. But still, I don't understand these memories. I know of no place in Alterra that matches what is inside you. And I don't know why, but two images seem to co-exist inside you. At times, you are not in one place or the other: *here* now, then *there* later on. At those times, I see you in both places at once."

"Am I losing my mind?" The words sounded awful out loud, but at least they were no longer rotting inside her.

Malvern shook his head. "I don't know." No hesitation, or any attempt to soften the blow.

"It's like you said," she went on. "When I'm in that place, it's like I'm there. When I'm not, it doesn't even exist! I don't travel to get there, and don't have any idea where it is or *what* it is. And I don't know who that *boy* is!" The last came out as an exclamation, and Eila suddenly realized she was desperate, angry, and afraid all at once. The boy had been dogging her throughout the terrifying mental interludes, showing up with the same dirty face, the same dirty clothes, the same white circles around his eyes left clear by the goggles slung at his neck. He was always waving, always calling. He *pursued* her. Even now, from somewhere, Eila felt watched, as if he were calling her on a different frequency. She felt that if she could flip her mind's tubes to his channel, she'd see him right now, plain as day.

"You don't know him? It feels like you know him."

"He's there when I sleep, waiting, like hiding behind a veil, and … "

"When you *sleep?*"

Eila stopped speaking, her pattern interrupted. "Yes."

"Does this *always* happen when you sleep? Is that when you go to this other place?"

"It doesn't happen *every time* I sleep but it only happens *when* I sleep. Why?"

Malvern chewed his lip, seeming to think. "Has it always been this way?"

"What way?"

"Going to another place when you sleep. Seeing things as you doze."

"Of course not!"

"Think carefully."

"No! Who goes to another place when they sleep? How can you see something when you sleep? It's like being dead. Do *you* travel when you sleep?" Eila asked it like an insult.

"No, of course not, but … "

"Is it a magic thing? Have you heard of anyone somehow … I don't know … *thinking* while they sleep?" It sounded stupid to say aloud, but she'd come this far. Any answer was better than none. Still, the idea was ridiculous. The mind shut down during sleep. By definition, you couldn't think when unconscious.

"Magic?"

"Yes! Magic! You're a psychic!"

"What I do isn't that different from what you, as a Builder, do every day," he said. "'Magic' is something for lore. And to answer your question, no, I've never heard of … " He stopped, thinking. "It just gives me a different way to think about it, because if you're asleep when you go away, it means … " He let go of Eila's hand to scratch his face, then took it again.

"What?"

"Do you quiet your mind when you receive objects from the machine at the Ministry? When you hear the Aether?"

What Eila did every day required a fair amount of training.

Builders learned to blank themselves so they were open to receive, but Building was done amid noise and chatter, the sounds of spinning gears and turning wheels. Quieting the mind was a key skill.

"Yes," she said.

"Can you do it now?"

"Maybe."

He nodded. "Try."

Eila closed her eyes, then slowly found herself sinking into the Build trance. She saw her construct behind her lids: a large, stark white, empty warehouse. She made the picture, then let the tip of her mind slip into nothing. Her final thought, before vanishing from her own image, was that she was almost *in* the warehouse, ready to receive from the Aether. In a way, it was about thinking while not thinking, as if asleep. The thought gave her chills.

Then she forgot it and everything else, and was gone.

Eila woke up to screaming. She snapped her head up and found Malvern pushing himself back, tripping over his chair, spilling it and himself to the floor.

"What?" she said, standing to see the psychic on the ground, his wide eyes now terrified.

"I can't help you," he blubbered.

Eila thought she might have heard Malvern incorrectly. It was the strangest thing for him to say as he slithered backward on his elbows.

"What do you mean?"

He slowly came up, his gaze again finding focus. He dusted his suit with his hands and righted the chair. "I said, 'I can't help you.'"

"Why not? What's wrong?"

"Your reality bends too far. I can't see meaning. But you *do* travel. You *do*, Miss Doyle. I don't understand it, but I'm not willing to return to where you just took me. Your mind has a missing division inside. It's as if you are insane … but also as if you're not. Your mind believes things that cannot be, and yet they *can* be. I don't know how I know that, but it's true. The unreal things you see are *real.* Somehow, somewhere. And I fear their approach."

This wasn't what Eila wanted to hear. It was terrifying to think about, and to see how frightened Malvern had become. He could back away from what he'd seen in her mind, but she could not. The visions came whether Eila liked it or not. Some of them held creatures from the darkest of Alterran lore — storybook monsters, the realm of the Citadel, goblins, more. She didn't want to be at their mercy, but without his help there would be no escape.

Malvern reached into his pocket as he had earlier and withdrew a second pale yellow envelope. Inside, Eila could hear the jingle of coins. He shoved it at her but did so cleanly, taking care to keep his hands from touching hers.

"Here. Now, go."

"But … "

"You must leave. I'm sorry. I cannot help you."

She took the envelope, then tried to force it back at Malvern. He retreated as if she were infected. "I don't want my money back," she said. "I want you to finish my reading!"

"Keep the money. Go. Just *go.*"

"I'll pay you double! I'll pay all you want!"

"I'm sorry," he said, now casting glances for his assistant. "It isn't a matter of money."

"It has to do with sleep? With my Building trance?"

"The trance gave me a door to open inside you. I did not like what came through. If I were you, I'd keep my back to that door, forever."

"I can't control what happens when I sleep!"

Malvern's assistant arrived at Eila's back and put a hand on her arm. The hand wasn't forceful, but its intention was clear.

With pleading eyes, in a softer voice, edging tears, Eila repeated: "I can't control what happens when I sleep. *Please.*"

"Then *watch* the door I opened in your mind, if you can," said the psychic. "Because there's something you can do that nobody should be able to do, and if you allow what's behind that door to escape —" He shook his head and bit into his lip, "— you'll change the world."

Feeling the assistant's grip on her arm, Eila began to step backward reluctantly, away from Malvern.

"I'll 'change the world?'" she said.

Malvern nodded. "Yes," he said. Then he swallowed. "Or destroy it."

Chapter Two

The Pianoforte

That night, Eila slept terribly.

She'd feared the strange visions since they'd started, but for some reason she'd never connected them with sleep. She spent much of her Ministry time in a sleep-like state, and those visions felt like walking through reality. Now that she'd realized, sleep felt like a dangerous place. Now, she had Malvern's odd warning to keep her frightened.

She'd met Cora at the Carnival of Curiosities and tried to forget what Malvern had said, dismissing it as the playful, scam-laden experience that Cora would say it was. They rode rides, played a few games with Cora good-naturedly grumbling about how they were rigged to make everyone look stupid while keeping her eyes peeled for pickpockets. Malvern never came up.

It should have made Eila feel better and allowed her to forget, but it did the inverse instead. Cora had felt violated, then ripped off when leaving the tent. Normally, that would get her grousing for hours. But she'd said nothing, which seemed almost like a conscious omission. Maybe she'd been more shaken by Malvern's prescience than she'd shown. Or perhaps Cora had disobeyed Eila's request to leave the area during her reading and had instead stayed near to protect her friend, possibly with an ear to the canvas wall.

Still, nothing was said as afternoon turned to evening. Eila stuffed the experience down, then in the fading sun left Cora with a promise to meet soon. She went home, had dinner with her family, and prepared for nighttime. Through most of the day, Malvern's words had stayed low. But as the sun fell, her experience grew barbs, reminding Eila in spurts of what had been said, and implied.

Malvern had said her visions were real. He'd suggested that she was broken, teetering at the edge of sanity's willowy rim. He'd said that she really *did* travel. That Eila could, somehow, be in two places at once.

By implication, it also meant that the boy in her vision was real. The boy who screamed in whispers and beckoned her closer. He *existed*, and was calling her to a place that was true. She didn't want to follow, him … but if he kept calling, she didn't know if she could refuse.

He was real.

The boy in the dark place who haunted her — watching, as if he were over her shoulder, or outside her window as skies over Waldron's Gate grew dark.

She'd laid her head on her pillow, closed her eyes, and feared traveling to that place. She'd been terrified of seeing those creatures, and of everything Malvern had said as she replayed the encounter repeatedly in her mind.

His frightened eyes, filled with terror and warning.

His suggestion that the creatures were coming closer, and that what was within her might change the world … or destroy it.

It was crazy. Insane.

And yet, unsurprisingly, sleep refused her.

Eila drifted and dozed in bits and pieces, then felt beaten thin overnight. She took her Crumble to settle her nerves, shared another meal with her family (she was nearly incoherent at this one, as if she were seeing the world through gossamer), and was preparing to spend her day's remainder in recovery, sleeping in the bright daytime sunlight where she'd be safer. But before she could lie down again, the Ministry called to announce that the machine was in Pianoforte — and that all Builders with no dire excuses were required to report immediately.

She rode the trolley to the Ministry with her father, feeling as if she were in a daze. Atwell was Head on the Enigma Floor (a separate section of the Ministry with a different schedule) and it was strange for them to take the same trolley at the same time, as necessitated by the mass summons.

Eila knew all about Pianoforte, but this was her first emergency summons and she'd never Built during one. She'd only been at the

Ministry for a month, since turning fifteen (the earliest age at which someone with an aptitude was permitted to Build) and Pianofortes came at random times. Nobody was exactly sure how they worked or why they happened when they did, so they were impossible to predict or plan for. All anyone knew — from lowly Eila to top scientist Rabbit Brampton — was that the best and most important Building happened during Pianoforte. According to legend, the first zeppelin had been Built during a Pianoforte. Same for the first locomotive, the map that became the Waldron's Gate city grid, the communication system, pneumatic and broadcast technology, and so much more. Even Crumble's formula was rumored to have been Built during a Pianoforte. And without Crumble, Alterra would be lost.

Once inside, Eila and her father parted. Atwell headed upstairs to the Enigma Floor, where the most analytical, application-based Building was done. Eila — who was just getting used to the enormous, sterile building of bright whites and vibrant colors, machinery gleaming from its many chambers — walked toward Aether Forefront, where the everyday of Alterra was crafted bolt by bolt.

The entire Ministry was in orderly chaos. The clear tubes snaking across the walls and ceilings were alive with activity, carriers dropping from their ends with the hollow thumps of released pressure. As Eila made her way through the central space, she watched carriers streak from one room to another. Well-dressed workers scrambled from place to place, most with huge clutches of paper and tattered books with overtaxed spines pressed to their chests. To Eila, everyone looked both burdened and excited. It was fascinating to see the workers' usually composed faces coming undone: men with carefully waxed mustaches tripping over women with orderly hairdos in buns.

Hard-soled shoes and heels clacked across the echoing chamber as Eila arrived to find Rabbit Brampton standing with his back to her, hands on his hips, fists against the sides of his expensive-looking gray suit. She tried to sneak by, but he immediately saw her and turned.

"Miss Doyle. So nice to see you. Took your time getting here, I see. It's not like there's urgency or anything. Please, have a cup of cafei if you'd like."

"I don't drink cafei." Right now, Eila wished she did. So many people swore by its ability to wake them. She'd tried it once, found it intolerably bitter, and hadn't tried again. She'd been told it was better with milk and sugar, but had yet to bother. If Brampton's sarcasm wasn't so thick, she might have tried it just to clear her sleep-deprived cobwebs.

"Maybe you don't realize it, but we're nearing Pianoforte," Brampton rushed on, not giving Eila a chance to defend herself. Not only had she been alerted quite loudly that Pianoforte was coming, but she'd been in Build training for years. It was her first Pianoforte as a Builder, yes, but Eila knew exactly what it meant, chaotic though things may have been. "Do you realize the impact each Builder makes during Pianoforte? Well, I'll tell you. Pianoforte is all about *resonance*, waves building on waves. A singer can shatter fine crystal by hitting a pure note and letting the vibrations grow … but in order to *stack* waves, we must *have* waves. Your ability to feed from the Aether into the manifestation engine is magnified greatly when the incoming waves, on the machine's end, hit a synchronized trough. Not to swell your pretty little head, but it means that each of you Builders become more like *twenty* Builders today. One bad man or woman on the array will shatter the resonance, and one short dims it twentyfold. So why are you not at your station?"

Eila resisted an overpowering urge to say, *Because I have to stand here and listen to your speech.*

"I'm sorry, Mr. Brampton," she said instead. "We were on the first trolley. We came as soon as we got the call."

Brampton's eyes rolled. He exhaled. He was tall, thin, and had short but immaculately coifed bright-white hair. He'd never seemed old enough to have white hair to Eila (he seemed to be in his late forties), so she'd assumed it had simply grown that way. Brampton was usually composed but cleverly insulting. On a typical day, you could come up to Brampton, have a throwaway discussion about the weather, and somehow walk away feeling like an idiot, like you'd put your blouse on inside out and had everyone laughing behind your back.

"Well you're here now," he said. His voice had softened, probably realizing that pressuring Eila — who needed serenity to do her work, not more to worry about — was counterproductive. "Go. Hook into your cradle and join the array. You know how to Build a series construct, yes?"

She nodded. They usually created individual constructs: her own large, empty warehouse, isolated from the world and open to receive whatever the Aether chose for Eila to Build on that particular day. But during Pianoforte, you were supposed to link your construct with that of the Builders to your right and left. For Eila, that meant creating the same empty warehouse but leaving the large bay doors open on each end. In a single construct, you could Build great innovations. But in a *series* of constructs, there was room for an entire team, working together, to Build enormous skyships, or to lay a locomotive's rails end to end.

"Yes," she said.

With a nod, Brampton gave Eila permission to leave. Then he stalked the entrance behind her, looking for more tardy employees to belittle.

On her way to the gantry, Eila passed the great machines the Ministry used to enhance the Builders' speed and efficiency. She wasn't sure how they all worked, but knew they'd been Built right here in this room. In the beginning, Building had been modular. Early Builders had simply received from the Aether, then used their skills to manifest what they saw. It had kept Building small and intimate, with Build teams often requiring session-end meetings to compare and combine their budding manifestations. But over time, the Builders Built the machines Eila was passing now, which helped them to Build without manual assembly. Thinking machines and recognizers improved simple creations without meetings and cobbling. And in that way, the Ministry had grown like a nautilus creating its own shell: from the core outward, the Builders Built the very things that allowed them to Build better. Manifestations became bigger … and bigger … and bigger. Now the entire complex — forged slowly from ideas generated in its own heart — was massive, systematized, and efficient.

Everything involved in Building had been born from the Blunderbuss — except of course for the Blunderbuss itself.

Even as Eila hurried up the gantry and down the row of cradles to her own, she couldn't help but pause to look up at the great machine. The Builders' cradles were arranged in a series of rings, stacked one atop another in open floors like a painter's scaffolding. The chamber was massive, with rings extending so high upward that the ceiling was almost invisible. The Blunderbuss was in the center, its titanic girth erupting from the bedrock somewhere far below to soar high above. It was enormous: fifty feet through the middle, chrome-colored skin covered in pipes and cogs, open in places to expose huge polished gears.

Like most machines, its works seemed to be run by steam. Here and there white clouds hissed like dragon's breath as chains and cams shifted, opening some vents as others closed. The largest cloud erupted from the very top, where the machine finally ended in a huge, gleaming, bell-shaped smokestack.

No one really knew how the Blunderbuss worked, because it had existed forever. According to history, the Ministry — before there had even *been* a proper Ministry — found the great engine long ago standing in the middle of a field of rock, half buried in the ground. Despite its outdoor existence, those early people had found the machine polished and as free of grease and dirt as it was now, showing no corrosion. And despite all the dials, gears, and pistons in its guts, it had not been made by human hands. The world had been explored by scientists and explained by natural laws, but those laws were all founded on a simple, unexplained leap of faith: *The Blunderbuss* always was. *The Blunderbuss* is, *and will continue to be.*

According to legend, the first Builder had stood by the Blunderbuss and seen a girder in his mind. He'd manifested the girder without effort, then laid it on the ground. Then he'd Built a second girder, and bolted it to the first. That was the birth of the Ministry, and the rest had followed. Piece by piece, the whole of Alterran society had been Built in the image of the great engine.

Eila slid into her cradle, lying flat on her back. The thing was usually restrictive (especially the top, where the cap for her head was not unlike a helmet made of steel, affixed to the table's frame), but today it greeted Eila like a hug. The padding felt especially soft. The pillow inside the cap was like the large pillow on her bed, holding her head like a cloud. Eila wanted to turn onto her side and sleep.

But she had work to do.

She tried to focus. At first fatigue made it difficult, but then the collaborative energy of the Pianoforte gave her a shove. She almost didn't *have* to focus. The collective — comprised of all the other Builders on the Array — had focused already.

She pictured her warehouse construct. The rest happened automatically. There was a sucking sensation and her mental picture seemed to snap backward, pulled by the will of the others. She saw the warehouse click into place, its open-door ends easily joining with the spaces on either side, like a segment of pipe slotting in and sealing on its own.

With her construct in place, Eila felt an immense force building inside her. The energy was as Brampton had described it: like a wave, impossibly strong. If she'd been standing in the open, she'd expect her long, slightly wavy hair to be standing on end, buoyed by an electric charge. There was an incredible sense of *possibility*, as if anything were obtainable.

And if she believed what was said about Pianoforte, anything was.

What would they Build today? Would it be a new breed of ship? A new form of broadcast? A building, a bridge, a great new device? It all seemed possible. Or rather, it all seemed *likely*. Eila was an optimistic, positive person, but her loftiest ambitions had always been held firm by the sensation of her feet touching the ground. Now, there were no limits. She could do anything. She could pluck any idea from nowhere and turn it into something real.

Mechanisms able to send people across Alterra without traveling anywhere between.

Entire cities, able to meet their population's needs with the pull of a lever.

A creature with arms that twisted and twined like the swaying of a long-limbed tree caught in the wind, feet like claws, mouth black like the yawn of night itself.

Eila jerked inside the cradle, her foot slamming out and striking the padded edge. She'd had the same reflex before — as if she was walking down stairs and had missed a step — but it came with the fringe of sleep, not Building.

She blinked. Clenched and unclenched her fists, shaking her limbs to stir her blood. She realized she'd curled sideways. She righted herself, shoulder blades pressed into the cradle below. She opened her eyes wide, forcing a blink. In her mind, the array's linked construct sagged and seemed to moan as her energy withdrew from the working collective.

Blink. Clench fists.

She couldn't allow herself to fall asleep. As her mind wrestled the collective's influence, she couldn't remember why that was important, but it was: *no matter what, she couldn't fall asleep.*

Unwelcome images began to flit through her mind. She saw a tent at the solstice festival. A frightened man with a white beard and salt-and-pepper hair. She felt a sense of a dire prediction, a feeling of herself in trouble. Then, with effort, she pushed it all away. Again she saw only the construct, and the collective.

She focused.

Build.

Inside the linked construct, she watched a shape form. It was long, floating in the middle of her mental warehouse. At first, it looked like molten metal floating in the air, but then it slowly found a rough form, a bulb forming on one end like blown glass, still hot, and curving down at the other end. Another shape formed beside it, then affixed to the first, slot-in-groove. She saw a pressure dial and the long line of a steam tube. A flat disc became a gear. It was the guts of some new machine, finding shape inside her mental space.

It boiled and bubbled as it formed, every Builder on the series wondering what the strange object would become.

Feeling the Pianoforte's rising power, knowing the wave's crests and troughs for what they were, Eila watched the Building with innocent fascination. She saw it as non-Builders must see it — or, perhaps, like a child. The Blunderbuss allowed them to make something from nothing. A nation of creations, spawned from the Aether itself.

In the space behind her eyelids, there was a white warehouse with a great object coming to life. And as it solidified, Eila saw something leaning against it: a boy in his late teens, wearing a long and dirty coat, black hair untidy, his face unusually white in circles — marks from the goggles hanging at his neck.

She blinked again. This time, nothing changed. The Pianoforte collective did not sag, and she did not twitch in her almost-sleep. The mental interloper — now raising a hand to beckon her as he always did — remained where he was.

Follow me. Eila heard his voice inside her head, not with her ears.

She couldn't resist. She took a step forward.

Follow me below.

She tried to respond, and found herself able: *Who are you?*

I am the white rabbit.

But Rabbit is here. Rabbit Brampton is my supervisor. He is in charge.

The boy laughed. *Not where you're going, he's not.*

There was a flash. All at once, Eila was no longer in the warehouse with the forming object. She was on a wooded path with the boy still in front of her, her feet bare, the moistness of leaves pressing into her soles with fetid insistence. It was dark, with a large gibbous moon overhead. She smelled something damp and rotten. She could hear a rustling, like the stirring of dead limbs or bones in a shoebox, but the sound was somehow far off, like a scuffle unworthy of notice, none of her business. It was so real, and Eila almost believed it all — except that someone had told her to listen and watch, and to never let the door open.

But it already was.

Snakes weaved between the boy's feet, his face filthy and cast in shadow. Beside him, on a greening tree stump, was a small man with a face like a dried-out apple, scruff of a black beard in patches on his chin. He was stunted and one eye almost protruded from its socket. In his hand was a pipe, its handle made from the bleached bones of a skeleton's finger.

Find us, said the boy.

Eila looked at the apple-faced man and wondered if "us" included him. It was hard to say. The small man — about the size of a dwarf, from a storybook her mother had read her as a child — was near the boy, but the boy was staring at Eila. He almost seemed to think they were alone.

She wanted to refuse, but instead she asked, *How?*

Convenience.

Another flash, and the forest was gone.

Eila found herself suddenly in a neglected section of Waldron's Gate, where papers and corpses of leaves filled the gutters. It was still nighttime, the same white moon overhead. The dwarf-man was gone, and the boy's clothing had changed. He had a dark, handsome face, but now his hands were covered with blood, and as he touched his chin, dirt blended with red and he became frightening rather than handsome, a filthy red thumbprint on his chin where a cleft should be. Behind him was an enormous contraption: half-polished chrome that shone blue in the moonlight, half covered in grime. Clotted with grease, like something from a ship's bowels.

Hurry, he said.

Something emerged from the machine — or perhaps from behind it — and wrapped the boy with large black arms made of smoke. Eila caught a flash of large yellow eyes with irises like lozenges laid on their sides from one side of his lean frame. Her breath was forced from her lungs. She fought for air as hands yanked the boy backward, his body contorting and twisting, arms and legs and torso bending at impossible angles.

Then he was gone. Into the machine, or somewhere beyond.

Eila heard a scream — its end sharply severed — and found herself back in her padded cradle, certain the scream had been her own. She felt sweaty and jittery, skin seeming to sizzle as her mind scrambled to find the Build construct.

She found it in time to watch the Pianoforte begin to collapse.

The in-progress project had fleshed out through her dozing, developed more completely in the constructs of her neighbors. Their innovations had bled into her warehouse, but Eila's absent attention was a weak link. Her space had filled with sloppy edges and warped surfaces that could no longer be smoothed. The machine they'd been building had wheels — at least one so far, a single corner end propped up on a strangely off-center axle.

She'd fallen asleep. Against everything she'd known she should and shouldn't do, she'd fallen asleep. Pianoforte relied on harmony. Her lack of resonance, as her mind wandered elsewhere, had soured it.

She heard a scream.

She jerked, almost forgetting that the cradle's cap was above her head. The bump reminded Eila to stay engaged, and lend her power to the collective from inside the array. But it was too late.

The decay she'd seen in her own construct was spreading like disease. Rigid pipes sagged and drooped as if made of fabric rather than copper. She saw the machine's wheel bend and become an ellipse instead of a circle. Down the line (almost invisible from where Eila was looking), another Builder in a separate cradle slipped at the scream. Something broke. Their minds were linked, and the shared project was glue between them. As the thing split and started to clang, it felt like coming insanity.

Eila gave up, realizing she wasn't going to be able to will herself into her trance as the screaming continued. Her eyes snapped open. She edged out of the cap and sat up, relieved with a look down the line to see that she wasn't the only one who'd done it. Some were sitting. Some were climbing out. Up and down the gantry, people were scuffling and hurrying.

The scream ceased, and Eila turned her head to see Rabbit Brampton a few cradles down, his gray suit counterpointed by the stark white coats of three lesser scientists. She caught a glimpse of something metallic as she rose. Edging closer, she saw it was a needle. The syringe they were giving to the screamer, of course, would be filled with a slurry of medical Crumble.

There was someone at her side. Eila looked over to see Victor, whose assigned cradle was just a few spots down.

"Who is it?" he asked her, looking toward the huddle of scientists.

"I think it's Bella."

"What happened?"

Eila didn't want to answer, but was pretty sure she knew.

"It fell apart," she said.

"*What* fell apart?" he said.

Eila wanted to cower and run. She was usually ready for anything — one of the benefits of being Head Builder's daughter and growing up with a prodigy's training — but now Eila felt like she was in someone else's skin. Cora spent her days drawing in her sketchbook and blabbing to her journal, attending plays and prattling on about boys by the handful. Eila had always played along with Cora, but she hadn't felt that childish for almost a year — certainly since joining the Ministry. Today, she wished to be innocent and silly. She wanted to obsess over her hair, and work on the extra pages assigned by a tutor.

Eila thought back to the thing they'd been Building (a skyship? Something for the ferry shaws? A military innovation destined for Stensue?) and watched a mental replay as it sagged and its edges turned untrue. Cogs had fallen out of mesh with cogs. The Builders were supposed to work as a single entity, but she'd ruined it all.

"The Pianoforte," she said.

"Pianofortes don't just 'collapse,'" said Victor. He glanced over with something between confusion and suspicion. Victor had serious brown eyes, an aquiline nose, and eyebrows that Cora said were too big and fuzzy. Usually Eila found him handsome and strong, but today she wanted to run — from him and everything else. Because somehow, she was sure he knew that it was her fault. They *all* must know. Soon Brampton and his scientists would finish pacifying Bella and come toward Eila. They'd diagnose her, inspect her, dose her, and send her off to Joffrey Columns. Everyone knew that former Builders were over-represented at the asylum of towers. Insanity, for them, was an occupational hazard.

"I saw it happen," she said.

"There must have been a fault. Something bad in the engine."

"Like what?" said Eila, dreading the answer.

Victor nodded toward Bella. Brampton had stepped back to clear the way, and the scientists in white coats were leading her away from her cradle, down the staircase and off the gantry.

"Ask her," he said.

Bella no longer looked frightened as they all watched her pass on the floor below. Now she looked serene, the Crumble an antacid to her problems. She'd be fine. Even if, after analysis, it turned out that Bella lost her mind, she'd never know it. The insane couldn't sense their insanity.

There was a tremendous groaning noise behind them. Eila flinched back, and the row of watching Buillders turned to face the machine.

The Ministry's prime engine usually billowed white smoke from its top, but now the plume had become a dull gray. Its cogs were slowing, its parts beginning to moan and whine as metal resisted the push of metal.

For the first time in years, the Blunderbuss was shutting down.

Chapter Three

Down in Forefront

THE SCIENTISTS — LED BY RABBIT Brampton, bustling back and forth while shouting orders — scrambled to the controls and tried to stop the shutdown, but the Blunderbuss had existed before the controls and machines that Alterra pretended kept it healthy. The machine helped the Builders Build, but anyone who worked closely with it knew the truth: the Ministry did not *use* the Blunderbuss to create. In truth, Alterra produced its bounty because the Blunderbuss *allowed* it.

It wanted to shut down. So it did.

The floor grew eerie in silence. Eila had never seen the Ministry without the Blunderbuss' constant thrums and clanging. Not hearing it now gave her a bone-deep unease, as if the ground had stopped pulling her down or the air had grown toxic. Without the clamorous clockwork and hiss, the entire world felt dead.

With no ability to Build — and with Pianoforte gone — the Builders were sent home. Brampton paced through the ranks, swearing at them as if each one of them was at fault. The Blunderbuss had shut down before, but not recently, and never so quickly or without so much as a warning. And it had never, *ever* shut down during a Pianoforte.

Brampton berated them for their incompetence. His perfectly combed white hair fell out of its coif. He didn't yell (even when he made his voice loud, it wasn't truly a yell); his manner was hectoring and insulting. When his eyes were elsewhere, the Builders around Eila traded half-hidden smirks. It was obvious to them all that if anyone was responsible for a collapse, it would be the man watching dials during the Build — the man whose job it was to midwife the

Ministry's manifestations from end to end.

But Eila felt differently. She had her own theory — her own *truth* — about what had broken the resonance.

Brampton called them worthless and barked for everyone to get out of his sight. He told them to keep one eye open and one ear listening, because the Build would resume the moment it could. Even if he had to wake them all at midnight.

Eila found her father high above on the Enigma Floor, his tall form bent over a machine with his battered, fifteen-year-old brown leather bag under a workbench nearby. Her presence so high on the circular gantry would have normally been looked down upon, but the same sense of resignation had bled upward, and the Enigma Builders had gone home as surely as their more creative counterparts in Aether Forefront. All except their Head, who would be working late, and maybe not leaving the Ministry before the others returned.

"You aren't supposed to be up here," said Atwell, seeing her.

Her father was merely moving his lips. It was clear that Eila's presence in rarified air didn't matter at all. Even the Enigma Floor was almost deserted.

"I came to steal engineering secrets."

"How did you find me?" he said.

"I asked for Atwell Doyle. It wasn't hard."

"Well," he said, then turned away as if the one-word sentence was finished.

Eila was tall, but her father was still a foot and a half taller. He had a long, lean frame and moved like an impatient spider when working. At home, he was a different man entirely. Instead of his usual way of speaking, which was brisk and direct (or "insulting" as those beneath him sometimes said), he moved with more purpose, and often in silence. Eila's bond with her father was half daddy-daughter and half teacher-student, and his constant instruction was one of the things Eila loved most.

But today, the lone word was all he had. His hands wore mittens of grease like an assembler's. It looked like he'd been working wrenches and bellows, not tending to controls and leading the Enigma Build as he usually did. He'd held onto his determined, almost arrogant air of purpose — but Eila, who knew him best, could see through his facade. Whatever had happened wasn't supposed to. Atwell's uncertain worry made Eila feel guilty.

"Do you need help?"

He turned to her. A two-day beard dotted his long chin, mostly pepper but speckled with salt. It was evidence of one of his quirks: not shaving until his latest, most pressing problem was solved. For a moment, his serious, deep-set eyes bored into Eila as if he didn't know who she was or what she wanted.

"What?" Then the stare broke, and he became her father again. "No, I don't need help. Head home, Rose."

Eila wanted to chide his use of the pet name (a tribute to the rose-lined street where he'd raised her), but she couldn't bring herself to do it. Her father was a hard, proud man, stretched too thin. Responsibility for uncovering the failure's cause would fall to Brampton, then the Head Builder below him. They'd work together or share the blame. He was facing a lot of pressure, compounded by the need to spend the next several hours holding hands with a man he loathed. If Father wanted to call her Rose — or even the detested variant "Rosie" — then so be it.

"When do you think you'll be home?"

He just shook his head.

"I don't want to go home," she said. "Can I stay?"

"No."

"I can turn a wrench, same as you."

Her father chuckled. It was insulting for higher-ups to act like mechanics, and it would have been polite for Eila to pretend she didn't know he'd been monkeying with the Blunderbuss's enigmatic works. Her affectionate sleight disarmed him.

"Go home. They won't let you stay, even though I'm your father. Heads are rolling tonight. I'd rather yours didn't make the pile."

Eila cringed. Her head probably should be at the top of that pile. She wondered if the scientists would be able to trace the Pianoforte's vulnerability and know she'd fallen asleep … or that her sloppy focus and damaged mind brought a fault into the Build.

"Was it bad up here?" she said.

Atwell nodded, unwilling to insult her intelligence by blunting the truth. "Yes."

"Was anyone hurt?"

"Hurt?"

"Bella was hurt. Downstairs in Forefront."

"Bella." His eyes rolled up, thinking. "Is she the one with the black hair? Moody?"

Eila thought she saw where her father was going. It was exactly where Victor had been going. *Ask her,* he'd said. Because if anyone was at fault, it had to be Bella. Bella was dark. She was moody. Bella must have gotten sloppy and introduced a fault. It wasn't fair, and Eila felt a desire to lay down on the gantry, to scrub the machine's works until hard work made her guilt disappear.

"She's just creative, Father." She paused. "Like all of us down there."

Atwell's head tilted. Then he came a step forward. "I didn't mean it like that. I was just trying to place her."

"It wasn't Bella's fault. I know it wasn't."

"I didn't say it was."

"Just because she's 'moody' doesn't mean that…"

Atwell closed the distance, then laid his big palms on top of Eila's shoulders. He seemed to realize at the last minute that the right one was covered with filth and pulled it back, but Eila wanted it back where it had been. She wanted her father to tell her that she wasn't at fault — a difficult proposition, given that he had no reason to believe she was.

"What have I always told you, Eila?" he said.

She didn't answer. She was looking at her shoes.

"Just because Enigma is high up does not make it better. It is simply a matter of geography."

"I know."

"We make analytical things because we are problem-solvers by nature. There are men and women up here who would tell you that pipes and purifiers and machines of defense are more important than what you Build in Forefront, but they are engineers. We can't help but be arrogant." He cracked a smile. Arrogance was one trait they shared, down to their bones.

"I wasn't saying that…"

"And for the *last time,*" he said, the left hand gaining weight on her shoulder, "I did not want you to be in my department. I wanted you where you were best suited, be it in Enigma or Forefront. It even makes sense, where you ended up — an extremely talented Builder who makes beautiful things. You are my daughter, yes, and that's why you're at the Ministry. But you are your mother's daughter, too."

Right here and now, with Pianoforte's blood still on her hands, Eila didn't want to hear the last. She loved her mother, but an Enigma Builder wouldn't have lost control of her Build to flights of fancy. The Enigma Builder she'd always believed her father wanted wouldn't have failed the entire Ministry (and possibly destroyed a fellow Builder's mind) because she'd been thinking about a *boy*.

"Can you tell how it happened?" she said. "Can you tell where the problem started?"

"Don't do that, Eila. Don't change the subject. You could have been in Enigma if you'd wanted, and I know it as well as Brampton does. But you chose Forefront and I'm *glad* you're in Forefront. We need both departments, and both departments are equal. Imagination and logic. Creativity and problem-solving. Pipes and comforts. Neither is better, and I want you to finally believe that *I* don't feel either is better. Do you hear me?"

Still looking down: "Sure."

The hand on her shoulder found the underside of her chin and tipped it up, and she found herself looking into her father's eyes. They were hazel now, but they shifted color when he Built. Nobody knew why. Sometimes they were piercing blue, sometimes green, sometimes gray and blurred at the edges.

"Listen to me, Rose," he said. "When the Blunderbuss goes down, it pulls Builders' moods with it. What you're feeling is natural, but you need to understand something, now and forever, and nevermind your petty fears that contradict it: *I am proud of you, no matter what you choose.*"

She pressed her lips together and tried to believe it. Little by little, she did.

"Now run home," he said, releasing her. "You were once my little monkey, but I won't have both of us doing monkey work." He held up his greasy hand, then turned back around.

Seeing his gritty hand shifted her thoughts. She found her mind straying back to the boy from her vision. She thought of his plea to find and follow him, and of his single word: *Convenience.* Inside the vision of horrors, she'd thought "convenience" referred to a state of being, but something now clanged inside her mind, and she remembered something her father had said about the city and what Enigma had built for its management. He'd told her Waldron's Gate wasn't all rose- and lavender-lined streets, beautifully angled homes and brightly colored buildings, or gleaming sky ships pocking the sky. *Every good comes with bad*, he'd told his eldest child, *and you should always keep that in mind. For every shining building downtown, there is grit in the ghetto. For every Blunderbuss, there is a Convenience.*

"Can I go see Cora?"

Atwell had turned to a bank of pressure gauges and was fiddling for something behind them. "What? Oh, yes, yes. Just be home for dinner."

"Will *you* be home for dinner?"

"I doubt it."

Eila fought her sigh. Dinners with Father were fundamentally better. Without him, it would be the same three siblings, the same mother, and the same handmaid scampering around in the background. Without Atwell at the table, discussion centered on flowers, clothes, and all things pretty. It was a love that her sister Penelope had inherited from their mother, but that despite her father's thoughts on the aesthetics of Forefront, Eila had never embraced in quite the same way.

"Can I stay at Cora's for dinner?" she asked.

"I don't want you imposing, Rose."

"'Eila,' Father." Enough was enough with the pet name. "And I wouldn't be imposing. They invite me whenever I see them, and seem insulted that I never accept."

Atwell stopped working long enough to stare at Eila. His eyes, no matter their color, could bore through metal.

"Without me around, your mother will be frazzled, and you know it. She doesn't sleep well when I'm away either, and she'll know I'll be a while when she hears a Pianoforte collapsed and the Blunderbuss shut down. You know how she gets. I want you there. Do you hear me … *Eila?*"

Eila sighed, then nodded dutifully.

She walked back down the gantry steps to the bottom, then out onto the floor. By the time she returned to Aether Forefront, the entire array was deserted. At least half of the lights were off, leaving the usually bustling line in shadow. It was spooky, seeing everything empty. There were on-shifts and off-shifts, and some Builders worked at night while most worked during the day. But as long as the machine was running and pulling inspiration from the Aether, Builders were needed to Build. Eila had never seen it so quiet, nor felt such a chill.

She walked outside alone, hailed a streetcar, then felt compelled to stand during the ride instead of sitting, as a kind of penance. Lying down on the job had caused a disaster, so she wouldn't rest again until nightfall.

She held the brass bar, swaying with the car to spite her fatigue, palm sweating more than it had any right to.

The car weaved away from the Ministry's round white form and eventually onto the central canal. It was only midafternoon and the sun was still reasonably high, its bright light occasionally dulled by stray clouds in the azure sky. Eila looked out the side of the car, sighted a patrolling skyship drifting toward the Fog, and wondered if it had launched from Stensue. Her father's department had Built many things that now resided in the seat of the Alterran military. Being Head Builder, Atwell even knew what many of those manifestations were and what they were used for. Eila had bothered him more about someday seeing Stensue than any other city, arguing that as the family's eldest child — and a Builder destined to rise in the Ministry — she should be permitted to go. She should be allowed to see the city with the world-famous waterfall and waterwheel, its legendary cliff pocked with structures and armaments.

For now, that was ridiculous. Eila was fifteen, barely past being an apprentice. And seniority didn't grant access to Stensue. That came from Prime Minister Morrison.

She thought of Stensue, and of her sleeping vision. The boy and the dwarf. The forest path, then again of the Alterran military. Why were her two thoughts connected? She'd been sparked somehow. The mundane had earned her curiosity. Maybe lights worked without anyone in Alterra questioning why or how, but Eila found herself wondering for the first time.

Where *did* water go when it went down the drain?

Why *weren't* the Builders usually allowed to see what they'd Built?

Why *did* Alterra have such a robust military if its primary purpose was patrolling the Fog?

If you believed Parliament, there was nothing in the Fog. It was but a damp, creeping horror, all brambles, thorns, and dark, echoing sounds. There was the land inside its circle, buildings of cogs and wheelworks in the cities, and sprawling farms beyond. That was the world. Alterra was vast, from the capital at Waldron's Gate at one end to Yon near the other. There was land and Fog. Beyond the Fog lay the ocean of Heaven in which Jonah the Whale God swam, if you believed in such things. Eila didn't believe in Jonah. But she believed in the ocean, for a reason she didn't entirely understand.

She thought of the vision, and of the boy with the dark hair mopped atop his dirty face.

Follow me below.

Who are you?

I am the white rabbit.

As Palpatine Malvern had said, Eila was sure she'd been to the places she'd seen. She'd been there *today*. But somehow, she'd also been in the Build array's cradle. Today's memories of the boy — as with *all* memories of the boy — were different from ordinary memories. They had fuzzy and missing parts. She usually had excellent recall (memory games and logic puzzles were a large part of Builder training, especially when your father secretly hoped you'd join Enigma), but Eila couldn't remember much of what she'd seen and heard, other than the most vivid bits. The visions always faded quickly upon waking. Already, the mental incursion that had ruined the Pianoforte felt very long ago, though it had just happened. She remembered only the white rabbit, and that he'd wanted her to follow. And the …

… the …

She almost had it. Whatever it was, she'd almost asked Father about it.

Eila gripped the bar harder, feeling the car shake underfoot, trying to force her mind into memory. How could she have meant to say something to Atwell just a short while ago, yet recalled nothing now? It was something having to do with her new questions about how things worked.

The lights. The water. The …

The Convenience.

Eila remembered. After her father had taken her aside and shared the burden of knowing that Alterra was not always pristine and that beauty created toxic by-products, he'd shown her pictures on the family's incandescent projector. He'd told her all about a system that Enigma had Built but that Alterrans tried to ignore. Everything Built was, by definition, flawless. If a vision from the Aether had flaws, it wasn't articulated. Yet not everything was Built, and people themselves were not perfect. They produced waste, and that waste had to go somewhere.

The waste, he'd said, was processed by a machine called the "Convenience," nestled deep in the pit of the Gate's inferior districts.

They'd sat in the parlor and her father had flicked from one slide to another, surely breaching dozens of laws by showing Enigma file images to an underage girl too young at the time to even lie in a Build cradle. He'd pulled each image of the Convenience up with the primary lens, then unfolded lens after lens in front to display the varied layers. Eila saw the image in three dimensions. She saw its pipes and its steam tubes. She saw its mixers and its aerators, spun by the wind to agitate the waste below and introduce oxygen. Scientists understood how it worked, but Atwell, though inquisitive, was not a scientist. He only knew that tremendous thought had gone into processing the less-beautiful aspects of Alterra, and that months had been spent on the Blunderbuss, Building the components of a vital thing that most citizens would never know about — or ever *want* to know about.

Eila recalled every image and every detail. She'd been in Build training for years by then, and had undergone her father's unceasing breed of pre-Build training prior to that. She remembered the machine's enormity. She remembered the aerial photos, captured by zeppelins, their twin airscrews visible at the image's peripheries. She remembered the way the Convenience sprawled for blocks. How it must smell, with its open pits and reservoirs. And she remembered asking why nobody knew about it other than those who had to live beside it.

And Father had told her:

Because nobody wants *to know.*

But Eila did. Because when she found it, she would find the white rabbit.

Chapter Four
The Convenience

THE STREETCAR STOPPED AT RAILTON Circle, and Eila stepped off. Her heart was fluttering for a reason she didn't entirely understand. She'd been steeped in thoughts of the deplorable and the undesirable, and before that she'd thought of her vision — the mental intrusion that had poisoned Pianoforte, shut down the Blunderbuss, and caused her father grief. She should be frightened or guilty or disgusted, but she wasn't. Her nerves were the pitter-patter of excitement, as if she were eleven, still waiting for Nils Parker to lean in and plant that first kiss on her lips.

She passed the connecting car that would take her home to Rowley Row on the Rose Belt — where cherry blossoms lined the streets to match the blushing white roses scattered behind every front lawn, and where she told her father she'd meet Cora — and stepped onto a different trolley instead.

The car was taking off as she reached it. She had to scamper a few paces to catch it, her feet uncomfortable in the low-heeled shoes her mother made her wear to the Ministry. She held her hand out to grab on. Several workmen reached out and took Eila's hand, then pulled her aboard, surprise on their faces.

Eila nodded her appreciation, then quickly looked away from their questioning eyes. They had to be wondering what business a well-dressed, obviously well-heeled girl from the upper crust had in their part of town. She was in her work clothes. They'd know (or at least guess) that she worked near or at the Ministry. A few, if observant, would notice the badge on her waist that marked her as a Builder.

She avoided their curious looks. Even if she'd wanted to tell them her plans, she wasn't too certain of them herself.

The ride seemed long, as the Gate's quaint, colorful structures downtown gave way to somewhat dingier, more muted buildings and homes. Her heart beat faster, but not from nerves. Waldron's Gate was (according to Parliament, anyway) safe from end to end. Part of Eila had expected the workmen on the streetcar to be rude or crass — she was away from her turf, young, female, and pretty — but they were mostly quiet. She wondered if it was always this way headed out of downtown, or if they were being courteous, stilling off-color tongues in deference to their strange young visitor.

When the trolley arrived, she stepped down, then looked around. Several workmen filtered past her, but one — a man with large, callused palms who'd helped her aboard — stopped beside Eila. He was as tall as her father, but twice as muscular and broad.

"Miss?"

Eila looked up. She usually felt older than her years, but with the trolley now departing, she felt much younger. Why had she come here? And what would her parents say if they found out she'd gone wandering?

"You know where you's going, Miss? Got a spot you need to be?"

"I'm a little lost. I'm not used to this part of town."

The big man chuckled. "Yar, you sure isn't. You sure you's supposed to *be* in this part of town? No offense, but I wondered if you'd gone wrong the minute you started chasing the trolley."

Eila wondered if she should be insulted. Was he asking if she'd mistaken the workmen's streetcar for the shuttle to the mercantile center?

"I'm quite sure," she said, a bit roughly.

"Well, then you should keep in mind that though it's nice enough here and you'll meet kind folks, I'd be heading back before the sun kisses the canal yonder." He pointed toward where the sun would set. "Ain't no part of Alterra's nice all the time, y'know."

Eila swallowed. Pretty pictures were painted downtown and in the Rose Belt, but weren't the workman's words the point of Father's lesson? Nothing was perfect unless it came directly from the Blunderbuss, and even then only from a talented Builder. He'd hinted that the Ministry's past had been plagued by rogues, and it was no secret that many Builders had found permanent homes in Joffrey Columns.

Confirmation that she might be somewhere unsafe (despite Parliament's claims) was unsettling, but Eila had to get back for dinner before the sun was halfway down anyway. If she wasn't, and her mother asked around and still found her missing, the Guard would be called.

"Of course," said Eila.

"If'n you want, I can escort you where you need to go."

"It's not dark yet."

The workman shrugged.

"Do you know where the Convenience is?" she said.

The man's head cocked to the side. He'd been quite talkative, but this was beginning to feel like pantomime with an intelligent dog.

"The machine that processes waste."

"Oh," he said, chuckling. "You mean the mudslinger. What you want with that boondoggle?"

"I'm … " Eila stammered. She didn't want to answer. "I'm here to repair it."

The man bellowed an enormous laugh. The other workmen must have been used to it, because none of the depot's few stragglers turned to look. "Sure you is. You can tell Al the truth. You meetin' someone?"

Eila felt herself blush. She wanted to stoop into the gutter, wipe filth from the cobblestones, smear it on her face and clothes, then drag her shiny hair into a ratty bun. Al was able to see right through her. A rich teenager in the city's armpit.

"No!" Her hand went to her badge, which she pulled away from her side enough to show the big man. "I'm a Builder, with the Ministry of Manifestation. I was sent here by my superiors to … "

"Without the machine, a kid alone in the gutter, yeah, that makes sense." Al flapped a big hand to dismiss Eila's retort before she could give it. "Fine, ain't nothing. What you want's that way." He pointed. "Take Hamford, not that pissant little alley betwixt the butcher and hot ironer's. Like I said, folks'll treat you nice, but that don't mean you should be goin' stupid places alone, bein' like you are." He gestured down Eila's length, and she wasn't sure if he was referring to her youth, dress, or physical appearance.

"That's where the Convenience is?"

He laughed. "Yeah. It's real convenient."

"Is it marked?"

He laughed again. "Oh, miss, if you don't see it, then you's blind. And if you don't *smell* it, then I can't help you. He tell you where to meet?" He corrected himself. "Sorry — I meant, did 'your superiors' tell you where you needed to 'fix summat'? Because the mudslinger's a big nelly. Goes for blocks."

"Yes," said Eila, having no clue. It hardly mattered. She didn't know why she'd come to the Convenience or what she hoped to find once there.

"Okay. Then Crownspeed to you."

Eila thanked the man, overcompensating for his religious sendoff by telling him she hoped The Crown shone down on him. Eila didn't believe in The Crown any more than she believed in Jonah (all of the god legends seemed as silly to her as the tales of elves living in Aerohead and leaving it haunted), but if Al believed, then good on him. Her father was a skeptic, but Mother had faith, and over the past year or so she'd come to respect that her beliefs weren't everyone's, and that nobody truly knew what was right.

Eila left Al behind and headed in his indicated direction, passing the small, relatively shadowed alley he'd told her not to cross. A block farther down was Hamford Road. It was wider, better lit by the slanting sun, and lined with quaint stands outside shops where merchants were taking advantage of the warm day. She saw a general foods market, a tailor, and a Tinker's shop. Walking close enough to glance over (but reluctant to stop, for fear the Tinker himself would begin to harangue and follow her until she bought something), Eila spotted an array of innovative creations. There were magnifying spectacles with a clutch of lenses the wearer could flip down (for what, she wasn't sure), a kind of two-ended work knife with a clockwork auto-sharpening sheath, a small oven for warming food and browning toast, and several things of mysterious wonder. If she'd been sure it wouldn't be taken as encouragement, she'd have nodded to the proprietor or swapped a few words. Eila Built amazing things with her mind, and the Ministry as a whole had surely Built the hodgepodge, piled-atop buildings and conveyance devices that composed this entire sector of town. But this man had Built things with his *hands*, using *tools* to create new things out of old scraps. It was quite different from manifestation via the Aether and the Blunderbuss, but it was Building nonetheless, and in its own way more fascinating to Eila than the Ministry magic that had birthed cities and ships and rails and most of the world around them.

As she reached the street's end, the shadows grew darker and open-air stalls started to dwindle. Her senses reset, and Eila realized what she was approaching.

The air stank, like waste.

The area felt like a corner because it was one; there was a wall of filthy metal and filthier tubes before her, looming far enough skyward to almost block the sun. A narrow road ran in front of the Convenience, but aside from that, the district seemed to be ignoring its presence. It looked like some great ship that had landed in the middle of town, hunkered down, and made itself at home.

By the time she'd gotten close to it, Eila realized that nobody she'd passed on the street had turned to watch her. All eyes stayed away from the Convenience. If a random girl had arrived in fancy clothes and fancy shoes to approach it, they weren't going to wonder why.

Eila wondered if Al had been wrong. She'd be quite safe here overnight if she just stayed by the waste management machine, invisible to the locals. When she left in the morning, they'd probably see her as untouchable.

Still, despite the gloom and stench, despite the dawning certainty that she really should have gone to Cora's as she'd told her father (Cora would probably want to arrange some photos in a book, sketch another portrait of her, and then go giggling off to the pond), Eila felt a bizarre need to touch the thing.

She walked forward and brushed her fingers across its surface. It was fuzzy with grime. Her fingers came away black, as if she'd dipped them in oil. She felt repulsed — yet fascinated to her core.

She'd had a vision of this thing. She'd seen it in her mind — not because she'd seen it in person or because it was a flight of fancy, but because she *would* one day see it. At least one thing from her visions had turned out to be real after all; the order of knowing was simply backward. Memory had come first, and experience had come second.

She stepped back, feeling ice wash across her. The sun was waning and leaving Eila in the last of its shadow. If she wanted to get home for dinner, she shouldn't dally long … although why would she *want* to dally?

Eila began to skulk around the massive utility, fingers dragging random, disgusting lines through its grime. She was vaguely aware that she was fouling herself with contact, but the moment made it not matter. This was the touchstone the psychic couldn't give her. She'd gone to Malvern to set her mental flights in reality, but he had only made her afraid. He'd told Eila that although her mind went away, it was a helpless journey, with no grounding in the sane world. But now, something from her vision was here. It was *real. Solid.* She could touch it, and so she did.

A shiver hit her, and Eila flinched back.

If this machine is real, is the boy real? And if both are real, are the monsters real, too?

She thought of the beast made of smoke. The flames she sometimes saw around her at night, in a place that recalled the bakery she'd visited in childhood, where kindly Carlo had died in a fire. She thought of the thing that was like a gnarled tree, its arms and fingers made of scarred bark. A creature with malicious yellow eyes; chimeric, indistinct presences made of mist and swirling ash. She'd seen things from Alterran lore, told by adults to children at night — or, when intoxicated, to each other: elves in the haunted city of Aerohead before it was haunted, horses with single ivory horns, great dragons with flaming lungs. And Eila had seen things nobody had envisioned alongside them: a beast that crawled backward on hands shaped like distorted feet, its skin green, mouth too low on its neck, seething with jagged fangs. A dark thing with a face of white eyes but no irises or mouth, seeming to swivel its head on its shifting body as if boneless, as if it couldn't decide where to face, or if it should face everywhere at once.

She touched the Convenience. *It was real.*

A few minutes' walk down the encircling alleyway, Eila reached a section that seemed somehow familiar. She recognized the array of pipes and dials; she could see a protruding cog and a manual pressure wheel intended to redirect something in the thing's guts. For the first time, she wondered who worked the Convenience, or if it worked itself. Piece by piece, it would have been made in the Ministry, then transported here in manageable chunks and assembled. Sometimes, inspirations given to the Builders by the Aether birthed thinking machines, and plenty of times they produced dumb clockwork and intermeshing gears that required a worker's hand to function.

There is so much about manifestation that is still unknown today, Eila's father had told her once at home, safely away from Rabbit Brampton's prying ears. *We are given items to Build, but have you ever noticed how some Builders Build better manifestations than others? And have you ever wondered why our cities are such a mishmash? Your mother complains about it all the time. But really, how can we create a unified look when we must take what the Blunderbuss gives us and guess at how to best arrange it in our lives?*

Atwell had been slightly intoxicated. Even in the privacy of his own house, it wasn't a good idea to ask such questions. Not when your daughter was a Builder's prodigy, destined to grow up wondering the same things.

Eila looked at the machine. It was a perfect example of what her father had said. The mercantile shops across the small thruway were charming and Old World — perhaps a bit behind the times, but quaint. And yet right beside them was this monstrosity from another world.

There should be a door here.

Holding on to anything from her earlier vision (the vision that collapsed Pianoforte, she thought with bitter guilt) was like chasing clouds, but Eila was certain that there should be a door on the thing, somewhere nearby. She didn't explicitly remember seeing one behind the boy, but the creature that had taken him away right before she woke up screaming had come from somewhere. If this blocks-wide machine handled the city's waste, it must touch the sewers. A door would be necessary. A door would let her down into those tunnels beneath the streets.

A voice inside her screamed. *Why would you want to go into the sewers?*

Eila wasn't sure. She *did* want to, but at the same time she very much *didn't* want to. There could be anything in the sewers. Even a creature like the one she'd seen take the boy.

Her eyes darted around. Eila had moved far enough from the shops that she was more or less alone. That couldn't be good. She wasn't supposed to be in this part of town. With her high-priced attire and impractical footwear, she stuck out like a sunflower in a grove of cow patties.

Eila had no way of letting Mother know she might be late — and no excuse for being where she was even if she could.

She should go. She'd found the Convenience. If she absolutely must try again later, she'd know where to find it. She'd even located the section from her vision, where she'd seen the boy. Where he'd beckoned her, and told her to find him, to find *them*, to follow him down. But there was no way in, no boy, and nowhere to go. Even if she'd wanted to explore the underworld on a foolish, reckless, dangerous whim, she couldn't.

Eila looked again, and saw a door where there hadn't been one before.

She traced its edge, her eyebrows furrowing. Again she looked around, still finding the area empty, save for some distant shouts and banging. The door was as plain as day, and yet Eila was certain the same space had been smooth a moment ago.

Open it. Follow the white rabbit. Follow him below.

But of course, it's not like the door would be unlocked. It's not like its knob would simply turn, opening to the casual passerby. Eila wouldn't have to resist doing something stupid, because the door wouldn't swing open at her hand's command.

But it did.

Chapter Five
Down the Rabbit Hole

Eila stepped through the door, brimming with excitement, fear, and something she might have thought of as *validation.* There was a distinct possibility that she'd lost her mind and was merely sinking deeper into madness, but given the feel and smell and sound of things, reality seemed more likely.

Her heart was whip-hammering hundreds of beats each minute, and it felt like her blouse should be jumping away from her skin from the blows. But still, Eila's every step took her from the hazy split reality she'd been feeling over the past weeks into something deeper, something genuine.

This was a terrible, terrible idea. Eila was more frightened than she could ever remember being. She was alone, and nobody knew where she was, heading into a dungeon. But at the same time, she was making sense from some of her vision: this place was scary, *but at least it existed after all.*

She took her first steps forward and heard the door clunk closed behind her. She turned to watch, not at all surprised to find that the door had more or less vanished. The inside was metal and rods, like the wall behind. It had to be there somewhere, but from where she stood it seemed as if it never was.

The die had been cast, one way or the other. Eila turned forward again and moved out from a small utility closet and into a larger room inside the Convenience.

The room was nothing like she'd have expected from the outside. It didn't look like the guts of a waste management machine. Rather, it looked like a smallish lobby in a well-appointed downtown hotel. There were fine rugs on a polished wood floor and fine etchings in frames on the walls. The walls themselves were smooth, seemingly made of familiar plaster and lath rather than gears and iron. There were ornate brass sconces along the walls, but most of the light was coming from standing cut-glass lamps in two of the room's corners.

Eila looked around in disbelief. The walls had baseboards and crown molding. And there was an end table farther in, situated beside a richly upholstered armchair not unlike Father's at home. On the end table were several scientific-looking devices beside what appeared to be a miniature telescope with interchangeable optics. A second device looked like eyeglasses, but with thick lenses that seemed multilayered. A ticking instrument was in the center, a kind of clock face on the front, oscillating back and forth like a round metronome.

Breath in her chest, Eila's attention turned toward the room's obvious exit — the only way to proceed farther unless she wanted to turn around and search the wall for the outside door that she was suddenly afraid might no longer exist. She faced a spiral staircase, glistening silver as it wound down and spilled into a heavily ornamented room.

"Time to go home, Eila-girl," she said aloud, stepping toward the staircase, as if her feet were not under her control.

She paused to touch the newel posts. They, like the rest of the staircase, were made of glossy metal, but they'd been molded in the shape of a round object and painted in blues and greens. She wondered for a moment at what the ball could be, then saw what was underneath: a man, nude, crouched and holding the huge ball on his back and shoulders. What did it mean? Who was this man, and what was the green-and-blue ball he strained to hold up?

Feeling the same blend of thrill and reticence, Eila began to descend the stairs. Their footing was as posh as that of the room above; the risers were solid hardwood, a runner pinned in the centers and cut to fit the turning spiral. With each step, Eila reminded herself how stupid she was being and begged her body to turn back for the door. The staircase spiraled *down*, and she'd started at street level. Nobody, save a few engineers, ever went below the streets. She knew there would have to be a few pipes just under the surface, but it didn't take Eila long to go lower. Below where the pipes were supposed to lie. Below where the water supposedly came from, and where sewage supposedly went. Below the sewers, so far as the citizens of Waldron's Gate understood them.

She should head home. She'd pressed her luck as far as it would reasonably go. Enough was enough.

But somehow, descent made her feel saner. *More* integrated. *More* whole. *Less* as if she were flying apart like a machine with loose bolts. Eila didn't want to be down here. And at the same time, she very much wanted to find the white rabbit.

Each ill-advised step was like an itch being scratched: stepping deeper felt so good, though she knew it could hurt her.

The staircase was narrow and tight. Her descent was rapid, and she wanted to look down to see how far the pit might go, but the spiral's center was blocked with the bulk of a huge spindle upon which stairs were mounted.

She seemed to be passing through floors as if she'd begun at the top of a tall building. Each was tiny and did not seem to sprawl far beyond the staircase. Each "floor" consisted of one open room (Eila could have stepped off into any one of them but felt sure the white rabbit was somewhere below) and nothing else. The remainder of the floor space consisted of a ring around the staircase that looked too close to the walls to squeeze around. The rooms themselves were intriguing, each fitting a particular theme.

The first's design scheme was unified enough to make her mother — the Ministry of Decorum's current Head — proud. It was nautical, as if from a day when people believed in an ocean beyond the Fog. She saw what looked like maps both on the walls and unrolled on an ornate desk, the corners pinned with instruments Eila didn't recognize.

The second room was military, as if belonging to a strategist at Stensue — a strategist who, it again occurred to Eila, would seem to have no purpose if the nation's only enemies lived in the Fog … which, she thought with amusement, was supposedly empty. Again she saw maps, but these ones were bizarre; one on the wall showed Alterra's tall outline, but then revealed more land beyond, as if the surface world spilled past the Fog. The office's absent occupant seemed well-prepared for some unknown conflict. The walls were crowded with weapons. Eila recognized several short blunderbuss rifles (each with a belled end, like their namesake) similar to those carried by the Parliament Guard. She saw swords and the blunderbusses' shorter cousins — dragon pistols, also with fluted ends like the machine. On the room's desk, someone was assembling strange, unknown contraptions. They were surely weapons as well, all tubes and seeming pneumatics, some with miniature pressure tanks hanging from their stocks.

As Eila descended farther, rooms passed in a strange kaleidoscope: A room dedicated to fashion — both the high-society kind Eila and her mother knew, with top hats and long coats, and something edgier, with black whale-bone corsets beneath cloaks of buckles and straps. A room filled with blades, some attached to gadgets. A room dedicated to tools — most of which Eila guessed, by the profusion of dirt on them and the floor, to be dedicated to digging. A room filled with black, grease-clotted gears combined into almost random configurations, as if the machinist disbelieved the laws of up and down, or cause and effect.

By the time Eila stepped off the staircase and onto a filthy stone floor, the staircase had become something alien and filthy. Her hands, which had held the smooth railing the entire time, came away black with the dust and grime of neglect. She could smell something putrid: stale, like a long-shuttered chamber, with a tinge of something burning. The lights had grown dim; she found herself having slowly become accustomed to gloom. As she'd come down, the rooms had become less posh, darker, more ominous. The last one she'd seen was filled with nothing but black rocks like shale and coal. Accordingly, the staircase had deteriorated underfoot. The runner was still in place, but it was now in threads and tatters, covered in filth.

How far down had she come? How many floors had she passed? Eila felt a sudden fright that time had slipped by in gushes while her mind went elsewhere, as if she'd slept and fallen into a vision. For a long, terrifying moment, she wondered if that was what happened. Had she really taken the trolley into the Doer district? Had she really found the strange Convenience? Had a door appeared from nowhere, and had she truly been foolish enough to enter, then walk blindly down a winding staircase filled with unrealities?

Eila made herself breathe. *Yes.* It had to be real. It was hard to recall her visions once they were behind her, but she felt sure that they'd never felt quite this authentic. Visions were swimmy, with their edges all soft. She held up her left hand, then used a fingernail on her right hand to drag a line across it.

Yes, it hurt. The pain was sharp. This must really be happening.

But then, was she so sure that she didn't *always* feel that way in her vision's grip?

Eila tried to place the time, then looked up at the staircase. If she wanted to make it home — and be sure to desert this part of town before nightfall — she would almost certainly need to head back now.

Eila stepped forward, away from the staircase.

Her eyes had fully adjusted to the gloom at the spiral's bottom, and picked out a door that had, of course, been there all along. She was sure that it hadn't just materialized, as she was sure that the door at the top had been there all along. Doors were either there or they weren't, and the moment Eila started believing they could show up out of nowhere was the moment she should admit that the visions owned her, and that she should pack her belongings for Joffrey Columns.

She thought of the time, and the sun she could no longer see to mark its passage. But even if she'd worn a wristwatch, she wouldn't have noticed the time or truly grasped the number of remaining minutes.

There was a door in front of her, and if the white rabbit was anywhere, he was behind it.

Maybe this was a vision, and maybe it was real. The truth hardly mattered.

Eila reached out, squeezed the knob, and turned it.

Chapter Six

The World With No Sky

THE DOOR SWUNG WIDE INTO another world.

At first, Eila thought she was still outside, with terrible weather descended. The sky — small, due to the abundance of tall, dark buildings — was thick with what appeared to be clouds. For the second time, Eila wondered how far down she'd come. How many floors had there been? A dozen? Two? She could remember a few motifs of the rooms she'd passed, but the number of floors escaped her. She'd felt dazed as she descended, giving no conscious thought to the length of her return climb. It was possible she'd come down twenty flights, thirty, more. If each flight was twelve or fifteen feet high (which seemed about right), Eila could be several hundred feet below ground — maybe as much as a thousand. Street level that high above could vanish into gloom.

Her gaze wanted to linger on the missing ceiling and strange clouds and explore the dark buildings around her. But her eyes were immediately drawn to a shape across a small opening, and Eila's mind surrendered because it knew she was in a vision after all, and that nothing was real.

The shape peeled away from the wall and revealed its true form: a boy in his late teens, leaning against a brick wall. Eila had heard hair referred to as a "mop" (Mother said it about anyone not perfectly trim), but in the case of this boy it was almost literal. His hair was jet black, long, and curling in a messy halo. He had a days' worth of stubble, thick and dark enough that at first she'd thought his face was merely filthy. As he came closer, Eila saw light cornflower-blue eyes under his thick dark brows. He was too swarthy for eyes so light, and the contrast disarmed her.

"Welcome to Pavilion, Eila." He extended a mostly clean hand, grit only caked deep into his palm. She had the distinct impression that he'd just wiped it, for her. She wanted to accept, but her feet felt like they were mired in sap, as if in one of her visions.

"To answer your question … " he began.

Eila felt tiny. The boy couldn't be more than a couple of years older than she was, but he held a lifetime behind those eyes.

"I haven't asked a question," she said.

A wide rascal's smile turned his grime and stubble into a white crescent.

"You're just as brash in person, I see. No, you haven't asked a question. But seeing as we've met before, I assume you're thinking that … "

"We haven't met."

His eyes, like his smile, were pleasantly mocking. "Or maybe I *shouldn't* answer your question."

"I'm sorry." Eila didn't know why she felt the need to apologize. Nothing made sense, and she suddenly wanted to be home, or with Cora, shopping and discussing her best friend's latest crush.

"To answer your question," he said again, "no, this isn't a dream."

Dream. Something about the strange word struck the back of Eila's skull.

"Are you real?" It felt like the stupidest question in the history of Alterra. The boy was solid before her, his voice crisp in her ears and as real as the air's acrid scent. Her visions had never been like this. Still, here they were, somewhere that couldn't exist in a rational world.

"I'm real. It's not a dream."

There was that word again. Eila suppressed the urge to ask about it, knowing its meaning more or less from context. Somehow, he knew of her visions. And somehow, he seemed to have shared them, from the other end.

"Where are we?"

He gestured, chin to sky. "Below your city."

"How did you find this place? How did you hide it?"

"I was born here." He chuckled. "To us, it's not *hidden*."

Eila turned to look behind her, sure that the unreality would help things make sense. It *had* to be a vision — or a "dream," as he'd called it. But also, it wasn't. And despite her hammering heart, being here made sense because part of Eila had known this was coming for weeks. What was worse — to believe in a strange truth or to remain helpless in the face of bombarding insanity?

The door she'd just come through was quite like the door she'd entered on the side of the Convenience. Eila's eyes followed the door, from its spot in the wall of a similar machine skyward, into the haze she'd mistaken for clouds.

"As far as we can tell, that behind you is the same machine you see up there, where you entered. Two halves to make a whole." He voiced a small laugh. "Not the only thing that works that way."

She looked toward the door, then at the boy.

"Who are you?"

"My name is Levi. Levi Meade."

"I've … I've … "

She didn't want to say it. Somehow, saying that he'd appeared in her visions felt like an admission of intimacy. Eila's thoughts were her own — and as a Builder, they were also her profession. Nobody should be able to control thoughts better than a Builder, and if Eila had felt anything over the past weeks, it had been "out of control." She'd followed his vision-self to this place, and yet she didn't want to say it, as if doing so would crack an unknown seal.

"You'll have a lot of questions," he said. "Fortunately, there are some answers. Not all, but some. Come, follow me."

Levi reached out and took Eila's hand. His was large and rough, like a laborer's — or a fighter's. But once his gentle tug snapped Eila from paralysis, she began to move. And once moving, she slipped her hand away. The daughter of the Ministry's Head Builder and Decorum's top officer would be led by no one.

"Where are we going?"

"To see a man who very badly wants to see you. His name is Daw."

"What kind of a name is Daw?"

"You'll stop asking that and start asking about the man himself once you meet him. Come on, it's this way." Levi motioned toward her hand, but she moved it back an inch — just enough to let him know it wasn't his for the taking — and moved up to walk beside him. Levi was tall and looked strong. Again, Eila felt as small as she did young. But she had followed her vision here. She could hold her breath a while longer, see how many of her odd visions unfolded into reality.

Unbidden, something Palpatine Malvern had said echoed in Eila's head as her low-heeled shoes clacked on the cobblestones: *There's something you can do that nobody should be able to do, and if you allow what's behind that door to escape, you'll change the world.*

She'd opened two doors so far. As Eila looked back, she noticed that this door, unlike the other, was still plainly visible. Rather than a reassurance that she could leave when she wanted, it made her nervous. If she could leave, maybe others could, too.

They moved away from the Convenience and into the town's streets. Everything was in shades of gray and black instead of the bright colors of Waldron's Gate, but otherwise it could have simply been the world Eila knew. After they'd walked in silence for thirty short seconds, her mind had already begun to forget that she'd come deep underground, that there was a ceiling above the sky, and that she wasn't simply walking through an industrial part of town on a very overcast day.

Walking beside her, Levi followed Eila's eyes as she watched the sky.

"Until I learned to recognize dreams for what they were, I never knew a sky could look different than this," he said. "In a way, it's a curse. Almost nobody down here knows we're underground. This is how it has always been. Our haze is generated by what you call the Convenience. We're fairly sure it's a byproduct of the machine's other functions, but it does a nice job of obscuring the rock. Pavilion's citizens might never question an eternally cloudy sky, but I sometimes wonder about the roof of an enormous cave. It's a question for the masters. How much can people accept? People say our society has been as it is for over a thousand years. If generation after generation lives in a cavern, would they even know it was a cavern? Or would they think that "rock above" is how the world is supposed to be? Would they even know it was rock, or find it odd if they did?"

Levi laughed, but Eila wasn't sure why.

She had a thousand questions, and each seemed naive. "You

know me," she said instead.

"Yes. I was looking for you. For those like you."

"Like me how?"

He shrugged. They were passing a brown building where a pleasant-looking plump woman was sweeping her stoop. She smiled. Despite her trepidation, Eila smiled back.

"That's not really for me to say. Daw will explain."

"Who is Daw?"

"Our Head of Dreaming. The white-haired man you dream about sometimes … is that the fellow 'Brampton'?"

Eila blinked, more disarmed by the idea that Levi had been cherry-picking her thoughts than the recurrence of the strangely familiar word "dream."

"You know Rabbit Brampton?"

"*You* know him."

Eila swallowed. "He's my boss."

"Daw is his counterpoint. On the other end."

"The other end of what?"

"He's a scientist, and he leads the Guile. He taught us all, and showed me what to look for."

"Is that why you're in my visions?" The sentence left before she could reclaim it. Not only had she just admitted to knowing that Levi had been tinkering in her head; she'd also admitted to visions. She'd only told one person about them, and that person had backed away from her in fear before kicking her out of his tent and predicting the world's doom at her hand.

Levi didn't take the question as odd. He kept walking beside her, his short black work boots clunking on stones. Dust and grime were everywhere, and Levi left a footprint with every step.

"Yes. I'm sorry. It's intrusive, like what the Dreamers do. Worse, maybe, because *they* don't know what they're doing, and I very much do."

"Who are 'the Dreamers?' What do they do?"

"Daw will tell you."

"How about *you* tell me?"

"It's complicated."

Eila felt annoyed. But annoyance was better than fear, which she should probably be feeling as well. Still, she found herself settling in, her once-thumping heart braking into a natural rhythm. The top of her mind had forgotten where she was, or that she was passing through something impossible. She was strolling through another city, beside an interesting stranger. The outskirts, though she'd never visited, couldn't be much odder.

"So you aren't going to answer any of my questions?"

Levi sighed, stopped a beat, then said, "Look. You've just discovered a city under yours. That's a big thing to realize, but nothing compared to what you are about to learn. I'm not a scientist. If I tell you the wrong thing or tell it to you in the wrong way, I'll … well, we're almost there, and Daw will do better. So please. Ask me questions I can answer."

He took a moment to follow as Eila resumed walking. She nearly laughed. She didn't know where she was going or what had come over her — only that she felt delirious with relief that she wasn't going mad. At least some of her insanity had been proven true. She wanted to know what else was true before whatever this was ended, or changed into something else.

"Why don't people from here try to go up?"

He shrugged. "Even if we could Tinker the parts for a borer, there would be no point."

"Why?"

"Nobody would believe us enough to let us try."

"Why not? You live in a cave."

"You don't understand. You know what blue sky looks like. You know what it's like to travel outside of your city. You have ferry shaws that move from place to place, spreading stories. We have none of that. If you'd lived inside a box for your entire life — but not just you; I'm talking about your parents, their parents, *their* parents, and so on for a thousand years — how would you even have any concept of what a 'box' is?"

Eila shook her head. "That's silly. Show them the walls. Blow away that haze and use optics to inspect the roof."

"'*That's the way the edge of the world is.*'" Levi's voice was probably supposed to imitate that of a typical Pavilion-dweller. "'*That's the way the sky looks.*' That's what they'd say. You can't possibly understand.

It's not about convincing people. They don't *want* to believe. Grow something in confinement, and it becomes used to confinement. Craves it even. How old are you, Eila?"

"Fifteen." She was almost sixteen, and for some reason wanted to say so.

"And how much history do you know?" He flapped his hands. "Well," he added. "*Your flavor* of history, anyway."

"'How much'?" she asked. *History* was a hard thing to quantify.

"How far back in time."

"What we learned in school, I guess. The usual. About the Fog. The legends. The finding of the Blunderbuss, and the construction of the cities."

"How many *years* of history? Since the Blunderbuss, I mean?"

"A thousand?" It was strange to realize it was roughly the same timeframe he'd given for all of Pavilion's history, though maybe he was being figurative.

"Exactly. All of your history, forever. All that matters, anyway. Do you see how long a thousand years is, and how much has changed since then?"

Eila's mind tried to flit back in time, to imagine herself at the dawn of the Blunderbuss. According to legend, Alterran people had been nomadic back then. They'd come across the great machine and realized that it could teach them to Build and create. She imagined being in that first tribe, finding the behemoth, looking up at its gear-strewn bulk as it gleamed in the sun. All she knew today had blossomed from that moment. Before it, nothing in their world had truly existed.

"Our entire society has been shaped by where and how we live," said Levi. "Other than in very small, very secretive pockets — and even then, only secondhand via a conduit, who understood the responsibility they carried — nobody has known about the world above. We do your dirty jobs, but we don't know they're yours. We sift your capital, but we have been told it all comes from us, or from another place. Our religions are based on how we've grown up and the world we find around us. Your people believe in The Crown, but can you understand how difficult it would be to believe in a god from the sky when we've never seen sky? Exposing the truth isn't as simple as cutting a hole in the roof to let the sunlight through. That knowledge would undermine everything we believe. Don't you see how completely it would destroy us … and your world along with it?"

"How would it destroy *us?*"

Levi looked as frustrated as Eila felt. But he seemed to be something else, too — perhaps angry or indignant. "Daw will explain," he said.

"What can *you* explain?"

"I'm not a theologian. I'm not a scientist. I'm not a philosopher."

"What do you mean by 'sift our capital'?"

"Daw will … "

"You tell me!" Eila blurted, feeling her cheeks flush. She felt something inside herself slip and realized with dizzying certainty that she was standing at the edge of a precipice. She'd felt confident and strong coming down here, but even as she'd done so, a deeper part of her had wondered why she'd been so serene. Now she realized the truth: she'd been calm because she was close to her breaking point. She'd spent weeks keeping a horrible secret and harboring a numbing fear. Her madness had brought the entire Ministry of Manifestation to its knees, and there was a distinct possibility that she'd be fingered as the responsible party. Something in her mind had terrified a genuine psychic, and she'd learned too many unknown truths to count — including, now, one that turned the world upside-down. She'd been calm because she had no choice *but* to be calm. Now her period of shock had ended and she was about to snap and turn violent, like an animal trapped.

"By 'capital,' I meant your *dreams*," said Levi, his face shocked.

"What are dreams?"

They'd been walking through a residential section of town. It was as dingy as the area near the lower half of the Convenience, but gloom aside, the lawns (how did they grow without sun and topside air?) had become friendlier. Houses — still darkly colored, surely for practical reasons due to the dust and filth of Pavilion living — had grown larger, and their architecture more elaborate. When Levi's eyes flicked toward the mansion fifty feet from where they'd paused, Eila found herself thinking that even her aesthetic-minded mother, if she could get past the muted colors and grit, might have been able to see it as beautiful.

They'd reached their destination. Whoever Daw was, she'd find him inside.

Levi swallowed. "Dreams," he said, "are what make the world."

Chapter Seven

Upside Down

Levi asked Eila to wait in a lushly appointed foyer inside the mansion while he ventured farther to find the man he'd called Daw — the scientist who might finally tell Eila where her mind sometimes went at night, how a boy from an underground city sometimes swam through those visions, and how she'd known to follow him to a place that existed in secret.

She had too many questions to count, and the empty seconds after Levi's departure felt stretched. With answers so close, every tick of an unseen clock threatened to spill her over the lip of insanity. She distracted herself by looking around the room.

The home, like Pavilion, wasn't nearly as oppressive as she would have imagined given its circumstances. Eila was already getting used to being underground and found that she barely realized she was. The cavern was enormous, and the city seemed to be almost as large as Waldron's Gate above. Once she opened new eyes and closed the biased ones she'd brought with her, it was easy to see Pavilion as just another city.

Daw's mansion, other than being shaded in browns and grays rather than the whites and brights Eila knew from above, belonged in the high-end district of any fine city. The man who owned it would be wealthy anywhere, and lived well. As well, in fact, as …

"Pretty, isn't it?"

She'd paused to examine an ornate umbrella holder made of wrought iron and bejeweled with some sort of dark, cloudy gemstone. The interrupting voice made her jump almost hard enough to fall over.

She spun to find a tall, thin man standing behind her. He had dark, serious eyes and a messy head of shoulder-length hair that looked plastered in a week's worth of unwashed oil. His large mustache was waxed up into a dramatic curl at the end. He was dressed in a parody of finery that, to Eila, felt like a mocking salute to his dusty but opulent mansion. The man wore a fine suit coat, cut long to fit his lean frame, a black bow tie, and a patterned gold vest. His clothing was formal but slouched, as if he'd been wearing the same suit for months as Pavilion spread dirty layers of living atop it.

"Very," she said. But Eila wasn't only considering the umbrella urn by itself. She was recalling a foyer much like this one that she'd visited as a child. Her own home didn't have a dedicated place for umbrellas — especially not one so extravagant. But that other foyer had — because as wealthy as the Doyle family was, that other was wealthier.

"If Levi were here, he could tell me what that odd look on your face means," said the man, "because he's been inside your mind. You wouldn't like for him to tell me, I'm sure. But that's the odd thing about his gift: Levi can't do what he does as an innocent. It is a violation. Always."

"I was thinking that your house has the same floor plan as Rabbit Brampton's."

The man's head cocked, like a dog's. "But you haven't seen my whole floor plan."

"I've seen enough to know." Eila touched the umbrella urn. "Right down to this."

"I suppose you got that trait from your mother. Your awareness of space and art. The Building — and perhaps the dreams — come from your father. Perhaps that explains your particular alchemy of elements."

"Explains *what?*"

"We're getting ahead of ourselves." The man took two steps toward Eila and extended a hand. His long, tailored suit pants swished a little as he approached, the coat moving as if tethered to his body. Eila could see the bow tie more clearly. It looked somehow withered, like a flower set near a fire. "My name is Daw Blackburn."

Eila looked at his hand, then decided it would be rude not to shake it. She met him halfway, touching his hand briefly and then letting her fingers fall. The ticking clock reasserted itself in the quiet split seconds between beats, and Eila realized that she was going to be late. She'd only make dinner at home now if she sprinted, but she was rooted in place, not wanting at all to move.

"Eila Doyle," she said.

"Oh, we *know* who you are. Levi had to swim for ages to find you, but when he did, he said you were a beacon. But yes, this house is like Brampton's, so far as our conduits' visions will say. It's something the Ministries seem to do, or the engine prompts them to do. They take what you Build and do what seems sensible at the time, setting it alongside other creations without really knowing why or possessing any master plan. They give two men whose jobs mirror each other, for example, the same house for an identical lack of reason." He nodded at the wrought iron object by the door. "And, apparently, gift them with the same useless umbrella urns."

"'Ministries?'" There were several, of course — Manifestation, Decorum, Culinary Arts, and countless others — but Eila doubted that was what Blackburn meant. Why would any Ministry give him anything, especially if Pavilion's existence was a secret?

"Come," he said, gesturing. "You must be tired."

Eila was suddenly very aware that she was in a strange man's house, more or less alone, and that no one knew where she was. She felt a need to stay near the door. Blackburn wore civility well, but to Eila its veneer seemed paper thin. His hair was matted on his head as if missing a top hat; on him it would look like a chimney sweep's rather than a banker's. He looked an inch from disorder, despite his quasi-finery.

"I'm fine," she said.

Blackburn didn't wait for her. He'd already turned, his black-coated back to the door. He was five steps toward his home's interior when Eila's paralysis shattered. She could — and probably *should* — let him go and head home, but she couldn't un-see what she'd already seen. If the day's many boxes stayed open with unanswered questions inside them, she *would* go mad.

She rushed to follow. It was as ill-advised as everything else she'd done and she didn't want to seem as eager as she felt, but if the man vanished, she'd have to call out — and she knew that if she did, he'd hold every card.

Scampering behind, she entered what appeared to be a study. Eila, with her Builder-trained memory, effortlessly placed it atop a remembered blueprint from the time when her father had taken her to Rabbit Brampton's home. It was the same, like the foyer had been.

There was a crystal decanter on a small wooden end table, flanked by two gorgeous tumblers. Unlike everything else in Pavilion — including Blackburn's wardrobe — the glasses and decanter were clean enough to sparkle. Inside the decanter was a bright-green liquid that practically glowed. Blackburn pulled the stopper and tinkled ice as he filled each glass with liquid.

"Do you know what this is?" he said.

"It's Thunderclap." Eila was pleased to pull the trivia from her head. It was an adult drink, usually not served or discussed around those underage. Eila knew of Thunderclap the way she knew about many forbidden things: due to her father's penchant for truth and well-timed bouts of slightly too much intoxication.

"Indeed." He held a glass toward her.

"I can't have that."

"Nonsense. You are in my home. I give you my permission." He shook his glass and tinkled the ice.

"I mean, I'm not old enough," she told him. "I haven't passed my assessment."

"Has it ever seemed strange to you," said Blackburn, still holding the glass toward her, "that adulthood is granted based on an assessment? Adult animals are those who have aged sufficiently to take care of themselves. Yet adult humans are judged by assessment, varying the age for everyone."

Of course it seemed strange. Her father had raised the same argument, always urging Eila to never accept anything without wondering why. But she didn't want to admit that to this strange man, so she kept her distance and repeated official Alterran rhetoric.

"Thunderclap is forbidden until a person is fully formed."

Blackburn's somehow oily eyebrows arched. "Oh? And why is that?"

"Because Thunderclap alters the mind."

He chuckled, then sat in the chair behind him. It was old leather

— a parody of finery that mocked the home's splendor as surely as the man's elegant but rumpled attire. He set Eila's glass on the end table, then leaned back, crossed his legs, and sipped from his own.

"And Crumble doesn't?"

Tentatively, Eila sat in the chair opposite Daw. She perched on its edge, knees pressed together, her hands atop them. There was the clack of shoes; Eila looked up as Levi entered the study. Without asking, he took a third chair and became one with the background.

"We know a great deal about Waldron's Gate, and about Alterra in general," said Blackburn. "Enough to know that our societies are similar in many ways."

"I thought your people didn't go up?"

"They haven't. Oh, I'm sure someone has found a way up at some point in history, but the tunnels explored by our Guile only go down so far as we've been able to find. We are not Builders. Our work is done by hand, through the works of Tinkers. You have a written language, but we do not. Not officially, anyway. Because we see the need to keep records, some among the Guile have worked a system, but it can't be widespread or comprehensive in the way that we understand yours is. So we don't *know* of anyone who has gone up even if they have. Until now, there's been no easy way."

"Until now?"

"Levi had to meet you in your dreams because that *was* the only way. Now that we brought you here, the seal has been broken."

"How?"

He took a sip. "You made a door."

Eila thought of her ease in unlocking the Convenience, and how odd she'd found it that there were no rumors of an underground city given the effortless entry. Then she remembered how at first there had seemed to *be* no door, then suddenly there was, as if she'd Built it. But that was impossible so far from the Blunderbuss.

Blackburn raised his glass. Eila still hadn't taken hers and noticed that Levi didn't move to pour any for himself. She could accept the Thunderclap as offered (she'd been curious since hearing of the drink's almost ritualistic secrecy among adults), but right now, as Eila sat in Blackburn's study, she had her discipline and nothing more.

"Thunderclap," he said, swishing the green liquid side to side, "is restricted. It is something the youth must wait for, and be protected from. By contrast, Crumble is safe. It must not 'alter the mind,' as you said."

"You're saying Crumble isn't safe?" The idea was absurd. Crumble was a part of Alterran life like sun in the sky. For convenience, Eila usually took her Crumble in capsule form, but she'd had black rocks crumbled into her milk and applesauce since she was a baby. Crumble was part of Crown ceremonies, coming-of-age ceremonies, dating, marriage, and childbirth. Not taking it was like not drinking water. If you wanted to live inside the Fog, you took it, or found yourself insane, locked up in Joffrey Columns. Legend said that Crumble hadn't been necessary before the Fog, but nobody really knew if the Fog had once been absent. Legend said it had been a thousand years. As long as the Blunderbuss had been known. As long, according to Levi, as Pavilion had lived beneath the city.

"Have you ever tried to stop taking it?"

"Of course not."

"Have you ever *had* to postpone a dose? Due to circumstances beyond your control?"

She had, of course. The experience was always acutely uncomfortable — again, like going too long without water. When she didn't drink for a few hours or half a day, she felt parched and needy and dry. Same with Crumble, only the parch was in her head. Thoughts became loose and easy to rattle, like a poorly maintained machine. It became hard to focus. After half a day without water or Crumble, any normal person would quit what they were doing and find what they needed, stopping at nothing to quench their thirst.

"Sure."

"Not pleasant, is it?"

"So what?"

"It's because you're addicted."

"I don't know that word," Eila said, annoyed to admit a failing. Blackburn was toying with her. Only glances at Levi seemed to set everything right.

"It means that you cannot go without it," he explained.

"I also can't go without food and water."

"True. But that's because you *need* those things."

"Same as Crumble."

Blackburn smiled and flicked his eyes to Levi. After a moment, Eila followed those eyes, looking at Levi as well.

"What?" she said. She didn't like this. It felt like they were performing a show, and it was her job to clap and wait for punchlines.

Levi said, "We don't take Crumble."

Eila felt her chin sag, but wouldn't allow her mouth to hang open or give either of them the satisfaction of her obvious disbelief — though she disbelieved it plenty. Anyone would grow mentally famished going a half day without Crumble. If you somehow went a full day, you'd feel out of your skin and barely able to concentrate. And as with depriving the body of water, it took just three days without Crumble before your mind would fail … at which point, if you managed to stay alive, you'd be stark raving mad.

"What I'm about to tell you," said Blackburn, "comes to us through special seers we call 'conduits' and is unknown to all but a very small, very select group. My official position is Head Scientist of the Ministry of Dreaming — counterpoint to your Ministry of Manifestation above — but my unofficial position, as has been true for all of my predecessors, is as head of the Guile. The Guile are, in essence, revolutionaries without a revolution, preparing for when one finally arrives."

Eila didn't want to engage with what Blackburn was saying (emotional distance seemed the best defense, other than her physical prowess with kicks, punches, and foot speed if necessary), but it all felt too close to scratching her itch. She didn't know what he was talking about, but for some reason Eila's mind didn't feel cleaved in half while they were saying. The promise of an explanation was worth staying for.

"On the record, I am a scientist for Governance, which is our version of your Parliament," he continued. "Covertly, I am what our authorities call a 'dirty scientist.' Such people are a well-known problem in our world. I traffic in lies and experiment in matters of the natural world and the human mind that ought not be trifled with. That is their version of things. But what they call 'dirty science,' I simply call 'science.' The Ministry makes the perversion. What happens *there* is 'dirty.'

"Our 'dirty' means have uncovered the truth. Contrary to what you've been told, Waldron's Gate is a pair of twin cities. Above is the world you know, open to sky. Below is Pavilion, which does not understand the concept of sky. Other than me, my predecessors, and the Guile — plus high-placed people in Parliament and at least one faceless mole topside, whose mind has been feeding us through our conduits — neither city knows of the other."

Against her intentions, Eila realized she'd settled back into her chair. Across from her, Blackburn's dark eyes were intense.

"Why?"

"Waldron's Gate is driven by innovation," Blackburn answered. "How does that happen? How do you develop the new things you need? How are your requirements met?"

"We Build what we need."

"Using the Blunderbuss. The engine that allows you to manifest what you cull from the Aether."

Eila nodded. The discussion was skirting the line of confidentiality, but she was only confirming his words.

"Levi," he said. "Pull up the Ministry, if you would."

Levi stood, crossed to an area along the wall beside Blackburn, and pulled a swath of lush purple drapery aside. Eila had noticed the drapes immediately, because they seemed so out of place. If Blackburn's house truly mirrored Brampton's, they hung on an interior wall, not one that could look outside. He pulled the drape's bottom away and tucked it behind a brass hook. Behind was a bulging contraption somewhat like the viewbox in the Doyle home. Its front was a bulky glass tube, rounded at the edges, fat at the back and asymmetrical.

"We receive some Built goods down here," said Blackburn, "but only when they are needed for a system that supports Waldron's Gate. Our waste management systems, for instance, are top-notch. The technology used to process waste is far beyond what we have for daily life or entertainment. It's because we process your waste and sewers as well as our own. Nobody knows that, but it's true." Daw pointed at the tube contraption behind the drapery. It's grayish-brown screen was warming with blue light. "This, on the other hand, was hand assembled by our Tinker. It's not as fine as something Built by someone like you, but … " He shrugged to indicate that they had learned to make do.

The image on the warped screen cleared, like an ordinary viewbox but slower, showing Eila an image of somewhere else. And to think: they'd put the thing together by hand? How was that possible? Even Eila, who had Built many boxes during her first month Building, had no idea how they worked. It was magic, powered by gears and springs, seemingly feeding off the Aether, no different from those she made.

Slowly, an image resolved. Eila saw rings of scaffolding surrounding an immense dark shape. Looking closer, she could see individual cradles, each occupied by someone who appeared to be asleep. Or in a trance.

Blackburn raised his eyes.

"It's the Ministry of Manifestation," she said. "Where I work."

Blackburn shook his head, then tapped the screen toward the bottom, where Eila saw something she hadn't noticed before. The massive machine stopped short of the floor, hanging above the ground, its huge metallic end fluted like the end of a rifle.

"The Blunderbuss," said Eila, her mouth finally unhinging. "It's upside-down."

"No," Levi replied. "You're seeing its bottom half."

Chapter Eight

The Dream Engine

EILA LOOKED AT THE CLOCK on Blackburn's wall, wondering if it kept the same time as the Alterra she'd always known. All she could tell for sure was that it was a quarter past forever. There was somewhere she urgently needed to be, but she could no longer remember where, or when, or how. Or, for that matter, why it mattered in a world turned end-for-end.

"Drink the Thunderclap," said Levi, his pale-blue eyes kind as he watched hers. "It will help."

Eila took the glass without hesitation, pulled a long sip into her mouth, then set the drink back on the table. She felt no different, but the small swallow she'd just taken would have, in the eyes of many above, made her an adult. It seemed appropriate.

"You believe your job is to receive ideas from the Aether," said Blackburn. "You are given an image of an object that is required somewhere in your world — a replacement propeller for a zeppelin, a new cog system for a water delivery machine, sails for a landship — and your job is to use your mental gift to make it real. You are told that the job of the Blunderbuss is to help this process. It harmonizes with your thoughts and helps you Build, adding your touches as if making art. It draws ideas to you. It hears what you require, and brings those things closer."

Again, Blackburn tapped the screen. One hand absently twisted his long mustache, firming the curl at one end.

"In reality, these people — at *our* Ministry, using *our* half of the Blunderbuss — are feeding you those ideas. But as with you and those you work with, the Dreamers here do not know there is another half to what they do. They don't realize they are passing you ideas, only that they are seeing and releasing them. Nor do they know where *their* ideas come from — the notions they use as raw material, before sifting and sending them on."

"Where do their raw materials come from?"

"From dreams," said Levi, sitting back into his chair.

"*Your* dreams," said Blackburn. "The dreams of everyone in Waldron's Gate and the rest of Alterra."

"What is a 'dream?'"

Blackburn cracked a smile. It was the most genuine expression he'd offered so far, as if recalling a pleasant memory.

"A *dream*, Eila, is a way your mind has of showing you memories that don't exist. A way of living things you've not lived. A mental performance, seen with closed eyes."

Her heart beat faster. Before Eila could ask what she had to do, Levi spoke.

"Your dreams made it possible for me to find you. I can swim through others' dreams — it's my gift, not unlike Building or Dreaming or being a conduit — but swimming in the minds of Waldron's Gate citizens — of anyone other than people in Pavilion, actually — is like fighting a current. But sometimes, Eila, *your* dreams are still. And somehow, you, from time to time, *you* are able to hold them."

"That's what my visions are? What you're calling 'dreams'?"

Too late, Eila realized she'd again spoken aloud about visions, and again wanted to reclaim her thoughts. But the way they were speaking, everyone down here was insane. They thought nothing of having visions, or seeing somewhere in their heads that was different from reality.

Levi nodded.

"How do I stop them?" she blurted. "Can you tell me how to make it all go away?"

Levi and Blackburn exchanged an amused glance. Blackburn said, "You're *supposed* to dream. Your goal lies in the other direction."

"Nobody has visions like mine!" Eila's panic seeped closer. The people with answers were spewing absurdity, and begging her to follow them into madness.

"That's not true," Blackburn said. "Everyone does. But in your world, people don't realize it's happening because their dreams are stolen before they can experience them." He tapped the screen, indicating the mirror Ministry and those he'd called Dreamers lounging in cradles like those used by Eila each day. "By them."

"How?"

Blackburn nodded. "*Crumble*. The drug you all 'consume like water' leaves a sort of back door in your minds. Dreamers, using the Blunderbuss, are able to sneak through that back door and take what belongs to you."

Eila found her eyes wanting to water. She barely understood what a "dream" was, but she'd seen how Blackburn's eyes lit at the mention. They were personal and precious. If his words were true, the trespass was a shameful violation.

"Why do they steal from us?"

"They don't know they're stealing," said Blackburn. "Like Builders and your relationship with the Aether, our Ministry tells Dreamers they're harvesting thoughts that simply exist in the world. In reality, they're not sorting from the Aether. They are stealing dreams from every citizen in Alterra."

Eila blinked. She wanted to believe it was all a lie, but she'd traveled hundreds of feet underground to follow a boy who'd appeared inside her mind unasked. She'd seen "dreams" that for some reason hadn't been stolen, and found a Ministry of opposites built around an inverted Blunderbuss.

"The Blunderbuss," said Levi, "is a kind of dream engine, helping Alterra to create what it needs. But only a select few know about both halves or the truth of how it works. It is this: whenever Alterrans sleep, the Blunderbuss leeches dreams out of their minds, through the 'back door' left ajar by the Crumble they take daily, then gives those dreams to our Dreamers."

"And if you find yourself becoming angry with the Dreamers for taking your thoughts," said Blackburn, "don't be. Theirs is a terrible job. There are only a few hundred Dreamers working at our Ministry, but there are *millions* of dreams that small group must process. You, as Builders, train your minds to manifest … but the Dreamers train theirs to *experience* and to *sift*. You, Eila, have experienced only a handful of dreams — those Levi was able to stabilize within your head. But Dreamers must Dream *thousands* of dreams every night. They are trained to fully experience each one of them, and to extract the ideas most worthy of manifestation. Those 'worthy' ideas are passed upward through the Blunderbuss to the Builders, and the process gives you the raw materials you need (supposedly "arriving from the Aether," as you are told) in order to Build."

Blackburn shifted in his chair. "But the Dreamers do not know the other half of the process, just as you didn't until now. Pavilion believes that what the Dreamers do is to clear away pollution. Filters strip toxins from our air, but we're told that without Dreamers, our 'psychic air' would be polluted with impure and unwanted energies — not unlike religious people in your world fear the dark influence of The Imp. 'The Aether is pressing down on us heavily today,' people here say when dreams stolen by the Blunderbuss are especially thick, much like Alterrans above speak about foul weather. On heavy days, Dreamers work especially hard to clear the air, sifting and sorting until all the 'pollution' is gone and Pavilion's people can breathe clearly again."

Eila thought of her work at the Ministry, trying to square it with Blackburn's words. When she imagined her empty warehouse construct from her Build cradle, ideas descended into the space as if from a queue. Her job was to make them reality. She'd always believed the Ministry's teachings (that ideas bloomed from the Aether, drawn by the Blunderbuss), but was it possible that ideas had actually been stolen from citizens, processed below ground like sewage, then sent back up once clean?

"You said the Dreamers 'sort' dreams."

Blackburn nodded.

"And that means only some ideas come back up for us to Build."

He nodded again. "Natural dreaming is messy. Sometimes, the mind finds inspiration, yes, but quite often dreams are simply the mind clearing its throat. A Dreamer's job — though they do not realize it and seldom complain — is a violation. They are forced to Dream what did not come from within themselves — scraps and fragments meant to be weighed and processed by another mind, and ill-fitting to their own. It's hard enough for a mind to master its *own* dreams … but to be piled under the desires, fears, insecurities, decisions, and perversions from *thousands* of other people each night?" Blackburn shivered. "Those things are the mind's garbage. And as with Waldron's Gate's *literal* garbage, the people of Pavilion are given the task to keep your fingers clean."

"If the 'garbage' isn't sent to the Builders, where does it go?"

Levi answered. "Into the Fog."

Eila's spine fluttered with chills. The Fog surrounded all of Alterra, but Waldron's Gate was at the oval's edge, almost flush against it. If Levi was right, did that mean the Fog was thickest near the city because that's where the Blunderbuss and twin Ministries were? And if what the men were saying was true, what of their 'mental waste' lived inside it?

Blackburn sighed. "The mind is a fantastic thing, Eila. Astonishing. When you are free to dream, it's as if manifestation happens by itself. Alterrans have come to rely on the Blunderbuss for everything they need, but for the few of us who see the whole picture, this system of instant gratification is a crutch. That viewbox there?" He pointed at the viewing screen behind the curtain. "That was created by a man named Willoughby Keys. Willoughby, like everyone in Pavilion other than those trained as Dreamers, has always been free to dream when he sleeps. We're given almost nothing down here, because we are not supposed to know that manifestation — what you call 'Building' — is possible. So we use our imaginations to create what we need. That tube may not be pretty, but it was crafted by a man and his hands, with no help from a Builder."

Blackburn shook his head. "People's most shallow dreams are filled with what they see around them already. But because you are not allowed to dream in your world, 'shallow' is as deep as you go. What has been Built by the Ministry and its Builders, according to what I've heard through my conduit and Levi, is fantastic. But still, I can't help but wonder what innovations might have been possible had human minds been required to think out their solutions instead of simply receiving them. What would have happened if you'd had to puzzle in directions *different* from those you already knew? A barbarian who wants a better weapon than his club would manifest a bigger club with help from the Blunderbuss … but what might have happened if that barbarian had been forced to *think* and *plan* and *figure* instead? Would his society have developed a gun instead of a club? Would they find alternatives to violence, and learn to resolve conflict?"

"We're not violent," said Eila.

"Not in a way that's obvious from where you stand," Blackburn argued. "But how accurate do you consider Parliament's media? And if you are as isolated as you are told — if all that's beyond the Fog surrounding Alterra is the ocean of Heaven, with Jonah swimming its seas — then why the need for a military? Why is Stensue nothing but troops and war machines and barracks and armaments?"

"It's not about weapons, Eila," Levi interrupted. "Daw and his fellow 'dirty scientists' — a few of whom preceded him in leading the Guile — believe the mind has a highly creative side. We see the creativity here, in minds like Willoughby's, where there is no engine to help us Tinker. It makes us wonder what's been stolen from you up there, *other* than dreams. What have been the Blunderbuss's side effects? Who might you have been without it? We wonder what it means that only those below are allowed to cleanse their minds, or dream deeply enough for fantasies."

"Fantasies?" Eila knew the word, of course (a synonym for fables told around fires and at children's bedsides), but it seemed out of place as used by Levi.

"We don't have a written language down here, so we tell stories," he said. "Does that happen in your culture?"

Eila started to reply, but found only hollow rebuttals. Cora was full of stories, as was her own mother. But stories and gossip weren't one and the same. Old books of fables held fragile tales — not just because the most ancient books were turning to dust, but because few new ones were written.

"Your fantasies never make it into your story as a people," said Blackburn. "They are lopped off at the knees before they can be fully articulated. You have heard of elves and dragons and trolls and ghosts? They were real, once. Now they are outside, cleansed from the world's memory and consciousness. Parliament and the Ministry see only what Alterra needs and what it has come to rely on as the means to get it. They don't see the way your collective mind is scraped without regard, like a plate's leftovers into a pile of compost. They don't see the torture inflicted on Dreamers, who must stay here and soak it all in, experiencing darkness and fear so you don't have to. They don't see how it has divided our society into an equilibrium so fragile that the mere *knowledge* of that balance would collapse us all." He paused, sipping his Thunderclap. "And perhaps most troubling, they don't see how the 'garbage' they toss out will one day consume them."

"The Fog," Eila said. "This is about the Fog."

Levi leaned forward.

"You are the first person we've found who can both Build *and* Dream," he said. "It was your aberrant Dreams that broke the resonance at the last Build — a wave we felt down here, in Daw's Ministry. We've been searching for someone like you. I found you, and you came to us. *You* were able to turn the waste management machine into a doorway. *You* broke the seal and blended our worlds, where no one else had. Everyone we've found has the ability to create or to manifest, but not both." He nodded at Eila. "Until now."

She felt a chill. "What does *that* have to do with the Fog?"

Blackburn waited a horrible moment and said, "Because we believe the dark things that live within it are beginning to realize the size of their large and growing number as it compares to our relatively small one." Then, after a curt nod, he added, "So *you*, Eila, must help us cross through the Fog and escape to the outside, before it consumes us."

Chapter Nine

Where Dreams May Come

Eila rode the streetcar home, feeling numb. The air had chilled with the sun's departure, and the brass pole at the car's edge felt cool under her hand. A good thing; a chilled pole meant her palm was still warm. It would've been easy to believe that it no longer was.

She was late, and didn't care. Her mother would be angry at best, frightened at worst. With Atwell at the Ministry, she'd be wrangling all three of the other children. Their handmaiden, Harney, would make the meal and clear the table while Juliette called Atwell and Cora's mother. She might even have called Rabbit Brampton, or the police.

Riding the streetcar, feeling the sway as it switched between tracks and made turns, Eila found herself unable to care. There were small spark lights at the trolley's edges, but the center was relatively dim. Twilight had draped a respectful shroud over the occupants, all of whom seemed tired and just wanted to get home without the burden of pleasantries or conversation. She didn't have to return curious stares from other riders with her own defensive gaze, answering unasked questions about who she was in her high-society clothing, leaving the low end of town. She didn't have to fend off well-meaning offers to see her home, as a young girl alone. She could simply ride, and feel her heart cool by degrees.

She'd held her stoicism through most of what Blackburn had said — or rather, what *Daw* had said, because the first time she'd called him "Mr. Blackburn" he'd asked her to be more familiar, implying that she might as well get cozy because they were all in this together. Eila lost her stoicism in that moment, suddenly wanting very much *not* to be "in this" with either of them — *any* of them if you included the yet-unseen, sure-to-be-unpleasant group of revolutionaries they referred to as the Guile.

Eila Doyle was a Builder prodigy, born and raised in the Waldron's Gate upper crust as naturally as a fish is raised in water. She was destined to work at the Ministry. She'd taken Crumble every day of her life. She knew streets underfoot and sun overhead. She'd been taught by her mother that The Crown ruled the sky and that the god Jonah governed the ocean Heaven beyond the Fog — and while some told tales of a time before the Fog, the concept made no sense to Eila. It never had. The Fog was there as it always had been. The Fog would be there forever. Superstitious people spoke of Jonah and his ocean, but Eila knew the truth: that there was nothing beyond.

She rode the car, afraid to stop at a talkbox and see if Mother had tried to contact her. She'd be home soon. The matter wasn't pressing. Not in the way the dirty scientist under Waldron's Gate and his ugly accusation were pressing, anyway. The scientist who lived in a world where nobody questioned their stone ceiling and walls or wondered if anything existed beyond them, because they had always been there.

Like the Fog.

Eila had pushed up from Daw's comfortable study chair and backed toward the door. Her hip had struck the wooden table holding the decanter of Thunderclap. She'd sipped at their insistence. Had they spiked it? Was that why she'd felt so suddenly lightheaded?

No. Eila had been splitting for weeks, barely held together for days, and actively fragmenting for hours. Daw's words had merely been the final straw.

You, Eila, must help us cross through the Fog and escape to the outside, before it consumes us.

There was so much wrong with that simple sentence. There *was* no 'outside.' The Fog was frightening, but it had been there for at least a thousand years (or for all eternity, in Eila's mind) and had never encroached or threatened to consume anything. Who were Levi and Daw to tell her any of it, anyway? Waldron's Gate was a vibrant city where Builders were given ideas from the Aether to turn real. There'd never been an underbelly to the city. There'd never been Dreamers who lived in psychological torture, forced to inhale fears by the thousands each night.

And for that matter, there had never been dreams. Only dark at nighttime, filled with stillness and quiet.

As the streetcar made its way toward the Rose Belt, Eila couldn't help but wonder at that last one: if her visions were, in fact, normal. She couldn't help but wonder at another thing they'd implied, too: that she, herself, might have been different if she'd been required to unpack her own mental baggage every night while sleeping, rather than sending it downstairs for others to deal with.

She thought of that day's vision (*dream?*) — the one that had poisoned the array and collapsed Pianoforte. She'd seen dark images within it. A shadowed path. Rotting leaves. The dwarf with his face like a dried apple, holding a pipe made of bleached finger bone. The dark shape snatching Levi into the Convenience's bulk.

Eila shivered. Her mind could learn to accept those things, maybe … but what must it be like to absorb them constantly, and by the thousands? If Daw and Levi were right, a Dreamer would normally have suffered that dream for her, once it had been siphoned through her mind's back door. Then, some time later, the sinister little man and the monster in the machine would have appeared out in the Fog, perhaps angry for their banishment, perhaps eager to worm their way back into Alterra, to their owner, where they belonged.

What else had she dreamed? What else might be out there? Snippets from the horrors her faulty mind had seen recurred in flashes like strobes: *Dark things with teeth. Great winged beasts, and demons. A world filled with fire. The haunting Citadel and its arena, from the storybooks her father had read her over Mother's protests.*

Eila shook her head. Closing her mind to the possibility that it might be true was the only way. Keep everything as it had been. It wasn't her responsibility. When Levi had walked Eila back to the Convenience's lower door (she'd gone ahead, and he'd stubbornly followed, despite her insistence that he leave), they'd found that door right where she'd left it. He'd nodded and confirmed what was said earlier.

You broke the seal.

If that was true, they'd be able to follow her up, to enter Waldron's Gate whenever they wished. If Pavilion wanted revolt, the so-called Guile could do it themselves.

I won't be back, she'd told Levi. *Ever.*

Yes you will, he'd said, *because your mind always invites me in. Because inside your head, you return every time.*

She'd thought that was a snarky, arrogant thing to say, but as Eila had climbed the many flights after leaving Levi below, she'd started to wonder if her own dreams belied her intention. She couldn't control the visions, could she? *He'd* been pursuing *her*, right?

The trip home was uneventful, as if The Crown had cleared her way up the staircase and to the trolley so she'd have extra time to think. Workman Al's warnings about being in his neighborhood past dark had amounted to nothing. Nobody even asked her for fare. She'd ridden the trolley for free, without meaning to, her capsule of silence unbroken.

She opened her front door to find Mother standing at the end of the brightly lit hallway, a talkbox pressed to her ear. Her eyes flicked toward Eila.

"Nevermind. She just walked in," she told the talkbox.

Eila worked to shake the cloud that had hovered around her for hours. She'd spent time in an expanded world where terrible things happened. Squirming back into her comfortable shoebox life was tricky. Having proper manners and sweeping her dress up under herself when she sat suddenly seemed so foreign. So wrong.

"I'm sorry I'm late."

Eila's mother met her daughter's gaze for a long moment after hanging up, one hand perched on her hip and her body turned side-on to Eila. The posture was very Juliette Doyle. Eila sometimes resented her mother's focus on appearances and beauty — even feeling the need to appear slim and elegant to her own disobedient daughter — but Mother couldn't help it. Eila had been born to Build, and Juliette had been born for Decorum.

"Well. You missed your chores. Harney had to straighten your room and set the table."

Harney was paid to straighten anything that needed straightening and to set any table that needed setting. Eila could point that out, but it was safer to let Mother have her say and move on. She wasn't spiteful, but did need Eila to know that she'd done something wrong.

"I'm sorry."

"Where were you? Your father said you'd be home over an hour ago. Were you with Cora?"

Eila waited, hoping her mother would give a hint of direction. She wasn't used to lying, and rarely did. She didn't want to get caught saying she'd been with Cora if Mother might have already called, but didn't want to get caught going to the Doer district even more. Neither a second city nor Thunderclap with a mad scientist were anywhere on the spectrum.

"I called Belinda. She said Cora was at the festival for the closing affairs."

"Oh, yes, we met there after I left the Ministry."

Due to Cora's quirks and Eila's schedule, they were mostly all each other had. Eila dimly remembered Cora asking her to attend the festival's closing when they'd parted yesterday, and realized she'd unintentionally left Cora hanging. If she checked, she'd probably find she had a talkbox message from Cora. Apparently, her best friend had gone alone. The image was sad and made Eila feel worse than she already had. More lying to do.

"I told you I didn't want you there for closing, Eila. The men who take down the rides … " She gave a disgusted little shiver. "I hear tales of their celebrations. It's not a place for young girls."

Eila wanted to tell her mother that she wasn't all that young anymore. She also wanted to say that she and Cora had sneaked into closing last year, and that those rumors were widely overblown. There had been pockets of intoxication, but many of the rides and games had still been running, and the midway had had a celebratory feel. First they celebrated the solstice, then celebrated the closing of the festival that celebrated the solstice. She'd found "the men who take down the rides" to be more amiable and amusing than threatening.

"I'm sorry. Cora … " She stopped, changing direction. She'd already abandoned her friend; she shouldn't now blame her for made-up delinquency. "… I had some leftover tickets and wanted to use them before the games were all closed."

Again she thought of Cora, hoping she'd made it home all right. The world was a surprisingly sordid place. It wasn't a good idea for a girl to walk home from the festival alone, her bag as heavy with coin as her mind was with fancy. There were those out there who would aim to steal both.

Mother held her fashionista's pose at the end of the hallway a few seconds longer, her strong blue eyes on Eila's. She'd placed herself under an overhead lamp, probably on purpose, and her long blonde hair shimmered in the glow. She'd gathered it away from her ears with a wide blue bow. Her earrings matched the ribbon, and her long azure dress matched the earrings. Her long fingernails were painted white, and Eila wondered why she hadn't gone with a predictable blue. Perhaps contrasting polish was in.

"Well, I had Harney hold dinner." She let her hand drop and returned her voice its usual softly brisk timbre. "I imagine it'll be just a few minutes. I'd like you to fill the water glasses."

"Maybe I'll have a glass of Thunderclap with dinner." Eila's words left without permission.

I need sleep.

Again, Juliette's piercing blue eyes held Eila. "Wash your hands before touching the glassware," she said. Then she walked away.

Eila found herself alone in the doorway, unsure whether she was pleased to have gotten away with her lie. She felt strange with the door to her back, as if one Eila had left this morning and a different girl had returned in her place. Behind her was a world she no longer knew — but the house, at least, was familiar: third from the corner, pink and yellow on the outside, all columns and decorative accents with peaked, faceted roofs like the bounty of colorful homes on Rowley Row. The Doyle home was clean and elegant on the inside, fine due to her mother's expertise, and the family continued its business as it always had. Vocations would continue to consume the days of the family's eldest four, and schooling would occupy the youngest two. For Eila and her only brother, school had given way to a job (Eila) and an apprenticeship (Nicholas). In time, they might spend their days at one Ministry or another, or work in the private sector if they chose to work at all — though under Atwell's guidance, nobody in the well-respected Doyle family would be permitted the sloth of an easy life.

The clockwork of existence would continue to click, but as Eila stood in the entranceway like a visitor, she wasn't sure that her cog would ever fit again.

She slipped off her shoes, then walked barefoot into the bathroom and splashed water on her face. She stared at the basin as water spiraled down the drain. She'd always assumed the pipes knew where to take the waste, thanks to some machine or another that some nameless Builders had created at the Ministry long ago. But now she knew about the Convenience and those who attended the waste in Pavilion, receiving everything the Gate didn't want: waste water, sewage, probably refuse. And of course, all of their dark dreams and psychic remainders.

Eila checked her reflection, wondering if her changed perspective showed outwardly like a wart. It didn't. She still saw the same smooth skin, the same head of wavy brown hair, healthy with shine thanks to her mother's sometimes overbearing assistance in grooming. She still had the same deep-brown eyes, which Eila now took a few moments to stare into as if they belonged to a stranger.

For the first time, as she looked into those eyes, she saw more than herself. Another person lived behind them. A spirit … the kind of thing her mother believed was kept by The Crown and went to Jonah when the body died. That was the part of her that was able to travel when she slept. The part that, Levi had said as they parted, traveled even during the daytime for people in Pavilion.

Daydreaming. Fantasizing.

Daydreams were different than dreams, he'd added, and Crumble wasn't always able to steal them away. And yet the citizens of Waldron's Gate didn't seem to do much of it anyway.

She brushed at her dress, surprised to see that no black under-city dust plumed from the fabric. She took a final check and walked out into the dining room, where Harney had, of course, already filled the glasses.

Her mother entered the room and began rearranging the already-arranged flowers. The younger children filtered in as she fussed, and the smell of food filled the air.

Eila sat, uncomfortable in her alien skin.

Dinner now.

Crumble later.

Then sleep, where dreams may come … and go.

Chapter Ten

Portraits on the Walls

Eila woke in the morning to a vicious clanging.

For five solid, fully awake seconds she had no idea where she was. She'd had a similar sensation only once, when they'd traveled up-country, out of Waldron's Gate and into the farmlands, to stay with her grandparents. There had been no city noise in those outlands, and she'd awoken from a sleep that was somehow too deep and too sound. She'd wondered at the strange bed, and stranger ceiling twisted into unfamiliar shapes. Only after surfacing from her momentary disorientation had Eila remembered the traveling, and bedding down in an unusual place.

But today she was in her own bed, not one in another house up-country. She saw her own pink pillow from the corner of her eyes. The ceiling was the same smooth plaster it had always been, painted a flat white and edged with molding. She could see the edge of a frame to one side. Cora had posters tacked to the walls in her room, but Juliette thought posters, hung naked, were trashy. So she had framed Eila's favorites, thus defeating the whole point.

Eila blinked. A few cobwebs cleared, but the clanging continued.

She looked up at her ceiling, covers seeming to pin her in place. She could move but didn't want to. Something was wrong. Maybe it was the light. Maybe the clanging.

The previous night, even after she'd settled into her routine, had been strange. Dinners were odd with Atwell away. He'd called from the Ministry to wish them good night, and as far as Eila knew, he was still there. They'd had roast duck and three kinds of jelly. Of course Winter and Penelope had slathered everything into a mess, and Harney had laughed at it all while refilling their water. Juliette had been irritated, but allowed herself a chuckle halfway through. Sometimes her penchant for elegance was irritating, but for some reason, last night, Eila had found it endearing. Her mother could be warm when it was needed. She was sometimes unfair in her criticism of Mother's way. None of them — Eila included — could help being who they were.

She'd had to lie a few more times during dinner, as conversation had proceeded. Winter kept asking Eila about the festival, and Eila had to keep nesting lies, each one dropping her deeper into her freshly dug hole. She'd be committed to the lie now, and might have to repeat it for Father. She wasn't sure what was worse: blame for disobedience she hadn't committed, or telling lies. Dinner had built the wall higher inside her mind. By the end, Eila felt like a visitor to the family: welcomed and accepted, but unfamiliar, and at a distance.

She'd felt the pull of Crumble through dinner, then felt it worse as she'd stood from the table and watched Harney gather the dishes. She'd consciously thought of Daw's warnings — what he'd said Crumble did and how he'd implied it changed the mind to hook its user — and, feeling defiant, had doubled her usual dose. For the first time, she'd also *thought* of it as a "dose." Crumble was a drug, yes, but it was also a staple. She took more the way she'd take extra powders for a particularly strong headache: she had a malady, and needed the drug to fix it.

That night of all nights, Eila hadn't wanted to dream. Somehow, she'd managed to hold onto a few visions in the past and wanted to forget them. She didn't want to see the dwarf or the path or the thing with the yellow eyes. She didn't want to see the dark creatures snapping branches in the damp wood. She didn't even want to see Levi, whose assurances had been running through her mind all evening.

If Crumble opened a door inside her and allowed the theft of her dreams, she wanted the door open as wide as it could go. It wasn't enough to pull a tiny plug from a tub and slowly drain the water; she wanted to knock out the tub's bottom, spilling everything into the sewers, where it would go somewhere else and become the waste managers' problem.

Still, she'd seen Levi for a brief moment after closing her eyes.

He seemed to be trying to stay with her but Eila watched him vanish nonetheless, victim to the Crumble's wide open door. And as Eila watched the flicker of the dream as it went, she realized she'd seen the same thing happen before. On some buried level, she'd seen occasional nighttime flashes — even before the visions had begun — of dreams being stolen.

That was her final thought before she'd fallen into darkness, her mind finally coming disconnected. She'd slept like the dead and lost her night in a blink, waking to that obnoxious, irritating, clanging of …

"Oh, damn," she said, sitting up.

Her earlier out-of-body feelings fell like a robe to the floor. She was back to being Eila Doyle, daughter to Atwell and Juliette, from an eminent Builder family, so recently out of schooling and following her father into the Ministry. Again, Waldron's Gate had become all there was.

Outside, the clock tower declared the time to be 9 a.m. She didn't even need to look out her window to know it, because the bells didn't clang before 9 a.m. — a city compromise designed to disturb comparatively few. Most people were awake by nine, as Eila should have been.

She hopped out of bed, then hurriedly pulled on a work dress that had been pre-approved as sufficiently *en vogue* by her mother. She snatched a complementing choker from her nightstand (black with a silver buckle), then fussed with her hair for thirty seconds in the mirror before deciding that its messiness actually matched her wardrobe. She took in the entire ensemble, declared it suitable if a bit fashion-forward for a Builder, and rushed downstairs.

"You're still here?" Nicholas caught her in the kitchen as she frantically rummaged for portable foods.

"*You're* still here?" she snapped back, not looking over.

"I'm off today." He leaned against the counter precisely where Eila needed to be. He was holding an apple, and bit loudly into it. "Doesn't your shift start at eight?"

Actually, after a shutdown, the unspoken rule was that all Builders should arrive at least an hour early to make up for lost momentum and time. And in fact, after a broken Pianoforte, the unspoken rule would probably dictate an even earlier arrival … if, that was, Pianoforte had ever broken before.

"You could have woken me," she said.

Nicholas smacked the apple. Eila shoved past him, grabbing a bag of nuts. Nuts for breakfast? Why not?

"It's not my job to wake you up!" he said. "Besides, I assumed you were already gone. Everyone did. Winter is raiding your cosmetics. Mother left. Like, hours ago."

Eila gave her brother an irritated look.

"I heard something happened at the Ministry yesterday. Father downplayed it on the talkbox, but I heard the engine shut down. What did you screw up this time?"

"Get out of my way, Nicholas."

"I'll bet you tried to Build something stupid. Like a pink propeller car. It was so stupid that the machine refused to make it."

"Move!" He was blocking the coldbox door. She shoved hard, and he slammed into the belt housing beside it. There was a clunk as one of the belts running the cooler adjusted, and for a moment Eila wondered if she'd broken the coldbox, too.

"You'd better get over there," he said. "You're going to be late."

"You think?"

Nicholas looked at the small pendulum clock across the room and made a quizzical expression. "Eight o'clock comes before nine, right?"

Eila wanted to shout at him for being annoying, but she'd already gotten her juice and had slammed the coldbox's door. She didn't bother responding or looking back — just groaned in irritation and stormed through the front room.

Outside, she scampered the few houses down to the trolley stop. She couldn't recall the streetcar schedule this late in the day, so she'd have to hope. At some point, the cars stopped running every seven minutes and ran every fourteen. If that had happened already and she missed one, things would only get worse.

Every second of waiting felt like an eternity, and the clock tower gave its annoying single quarter-hour bong before the first car arrived. Eila tapped her foot through the ride, urging the trolley to hurry. But in the end, she was an hour and a half late for her shift (two and a half if you counted the implied early arrival), and an extra two or three minutes couldn't possibly matter.

The ride itself was less than ten minutes total, but because she could only wait, her mind wandered and blustered. She recalled Pavilion, now seeming days distant, buried behind her current rush and likely reprimand. She recalled the day before Pavilion — and *that* day felt like an eternity ago. She recalled Levi: in her Dreams, as an intruder, and in front of her as an implied ally. He was taller in person. Darker in tone. She had extra sensory inputs now, and when Eila had seen him flicker last night, she couldn't help but apply them. Even his smile's glint was different, and Eila thought she knew why. In the past, he hadn't smiled. Before they'd met, he'd been a summoner. Now, he probably fancied himself an acquaintance.

But she was *never* going back.

She remembered Levi's expression twisting as the dream had bent inside her, trying to drain away. The whole image had been a ship into a vortex, and Levi had tried to hold on, his mouth wanting to speak but unable, thanks to lubrication from Eila's extra dose of Crumble.

Help us.

No, they'd have to help themselves.

Eila ran into the Ministry building as quickly as she could without foregoing her dignity. She found the floor surprisingly quiet, the mood surprisingly docile. On the main floor, she looked at the Blunderbuss to see arrays of Build cradles that were still mostly vacant. Her eyes drifted upward as she approached, through the center of the circling floors. Steam belched from the engine's belled top as always, meaning the Ministry had managed to get the machine running again. But the steam was an iron gray rather than its usual bright white.

"Getting there, anyway," said a voice beside her.

Eila turned to find herself facing Victor. He was close, his breath practically at her shoulder before she'd looked, and she felt compelled to fall a step back.

"What did you say?"

Victor nodded upward. His face had a heavy shadow of stubble, though he was usually clean shaven. Seeing it made Eila feel like she was seeing something private, as if he'd only just woken and was still in pajamas. She felt guilty. Victor must have raced from his home, foregoing grooming, to help the Ministry fix her mistake.

"The Blunderbuss. It's getting there. Much better than it was."

"What do you mean?"

"The smoke. Have you ever seen a startup?"

Eila shook her head, keenly aware that she had just arrived in Mother's couture while Victor worked unshaven. At least she hadn't bathed. Quite the conundrum: if she reeked, he might respect her dedication. But if he smelled her ... well, that clearly wasn't ideal.

"The smoke is pitch black at startup. Like a coal furnace. That's actually why the roof is fully retracted now instead of being closed and screened like normal — the smoke is so thick and disgusting, it actually stains the ceiling." He looked over at her, running a quick glance up and down — the kind of once-over that boys somehow thought girls wouldn't notice. "Anyway, it's getting close. Some people are already hooking in. I wouldn't, though."

"Why? Is it different?"

"It's like swimming when the water is cold." Victor shivered. "You can get in there and Build, but it's not very powerful. Why not wait?"

"Good," she said. "I overslept. I was afraid it would be all hands on deck."

"I know." Victor nodded. "Rabbit was yelling about it. I told him your father had called you up to help at Enigma. That shut him up."

Eila looked over. "You did?"

"Yeah. Might want to tell your father that, though. Not sure if he goes along with lies."

He didn't, but he *did* go along with anything that made Brampton look bad. They were allies in name, but adversaries for all practical purposes. Brampton knew that Atwell was in line to replace him and held his position like a dog with a bone. It wouldn't matter that Brampton would move up when it happened; he sometimes treated spite like a cause. It was either that, or professional pride. The Ministry chief was called "head scientist," and while Atwell was already a Head, he hadn't been trained as a scientist. It wouldn't matter that the actual science happened at lower levels; Brampton would resent any layman in a scientific position.

"Thanks," said Eila, feeling warm.

"There was no need to be here early. We just sat around drinking cafei and talking. Except you, of course. You were hard at work up on the Enigma Floor."

"I do good Enigma work," said Eila, wishing immediately that she hadn't said it. Despite yesterday's assurances, she found herself recalling her own deep-seated surety that her father had wanted an Enigma Builder as his heir, rather than one in Aether Forefront.

"Sure you do," he said.

Eila looked up at the smoke, already so much lighter. "How long before it's ready?"

An annoyed bark from somewhere behind them echoed up the Blunderbuss dome before Victor could answer. They turned to see Rabbit Brampton, bustling upon approach.

"I guess it's ready," Victor said. "See you up there."

Eila took a moment to store her bag, earning a long stare from Brampton for not heading directly to her post. The stare — cocked eyebrow included — also said he didn't precisely believe that she'd been on time and resented it, regardless of whether there had been any reason to do so.

Eila took her place on the array, laid back in her cradle, and found a comfortable position with her head inside the overly large helmet-like cap. She closed her eyes as she felt the other Builders' waves begin to swell. It wasn't remotely as strong or resonant as it had been during the Pianoforte, but Eila could still feel their energies gently tugging at her, like the call of distant friends playing somewhere and summoning her to join them.

But even after she'd settled back, begun her breathing, and closed her eyes, Eila found her usual construct elusive. The warehouse didn't want to form. She got glimpses of white walls, smooth corners, and even the large doors on each end that she'd always wondered about but had only seen opened yesterday, when they'd joined spaces to siphon from the wave's trough. But that was all.

For the first time, Eila thought, *What is Pianoforte?*

It was a period of synchronicity. That much had been explained during training, but not much else had been. If Daw was right (And why wouldn't he be? Daw, unlike Rabbit Brampton, was a

Blunderbuss Ministry Head scientist who actually *knew* the machine had two halves), Pianoforte seemed to be about dreams, not Aether.

Pavilion's workers took dreams from Alterra's surface-level citizens (not just those in Waldron's Gate, but the entire country), Dreamed those dreams as if they were their own, and sifted out the concepts most worthy of Building. Eila and the others then received their own worthy dreams right back after they'd been lived by — and then ripped violently from — the Dreamers below.

Perhaps Pianoforte was about the collective unconscious. Perhaps somehow, Alterra's dreams synchronized from time to time, and they all found themselves seeing the same things for a reason only the topmost of scientists might understand — or, likely, that *nobody* understood. Perhaps Pianoforte happened when the Dreamers felt that synchronicity on what *they* thought of as the Aether. Would that make things easier for them? Or harder?

The construct formed. Inside it, Eila saw the Convenience door that led to Pavilion.

She focused and drove the image away. Yesterday, she'd fallen asleep and seen the Convenience. This was different. She was trying to Build, and needed to focus on nothing. A Builder's job was to empty her mind so the Aether could present her things to manifest. But this time the *Aether* hadn't put the door in her construct, and an errant Dream hadn't drawn her in. *She* had put it there, and it had to go.

She found herself thinking back to the real Convenience, out in the real world — and with the thought, she realized the truth: there *hadn't been* a door in its side before she'd shown up. She'd made it. She'd Built it. Out of nothing.

Everyone we've found has the ability to create or to manifest, but not both. Until now.

Eila pinched her eyes shut harder and slowed her breathing. The construct reformed, empty as it should be, and she waited in the vacant-minded trance she'd learned at Father's knee, then later in formalized Ministry training. It was like a relaxing of the eyes: a willingness to see by refusing to see what was in front, and instead see what lay behind.

A small object appeared in the middle of the warehouse. It was

like a pair of goggles, but with a set of micropneumatics on the side. Eila couldn't imagine what the add-on did — what functionality it added to the goggles — but her job as a Builder was to Build, not understand. And so, clearing her mind, she began.

Eila straightened lines as a sort of second image was laid over the first, because straighter lines refined the articulation of the raw thought as she saw it. When in a Build trance, you didn't precisely see the idea because ideas, in themselves, had no shape. You only saw your *interpretation* of that raw idea, and your job when Building was to purify and idealize that interpretation. Every Builder had a signature, like a voice. And as Eila laid her own more perfect image of the goggles over the first, it was as if she was collaborating with the Aether's idea. First it was given, and secondly, Eila's style improved it.

Her perception of the idea began to change. She held the perfected (yet incomplete) Build image over the underlying idea as she'd received it, but now started to see the idea for what it was. An idea without a mind was as alien as a head without a body. It was a thought without a corresponding thinker.

How had the truth eluded her for so long? The realization was like solving a visual puzzle; once she saw the pattern, she'd see it forever. What others thought was just a jumble would make sense to those who'd solved the puzzle before: a steamship in a mess of lines, a three-dimensional face emerging from a nonsensical collage of shapes. Eila looked at the goggles with their micropneumatics and wondered at the mind that conceived it. Had it come from a welder who'd dreamed of a way to better shield himself from sparks? Had it come from an skyship captain who dreamed of enhanced visibility? Had the idea been dreamed by an underwater explorer whose mind wondered at a way to combine breathing with seeing in a single device?

The thing in the warehouse began to unfold like a puzzle box, its insides flipping outward like a vision of something sharp exploding in slow motion. It grew as it opened, insides spilling with each unfolded iteration, all ochre black. It filled half her vision before Eila realized she was seeing a true Dream — a new kind of Dream, gripping tight to hold out from her Crumble, combining with what she saw on the Aether. A vision with purpose.

Levi had spoke of swimming in dreams, and as Eila's mind expanded the metaphor began to feel right. She felt herself beginning to swim. Only she saw herself swimming *upstream*, into the great engine's mouth, tearing at the Aether's one-way flow of ideas, moving toward their source.

Eila blinked internal eyes. All was quiet. The Blunderbuss was suddenly upside-down, its belled end pointing at the floor instead of skyward. When the end she felt herself nearing belched steam, it rose in hot waves that made the Dreamers — bound to their cradles, she saw — sweat like wet sponges. And when it was starting up, as it had this morning, its smoke would be acrid and black, enough to make them cough and water their eyes. In the Ministry of Manifestation, the ceiling opened because black smoke would stain the roof. But in the Ministry of Dreaming, it would stain the workers themselves. Dreaming, unlike Building, allowed no holidays. She somehow knew that the array was always full, shifts coming and going. They laughed and joked before their work, but often screamed during. Whether they forgot the horrors by the end or not, she couldn't tell. But the Dreamers came away gray, their job for the day well done, their wounds a few hours deeper.

Eila saw the goggle-shaped idea she'd been chasing far in the distance. A picture on top of a picture, seen by her perception as a pair of streams. Her mind followed it, using her Build training like a bludgeon to smash upstream. She'd wondered about the notion's source. She wondered who had Dreamed that particular Dream.

Eila fell back a few moments in time. But ideas were like any other thought; they had memory built into them. She looked back as if recalling her morning — but now that morning was no longer hers. It was *someone else's*. Another's mindstream, dumped into a repository with no filter.

She was inside a Dreamer's mind, no longer herself at all.

The Dreamer was a woman in her thirties, judging by what Eila could see as a panorama of how the Dreamer saw herself. She had a husband and two children. It was easy to pick them out; her mindspace was like a well-furnished living room with portraits decorating the walls. But before Eila had a chance to wonder if the living room construct was her own or the Dreamer's, the room itself expanded, stretched like a ribbon of taffy. The back wall retreated. The side walls grew long, and with the departure of the overhead light the room grew dim. The floor was no longer hardwood. Now it was like sap, or tar, or thick black blood.

Eila, as present in the room as she'd been in her visions, stepped back.

Something was coming.

It came in the way ideas from the Aether usually came to Eila while Building. Only this inspiration wasn't *inspiration* at all; it was black and haunted, burnt at the edges. It smelled like rotted fruit and had a taste, in the back of her throat, like bile. She could feel its presence before it arrived, and realized with panic that there was no way to stop it. It was coming. Eila couldn't even brace because her body and mind were strapped down. She was this other woman; she was a Dreamer. It was her job to take what came and sift it for gems. But as with the search for anything fine, there would be much more waste than treasure.

Eila felt herself as the Dreamer — the woman who, not long ago, had experienced all of this for real, deep in the bowels of Pavilion. Eila wanted to pull back, retrace her steps, follow the normal flow of thoughts through the Blunderbuss engine from bottom to top, re-experience herself as Eila and only Eila, feel the arrival of only *good* things from the Aether.

But she wasn't Eila anymore. She was

(case my name is case)

someone else now, and whatever was coming was coming and could not be stopped.

She knew, because she was the Dreamer, that visions on the Aether were always like this. Every day, in and out. But if Dreamers didn't clear the waste, everyone in Pavilion would suffer.

(carson lily hunter)

Eila could feel the woman — the Dreamer whose mind she'd leaked into as Levi had leaked into hers, back when she'd had one of her own — use the three names as a shield. She saw glimpses of the husband and two children flash in front of her eyes like photo strobes. She was steeling herself with a sense of grim duty.

If I don't clear the air, they will suffer.

It came. *Again.* It came as the dark force *always* came — as it came to Case, the Dreamer, for the four hours she strapped into the Dream cradle every day of her life. This was nothing new. Case was used to what was about to happen, but being accustomed to a knife's edge didn't dull the pain of its cut.

The room turned black as a shadow descended. There were windows; they went dark with a swoop, as if draped in velvet or leather. The living room construct, horribly distorted already, began to further twist and fold. A table grew animal legs and started to stumble. A candelabra became snakes with no eyes.

Images slammed into Case/Eila, their force like a steam piston. She felt it in her gut, like a wound in her brain's most delicate corners. Not just images. *Feelings.* Beautiful visions made terrible, as if the dark force knew just which sensitive memories to twist.

She saw the woman's husband and children killed repeatedly in seconds. She saw torture and pain. Walls parted to a forest of horrors, dark paths sprawling in every direction, desperation lying in wait at each end. She saw the walls of a maze, knowing an impossible puzzle lay at its center.

Eila wondered at her existence. *Doubted* her existence.

Her mind splintered, drawn in a hundred directions at once. She felt lightheaded, out of breath, suffocating. Mockery descended. Cruelty. She felt herself fall, then tumble. Something with yellow irises beckoned, promising relief, but there was a demon's gleam in its eye.

There were creatures. There was horror and pain and blackness and …

Eila had curled up inside the woman's mind, but now saw the air beginning to clear. The room was now gray rather than black. The walls had become less stretched. She saw Case — some version of herself, battered and bruised and humbled — sending out some sort of energy, forcing the visions to retreat.

The Dreamer looked toward Eila but did not see her. Eila's presence was silent. That was a good thing, because Eila was more than an intruder. As a Builder above, she was this woman's *exploiter.*

Eila's mind's eye looked up and watched as the last of the darkness retreated, going out to the Fog, to thicken the wall of detritus and

garbage that Alterra didn't want fouling its soil, rock, or minds. Several hundred unknowing surface-dwellers had just been purged at once, and now they would no longer be troubled by what Levi had called nightmares.

Exploiter.

It wasn't fair. Eila hadn't known what she was doing to these people. None of them had. They weren't complicit. They hadn't known what kept their minds as clean as their city. They hadn't known why they, themselves, didn't have to face down their demons each night, or that those demons even existed. They hadn't known others were doing it for them: sending those bad things outside, where they wouldn't hurt anyone.

Until, if Daw was right, those bad things turned around and hurt them *all.*

As the air cleared, Eila watched two shimmering objects surface from the gloom and begin to float upward. One was a long object with cams at each end, and the other was a pair of goggles with micropneumatics on one side. The same goggles she'd chased down here, seeking their origin.

We did this. We are doing *this. We are the origin.*

Eila watched the googles and the rod object float upward, out of the mental construct.

Two ideas. There had been thousands of horrors in that deluge, but only *two ideas* worth Building in the Ministry above.

Eila felt herself released as the Dream that wasn't exactly a dream began to end. She was moving upward. Following the idea she'd followed before, now in the other direction.

The last thing she saw before her awareness returned to her body above was the woman. The Dreamer. *Case.*

The woman wore a small smile. It wasn't the smile of someone who is happy, but of someone who has done a job — no matter how unpleasant — and done it well. It was the look of a defender. Of a martyr who is, day by day, placing herself in the line of fire to save the world for those she loves.

She didn't look angry. Or beset upon. Or even burdened.

The woman looked wounded and beaten, but satisfied. Because she was doing her part of what needed to be done.

Because this was life.

The cruel world gave everyone a burden to bear, and no one was to blame.

Chapter Eleven
The World on His Shoulders

It took Eila a while to stop feeling sick to her stomach — and a while longer to stop fearing that a dark hand might tap her shoulder (or stab her throat) while her eyes were closed and her attention was focused inward. Her body slowly lost the feeling of being in another's skin, but it was probably an hour before her head cleared enough to resume Building at a reasonable pace — something she thought Rabbit Brampton, at his bank of viewboxes, had probably noticed.

Halfway through her shift, she stopped imagining every idea "from the Aether" as coming to her covered in blood. And after that, things became a little easier — once she was able to pretend that an idea was magic as it had always seemed before, rather than filtered from horror and muck, leaving a fellow human with a fresh mental scar.

Even after that, though, she couldn't quite shake the feeling of being a thief.

Usually, Building was a kind of divine play. She felt like a creator when she was working — a developer of notions who recognized brilliant things that hadn't yet been born and gave them life. Without people like Eila, ideas were merely air. Builders made everything *real.* She'd felt such joy the first time she'd taken her place at the Blunderbuss, and such pride in her father and grandfather as Builders before that.

Most people simply *existed* in the world, but never Builders. Builders *created.* Builders *made something from nothing.*

But now Eila knew that ideas *didn't* come from nothing. They were dreamed by real people — fleeting sparks of genius buried in otherwise disorderly minds, plucked like a lone daisies from fields of weeds by Pavilion's Dreamers. If anyone was *creating* an idea, it was the unconscious Alterran who's mind had birthed it. If anyone was *finding the glory and beauty* in an unappreciated idea, it was the Dreamer.

Builders were merely producing what they were given. They were not creators, making something from nothing. They were stamping machines, delivering blueprints. They were plagiarists — cutting brilliance from the chests of mute geniuses and selling it as their own. They were exploiters, clutching profit while the geniuses bled to death.

A new object came into Eila's warehouse. She did the least she could with it, like any good duplicating machine. She didn't need to add anything to it. There was no flair, no inspiration, no need to collaborate and bring out its very best.

Someone else had drawn the picture. Eila was just tracing.

When her focus first returned from the lower half of the Blunderbuss, fresh with Case's horror and pain, Eila wanted to stand, leave her cradle, and run. The truth was behind her in the way the darkness had recently been in front, and if she ran fast enough, she felt like she could outrun it. Now that she knew the truth, she couldn't face herself in a mirror. She couldn't face her fellow Builders. They were all monsters, even if they didn't know it. All had blood on their hands, and she couldn't tell them about it. Because who would believe her? And even if they did, how could Waldron's Gate survive without the Ministry? They weren't a society of Tinkers, able to build with their hands. Daw was right; the problem wasn't just the theft of dreams or the plight of the Dreamers. The cycle had neutered Alterra. The whole nation was as hooked on the Blunderbuss as surely as she was hooked on Crumble.

She *couldn't* bolt upright. She *couldn't* leave her post. She *couldn't* run.

After a few minutes — after the sick feeling of being someone else started to fade and the worst of the darkness left her mind — she saw that. Her grandfather and his mother had been well-respected Builders. Her father was a Builder, and was second in line at the Ministry. Atwell loved what he did, and was good to the people under him. He rarely Built anymore, because he was now a supervisor and a planner. He'd been working toward the position his entire adult life.

Eila had been born to Build. A pure Build trance — if she could ever forget what she'd just seen — was the best sort of euphoria. At her core, she didn't *want* to give it up. The thought of never Building again filled her with existential horror. Most Alterrans — even Cora, who thought sketching was about self-expression — could never know that level of creative bliss. Only Builders delved deep enough and articulated fully enough knew *true* expression — at, apparently, any cost.

So despite the crawling of her skin, Eila kept working. She didn't make waves. She felt the weak, non-Pianoforte resonance of the Builders in the array and allowed it to lift her. She breathed deep and watched her empty warehouse construct form. It was dirtier than usual — dull instead of pure white, dusty like an assembly house rather than sterile like a lab.

The engine sent Eila ideas to articulate, so she did.

Next.

Next.

Eila was one of the gray-faces working an assembly line, putting one Blunderbuss-Built part next to another. Someone, somewhere had to attach propellers and rudders to sky ships. She was that person, doing a monkey's job.

When her shift ended and a whistle reminded her to surface from her trance, she stood from the cradle like dropping an ox's yoke. Usually she left the array reluctantly, wishing she could continue her Building. She'd always felt accomplished as she left, as if she'd purged her own mind and washed it clean. Now she felt the opposite. She felt dirty. All of them were — and they'd never be clean, because it was the kind of dirt they couldn't even see.

She trudged past Brampton. His eyes were on her, from the gantry down across the floor. She saw him from her station as she walked, standing in his open office door with his arms crossed over his chest, trim blue suit immaculate and white hair perfectly in place. Brampton didn't know what he was leading. Should she hate him? Eila decided she wanted to, and did. She watched his accusing eyes — *oh yes*, he'd noticed her lackluster output today — and wanted to hit him. But she resisted a confrontation, because it would be foolish.

Brampton was a grown man. She was a little girl in a dress that was too fine for her, and felt it.

Outside, she found a pleasant but somehow unwelcome surprise. Today of all days, Cora had taken a trolley to the Ministry to meet her.

"Hey E!" she shouted brightly, standing from her seat on the stone steps to trot forward. She was wearing a light, summery dress that came to her knees — the opposite of what Eila was wearing, down to the spaghetti straps where Eila had worn the black choker. If anyone saw the pair from a distance, they'd look like mother and daughter — a carefree girl beside a serious worker who bore the world on her shoulders.

"Oh. Hey."

"Missed you at the festival closing last night." Cora wore a wide smile. To Eila's dour mood, her expression looked stupid. Her most sensible part wanted to hug Cora — perhaps too tightly, like clutching a treasured childhood toy — but a larger, more dominant part wanted to shoo her away. Eila wasn't in a light or playful place. Her soul wanted a hug, but her surface felt iced by annoyance.

"I'm sorry. It was a Ministry thing."

"I heard the Ministry shut down." She said it without accusation. Still, guilt chewed into Eila. She didn't like lying, and it was already becoming easy.

"A different sort of Ministry thing."

"Oh, I'm sure." Again, the bright smile. Cora's teeth were white, her skin was pale, and her hair was so blonde it seemed bleached. It was almost as if The Crown was taunting Eila with her presence — if, that was, Eila had believed in The Crown.

"I got off early," she added when Eila didn't respond. "I thought I'd come over to pick you up."

Eila wanted to shout at her. Cora had "gotten off early" because she didn't actually work. She could come and go as she pleased, even if she was in the middle of what passed for urgency at her job that wasn't a job. Her position was worse than useless — the kind of job that was made up to give a spoiled rich girl something to do.

Eila tried to shake it the feeling away. *She* — Eila — was also a spoiled rich girl. Atwell had worked to sharpen his children's edges, but the Doyles had been wealthy for generations and nothing would change that. Her mother's family had a humble background, but Eila had certainly never felt its brush. It wasn't Cora's fault that Eila's life was stuffed with such particular lessons. Had Eila really been as silly as Cora once upon a time? Almost certainly yes, though it was hard to believe. Two days ago, Eila had still believed that she Built what came from the air like motes of beautiful dust. But today, that time of naiveté felt an eternity distant.

"That's nice," said Eila. She forced herself to pause on the steps, feeling the pull of something unarticulated as it cried out for her to keep walking. Was it the pull itself an idea she'd inadvertently ripped from a Dreamer? It seemed unlikely, but everything felt tainted, as if the sun itself had been draped in dark silk.

"I thought we might go shopping," said Cora.

Eila sighed, failing to blunt its condescending edge. *Shopping? Really? Now?*

"Oh, I don't know, Cor. I'm pretty tired."

"They're getting a new shipment down in the mercantile district." Cora looked over at the clock tower — a different face than the one that greeted Eila at her window. "In just about an hour, actually." She stopped and looked around, craning her neck to peek along the skyline as if searching for something. "Well, I guess we can't see them yet, but there's supposed to be a pair of ferry shaws coming at six."

"Oh."

"'Oh?'" Cora repeated. She rolled her eyes. "That's *it?* I thought you'd be excited. First the solstice festival, then an extra shaw run. I thought we'd have to wait until autumn."

"I'm not really in the mood right now, Cora."

Cora pouted and grabbed Eila's arm theatrically. "Oh, but it's our *thing!"* she whined. "New stuff arriving from places unknown. Cute ruddermouths arriving for chatter. We can make an evening of it. Ring your parents. They won't care, will they? We can have dinner. Maybe get one of the pilots to join us."

That was a laugh. The "mouth" in the pilots' "ruddermouth" nickname was there because they told such fantastic tales: journeys on their giant ships carrying specialty goods to other regions for sale. Ruddermouths were usually cute, as Cora had said, but much of their charm — and the biggest reason they were always mobbed by local girls — came from their stories. The chances of Eila and Cora dining with one was remote. Atwell had declared that most of the pilots' stories were rubbish, created to help them hawk more of whatever they'd crammed in their shaws. But Eila, who was younger and less steeped in the world's ways, felt differently. Whether the ruddermouths spun yarns of dancing mobs, haunted villages, or creatures in the northern Fog, Eila always found herself believing them.

"I'm really tired," said Eila.

"Oh, come on. You'll wake up on the walk."

Cora was still gripping her arm, now actively tugging Eila down the steps. Eila had to fight the urge to snap at Cora — to tell her to go away and take her silly, meaningless babble elsewhere. Didn't she realize there was torture being done in the building behind them?

"No, Cor. Seriously. I'd just be a bummer. Maybe you could go with Clementine?"

"Clementine! Now I *know* you need to come with me. You're so tired, you're losing your mind! Come on, Eila. I'll buy you a nice little ensemble."

"I don't need you to buy me anything." Eila wanted to shake off the pall that had draped her, but it wouldn't leave. She couldn't watch the shaws arrive, shop, then dine and giggle about pilots knowing what she did. Her mind was on Builders and Dreamers, up and down, innovation and theft. And Crumble. Perhaps Crumble most of all — a door that allowed looters to loot, same as the door she'd made to Pavilion.

The door.

She wondered if it was still there. It would be, of course. She'd broken the seal. If Daw and Levi and this "Guile" wanted, they could march topside right now. Come to the Ministry and stop all the thievery. It would topple the country and ruin her family's life, but a part of Eila's didn't care.

"Fine, then you can buy things yourself," said Cora. "Come. I don't want to miss the shaws' arrival. When they glide overhead, and you can look up and see those big wooden propellers while they block out the sun?" Cora shivered. "Oh, it just gives me chills."

A random thought hit Eila: once they were a few years older, she would need to protect her friend. At seventeen or eighteen, they'd both have a shot at snagging the pilots' attention … and given Cora's swooning, she'd be a big, pliable target for any pilot, willing to go anywhere or do anything.

"I *can't go*, Cor. I'm sorry."

Cora still pulled. "Oh, yes you can. You're not getting away from me, Eila Doyle."

"Cora … "

She added, "Not after abandoning me last night."

Eila felt punched. Worse, she felt punched in an already-bruised abdomen. Cora had said that last bit like a joke, but it was true. Eila had cut their time at the festival short after visiting Palpatine Malvern, had refused her festival time the following night, and already wanted to run off again. They were best friends and neither really had anyone else, but Eila couldn't think about that now. She could only think of the people who didn't exist to the world Cora knew, and how they suffered.

"Don't say that," Eila said.

"What?" She'd already forgotten the offhand remark.

"Look … I'll make it up to you. Promise. We'll go out tomorrow."

Cora stopped tugging. Her face changed, realization dawning. Up until now, she'd thought Eila's protests were play; now, she saw them as the refusal they were.

"You're really not going to come with me?" Eila felt the sting of the final two words: *with me.* Even *You're really not going to go?* would have hurt less.

"I have something I need to do."

"Right *now?* E, it's the *ferry shaws!* They only come twice a year. This might not be an *extra* run; it might be an *early* run. They might skip autumn! We might have to wait until winter to see them again!"

For a second, Eila considered relenting. She could make Cora happy and go. But it wasn't just about delaying her errand; it was about suffering through an evening of artificial joy. She couldn't just *go with* Cora. She would be expected to laugh, to chatter about the pilots when they docked and clomped down the planks, and to be excited over buying more clothes that neither of them needed. Cora was right; it usually *was* their thing. But it was as if she'd grown up all at once, and it all seemed so suddenly childish. She couldn't pretend. Faking excitement was more of a betrayal than not going, and it would gut her sore insides to try.

"I'm so sorry, Cor." She really was. It hurt to say it.

Cora's face had already fallen from good-natured goading to disappointment. Now it soured into offense.

"Oh, I see. What, are you meeting someone?"

"What? No, of course not!" Eila decided to take a risk and added, "I'd tell you about something like that."

"Sure. Sure you would. Just like you tell me everything recently, right? What did you talk to Malvern about, by the way?"

"I can't … "

"What's been bothering you lately, then? When you come over groggy, and your hands are shaking? You're up working on something, right? What is it?"

"It's not that, it's … "

"Oh, and I make fun of you about Victor, but that's really happening, isn't it? Only you won't tell me about that, either. And yet I told you all about that thing with William."

"Cora, you're being ridiculous."

Cora nodded. "Yes. I guess I am. Cora is always *ridiculous*. While you have something *very serious* going on." She made a mock-stern frown. "It's been like this ever since you started working at the Ministry. I swear, when you promised that it wouldn't change things, I believed you. But now it's like you're too good for me. You with your Builder friends."

"I don't even talk to the other Builders!" Except that she had, just today. And, for the double-punch, that Builder had been Victor.

Cora shook her head. "My mother warned me that the Ministry might change you. We've nothing but respect for Builders; you live where there are roses while our section reeks of too much lavender. It wasn't a big deal when we were merely girls who had known each other since our mothers were taking birthing classes and acquainting us as pre-borns, when my mother had her own social standing and yours was still just a few years from being a tailor's daughter. You were a Builder's daughter and I was 'just' a society's … "

"Knock it off, Cora!"

This wasn't fair. Eila already had the weight of the world on her shoulders, and

(Like the man on the newel post at the top of the staircase behind the Convenience door; that was the world he carried on his.)

now Cora was heaping guilt atop the burden of responsibility. It wasn't fair. If she was a true friend, she'd back off and let Eila process what she had instead of making things worse. But that could only happen if Eila told Cora what she knew … and she couldn't, because that would be unfair to *Cora*. She'd be setting the world atop *Cora's* shoulders. Just like the world sitting atop the man's, at the top of the newel post behind the door.

(Atlas. The man's name is Atlas, and he carries the weight of the world on his shoulders.)

But the world wasn't a ball. The world was flat and long, and beyond the Fog lay the ocean of Heaven.

(Or perhaps one filled with monsters of mankind's making.)

The thoughts were like whispers, but they hit Eila like punches, besieging her from one side while Cora struck from the other. She felt the weight of what she'd seen during her shift, bearing down like a world large enough to be an enormous ball.

She shook it off, re-focusing on Cora. Her stare was hard — a strange contrast to her innocent, childlike look.

"I guess now that you're a Builder, you've outgrown me," said Cora.

"Cora … "

But Cora was already halfway down the wide stone steps and moving quickly. Eila knew she should give chase and apologize — or issue a *mock* apology, since she hadn't actually done anything — but could only stay frozen. Ministry employees passed without glancing as newcomers ascended steps in the other direction. Eila felt besieged, her motor controls taken over by something else. She was like one of those ferry shaws that Cora had desperately wanted to see — steered by a pilot and bound for *his* destination, not her own.

She watched Cora reach the bottom of the steps, still paralyzed. Her mind was confused, hurt, flipped upside-down. Then, before boarding a waiting streetcar, Cora turned. Eila wished she hadn't. If

Cora had simply gone, that would be bad. But her small glance back — one that, with childlike hope rather than anger, seemed shocked that Eila hadn't followed — hurt so much more.

Then Cora was gone, and still Eila stood rooted to the steps like a tree.

There was only one thing she could do now. Only one place to go. So she called her mother, another lie spilling from her lips with nauseating ease.

And then she went.

Chapter Twelve
The Mind's Dirt

Eila reached the Convenience without incident, not raising a single eyebrow and speaking to no one. It was as if she were a ghost, invisible to all she passed. She almost wanted to linger enough to make people on the streetcar push past her, to feel the press of bodies and be reminded that she herself was real, and alive.

When she arrived to find the door right where she'd last seen it (where her mind had *created* it, if she believed Levi, Daw, and her own niggling suspicion that she hadn't simply "missed" it on arrival), Eila did something she hadn't done in years. She knelt on the street, heedless of soiling her fine dress, and prayed.

"Please, if you're up there," she said to the invisible Crown — to the god her mother believed in but that Eila usually did not — "help me. Help me to see the truth and know what to do. But if you'd be so kind … please don't crush me along the way."

She stood quickly, glancing around and feeling ridiculous. A being in the sky was as absurd as a whale god swimming the ocean beyond the Fog. The Crown watched over them and Jonah's belly gave them a place to go after death. It seemed arbitrary, naive, and overly convenient to believe in such tales, but if Eila had learned anything, it was that stories were sometimes more than they seemed. Alterran lore — told by toothless old men but quietly respected as the culture's underpinning by pretty much everyone — spoke of elves and demons and dragons — mythical beings that had inhabited the land before humans. Even those who believed the tales thought they were just stories from the past, but Eila had been given a reason to believe otherwise.

Worthy thoughts from Alterran dreams were Built and became

devices like the mammoth machine before her. Unworthy thoughts went into the Fog. A dream of the Convenience had made it real, so why wouldn't the same hold true for the legends?

She brushed her hands, nodding skyward. If there was no Crown, what she'd done would hurt nothing. But if there could be steam-powered machines and monsters at their borders, couldn't there be a god in the sky — not because it was logical, but because it had been dreamed?

The door opened with the slightest tug. Anyone could go through. The door was subtle, and you had to be looking at the machine's side just right to see it, but there was no question it was *there*. Any person with a reason could go down. And if the Guile had found their guts and reasons in Pavilion, they could come *up*, too. Because the seal had been broken, by a Builder who could Dream.

Was that what I did today? Did I Dream, along with Case?

She'd traveled the length of the Blunderbuss. Eila had never, to her knowledge, done the kind of "Dreaming" Daw had described, but she'd managed the more ordinary sort. Although most of her dreams had been stolen away like everyone's, a few had remained. Maybe it meant something. Maybe it meant nothing. But after 24 hours with new eyes on Waldron's Gate, she'd realized her answers wouldn't come from above.

She touched the newel post, feeling the molded shape of the man

(Atlas)

carrying the giant ball

(the world)

on his shoulders as her fingers brushed it.

She walked down, taking her time, in no rush to pop the bubble around her. She'd felt lost, back at the Ministry. Soon, after finding Daw, she'd probably feel confused, beaten, or beset-upon. But now, in the sweet honeymoon between the two, she felt neither. Everything was possible, and anything could happen.

Eila passed the strange vacant rooms, again wondering at their purpose as she descended.

One for gadgets.

One for war.

One for fashion.

One for machines.

After an unknowable time, Eila opened the final door and emerged into Pavilion. This time, Levi wasn't there to meet her. She looked up at the sky, seeing turbulent steam that roiled and bubbled in slow motion, gray clouds rolling in lazy whorls. To her far left, she saw a building she hadn't noticed before. It was tall, with a flight of wide stone steps leading up to its door and so tall its top vanished into the faux clouds. Nobody down here would question the way the building had no visible top because it was the way things had always been. How could you know you were in a box when you didn't understand what a box was? Pavilion was like that. A society fooled into believing that their walled-off, squeezed-in existence was all the world had to offer.

The building's lower half — before its architecture began to stretch skyward — looked like the Ministry of Manifestation, only darker. She thought of Daw Blackburn's house and how it had the same blueprint as Rabbit Brampton's.

Daw is his counterpoint. On the other end.

Of course Eila was seeing the Ministry of Dreaming. Smokestacks jutted from the building at odd angles, protruding skyward at its sides, belled like the top of the Blunderbuss … or, here in Pavilion, like its bottom. Thick, black clouds issued from all of them. Of course. The engine's top half plumed white steam, so it made sense that it would spill black from the bottom.

She stared at the smokestacks for longer than she'd intended, wondering how the air was cleaned and how clean air was piped down to Pavilion. Perhaps the air was handled by the Convenience. It all seemed so implausible and strange to Eila, but she was from Waldron's Gate, where everything was right-side up. Given enough time and generations, people could get used to anything.

She walked, her feet remembering the way to Daw's.

As she'd done topside, Eila passed small swarms of people without turning a head. She should have elicited more surprise than yesterday, owing to the improved finery of her dress. But she didn't. People went about their business, none seeming downtrodden. It was almost as if they didn't know they were being oppressed … but then, wasn't that why the worlds were kept isolated? Blackburn knew the truth because an unknown Ministry mole was feeding him information through a kind of psychic he'd called a "conduit." Parliament must know, at least in part, and the same for their counterpoint in Pavilion. Surely, Prime Minister Tillet Morrison knew.

She almost tripped as she thought, *Does my father know?*

Definitely not. Father was second in line at the Ministry of Manifestation, but she'd be able to tell if he knew something that troubling. They'd had a lot of long talks, many of them unadvisable, almost as if Atwell were training his daughter in the art of disobedience and teaching her to think outside the box.

Eila shook away the thought. No. Father didn't know. But Rabbit Brampton might. He was Ministry Head, and a scientist.

Then again, Brampton was unabashedly, vocally proud of Ministry accomplishments. He was always in the public eye, loudly boasting about the amazing things Built by his team. More than Built; *conceived*. Brampton saw the Ministry as his extended body and mind — probably why he was so reluctant to surrender the reins to Eila's father. His ego centered around the Ministry. He didn't behave like a man who had power and reveled in it; he acted like a man who'd done great things and used them to define his personal worth. Brampton seemed to believe that the Ministry Built from nothing. He took credit for the Builders' innovations … in a way that implied that he did, indeed, see them as *innovations*.

She passed a few more groups of people, none taking notice, and found Daw's opulent (for a soot-covered city) neighborhood. His house was the largest and most luxurious. Eila approached the front door, wondering at the grass. Was it irrigated? And how did it grow without sunlight?

Daw opened the door before she touched the knob and extended a glass of Thunderclap.

"So you came back." He didn't continue with the *I-told-you-so*.

"I need to understand some things."

He nudged the glass of green liquid toward her.

"You seem so insistent on me drinking that. How do I know you didn't poison me yesterday? Make me confused? Get me to see or believe things that aren't really true? Maybe I've had a hallucination."

"What's a hallucination, Eila?"

Why did it feel like Daw was constantly on duty, always testing her? He was like a teacher questioning his student.

"Something crazy people have. Like the insane at Joffrey Columns."

"What does it mean to be 'insane,' Eila?"

"To see things that aren't there. Believe things that aren't true."

Still standing, his attire as rumpled as the day before but in new, similarly stylish fabrics, Daw took a sip from his glass, which he'd set on a table before opening the door. "I'd say it means to see things differently than others see them."

"You make it sound like insanity is a matter of opinion."

Daw shrugged.

"Can I come in?" she said.

"Of course. I wouldn't have opened the door for you otherwise. That would have been insane of me."

He stepped aside, allowing Eila to pass, giving her the lead inside his house. She knew where the parlor was (she'd have known even if they hadn't sat there yesterday; it was the same as in Brampton's and she had a photographic memory), but her steering them there seemed like a trap. If she led, it would forgive Daw for his lure.

Eila stopped and looked up at the scientist — the practitioner of "dirty science" as he'd called it. He was tall enough to make her feel short. His mustache had the same waxy shape, curled up into near circles at its long ends.

"What you did to me wasn't fair," she said.

"What did I do?"

"Brought me down here. Piled all sorts of information on me that you knew I wouldn't be able to handle."

"And yet here you are. Alive. Back for more. Voluntarily at my home, same as yesterday. Just like how you voluntarily opened the Convenience door, and voluntarily came down the staircase."

"How do you know there's a staircase inside, if you'd never been able to open it before?"

"It's complicated. Nature of dreaming."

"Why doesn't anyone seem surprised that I'm here, if nobody from above has been here before me?"

"You assume a lot. Did I say that nobody from above has been down here before you?"

"Has there been?"

"Of course not. But you assumed nonetheless."

Eila rolled her eyes. He was exasperating. She wished Levi were here to rein him in, but he didn't seem to be, and Daw was acting like he'd drunk too much Thunderclap.

"Why don't we go into the parlor and sit?" suggested Daw.

"Fine." She felt annoyed, but that was better than feeling like a helpless little child.

"Do you want your Thunderclap?"

"No."

Daw shrugged. "Your choice."

She picked up the glass, wondering why. Probably because it seemed contrary, and in defiance of Daw's willingness to let it sit. The glass was cold. Yesterday's few sips had caused neither confusion nor hallucinations. Based on what Eila had felt, the drink did nothing at all. Its restriction above was arbitrary, as Daw had implied. It was the magician's right hand, distracting the audience while the left made manipulations unnoticed.

Daw led her into the parlor and sat in the same chair as the same sense of oddity slinked through Eila's mind. Who *was* this man? And why was she sitting alone with him in his home, drinking something he'd poured, without anyone above knowing where she was?

She set the glass aside. Safe was better than sorry.

"No one finds your presence strange because we are all used to strangers," he said. "It's not unusual for people to simply 'show up' in Pavilion. Our population is quite large; nobody assumes they must know everyone else. But the Guile and I have seen the way strangers arrive without memories. Our city keeps no records, beyond those at the Ministry of Dreaming's highest level, so such people fade into the fabric. There is no census, no official property ownership. Pavilion owns everything and gives us what we need. It's easier to hide what is Built, what is Tinkered, and what is taken away."

Eila felt played with. She'd asked the question, but Daw had been ready with the answer as if he'd planned for her query. She felt like a puppet who knew what strings were, yet believed she had none.

She'd come down on her own, and yet she felt dragged.

"Could you go up on your own, and be strangers above?"

Daw nodded slowly. He set his glass aside, delicately folded his arms, and spoke as if measuring words.

"I think so, yes. Now that you've been here, we are able to open the door where there was no door before. A few of the Guile poked their heads inside and looked up."

"So why don't you?"

"It is not time."

"I did what you needed, so what are you waiting for? You said I made a door. Fine; it's made. Now you can go up and … " She trailed off.

"And what, Eila? I am one man. Levi is another. The Guile number six. You tell me: how will eight crusaders change the world?"

"That's not my problem."

Eila heard her petulant tone. A juvenile part of her wanted to stand up and stomp her foot, despite the act's impotence. She had an inkling about the grown-up way to handle this situation and wanted no part of it. She was just a girl. This man had reached out of the ground and slid his fingers into her mind while she slept. Maybe her current situation was all his fault and maybe it wasn't, but Eila's presence at his home certainly was. The world might be tearing at some hidden seam, but why did *she* have to know about it? Eila would have been so much happier to continue dreaming barren dreams, Building as if the creations were hers alone. Instead Daw had ripped open a wound inside her, then left it to fester.

See? Now do you notice how badly it hurts?

"Maybe not." Daw uncrossed his legs, then crossed them in the opposite direction. His posture was oddly formal: long limbs crossed at the knee rather than farther down. "But you're wrong when you say you've done what we needed. Forget the Fog for a moment, and think only of Pavilion and Waldron's Gate. How could the two worlds possibly mix? They have not been made ready. We would be interlopers up there, unable to do a thing. We'd be arrested by those who know the secret, or shipped away by those who didn't. You cannot simply break open a dam between villages to usher in a change. Until both sides understand the concept of a river, a shattered dam will only ruin one village and flood the other."

Eila wanted to leap up and storm out. Her body tensed, but then she remembered her long day at the Ministry, her questions about Father's involvement or his knowledge as Head Builder, and the unfortunate quarrel with Cora. She'd become a puzzle piece that didn't fit, and there was no way to numb her edges or slide back into place. Pavilion was a foreign land with no map, but Waldron's Gate was no longer home.

She didn't want to hear another word from Daw, but how could she look her father in the eye again without getting some answers? How could she tolerate another of Rabbit Brampton's glorious media speeches, blathering on and on about the Ministry of Manifestation's latest accomplishments? She'd never be able to have another ordinary dinner, or see the ferry shaws again with Cora. Because how could she giggle and point (or care about handsome ruddermouths) without wondering whose mind the great ships' propellers had been torn from?

"Stop speaking in riddles," she told Daw.

"Tell me, Eila, how would you *like* me to speak?"

"I want the truth. Plain." *But be gentle,* her thoughts added. *Tell me that everything will be all right, and that all will go back to how it used to be.*

"All right," said Daw. "The truth is that you are a Builder who can Dream, which makes you a self-contained creator. Right now, you're but a fraction of your full potential, because you've been neutered like everyone else above. You were able to dream enough to allow Levi to find you, and to dream a door into our world. But even so, you don't know what's possible because you haven't experienced true dreaming. You haven't had the same sleeping experiences that we do each night. You haven't truly, with all your head and heart and psychic body, stepped into a dreamscape that's as real as walking in another place. You haven't had dreams of joy and excitement. You've had no dreams of love. And not a single nightmare."

"Nightmare?"

"Horrors. Dreams that cause you to wake in a sweat or with a scream. The mind's dirt working upward, percolating out in order to cleanse you. Or perhaps to soil you, because sometimes our wounds make us who we are." Daw uncrossed his legs and leaned forward, now hands-to-knees, lightly clasped. He was near enough to touch her, but met Eila's eyes like a reluctant teacher. "Right now you are like a girl with her eyes closed who believes she can see the world with her hands. But if you don't open your eyes, you will never know the meaning of blue."

"Riddles," Eila muttered. "More riddles."

"You must stop taking Crumble," he said.

Eila had blinked down, frustrated. Then her eyes came back up, meeting Daw's. He was staring through to the back of her skull, as if peering into where her dreams might be hiding.

"What?"

"Stop taking Crumble. Today. Close the back door in your head. Keep your dreams for yourself, and close them to the Dreamers."

Like a doctor tapping her knee with a hammer: "No."

Daw cocked his head. For the first time, Eila felt as if he was seeing her as a child. It made her realize the opposite: that up until now, he'd treated her as an adult. She didn't know whether to be flattered by his trust in her maturity or insulted.

"No?"

"I can't stop taking Crumble." The words spilled from her mouth in a rush as part of her panicked. "I won't. I'd never do that. You're insane. Why would anyone stop?" She looked around, as if missing something. "I need to go. I need to get home for dinner."

It was past dinner, she'd made her excuses to Mother already, and even though she didn't want to stay, she absolutely did not want to go. But her only likely savior had just asked her to shove a knife in her eye if she wished to keep playing the game.

Without thinking, Eila's hand stole into her handbag's outer pocket. She removed a capsule, slid it between her lips, and swallowed it dry. It was a spontaneous act of defiance — taking Crumble the minute Daw had told her to stop — but she felt none of the righteousness that so often followed a saber's rattle. Instead, she felt more defeated. She hadn't asked her hand to do what it had done, and the unconsciousness of the action reminded her again of being a puppet.

"Why did you do that, just now?" Daw said.

"I won't stop taking it," she said. "Please."

"I'm just asking you a question. Just now. Why did you do that?"

"I … I … " Eila blinked twice and then held her eyes closed, feeling beaten.

Then, the new Crumble's bright wash began to work on her. Her jitters began to ease. An edge of sharpness returned to her thoughts, like snapping fingers striking against each other rather than slipping. She felt readier to face what Daw was saying — ironic, since his words contradicted the feeling growing inside her.

"You don't know," he said.

"I've been off it before," Eila replied. "It was terrible. You don't know what it's like up top. I don't know anyone who would deliberately choose to do something so … so …" She wasn't even sure how to finish the sentence. Her argument was lame, and she felt defensive. Why *should* she know? Why should she *have* to know? And why should she stop? She could make her own decisions. Daw Blackburn was a man who had only surfaced from the sewers to invade her headspace. He had no right to order her around.

"You're *addicted*," said Daw, "as I told you before. You don't have that word topside, because they don't want you to know that Crumble has hooked you. It does its work to open your mind, but it also digs in so you don't want to stop. The Guile broke down its mechanism years ago. Ironically, Crumble's formulation seems to have been Built at your Ministry."

"Crumble has been around since the first days."

"That's not true." Daw shook his head. "Not as far as we know. Not many here understand written language enough to keep records, but we've found our ways. Conduits have learned a little of your writing through their unique mental gifts and have taught it to others. We had a sort of scratchwork of our own before that, and those records peg Crumble's age at three hundred years, give or take."

Eila shook her head. "Lies."

"I don't lie, Miss Doyle. The truth is too rare."

Eila felt her head wanting to swim. Daw *was* lying. Worse: he might be crazy. She'd come into his house; yesterday she'd drunk his drink. She knew the way home, but what if Daw wouldn't let her leave? He had a quiet way about him, but Eila couldn't shake the sense of something violent bubbling under his surface. From top to bottom — from Daw's odd rumpled dress and mustache to his measured, circular speech — he looked like a man who'd painted a veneer of normality atop unstable bedrock. A man with more responsibility than he could handle, soaking it with denial in hopes of escape, pretending to be dignified and knowledgeable while cracking beneath the surface.

He might as well have said the sky, above in Waldron's Gate, was red. The idea that anyone could have survived without Crumble — *ever* — was as mad as Daw must be.

"Then you're mistaken," she said.

"I'm not."

He continued to hold her eyes. A big, crazy mustache drooped beneath his stare of insanity. And then, in a moment, Eila had it: a way to collapse Daw's argument with its own sharp edge.

"You said you need Crumble to steal dreams! You said we can't Build without it!"

"According to what the Guile has learned throughout its history," Daw said, "your minds have developed a callus. Do you know calluses?"

He began to unfold his hands to show her, but Eila waved him away. Life in Waldron's Gate was not so coddled that every man's hands went barren of patches.

"Of course." Eila crossed her legs, closing herself off. The desire to stand and walk out — especially now that she doubted Daw's sanity — was still strong, but her craving for answers was stronger. She kept thinking of tomorrow's shift on the engine. And the next day's. Then the day after that. She couldn't go back. She was at a precipice, needing to tip in a single direction, for better or worse.

"We believe that dreams used to float freely through the air (or through the Aether if you'd like; both worlds seem to believe in the Aether), and that in those days, you *did* dream. You believed in more lore. It was not impossible to accept that there were elves in Aerohead, for instance. Today, the people of Nascent are considered superstitious for believing those old tales — and for believing that Aerohead is haunted — but there was a day, according to our conduits, when you *all* believed all of that and more. A time before Waldron's Gate was filled with all the Blunderbuss had created. Back when your methods of Building were immature. Before the systems and machines."

Eila leaned closer to Daw, unable to help herself.

"Have you never wondered why the old settlements, farther from Waldron's Gate, are more backward? It's not because their dreams aren't stolen, because the Dreamers don't know distance. They seem backward because those outland places are forced to dream *for real.* They don't receive Built goods as readily as the cities. Their air is still fringed with fantasy because they must Tinker to have what they need, and imagine as they do. They dream jagged dreams, and take less Crumble."

"You claim to know a lot about a world you've never visited," said Eila with spite.

"We are fed information from above."

"From whom?"

"We've never known. Conduits only see what is offered to them, not the faces that offer it."

"They could be seeing lies. Something fed to you to deceive you."

Daw chuckled. "When you have heard as many lies as we have, you learn to tell the difference."

Eila shifted, unsure what to say.

"As cities Built," Daw continued, "dreams from those in the cities became tinged by the Building. You Built steam locomotives, and when people of the cities looked upon them, they dreamed of larger and faster steam locomotives. Balloons operated in the cities. City dwellers began to see them and imagine larger balloons. They made zeppelins, then powered skyships. Have you ever wondered at your city Stensue? Why there is a military city when there is no enemy?"

"My father says they settle disputes."

"Between whom? Between Yon and Alseer? Is that why they have a vast armada?"

"I … "

"No, Eila. They proliferate for the sake of proliferation, like all of Alterra. Most areas outside of the cities are not used to receiving Built goods, so they craft with their hands. But the Waldron's Gate brain grew used to the constant, subconscious theft, and grew protections — like a callus — to stop it. You dreamed less, and hid the few dreams you had. Crumble is *worse* than a back door into your minds

— it's a surgeon's knife slicing you open like overripe fruits every time you close your eyes."

"You don't make sense."

"I'm asking for a leap of faith, Eila. Stop cutting yourself open. See what grows inside. See what your mind is able to feel. Experience what *your* mind, in particular, is able to do."

"Crumble protects us," she said.

"From what?"

"From the … " She didn't want to say it.

As a child, Eila had been told what most children of Alterra were told: that Crumble kept The Imp from sinking his fingers into your soul and dragging you into The Pit. Not everyone believed in The Crown and The Imp, but even those who didn't believe still repeated the tales. There was no way to explain insanity to a child; The Imp seemed as good a boogeyman as any. Once older, Eila simply accepted Crumble's protection and never wondered on the whys. Scientists like Brampton understood, maybe, but any citizen had only to miss a dose to know Crumble was protecting them from *something* horrible.

"From The Imp?" said Blackburn.

Eila looked away.

"Levi tells me that you don't believe in The Crown and all that come with him." A smile crept to the corner of Daw's mouth, twisting under his oily mustache. "And yet he told me that moments before you came here today, you knelt down and prayed to Him. Why?"

Eila stood violently enough to push her chair back a fraction of an inch.

"You want my help, and yet you continue to spy in my mind?" She felt furious, her cheeks flushing red. She wanted to storm from the room, knock things off of shelves, gather the many instruments — surely hand-Tinkered — and hurl them.

She wanted Daw to answer for his intrusion.

"Sit down, Miss Doyle."

"Where is Levi? Why isn't he here to look in my eyes and tell me what he's found inside me? What did I have for breakfast? What trolley did I take?" The cut felt too deep, too private. She forced herself not to go on: *What have I written in my journal? What have I thought about Victor? Which undergarments did I put on this morning?*

"Sit down," he repeated.

"I did not ask for your intrusion! I did not invite you inside! You had no right!"

"Sit down!"

Eila met his eyes in quiet, but refused to sit. The door was within sprinting distance. She longed to run, but that maddening tether held her fast.

"You are not allowed to be righteous here," Daw snapped, words suddenly icy. His paternal demeanor had vanished. He was a sharp piece of iron in search of something to cut. At least she could see past his facade now, into the madness beneath. Daw had a goal, and she was something to help him achieve it. Eila wouldn't be handled deftly. She'd be handled in whatever way got him the result he wanted.

"You did not realize it yesterday, but now you know you're part of a brutal system — one cruel enough to dig humanity's grave. *Yes*, we've trespassed in your minds … but so have you trespassed in ours. Not everyone here is a Dreamer, but we *all* feel your boot. You've seen sky. You do not fear with every moment of your life, as do the Dreamers and those who love them. So I'll ask you again, *Builder*: Why did you pray to a god you do not believe in?"

Eila blinked, unable to process the change in Daw's demeanor. She felt chastised and found herself obeying an engrained compliance as surely as she'd followed Levi Meade to the Convenience door. Guilt — justified or not — bubbled in her stomach. Slowly, she sat back down.

"I don't know."

"You *do*. Trust me, Miss Doyle. While you remain on Crumble, I know you better than you know yourself."

"I … I thought … " She tried to remember the feeling she'd had before kneeling on the stones outside. She'd thought of the Fog. And of new possibilities not yet imagined. "I thought we might have *made* Him real."

"So you believe. In what I said yesterday."

Eila nodded. *Yes*. After today — after what she'd seen inside the Dreamer — she couldn't *not* believe.

"I don't know if there's a Crown, or whether there's a Pit somewhere below," said Daw. "But I *do* know that what you feel —

what you've become numb to after a life of Crumble addiction — is a fear of your own power. Not just you, Eila, but *everyone* above. We are all creators. My Tinker makes amazing things, created from his mind. He has never hooked into the engine, nor taken your drug. Our dreams are not stolen. We face what you fear every day. Not just in nightmares at night, but in daytime trembles, in a thousand small disturbances of the mind. Unarticulated thoughts — those that aren't purged and swept like detritus from a shattered vase — rattle within us at all times. We are halves of a whole. Trust me," he said, a small, bitter smile finally returning to his face, "a person gets used to it."

Eila wasn't so sure. She'd missed a dose of Crumble once while traveling, when the vial in her bag had run dry. She'd only been nine or ten at the time, and her father had been in a foul mood. She hadn't had the courage to break the tension and beg Father to take her to their stowed luggage for more. A half hour after her missed dose, she'd felt uneasy and confused. After an hour, her mind had swum with a thousand loose and swirling ends. Staring outside their train car, she'd seen shadows and imagined them as shapes of real things, as if they might come alive. Clouds became demons. She'd looked at her hands to avoid the window, but it had only made things worse because she saw her clenched fingers as curled claws. Darkness had stabbed at her heart whenever she blinked. It was two hours before they arrived home and she was finally able to dose, and by then she'd been seeing dark specters in every closet, hearing the echo of footsteps across the house as if intruders had come to take her away. She'd huddled in a ball on her bed after stuffing her mouth with raw powder, waiting for the swirl of thoughts and images to end.

The idea of "getting used to it" was ridiculous.

"No."

"Everything depends on it," Daw said. "You know it does."

"I don't. I won't."

"You're the Dreamer who Builds. The Builder who Dreams. And you're but a fraction of who you're supposed to be. You're a boiler with an open valve. You can't build the pressure required to run a machine unless you close the valve and allow the force to build inside. We need you to move mountains. We need you to *Dream*."

"I'll go insane."

"You won't. We don't, down here."

Eila wanted to argue. Daw seemed plenty insane to her.

"I've been off it before. It was terrible."

"Because you're not used to it. Because you've only known a clean, orderly mind, and … "

"And you want it disorderly?" She was feeling less afraid, angry again. She didn't lose her temper often, and may never have been quite as mad before as she felt herself becoming now. It was an out-of-control feeling, but Eila was starting to find that she liked it. She was smaller than Daw by a head and some shoulders, but was beginning to feel like she could tear him in two with her mind, if necessary.

"Yes," said Daw, nodding.

"Everyone knows what happens to people who go off Crumble," said Eila, her skin crawling with the thought. "They go to Joffrey Columns. They are walled in the spires, left to rant and rave."

That wasn't all, though. What the children said about the asylum was probably more rumor than fact, but those rumors were terrifying. Whether the absence of Crumble let The Imp inside or merely opened floodgates to the mind's trash, the tales she'd heard about Joffrey doctors sent chills up the spine. They used a metal spike, sent through the eye at the corner, to spear the brain into compliance. They subjected the mad to machines — steam calliopes flashing terrifying images to force their minds into overload. Shock treatments. Great engines that immersed patients in their worst fears in order to force (then fuel) their denial. "Integration treatments" that sounded more like fragmentation. And tales of monsters in the dungeons.

"How do you know the people in Joffrey are not ranting and raving the truth?" asked Daw.

There it was again: The implication that sanity was arbitrary. Eila glanced at the door, wondering if it had locked when he'd closed it. If Levi had told Daw about her prayer, was he still here somewhere? He'd seemed more balanced than the scientist, but maybe she'd only thought that because he was younger and better-looking. For all she knew, he could be somewhere in the basement, preparing a table with straps, and sharpening knives.

"It's *not* the truth."

"How do you know?"

"Because this is the truth!" She slapped the chair's arms. "This! Here! Reality, here and now!"

"How do you know?"

"I can feel it!" Again Eila slapped the chair, emotions still swirling. Had she really taken that Crumble moments earlier? It felt like she'd missed, like her mind was unhinging as it had in her memory. She felt sweat wanting to bead, though the room was cool.

"Have you ever had a dream you thought was real?"

She stopped.

"What would you think if I told you that you weren't sitting in a chair, but were instead on a camel's back?"

She looked down. The chair remained a chair.

"I would think you were insane."

"But it's your word against mine. I believe it's a camel. You believe it's a chair. What makes you right and me wrong?"

"It's … "

"What if Levi were here and agreed? Would you think us *both* insane?"

"I'd … "

"If your family were here? Your co-workers at the Ministry? What would it take, Eila? How far can a vote swing before you believe it's *you* who is wrong, even when you're certain you're right?"

Eila was mute. She had no reply.

"Sometimes the mind breaks, Miss Doyle — but sometimes, it merely dreams. And though you dream one thing and I dream another, neither of us is right or wrong. You've grown up in a black-and-white world. Without Crumble, you will see many shades of gray, as we do down here. At first, it will be difficult for your mind to assimilate. Some who go off your drug cannot take the assault. Here, we grow up with uncertainty and fear, darkness and nightmares. We learn it young, while our minds are pliable. It would be hard for your father to go off, or any adults you know. But you may yet be young enough to take it."

"'May?'"

"Anyone *can*," said Daw, "if they decide to. If they know what is real and keep it in mind. But children find it easier to fantasize.

To accept the unreal. Your mind is especially strong." He hesitated, clearly unsure whether he should say the next thing. Finally he added, "Levi has seen that in you, and believes."

"But he's not sure."

"Nobody is sure. Of anything."

"I won't do it," Eila said.

A bridge had been crossed; she could feel the room's new mood. They were done with lecturing and asking and telling. Another wound had been opened, and her mind couldn't close it. She'd come for some sense of assurance: that she could find a way to make peace with Building, that the Guile were coming topside to make changes so she wouldn't need to, that she could purge her mind and learn to deal with what she'd heard and accept things as they were. But she'd not only been denied that assurance; she'd been given even *more* to fear and do and be.

Daw wasn't going to tell her that everything would be fine. He was going to heap the world onto her shoulders and leave it for her to decide between a slow descent into madness or a quick one.

She stood. They were past discussing Crumble and its function. Now, only urging and pushing and convincing were left.

"You have to," said Daw. "You can't go back."

"I can refuse to come here again. I can forget you exist. You'll either come up or you won't, but it won't be my problem either way. You can have your revolution. I'll stay in the system, as part of what you'll revolt against."

"You won't."

"I will." Eila looked over her shoulder and began walking backward. "I'll return to work. Force myself to forget. I'll take more Crumble, not less. I can even keep Levi out if I take enough; I saw that last night. I'll get used to what I know. I'll go to the mercantile with Cora. I'll … "

Daw rose and approached her. His voice was softer when he spoke next — almost sad, as if trying to offer comfort where there was none. He sounded like a doctor informing a woman that her husband would die, and that nothing could be done to save him.

"I'm sorry, Eila."

"I can't stop taking Crumble."

"You must."

Her foot struck a wrinkle in the rug as she retreated, and she half stumbled, grabbing the parlor doorway to steady herself. Daw came closer again and took a hand. She snatched it back, unwelcome tears starting to leak from her eyes.

"I can't."

"You must."

Her feet stopped moving. She avoided the scientist's eyes, now looking down. A tear fell from her nose to the rug, splashing from the side and onto the floor. It made a starburst, spiked edges on the hardwood. Holding herself erect over the past two days had been like holding a weight above her head. Eila was fatigued, and surrender promised to make everything simple.

Another tear fell, her chest wanting to hitch. But she wouldn't let it happen yet. She sniffed the tears back and looked up. Daw was watching her with compassion, her hand finally in his. Aside from the man's ridiculous waxed mustache, his madness had departed.

"If I stop taking Crumble," she said, "what will it be like?"

"It will be hard. Then you will adjust, and it will be like opening eyes you didn't realize had been closed."

"And then I'll feel good again. Normal, like all is all right. Like everything will be okay."

Daw shook his head. "All will not be okay."

"You said I'd adjust."

"You will adjust to how it will become, not how it was."

She sniffed again, refusing to snatch her hand back to wipe her eyes. "Just tell me I'll be fine. When it's all said and done, tell me that I'll be fine."

Daw continued to slowly shake his head.

"I can promise only two things," he said. "The first is that everything will be different. Not good, but not bad either. *Different.*"

"And?"

"And I can promise that you, Miss Doyle," he said, "are our only chance."

Chapter Thirteen
37 Pills in a Dish

Eila arrived at home to find that Mother — which was to say Harney, the handmaid — had held dinner again. Atwell had to spent a few extra hours at the Ministry, but he wouldn't have to pull another all-nighter. Juliette, despite her occasional seeming indifference, loved Atwell with an almost furtive affection, as if she found it undignified. She cherished and protected her dinners with Atwell. It was something, through her abundant arrangements of flowers and lit candles on the dinner table, that she always made beautiful.

"Oh, lovely," she said, seeing Eila step into view. "You're back already? Did you even see the shaws arrive?"

Cora was apparently too hurt and angry to discuss what had happened on the Ministry steps with any of the Doyles, and Juliette didn't care a whit about the ferry shaw schedules. She bought her own clothes (and her children's, when they allowed her) from extravagant tailors downtown. Eila could lie all she wanted about her supposed evening with Cora. It was as if her best friend no longer mattered — a thought that nipped at Eila's mind like a yapping dog.

"Yes, we saw them arrive and dock. But I left when they began to unload."

"That means the pilots ignored them and went with older girls," said Nicholas, entering the room holding a breadstick. Juliette's eyes flicked toward the boy, her gaze disapproving of his breach of decorum as crumbs spilled from his mouth.

"Shut your face," Eila said.

"You'll be too ugly anyway," he answered. "Even when you're older."

Eila punched Nicholas too hard in the arm. He flinched back and looked for a moment like he might cry or complain to Mother, but he was thirteen and nearly too old for both. He moved to punch Eila back, but Juliette stepped between them.

"Nicholas, go put that breadstick back on your plate. We will wait for your father. Go. Now."

He sneered at Eila and walked back out into the dining room.

Juliette turned to Eila. "I didn't realize you'd be home. I didn't have Harney set a place for you. Would you tell her? And please get yourself a glass?"

She said the last like a question, even though it was a request. But the normality of speaking to the handmaid and filling a glass with water had an undeniable appeal to Eila after her time below. She wanted to latch onto both chores and hug them. For a few moments, they'd kept her from thinking about what she'd done: skipping a dose of Crumble when she'd felt the need nipping at her on the trolley. Her capsule at Daw's had only been a partial dose. She needed more and was now feeling agitated, and empty.

She only had to make it through the night. She only had to see what her dreams would be like without Crumble. If she'd just had a few dreams so far — and if they'd been halfway things — what would *real* dreaming be like?

The thought was terrifying, yet somehow exciting. Like stepping off of a cliff.

Eila grabbed and filled her water glass, then went into the dining room to set it on the table. She found her father and two sisters in place: Atwell at the head, Winter and Penelope on either side. It had always seemed annoying to Eila, the way her sisters clamored to receive the most of their father's attention, but her experience at Daw's had given her new perspective. She couldn't help but see the girls as innocent and Atwell as their protector … and yet none of them knew what they were innocent of or being protected from. Unless Father knew truths she didn't want to believe he might know, given his senior position at the Ministry.

"Eila!" he said, looking up. "I thought you were shopping with Cora."

She pulled out a seat and sat, ignoring Winter's snotty look.

"We finished early. I didn't know Harney would hold dinner."

"Your *mother* held dinner," said Atwell.

Juliette had "held dinner" by telling Harney to wait. It didn't seem heroic to Eila, but then she and Mother saw things differently. Juliette had been born with an eye for beauty, whereas Eila didn't care much about aesthetics. Her room was always disorderly when she left and clean upon her return — a tidying service her mother thought of as a gift but which Eila saw as a minor intrusion. But for some reason, even that wouldn't bother her today.

"That was nice of her," said Eila. She didn't add what she was thinking: that her mother had held dinner for Atwell, not her. But even that thought wasn't fair. She'd hold it for Eila if Eila wanted, but the family's eldest child was belligerently independent, and seldom asked.

"You went to the mercantile district?" Penelope asked.

Penelope, at age nine, was most like Eila. Nicholas and six-year-old Winter both seemed to be cut from their mother's cloth, and from a different swatch than Eila and Penelope, who were more like Atwell. From a high enough perspective, Eila was sure everyone in her family loved each other and agreed on what mattered most, but sometimes the differences and petty irritations were annoying enough to veil it.

Eila nodded. As much as she hated lying to her mother, she hated lying to Penelope even more. But now she'd dug herself a hole and would be held responsible for climbing out.

Strangely, the lies were practically falling out of her tonight, and not just because she'd gotten used to deception. It was also the Crumble — or its lack. The drug's absence in her blood was making her almost lightheaded. She could see shadows making shapes and playing along the walls. She saw a fluffed-up cloth napkin and thought how it looked like some sort of animal. The way her father used his napkin to dab at his mouth seemed funny in a way that it never had before. She felt intoxicated. Was it the Thunderclap? Should she have refused?

But it couldn't be that, because today Eila hadn't so much as sipped the Thunderclap.

Her mind felt as untidy as her room. Every small thought

competed for attention and jumbled her focus.

"Did you see the ruddermouths?" said Penelope. "Did they tell any tales? Where had they been last? Have they been to Yon? Is the Fog near Yon like the Fog here?"

Penelope's questions were innocent, but Eila felt herself shiver. She'd never really thought much about the Fog prior to her time with Levi and Daw. She'd accepted it as a fact, as did all Alterran citizens — there like the sky and clouds. But now, with Crumble draining from her system, she thought of it in a way that was exactly the opposite of Penelope's question.

She'd seen it in person just once, when she was eleven years old. Mother had taken her to the outskirts of Waldron's Gate and held her hand as they stared at a place where a footpath vanished into an opaque mist.

Never take for granted the protection The Crown gives us, she'd told Eila, who'd stood shivering beside her mother.

When Juliette had taken her to the border — a line that sometimes waxed and sometimes receded, like mythical ocean tides — Eila had accepted the Fog as a religious experience. Some said The Imp lived inside, while others said it swarmed with monsters. According to Parliament, it was empty. But regardless, looking back, the trip to see the Fog had seemed more like her father's move than her mother's. But it had been Juliette who'd taken her as surely as she'd once taken Eila to the bakery — to Carlo's place in the city, before it had burned to the ground with Carlo trapped inside. Maybe, in some ways, her mother wasn't as orderly as she seemed.

Even today, thoughts of how that footpath vanished into nothingness gave Eila chills. *Especially* today.

"Penelope," said Atwell, his tone warning Penelope to mind her topics. His eyes ticked toward Winter. The family's youngest wasn't visibly shaken, but she had her mother's demeanor. Atwell, Penelope, and Eila were open books, but you could deeply wound the other three members without them showing a mark. Winter was only six. There would be a day that Juliette would take her — and Penelope, for that matter — to the Fog's wavering border to show them what they should appreciate being saved from. But not yet.

"The pilots, then," said Penelope, undaunted. "Did you see the pilots? And *did* they tell tales?"

Eila gave her sister a soft smile. Despite the way her thoughts swirled faster and faster in the back of her mind, Penelope's simple, eager questions calmed Eila's heart. It was sweet, the way she still believed in the world's beauty. Perhaps that was the primary reason for the gap between Eila's and Juliette's ways of thinking: even before Eila had learned the Blunderbuss had two halves, she'd known life's experiences ran deep. Juliette, however, stayed at the surface, tending lilies and clothing and candles.

"We didn't see the pilots, Pen." Eila blinked the guilt from her face, then continued. "I'm sure they were too busy."

"Or you were too ugly," said Nicholas, arriving to sit beside her. Juliette was behind him and took her position at the short table's other end.

"Nicholas," said Juliette. Mother's single word was so soft as to carry the correcting force of a pillow, but her son stopped anyway. Juliette looked to her husband. "Would you say grace?"

Winter started to eat the second Harney set a plate in front of her. Atwell looked over and, deciding not to demur as he normally did, rushed ahead as if to beat his youngest daughter to the punch. Father didn't believe in the gods, but Mother did and always had. Perhaps he could save Winter's soul if he finished grace before she ate too many peas.

A thought flitted into Eila's mind: *How many peas, eaten before grace, damn you to The Imp and His Pit for all eternity?*

She couldn't help it; a giggle escaped her lips as Atwell opened his own to speak. Both adults looked at Eila as she put a hand over her mouth. She'd never laughed during grace. Nor had she, in her mother's presence, had such a sacrilegious thought. Where was this giddiness coming from? Was it her lack of Crumble? And if so, what had she been so afraid of?

With a final glance, Atwell clasped his hands on the table and began.

"Dear Crown, as you rule the sky above and the ocean beyond, as your companion, Jonah, keeps our souls and saves us from The Pit's endless temptations, we thank you for this food on our table, and for all we are given."

"Let's eat," said Nicholas, tucking in. But Atwell's eyes had returned to Eila, seeming to see whatever oddness she felt.

"How long were you in the district, E?" he asked.

"Just an hour or two."

"When did the shaws arrive?"

She couldn't remember. Cora had told her, but then she'd offended Cora, destroyed their friendship, and sent her raging off to cry. A bubble of guilt rose in her chest, and she inexplicably found herself thinking of her father's grace.

Save us from the temptations of The Pit.

And from the Fog.

Eila didn't believe in The Imp or His Pit any more than Father did, but today of all days, she believed in the Fog with all of her fragmenting heart.

"Just as we got off the trolley."

"How many shaws were there?"

Eila had just shoved a mouthful of Beef Applebee into her mouth. She took her time swallowing, trying to pretend she couldn't see the piercing insistence in Atwell's eyes. Juliette saved her as she swallowed, asking Atwell to pass the butter and breaking his stare.

Eila found her thoughts sneaking back to the Fog. Normally, she could push an unpleasant thought away. She'd had to do it often after that first trip to the Fog, and the strategy had come easily enough. But now she couldn't shove the thoughts an inch from her mind. She found herself thinking again of that first night and how easily she'd slept — and for the first time, wondering if she'd dreamed of horrors in the Fog after all. Perhaps she'd dreamed of dark shadows and trees with limbs like reaching arms, but those dreams had been stolen from her. And perhaps, instead of young Eila facing those night fears, someone underground in the Ministry of Dreaming had faced them for her.

"Father," said Penelope, "do the shaws fly all the way to the borders?"

"I think so," Atwell said.

"Yeah," Nicholas agreed. "Kids at school were talking about it, and … "

"Well, if they were talking in school, it must be true," said

Penelope, clearly resenting her brother's attempt to answer a question intended for Father.

"They're daredevils," said Nicholas, undaunted, looking around at each family member as he continued. Speaking too much about the Fog at the table would eventually raise Mother's ire, but he was still in her margin of tolerance, and seemed to think his story was worth testing her limits. "That's why they're called ruddermouths. They like to travel. Who else would want to head to the north's haunted cities? They even visit the asylum city; did you know that?"

"Nicholas ..." said Juliette.

"I heard they fly right up to the Fog. They say it goes upward as far as a shaw can fly, so they can't go over or see past it. Zeppelins, too. I know this kid who ... "

"Nicholas!"

Juliette's fork plinked on porcelain as she stared her son down. She looked to Winter, to see if the youngest was bothered, but her eyes found the eldest when her facade finally broke.

"Eila?"

Eila could hear her mother's words and see her eyes, which had grown somehow softer than usual. But she could also see the Fog in her mind, stretching from the ground to the world's ceiling, the hinterlands of Alterra below a zeppelin's bulk like a patchwork quilt. The thought made her feel walled in. *Trapped.* They were animals in cages. Alterra's size didn't mattered. There was no way out — and if Daw was right about the Fog, it meant they'd forged their own walls, brick by brick.

"Eila? Are you feeling all right?"

No. No, she wasn't. There was a dish of Crumble capsules on her dresser upstairs. There were thirty-seven pills in that dish, exactly, and a glass vial in a kitchen cabinet that was half full. Another in each of her siblings' rooms, plus one in her parents'. Eila had more in her bag. She felt each pill call to her, plus the loose block they often broke into dust and sifted into Harney's cooking. She felt surrounded by light emanating from the drug, and stupid for closing her eyes to its brilliance.

She saw the Fog. A beast inside with yellow eyes, its pupils like capsules laid on their sides. She saw a thing with great claws. A dark black shape that flew in a long cloud like a ghost with a tail. Of *course* the old lore was all true. There *had* been elves in Aerohead. There *were* specters haunting Yon's outskirts, where there was no Parliament Guard to protect the people at night. It couldn't be any other way. *They'd* made those things. *Trolls. Demons. Creatures.* Unarticulated and incomplete thoughts. Dark horrors with no faces, lurking behind half-closed doorways. Sometimes, the dream theft wasn't as efficient and facile as it could be. Sometimes, for seconds, terrors lingered. *Like now.*

She had to flee the table. There was something under the butter dish. She could see it moving, an edge peeking up and a sliver of darkness beginning to show with the white speck of minuscule eyes. She stood in a single fluid motion, the force of her lower legs knocking the chair backward. But the chair's legs didn't move smoothly on the rug. They caught, and Eila found herself falling, tripped by the force of her motion. She landed in the chair's cross-bracing, wood and flesh diving for the floor at the same time.

Her father stood with a loud crack, a moment before Nicholas. Mother was frozen, her hand finally stealing up near her open mouth. Penelope disappeared, her face masked by the table now looming above.

"Eila!" said Atwell, coming forward.

The drape of the tablecloth was long and nearly brushed the floor. Eila's lower legs, bare beneath her dress, had skidded beneath it as she'd fallen. There could be anything under there. A beast with razors for teeth. A thing with eyes on its fingertips, crawling on all fours, snapping up table scraps. A portal to tunnels. The tunnels Daw had told her about, that she was suddenly sure were teeming beneath Pavilion, showing even the Guile's most courageous their limits.

She snatched her legs back, bringing them into the safety of the dining room's light.

Atwell reached down. He didn't grab her; he allowed her to take his hand. Blinking, she did.

"Look at me."

Eila couldn't. The tablecloth. The darkness. The tunnels into the ground. The Fog. The specters that awaited her at night, when she laid her head on her pillow.

"Look at me."

With effort, she did. Father's eyes were now a deep blue, but Ministry rumor said that when he Built, his irises fogged at the edges, becoming indistinct and gray. Eila had always thought it was good-natured tomfoolery — a legendary joke on the Head Builder — but saw it now as he stood above her. Little by little, her spooks drained away and she was again just a girl lying on the floor, her father's concerned face hovering above.

She stood.

She looked around their ordinary, everyday table, but those around it were not her ordinary, everyday family. The table sat five people who, right now, looked like they were watching a loved one burn in a fire.

"I'm fine," she lied.

"What's wrong, Eila?" her mother asked.

"Nothing. Nothing is wrong."

Juliette's lips pressed into a line. "You're sure?"

"I'm sure. Really." Eila tried to right her chair, but the bracing had been shattered, and the seat now wanted to sag in the middle. She went to grab a replacement chair from another room and took the broken one with her, feeling as if she were gliding on ice. Everything was moving past her too quickly. She could hear whispers from behind and wanted to shout them down. But she couldn't, nor could she stop moving.

The chair. She had to get the chair.

Eila returned with the spare seat, placed it in her spot, and sat. She looked at her setting, seeing now that she must have snagged the tablecloth on the way down. Her glass had spilled, liquid dripping onto the rug underfoot with a soft pattering. She righted the glass.

Juliette said, "Let me get that."

"It's fine." But it wasn't fine; she'd set the glass atop the knife's edge. Again it nearly tipped over. She set it more deliberately, despite her shaking hand.

"Give it here. I'll fill it again for you."

"I have it. It's no problem."

"Eila … "

"I'm fine!"

Her head snapped up, suddenly seeing her mother as some sort of a nymph. Something innocent and naive. Something that could never hope to face what was coming. Then, in a blink, she was back to Juliette Doyle.

Eila turned to her plate, then began to saw Beef Applebee with her knife and fork. She cut off a bite and stuffed it into her mouth. Another. Another. She realized it was too silent and looked up to find that no one was eating. Everyone's eyes were on her.

Eila's mind seemed to split. One part realized that something was very wrong and that she must seem insane. The other half buried its head in the dirt and kept her eating.

Keep doing what's normal, and it will all go away.

"Eila," said Atwell. "I need your opinion on something."

She looked over. The hopeful half of her split perception saw what he was doing while the cynical half began raising its wall. But with the flash of darkness gone, the first half was getting stronger. With effort, she said, "What?"

"I'd rather speak in private." He looked around the table, doing a better job of keeping his face impassive than the others. "It's about the Build."

"I'm fine. Really."

"I know you are. May I have a few minutes?" Then he reset his expression into something more businesslike. "Please?"

Eila stood — carefully, so as not to trip the chair's legs again on the rug — and set her napkin delicately on the table. Father led her into the other room, and Eila tried to pretend she didn't see the concern she was leaving behind her. Even Nicholas looked worried, and for some reason that bothered Eila more than his usual taunts and scorn.

They moved into Father's study. Leather assailed her nostrils, but it wasn't an offensive scent. She'd played on this floor thousands of times growing up while her father shifted paperwork on the desk above. The smell was a welcome childhood comfort.

"You know about the Pianoforte," he said.

"About how it collapsed?"

"Yes."

"Of course. I was there." *I caused it*, her mind wanted to add.

"We've gotten some information back."

"From Mr. Brampton?"

Atwell shook his head. "From the engine."

"From the Blunderbuss?" Eila cocked her head. "I didn't know it gave you 'information' about the Build."

"It's an odd thing," he said. "We get something like reports here and there, but it seems to happen almost at random. But really, *not* randomly. Honestly, Eila, when the Blunderbuss gives us reports like this, it comes off like spite."

"Spite?"

Atwell nodded. "My Enigma people get it when it happens. They say it feels like the machine is … well … 'angry.' It hits them, while they're in their cradles, as feedback. The word we use is 'complaining.' 'The engine is complaining,' is what someone will say."

"What does that mean?"

Atwell shrugged. "There's a lot about the Blunderbuss we don't understand. Complaining isn't usually a big problem and feels more like a locomotive venting steam. Like it doesn't want to run but does anyway. But those … *bursts* … sometimes give us insights into their cause, and it's usually from some kind of imbalance. Too many Builders, too few Builders, Builder preferences being weighed too heavily in the Build, as if not respecting the ideas coming in from the Aether. It's supposed to be about working together, but some Builders grow arrogant and want to switch a part on something they're Building from here to there because they believe it will look better, not caring if it alters function. Things like that."

Eila nodded. She knew a few Builders who fit that description.

"But last night's burst, after the shutdown, told us something else. So much of this is guesswork, seeing as it's just images that gurgle back to someone working up top, but Bolster received this one, and his words were, 'It's like the thing is contaminated.'"

Eila thought of Victor, right after the shutdown, proposing that a fault had broken the resonance. She'd heard of this sort of thing before, and had learned it during training. Sometimes, when a Builder's focus was particularly bad, the Build in a given sector would proceed as if missing a wheel.

"From where?"

“We’re not sure yet. But whatever it is, it’s lingering.” He sighed, then seemed to choose his next words carefully. She knew the gesture: he was trying to find a way to say something to Eila that needed to be said, and that he sincerely hoped wouldn’t bother her. “And it went away at five o’clock today.”

Eila’s earlier disorientation was replaced with one of mounting defensiveness. The new emotion was actually an improvement.

“When my shift ended, you mean.”

Atwell shrugged.

“A lot of shifts ended at five. Not just mine.”

“And maybe all of those people are now showing signs of Depth Syndrome,” Atwell said. “But I can only speak to the one I know about.”

Eila wanted to shout. She’d been trained formally by the Ministry and trained informally by her father for years before that. She knew more about Building than most of the Builders with a half decade on the array — including how to recognize and avoid overstimulation and neural fatigue disorders.

“I said I’m fine.”

“Don’t posture with me, Eila. You’re smarter than that. Stop thinking about your emotions and examine the facts.”

For a moment, Eila resisted, but this was one of Father’s classic themes. Sometimes, you just wanted to hit the boy who pushed you down, but it was usually smarter to think things out and realize that nothing would be solved … if you could force yourself to do it. Having a father who only coddled when absolutely necessary helped. Eila supposed it made her stronger and more self-reliant, but in her worst moments she still wanted a sympathetic pat on the head from Daddy more than anything.

Eila forced herself to see how she’d been lately as if from his perspective — or Brampton’s perspective, or that of anyone who might have watched her last week at the Ministry. Depth Syndrome occurred when Builders over-immersed in deep Build constructs and their lower minds forgot the trick of telling reality from the Build. She’d never done that, Eila was certain, but supposed that becoming lost in a dream — which her father had no reference for — must look very much the same. Especially without the safety valve afforded by

Crumble.

Eila felt something deep inside her protest like an empty stomach. Her lips felt dry. Her mind felt hungry. She had an almost irrepressible urge to dive toward his desk and fish out the pile of loose Crumble she knew he kept in his top drawer.

Knowing her actions would look like the panicky movements of a Depth Syndrome sufferer kept Eila in her seat. That, and the coat hanging on the hook behind the desk. It looked like the wings of a gargoyle, and Eila was sure she could see the creature's head peeking out from the folds.

Her heart began to beat faster, threatening to betray her.

"I've been tired."

"Just tired." It was a statement, but she heard the question within it.

"Cora and I were out late, and … "

"Which night?"

"At the solstice festival. We saw a psychic, then rode too many rides. It unsettled my stomach, and I had trouble sleeping."

"Remind me. Was that the night of the Pianoforte?"

"It was the next day."

"Uh-huh. Because I thought you came in late the following day."

"Oh. Well, yes."

"So you were at the festival on the *same* day as the Pianoforte."

"Yes. Wait. No." She was confused. Which, of course, was Atwell's intention. And to think: Eila had believed she'd gotten away with all of those lies.

"Which was it?"

"I was tired on both days. The festival was first. The Pianoforte was the next day."

"And you were tired on the second day, too."

"Yes."

"Because you went to the mercantile with Cora."

"Yes. Wait." That was just today. Had she really rebuffed Cora so recently? Eila felt like she'd been ruining their friendship for a week, maybe more. "No. Stop it. Stop playing games with me."

"I'm just trying to get the story. The *real* story."

"I was at the festival with Cora."

"Again? On the second night? I thought that was the first night."

Eila met Father's eyes, more angry than confused. Angry enough to face the gargoyle behind his desk and take the Crumble that would murder the beast. She looked at it and saw its neck crane up to meet her stare with malevolence. Then it was only a coat again.

"I went twice."

"You're sure? Maybe we could ring Cora to verify." His hand moved toward the talkbox.

"Stop it!"

Atwell shrugged. "Stop what?"

"Stop testing me! Stop *interrogating* me!"

Atwell turned. Demeanor shifting, he laid both palms on her shoulders. "You're my daughter, Eila, but you're also my employee. It doesn't matter that you work directly under the Ministry Head; I'm the Head *Builder*. And *you're* a Builder. That makes you, like the rest of the Builders and the Build itself, my responsibility. I don't just mean responsibility in the sense of making sure things go smoothly for the Ministry. I mean it in that I am *responsible* to you. I need to take care of you, and ensure that you stay safe and healthy. That duty doubles with you as my daughter."

"I'm fine."

"You keep saying that."

"Because I *am!*" Eila wanted to rush off to her room and be alone. What happened at dinner was irrelevant. It should have been over hours ago anyway. By leaving, she'd be obeying the normal schedule, making the rest of them the oddities.

"Something is wrong, Eila. I can tell. You can talk tell me."

"Nothing is wrong." His caring eyes made it hurt to lie, but the truth would hurt far, far worse. She had to give him something. "It's just … Cora. I had a big fight with Cora."

"At the mercantile?"

Yes, she supposed that made sense. Eila nodded.

"What about?"

"Girl stuff."

"Anything that would poison the Build?"

She shook her head. "I don't know. I don't think so."

Another necessary lie came rolling out. She hated it, but was in too deep.

"Besides, our fight was just today. After my shift."

Atwell sighed, dropping his hands from Eila's shoulders. "Then what was that at dinner?"

"Girl stuff," she repeated.

Now Eila wasn't just lying; she was being manipulative. Like most men — and especially most fathers — Atwell would never want to discuss anything with Eila that she emphatically labeled as "girl stuff." He still thought of Eila as a little girl, and the thought of her growing up had to be a unique variety of pain. If necessary, he might ask Juliette to intervene, but as far as Atwell knew, girls needed to handle any of the stuff that was foreign to his gender.

"You're sure?"

"Yes."

"You're feeling okay? Other than … " he trailed off.

"Yes. Fine." Eila felt her voice soften. Her mind was still churning, but Father gave her something to focus on. She focused on feeling guilty for lying, feeling bad about Cora, and feeling besieged by the weight of Daw's request. She could lose her mind when she was alone.

"Well. Sure," said Atwell. "Just … just let me know if you're having any more trouble sleeping, okay? Because I'm not kidding. Lack of focus can pollute the Build. But of course, you know that." He turned away, embarrassed.

"Of course."

"Should we head back in to dinner?"

Eila looked toward the study door. They could walk out, cross the hall, and re-enter the dining room. Or, instead, she could turn into the hallway, walk upstairs, and go to her room. Everyone would wonder what was wrong, but she now felt sure that Father, in whatever shambling way he managed, could explain what had apparently gone wrong.

"Maybe it would be best if I turned in early," she said. Then, throwing him a bone: "You know. To make sure I'm fully rested for tomorrow."

"All right," he said, rising to leave and return to dinner. "Sleep well, then."

But of course, she didn't.

Chapter Fourteen
Crumbled Reflection

By the time Eila was ready to lie down, she'd been off her Crumble for nearly seven hours — twice the time she'd been deprived during the family trip. Now the room was dark and she was alone, her symptoms exponentially worse.

She tried to putter in her journal, but her thoughts were jumbled in terror. She would feel good for a few minutes, then look back and find her handwriting manic — all edges and urgent points, nothing like her usual soft, flowing script decorating the other pages. Looking at those pages, she thought the words looked like the scribblings of a madwoman … and when she read them back, she found she barely remembered writing what was there. She'd dipped into a fugue, recording without even realizing it: thoughts of the Ministry, Pianoforte, and the dual-ended nature of the Blunderbuss. The horror of dream theft as she'd felt it herself, followed by the terror of Dreamers below forced to sift the unconscious thoughts of Alterrans. It was as if the pages had been written by another — someone, it seemed, whose mind was unhinging.

Eila tried to read, but everything made her uncomfortable. The book she'd been enjoying all week felt predictably boring, every twist and turn obviously rehashed from the millions of other books that began, proceeded, and ended the same. She had a few fairy tale collections from childhood boxed in her closet, but when she began to flip through those instead, they filled her with terror. She forced herself to turn the illustrated pages for a while, shocked that such tales would be told to children. She was fifteen now, well past those early ages. How had she grown up normal, hearing these stories for the first time at just a few years old? How could *any* Alterran child grow up thinking of them, without trembling in the dark?

She'd heard rumors about the north of Alterra, where the city surrendered to country and such tales were still traded, as if true, even among adults. *Those* stories, if they were the evolved forms of fairy tales told to children, would have teeth, and would keep villagers burning midnight oil just so full dark would never fall. And what of those who actually lived near the Fog? What would they believe? What would they see?

Eila turned on every light in her room, even adding a few gas lamps to accent the electric. When the lamps couldn't kill all of the shadows, she lit candles. Their wavering flames gave the room a flickering double light, dancing shadows washing atop yellow incandescents — like an image atop an image, or a dream atop reality.

She stared at herself in the mirror, seeing herself in the shifting light as if she were two people. Looking at her reflection, she suddenly realized that she was — and had always been — too tall. Or too short. Too slim. Too fat. Her arms were too stubby. She had a crooked nose. She had a nose that was too straight, too perfect. Her hair was flat and dull. Too shiny, too curled, too light brown and bouncy. Without Crumble in her blood, there was a new person behind Eila's old eyes, seeing new things and wondering at every one of them. Everything was in doubt. Reality had evolved, now filtered through a distorted lens.

Or — and this was terrifying — maybe nothing had distorted at all. As Daw had implied, perhaps this was what life and her mind were *supposed* to be like. Maybe if she stayed off Crumble, this could become her everyday way of being.

She wanted to shatter the mirror, but the noise of doing so would bring her parents running. So she draped a blanket over it instead, but looking at the blanket-draped mirror was in itself frightening. What was she hiding? Was her double (her too-slim, too-fat, ugly/pretty double) still hiding behind the fabric, inside a darkened plate of silvered glass, gibbering from behind the pall like a phantom?

She pulled the mirror from the wall, not daring to remove the blanket for fear of what she might see. She opened the closet door to shove the thing inside, but seeing inside the closet somehow chilled the back of her neck, so she shoved the door hard to latch it after quickly leaning the mirror in the back with its face toward the wall. And even still, she was sure she could hear her reflection trapped inside, laughing at her.

"There's nothing to be afraid of," she said aloud.

A dry, cracking voice whispered inside her: *That's right. So go to sleep and find out what doesn't await you.*

She sat on the bed, knees to her chest. Blackness yawned beyond the bedroom windows, which had no blinds. Even with the streetlights outside, there were too many pools of darkness. She glanced out, after the house had gone still, and saw something snakelike sliding along in the gutter. But then it was gone, and all that remained were the shapes of three impossibly tall, impossibly thin strangers with black cloaks, standing in the garden across the street, their long fingers idly laced through the neighbor's roses.

Eila turned and faced the wall, willing her mind to adjust, as Daw had promised it eventually would, while wondering how far a mind could stretch before snapping. She wondered about Joffrey Columns, and the treatments given to their patients. Those treatments sounded like more torture than treatment. Or maybe they were only rumors.

She had a block of Crumble in her desk. She had those thirty-seven capsules, their shapes long and neat for taking on the go. She removed them from their normal places, laid the capsules and the block on a small white cloth, then placed the cloth on her bed. She sat away from the window, knees up, watching the Crumble as if it might move. And why wouldn't it? Everything else had.

She had to stay strong. Daw had said that Crumble was blunting her gift. She was a Builder who could Dream. A Dreamer who could Build.

You are our only chance.

One night. She could make it through one night. She had to. She was in the middle of a tunnel, and there was no direct escape. If she wanted out, she had two options, equally unappealing: she could keep going deeper, or she could try to go back to where she'd come from. The first was uncomfortable; the second wasn't an option. She couldn't Build again. She couldn't lie in a cradle and turn thoughts into reality any more. Not now that she'd seen the place those thoughts were born, and what the process did to the Dreamers. And to Pavilion. And to — if Daw was right — Alterra itself.

The Fog.

That day, eleven years old, Eila had sworn she'd seen a small, dark shape moving in the mist not ten feet from the Fog's white edge. She'd flinched back and told her mother what she'd seen, and Mother had said it might be nothing. *Might.* But even if it *was* something, it couldn't emerge . The Fog kept to itself.

They'd stayed for fifteen full minutes, staring into nothingness, watching the path descend into forever, seeming to see the trees and plants writhe as if moving on their own. And as her mind had wandered — as it had tried to flee what they were watching — her memories had traveled back to the last time she remembered her mother holding her hand so firmly.

Eila and Juliette had never been as close as she was with her father, but they'd had one ritual when she'd been younger: trips into the city each Sunday to buy pastries from the small bakery with the striped awning, where the air always smelled of cinnamon. Eila could recall the smell of the place, that day as she watched the mist, just as clearly as she could recall the comforting feel of her mother's hand over hers. She'd loved those trips — handled in secrecy, with Mother and Eila devouring one pastry each before bringing the rest of them home, giggling, swearing not to tell the others they'd done so. But as Eila had stared into the mist at age eleven, she'd felt the Fog's energy begin to sour those old memories. She found herself forgetting the gentle times and instead remembering only the fire and seeing the charred bakery the next week, knowing how friendly Carlo had died. As she'd stared into the Fog, she'd only been able to imagine what his final hour must have been like, as he'd found himself trapped in the flames.

And on the heels of that, she'd realized how their only mother-daughter ritual had died along with Carlo. They hadn't held hands this way since the fire — now under decidedly less pleasant circumstances. Just like that, her cherished memory had been replaced by a horrible replacement. It was as if the new vision had eaten the old one, as the first died screaming.

As they'd stood watching the Fog, Eila had asked, *Why do we have to be here at all?*

And Juliette had answered, *So that you will remember that you are here by grace. By Providence. And that you must appreciate the life you have, because the worst trap is one you refuse to acknowledge.*

Her mother. Her father. Two different people who loved her in the same ways. Who loved all of their children and wanted them to be safe, to be protected, and to be prepared.

But prepared for what?

Eila watched the Crumble-covered cloth. There was an abundance of drug right in front of her. She could take a pill now and make this all go away. It would even happen fast. Childhood lore said that Crumble kept The Imp out of your mind, and rational people like Atwell — like Eila *used* to be — would say it kept the otherwise-wild brain stable. Without it, the mind tore. But for the first time, Eila found herself wondering if that logic, from a rational standpoint, made any sense. Crumble was manufactured, not naturally occurring. How had humanity survived before the Blunderbuss had made everything possible? Was it really rational to believe that the mind was unstable in its *normal* state? Crumble was everywhere now, but once upon a time it hadn't been. The people in Pavilion didn't take it, and never had.

As Eila watched the cloth, she saw the pills grow legs, like insects. They began to walk around, then climb the drug's solid block. But by the time Eila reached for the cloth to stop them, they'd become mere pills again. So she set them aside, climbed into bed, and closed her eyes. *Nothing could hurt her.* She had to keep that in mind, just like how Mother had promised that the Fog couldn't hurt her as long as she didn't walk into it.

Eila *was* walking into it now, though, by skipping her Crumble.

Her mind drifted. She found herself floating, on the edge of sleep. The sensation was foreign; it wasn't how Crumble normally put her to bed. Usually, she closed her eyes and vanished more or less instantly. Tonight, well past midnight and with the others already asleep, she heard her home's every sound. She heard ticking clocks — even those in the hallway and other rooms. Light played behind her eyelids now that she'd snuffed all but a single lamp, and she saw it as a wavering shadow.

Rather than being terrified, Eila found herself mulling all she'd heard from Daw. Now that it was free of the Crumble's neat, boxed-in way of thinking, her mind moved on its own, puzzling solutions as if Building on the Blunderbuss. At those times she'd been collaborating with another creator: some said the other party was the Aether itself, but she now knew it to be a Dreamer. During those sessions, there was always interplay. She solved Build problems by proposing solutions to questions of design, and the other intelligence (or perhaps the idea itself) pushed back, lending Eila alterations to obey or counter. It made sense when in a Build trance, but what about now? Was her mind really playing both sides of that coin — both asking *and* answering questions?

Was this what thought was like for the Tinkers in Pavilion? Or sometimes for those in the outskirts, whose "calluses" weren't as thick as Eila's, who'd grown up in the dream engine's shadow?

After a while — after she began to surrender — the duality of thinking began to feel comfortable. Maybe even *empowering*. It was as if she'd found a missing half of herself she hadn't known was absent.

Then she saw herself standing at the Convenience door and realized she must be dreaming.

There was someone by her side. It was Levi Meade. Somehow, she knew this wasn't the real Levi — that this wasn't the dream-swimming from before. This was a Levi of her own creation. A figment. She wasn't given that information; it simply appeared in her mind as if it had always been, as if she and this false Levi had traveled here together over the course of many hours.

His wild black hair was stuffed mostly under a hat, his clothes dirty but different than before. Again he had goggles slung around his neck, and Eila realized she'd never thought to ask him why he owned them. She knew he could float through dreams, but that was for Daw and the Guile, as part of the underground. What did he do for a living? Did he work a large machine? Did he drive a locomotive? She wasn't sure.

Open the door, he told her.

Eila looked at him, annoyed. He was standing between her and the door with his hand on the knob, and yet he wanted *her* to open it, as if she were his slave.

You *open it,* she said.

But of course, he couldn't. The real Levi — or anyone else, come to think about it — could open the real door of the real Convenience in the real world, but this door was something different. It was a symbol of something on which the seal had *not* yet been broken. Something Eila's mind was still trying to protect, because it feared what might be released.

She came forward. He stepped aside. The door opened.

They didn't need to descend the stairs. All at once, they were at the bottom, in Pavilion. It should have seemed strange, to simply relocate without traveling the places in between, but it didn't. Eila's mind accepted it, just like it accepted the newly broken seal. Now she could go to other places. She was free, and could see other things she'd been keeping at an arm's length.

She was no longer afraid.

Where are they?

She wasn't sure what she was asking about, but part of her knew. *The tunnels.* She wanted to see the tunnels.

You know where they are.

And he was right. Dream Levi, not-really-*Levi* Levi, knew where the tunnels had to be just the same as he'd known, as *she'd* known, that there were tunnels in the first place. She felt a strange sense of doubling, as if Levi were another part of herself. But of course, he'd have to be. She was Eila. Levi was Eila. Everything she was seeing was, somehow, *Eila.*

She watched Levi, his mop of thick, black hair moving slightly, as if in a breeze.

Daw's, she told him. *We need to go to Daw's house.*

Above, clouds made of steam and vapor began to roil like boiling oil. Eila looked up. There were by-products in those clouds, purged by the Blunderbuss. They had become dark thunderheads and were starting to crackle with lightning and shower them with rain.

It rains here? she said.

Levi looked up. Then he held his hands out, palms up, face fascinated. *I've only ever seen rain in dreams.* His eyes met Eila's. *Everything is different now.*

There was another sensation of movement without travel, and Eila found herself in Daw's mansion, but the walls were long and distorted, like a festival funhouse. Everything jutted from odd angles, the house now a maze with dozens of intersecting hallways crashing into darkness. She found herself alone in the brightly lit center, where the hallways met. The floor shifted underfoot, and Eila looked down to find that she was standing on sand. The space had already expanded, and brightly colored bunting hung around the edges. The ceiling was no longer plaster and molding. It was now striped fabric raised high by poles, like an enormous tent.

Daw was walking toward Eila, dressed like a circus barker. His usually rumpled formal wear had been replaced by a bright showman's uniform. He had bright-white gloves, their pristine palms stained with something bright red, like paint. From the neck up, he was exactly the same — waxed mustache curled up at the ends, as appropriate to this surreal Daw Blackburn as to the one she'd met twice in his parlor.

Hurry, hurry! he bellowed. Then he waited, as if it were Eila's turn to answer.

She looked around the space, now seeing that it was clearly a circus ring. Somehow, she'd mistaken it for Daw's foyer, but that was probably down one of the hallways from the center ring. As was the kitchen. None of it seemed strange. Instead of asking Daw what he meant, Eila said the next words in the only way that made sense.

… step right up.

Daw shook his head. Of course he did. *Up* was the wrong direction. He pointed, and as Eila followed its length toward one of the hallways outside of the ring, his arm seemed to stretch an impossible distance. She only saw it from the corner of her eye, because a second later she was in a different hallway, her feet moving as if they'd never stopped. Daw's hallway, the same as she'd seen it twice before. Like Rabbit Brampton's house. The living room would be ahead and to the right. Basement access would be straight ahead, behind the white door.

She walked down a dark stone staircase, going beneath even the world of the underground.

The basement was abandoned, but Eila could see evidence of others having been there recently. There was a table to one side of the well-appointed room, covered in handwritten maps, a few mugs, and an odd deck of playing cards. Corridors led from the main area into side chambers, just as on the upper level. She could see into one of those side chambers to a workbench covered in devices that might have spun from Builders on the Blunderbuss, but that Eila knew had been Tinkered by hand. They were the work of Willoughby, the Tinker mentioned by Daw. Eila wouldn't dare herself closer but saw how very like Blunderbuss inventions they were.

How did the Tinker do it? Where did his ideas come from? How did he receive the templates for his inventions? What Aether force was he collaborating with to make them?

But those questions were unimportant. Eila felt herself drawn forward, and a moment later was standing in another well-appointed basement room, floor covered in rugs as if the room lived on the surface (*the surface of the subterranean city,* her mind amended). There was a second door at the room's opposite end. It looked like the door to a closet, and it was open.

The closet was empty, a few feet deep, with nothing stacked on its floor, hung on its hooks, or set on the narrow shelves to either side. Its most striking feature was the gaping hole in its back, leading into a rock-lined corridor strung every dozen feet with lanterns.

Levi was back, standing beside her.

Is this real?

Levi shrugged. *That's a matter of opinion.*

Into the tunnel.

Down the tunnel.

Darkness descended; the small lanterns were not enough to banish the underground gloom.

Eila looked down to see that she was dragging both feet. Something was pulling her. She turned toward her companion, panic swelling. But Levi was gone.

The tunnel began to slant downward.

Deeper.

Deeper.

The lanterns spread farther apart, then vanished.

Pressure began to build on her dream-ears, very real. The air was heavy on her, but it was more than that. The press came mostly from memory. From mentality. A part of Eila was awake to the idea that this was still a dream, but that part was shrinking, and it slipped like mist through her fingers.

Her mind began to spin as the light died. Nobody was supposed to go this deep. There were no lanterns here because nobody had dared to come so far.

She felt herself moving faster and faster.

Somehow she could still see, but it seemed she was only given enough vision to ensure she knew exactly how frightened to be. It was as if her eyes had adjusted and were able to see without sight, like a bat; the true air was blacker than pitch. She could sense corridors branching away from the main one, knowing they'd snake in unpredictable patterns, some rising above, others descending, the entire tunnel structure serpentine and alien. They'd been pitted from the rock in the way ants might build a nest. Or perhaps they'd been made by people, though certainly not the Guile.

The tunnels had been here forever, as surely as the Blunderbuss itself.

How do I know that?

There was no one to answer her. Maybe Eila was Dreaming, like Dreamers Dreamed. Maybe there was a mind above them all, accessible by the ordinary girl who wanted everything to end but now could never go back. The girl who, now that she was into the blackness, could only go farther if she ever wished to escape.

She moved faster. Around her, the tunnel blurred.

Then the passageway began to move upward. She'd lost her sense of direction, but somehow still knew where she was going. It was possible there was a place outside of Waldron's Gate where the tunnels surfaced, but Eila didn't think so. Who would make tunnels that merely led underground? And if it was only a matter of walking on in order to come upward in time, why hadn't those who'd strung the lanterns farther back kept walking their way to freedom and natural light?

She wasn't headed to the countryside just beyond the city.

Her heart began to thunder as she realized she was going to surface inside the Fog.

Another mental skip, and Eila found herself on an earlier path, leaves wet under her suddenly bare feet, standing in a mildew-scented wood. The knotted tree stump that had held a dwarf the last time she'd seen it, his face dried and twisted like a rotted apple, was empty.

The wood was deserted.

Hello?

She felt foolish speaking aloud, and more so when there wasn't an answer.

She was standing in the middle of a small, mostly empty circle, the air rotten with decay. Around her, at a distance of maybe ten feet in all directions, was a thick white mist. It had to be an illusion, because when you stood in the middle of a fog bank, you could see for a few feet before the fog became too thick to peer through. The fog — or, in this case, the *Fog* — wasn't keeping its distance; in reality, it was everywhere around her.

Eila felt a chill. With a sensation like a weight dropping in her chest, the dream became both transparent and sharp. She knew it for a dream in a way she hadn't before, yet still found herself frozen. Knowing she was still inside her mind rather than in the actual Fog should have felt comforting, but it made her feel the opposite. The world around her wasn't indistinct and soft; it was crisp. She could feel the moist leaves against the flesh of her feet and the mist kissing her bare, pajama-clad arms and legs. She could hear the rustle of a light breeze stirring branches, and see every detail on a tree that looked like it had been tortured while still clay in The Crown's studio, its bark in whorls, branches twisted into a parody of sharp-cornered ellipses.

She was dreaming, and yet *here* was as real as real could be.

Things began to move at the limit of her vision, made indistinct by both the Fog and the oppressive nighttime darkness.

She saw a creature with six pairs of legs, its body tall and upright like a procession of people joined together in a tube. It moved in a wave, dipping and swaying. One end — at the end of the thing's trudging, twig-snapping progress — seemed to be a head too weighty to stay fully upright, so it sagged and dragged along the ground.

She saw something slither in the trees, up high. But the slithers were strangely coordinated; every flicker of motion in eight or nine trees happened over and over at the same time as the others. She couldn't make out their shapes, only that the branches ticked and snapped from a half moon of directions. The thing (or things) made a bone-rattling exhale, soft but resonant, and she heard it from every horizon at once.

She saw a man pass her near enough to see. She almost called to him for help, but he turned to stare before she could. He had a single eye in the center of his forehead. No nose, ears, or mouth. His eye was normal-sized, like Eila's. The image shocked her, but otherwise, the man was only a man, stealing her heartbeats with the movement of his pupil, as if it were trapped inside, trying to escape as the body marched past.

Something was behind her.

She spun but saw nothing. The Fog was thickening, approaching in tendrils. At first, it had simply been mist, but now it knew she was here. It was reaching out to her. Because she was familiar.

She ran.

The landscape changed as she moved, strobing in a portfolio of images. The woods surrendered to a path guarded by stone walls, their tops tall and nearly out of sight, a moon overhead, illuminating the Fog in all directions rather than truly piercing it. She was forced into a dead end, her bare feet scrabbling as the tendrils advanced. Eila held her breath, her eyes closed and waiting. A second passed. Two seconds.

Slowly, she opened her eyes.

The Fog was gone. She was inside a kind of castle courtyard, ramparts crumbling with age as if long since abandoned. But it *hadn't* been abandoned; now that only the gloaming obstructed her eyes, Eila could see movement on the walls and in the receding corridors, lit by the moon's glow enough for recognition.

She paced, afraid but somehow fearless, knowing what she'd find before she found it.

She was inside the Citadel.

She walked the large, open-air circle with a sense of awe. She knew the place as if she'd been here before — as if it were real or had ever been. She remembered it from the storybooks her father had read her as a young child.

Even now, nestled inside a dream's vision, she could imagine those illustrations.

There, across the space, was the row of iron circles where handlers tethered dragons, only the rings weren't pristine and silver as they'd been in the story. Now they were rusted and flaking.

Across from her was the raised platform from which the Dark King would watch the battles, his cruel hands curled around a scepter topped with a knob made of quartz. But instead of being ornate and elegant, covered in a sunshade as it had been in the stories, the platform was crumbling in a place that boasted no sun.

She had spent so much time here in her younger days. Most Alterran children had. As she looked around, touching the rock and dragging her foot across the fetid dirt to feel its reality, she felt old memories resurface. Her father on the bed beside her, any one of a dozen large books open wide. Eila remembered the feeling on those nights, when Atwell would read the Citadel books aloud. She remembered the way the spell always broke when Mother caught him doing it, lecturing with her nose turned high that the tales were sinister, inappropriate for eyes and ears so young. But when she left, Father always resumed the tale and told it to the end. They were the same stories over and over and over, until Eila knew them by heart.

No matter what her mother thought, the books didn't frighten her. Or rather, they *did*, but in a way that was wonderfully fun.

There would be — or had once been — trolls in the corridors below the half-buried castle. And when the sea had risen to bury the Citadel (Eila recalled from those big books), it had flooded the sub-basement below even those chambers. It was still flooded in her childhood stories, and Atwell had told to her about things living in the depths. She remembered how the king's men called the flooded dungeon *Leviathan*. Nobody went down there. A squire was elected to feed the imprisoned beasts through a trap door laid into the floor. Sometimes, through an accident, the squire vanished. It didn't matter to the Dark King, or to the others. It was only a squire, and the Leviathan sometimes demanded its sacrifices.

Now, standing inside what should have been only a childhood story, Eila looked down and saw an ivory shape, its sides grooved like something worn through use. The thing's top was like a dull blade, shaped like the head of a garden hoe. Below was a cylindrical base, as if the thing were meant to be held. She picked it up. It was the size of her hand.

It's a dragon's tooth.

With a wince, she laid the tooth down and began to walk, eyes now attuned for more childhood relics. She saw claw marks in the dirt, bones from fallen combatants, and what looked like a brooch. But when she picked the supposed brooch up and twisted it in the moonlight, she realized it was actually a dragonstone — red in its heart, dark blue at the edges. The gem would have to be cut before it could sparkle, but even with its haze of dust in the dim light, the rock's gleaming promise was beautiful. In stories, warriors took their chances in battle because if you managed to slay a dragon, you could pull a dragonstone from the fallen beast's neck. A dragonstone, Eila recalled, was the only offering a warrior could make a Nobleman that would grant his daughter's hand in marriage.

There was a noise across the deserted arena.

Eila turned and saw the gate at the far end of the battle yard opening, as if on a breeze. Metal squealed against metal as hinges protested. She looked ahead, seeing the way the gate opened into seething blackness, a damp wind wafting from it like vented breath. She couldn't see movement there, but she could hear a sickening noise: a wet sound, like a pair of hands mixing raw meat.

She slipped the stone into her pajama pockets, remembering that she was an interloper in a dangerous world. She wasn't supposed to be here. Because this place shouldn't exist.

Opposite the open gate, two wooden doors opened in the Citadel's courtyard wall.

It isn't abandoned after all.

Spiders seethed from the yawning doors. Eila lost her fascination and ran.

The dream held her feet. She seemed to be running in syrup, a thick goo yanking her back. She didn't want to run into the black mouth beyond the gate, but she had to. If the spiders were still here, the trolls would be too. Along with the sea creatures below. And the Dark King himself, or his core of magicians.

Eila's feet came free of whatever had been holding them and she tumbled forward, but her feet were no longer carrying her. Now it was her mind that propelled her forward. She felt an odd power bubbling inside her, and on the heels of it, a thought arose: *I've beaten this before.*

Juliette had been right; the Citadel books her father had read Eila as a young girl had frightened her. But they were only stories, and she'd slept through the night even then, her mind vacant of nightmares.

Because those nightmares didn't stay in my mind to frighten me. Because of the Crumble, they came here instead.

The thought screamed by her, and Eila found herself flying toward the path ahead, strangely fearless. She could move past it. She'd moved past those terrors years ago, and she could do it again. Even though she'd never seen this place in quite this way, she merely had to move on. Because Dreaming was just Building. And Building was just Dreaming.

She saw darkness, then re-emerged into the Fog, suddenly sure she'd just passed through its vivid center. But if Eila had passed *into* the Fog having passed *through* its middle, then that would mean …

The Fog parted before she could complete the thought, and as suddenly as she'd been startled in the Citadel, she found herself in the open air, apparently safe. She saw a strip of beach, gentle waves lapping onto the shore. She took a few tentative steps forward, her senses still thick and sharp, and let the water splash onto her bare feet.

She looked back. The Fog was behind her. As was Alterra, on its other side.

Unafraid, Eila took a deep breath. The air was clear, its scent somehow tinged with salt. She looked to the right and left, seeing the unbroken wall of Fog on one side and water on the other. In some places within her line of sight, she could see land protruding beyond the Fog. In other places, the Fog was over the water. In the distance, Eila could see what looked like a small town on a peninsula, its shores lined with small specks that had to be boats.

She strolled the beach in a single direction, finding a tree-pocked finger of land, then wove between the trunks, exploring. There was movement in the underbrush out here as there had been in the Fog, but this movement wasn't frightening. She could see shapes beyond the trees, including a trio of what looked like white horses. But she felt no need to follow, or look, or see.

Eila sat on a rock.

Something shifted to one side. She looked over to see the same dwarf she'd seen earlier. His face was macabre; patches of beard fought for space amid his twisted features. As Eila looked over, he raised a bone pipe to his gnarled lips and took a slow puff.

She found the courage to speak.

Is this place real?

That, said the dwarf, *is a matter of opinion.*

Eila jerked in bed, her feet trying to find purchase as if missing a step in a staircase. Her eyelids snapped open, and she found herself looking at her bedroom ceiling. The cloth holding the block of Crumble and the thirty-seven pills was still where she'd left it, across the room. The mirror was still inside a now-ajar closet, its hidden front still covered with cloth. The shades, on the windows that had them, were drawn. But the early-morning sun was shining through even those, mocking their lack of substance and washing the room in light.

Eila rolled over and took in her room's disorder, feeling foolish. Why had she been so afraid? The darkness had made everything terrifying, allowing her mind to wake-dream things beyond rational comprehension. But now, in the daylight, the night's fears seemed as insubstantial as … as …

She'd had an image in mind. Something from her dream. But what had seemed so obvious a moment ago was already draining like water from an unplugged sink. She felt a rush of panic — somehow, even without Crumble, her dreams were being stolen!

She tried to hold onto the images. She'd been with Levi. They'd been in Pavilion. There had been tunnels? Yes, she was almost sure there *had* been tunnels. She'd seen the Fog, then a place that was familiar from long ago.

But where was it? *What* was it? And where had she gone next?

It was no use. Within two minutes, all she remembered were the feelings. She remembered that she'd been afraid, but not exactly why or whether those same things would be frightening now, in the light. She remembered feeling somehow empowered, but not why. She'd entered the Fog. But how had she come out?

She rolled over, groaning. It was gone. Whether the remnants of her dream were being stolen or simply evaporating like — well, like a spring fog — she had no idea. But it didn't matter.

She was awake — and normal life, such that it was, beckoned.

She closed her eyes, sighed, then rolled back the other way. But she stopped when something hard pressed into her hip, pinching her skin between bed and bone.

Eila sat up, searching for the offending object, but the bed was empty because the thing that had pinched her was in her pocket. Confused, she reached in and fished it out, then held it up in the sunlight.

It was a beautiful stone, red in the center, and dark blue around the edges.

Chapter Fifteen
A Deep Cut

Daw Blackburn didn't have to send Levi into Eila's mind the next day for her to know what had to be done. The scientist had told her that she had to give up Crumble for her gifts, and he must have known — or at least suspected — what would happen.

Levi had seen inside her; he'd know (or, again, at least suspect) what she was capable of.

She'd skipped her Crumble. She'd dreamed. And she had, apparently, manifested something from the dream. Without help from the Blunderbuss, she'd done exactly what the dirty scientist had said she could do: she'd Dreamed, and she'd Built.

Daw had been right.

As soon as she awoke, Eila stowed the dragonstone in her dresser under a pile of socks, broke a hunk of unpackaged Crumble from the block, and jammed it into her mouth like candy. The taste was hideously neutral. Crumble's current formulation was designed to disappear into any food (you couldn't have your kids going insane because they refused to eat or drink it), but that neutrality made the brittle making its way over her gums and tongue like eating something that both was and wasn't there. It was like air with substance — a giant wad of tasteless gum.

She swallowed without so much as a drink, hoping its undiluted dose would cause it to work faster.

There was a quenching as the drug landed in her stomach. Then, within seconds, she could feel her thoughts falling into their familiar, comfortable order. It was like watching a room become organized of its own accord: books and clothes finding their proper places without effort. She lay on her back with her eyes closed, watching with defiant pleasure as Daw's backdoor re-closed inside her mind.

To The Pit with her gift. To The Pit with the Guile's grand plans. She'd done her trial night of drugless penance. She'd had her dream, and it had slipped through her fingers as surely as it always did with Crumble. What use was her night of horror — or the paranoid evening spent scaring her parents — if she was unable to think past her own disorder?

She'd accomplished nothing.

Except for the stone in your dresser.

What stone? she almost said aloud.

It was Saturday, and she didn't have to work. She was a girl with a mind that was again becoming as closed or open (according to perspective) as it ever had been, the same as anyone in Alterra. Why should she have to shoulder an extra burden? Right now, she just wanted to giggle about boys, and about how Victor had approached her the other day, talking to her as he'd talk to anyone — or maybe in a more engaging, handsome way than he'd talk to others. She wanted to go down to the mercantile district. She wanted to watch the ferry shaws arrive, and goggle over the ruddermouths' stories.

They'd still be there, too. Shaw pilots always stayed the night after the crews unloaded their untold tons of merchandise from the last district and packed their ships with wares from the current one. They partied hard and ended up too intoxicated to fly. The shaws' departure was always significantly less interesting than their arrival, but still it was something — and it was all Eila had left in the way of normality.

She threw on a summery, almost childlike dress and sneaked from the house, stuffing her bag full of Crumble so she couldn't possibly run dry. Her parents were in the kitchen with at least one or two of her siblings, but when Atwell called out to Eila (probably to see if she was feeling okay, following her idiotic and never-to-be-repeated decision to skip her Crumble the evening before), she yelled something noncommittal in return — something that didn't answer Father's question, but that she could plausibly argue was an answer to what she'd thought he'd asked.

She left the house with nothing to hide. She wasn't suffering from Depth Syndrome; she wasn't at a loss for focus; she wouldn't be having any more visions; she *definitely* wasn't going to have any more dreams. Nobody dreamed, because dreaming wasn't normal. Not in Alterra, anyway.

She trotted down the street, to the other end of Rowley Row where the houses were lined with lavender rather than her own home's roses. She stopped in front of a grass-colored house, trimmed in forget-me-not blue. She rapped the knocker, then asked the housekeeper if Cora was home. She was not, but the housekeeper told Eila where to find her.

Eila rode the streetcar into town, feeling a suspicious euphoria that part of her knew was due to taking way too much Crumble. Crumble was more or less binary; it either kept the mind satisfied or it did not. There was little reason to overdose, but Eila had done so, accidentally, once or twice. The only side effect was an excess of optimism, but it was slight and subtle. She felt it now … but rather than feeling unadorned positivity, she found herself feeling guilty. Her optimistic haze was phony, and she knew it. Last night (though it seemed foolish now, and she didn't want to think about it), Eila had felt the raw edge of unblunted emotion — possibly for the first time in her life. It made her realize that the Crumble mania was a poor substitute for the real thing.

She found Cora in the square, buying fancy cafei beverages for her parents like a dutiful young girl who played by the rules, rather than one who lied and ran off to strangers bearing glasses of Thunderclap, to aid conspiracies.

"Cora!"

Cora looked over, then turned back to the cafei merchant. She slid her coins across the countertop, and began gathering the cups into a carrier.

Eila walked closer. Cora's face was set, pretending that her best friend didn't exist.

"I'm sorry about yesterday," Eila said. "Did you go to the mercantile?"

Cora moved the cups to the side table near the counter, opened lids one by one, and began adding sugar. There was a marking pen near the sugars, and Cora wrote on each of the paper cups: *Father. Mother. Me.*

Eila looked at the last. "Since when do you drink cafei?"

Still not looking at Eila, Cora said, "I guess there's a lot about me you haven't noticed lately."

"Can I join you?"

"You *don't* drink cafei. That, I actually know."

"Maybe I've started."

"It's possible. So much has changed."

Eila reached out and lightly clasped Cora's left arm. "Look. I'm s—"

Cora snatched her arm away and resumed sugaring the drinks. "Yes, you said that."

"Don't be like this." Eila's false euphoria was turning to vapor.

"Like what?" She faked a realization. "Oh, you mean like *you?"*

"I said I'm sorry."

"Yes." She capped the drinks. "I'll see you later."

"You're angry."

Cora laughed. "You think?"

"You have a right. I'm sorry. I was so rude. It's just … a lot has been happening."

"Life's tough for a Builder like you. I can imagine." Cora looked around as if contemplating something. "No, wait, I can't."

"It's not about that. I … " A terrible, horrible, worst-idea-ever formed in Eila's mind. "I can *show* you."

"I'm not interested."

"Look, please. Cora, *please*. Just sit with me for a minute, okay? You're mad. You have every right to be. I've been so terrible. But I swear I have a good reason, and it has nothing to do with you, or Building, or whatever. Well, it has a *little* to do with Building, I guess, but … "

"But what? But you know I wouldn't understand?"

"Can we sit? Please?"

Cora rolled her eyes, but at least rolled them toward Eila. Progress. "Fine."

Eila went to the counter, bought a plain cafei, then went to the side table, dumped out a third, and topped it with rich cream and six spoonfuls of sugar. She heard a noise like a snicker from Cora behind her. When Eila turned, her face was straight and composed, as if she didn't want to confess weakness in her anger.

They sat in the sun. The morning was warm but pleasant. Crisp, like after morning rain.

"I've had a lot on my mind," Eila said.

"I'm sure."

"I still want to go to the shaws. I'll make it up to you, okay? I'll buy you something nice."

"No thanks."

"Come on, Cora. Haven't you ever had a bad day? Aren't we better than this?"

"*I* am," she said. But then, unable to help herself, puffed laughter.

"Of course you are. I'm the idiot."

"You are."

Eila sipped her cafei, finding it gross and bitter despite the cream and sugar. How did people drink this? She looked across at Cora, who'd looked away, out at the people on the street, not being defiant but refusing to meet Eila's eye. They were in one of those lulls they sometimes shared, where the unspoken settled to the bottom and left only what had to be said. Eila would be on thin ice for a while, but she'd be allowed back in. Good — because more than ever, as Eila tried to forget so many other things that shouldn't be spoken, she desperately needed a friend.

Eila studied Cora's profile, wondering what she'd been planning to do. Did she really just want to fly off to the mercantile district and talk about shopping and gossip? Was that possible? It had sounded brilliant after she'd downed all that Crumble upon waking, but now that the wave was fading, she wondered. Unless Eila planned to overdose on Crumble for the rest of her life, she couldn't turn away from what she knew. Her choices weren't truly to go on with her old life as it had been or to dive into the life that beckoned from Pavilion below. Her choice was simpler and far less appealing: she could live in uncertainty and fear by leaning forward, or in denial and as an accomplice to torture by burying her head in the sand. Every terrible option seemed to be weighted, as if The Crown were already dispensing judgment.

"I have something to tell you," said Eila.

"What?"

Eila hesitated. "Promise not to get mad at me?"

Cora shook her head. "No promises."

"What do you know about Building?"

Cora paused before replying, the topic of their differing social statuses still a sore spot from yesterday. "Nothing."

"Oh, come on. You've seen Rabbit Brampton blabbing on in the media, same as everyone."

Cora sighed. "Fine. You hook into that big engine and use it to make things. Things that come to you. And that Brampton guy, he … what … steers it?"

"He doesn't do anything, Cora. He's a blowhard. Builders do most of the work, and there are Assemblers who go out and put those things together, but they're just workmen, not highly regarded. It's not like anyone is giving Assemblers credit. Builders Build, and someone else puts those things in place where they seem to belong. That's it."

"Okay. Fascinating." Cora's face was already bored. Maybe Eila should have held her peace for longer. Maybe they should have gone to the mercantile as she'd first intended, spent a day bonding, and only then launched into this discussion. But over and over, Eila, who had her father's self-awareness, had confronted the truth of her selfishness. She'd managed to get Cora's attention, so a trip to the mercantile (which would have been what *Cora* wanted) had become less necessary. Eila had wanted a discussion, and now she was going to get it.

"There's something we're supposed to do at night — all of us, not just Builders," Eila continued. "It's called 'dreaming.' It's like you go somewhere else, or see things in your head. It started happening to me a few weeks ago." She shook her head, distracted by an intrusive but probably accurate thought. "Maybe it was because I'd started working at the Ministry and it was stimulating my mind; I don't know. I've never heard of it happening to other Builders, but I'm … well, I barely know where to start."

"You were … seeing things?" Cora already looked more concerned than angry. That was Cora: thinking of others and their welfare, unlike Eila.

"It's not like that. I guess we're *supposed* to dream. It's natural."

"I've never seen things. Do you mean you sleepwalk and go other places?"

"No, Cora. Like on a screen, only you see the pictures with your own senses. You can go places, but they aren't real."

That wasn't entirely right. It was *supposed* to be, though — the red/blue stone under a pile of socks in her dresser notwithstanding.

"That doesn't sound healthy, Eila. It sounds like something that happens before you get sent to Joffrey Columns."

There was no place to start. *Everything* was a loose end, and Eila held only a thread.

"Let's go back to Building, then," she said. "You know a bit about how that works. How it *officially* works. The Blunderbuss plucks ideas from what they call 'the Aether' and sets them in front of us in a kind of mental workspace. We take that mental picture and flesh it out, making it practical to exist in the real world rather than out in the air with The Crown or whatever, and our … well, I don't know the exact process, but somehow what we've trained our minds to do, with the Blunderbuss's help, makes those objects manifest as real objects. That's why it's the Ministry of *Manifestation*."

Cora looked insulted. Eila had gone too far, giving her the picture book version of Alterran technology. She pushed on.

"But like I said, I've started to have these 'dreams' on and off while I'm nowhere near the Ministry, and I think it's because someone has been pushing them into my head, so they're stronger than regular dreams."

"The 'dreams' we're supposed to have, you mean." Cora said *dreams* same as she'd say *snot* or *vomit.*

"Yes."

"But we *don't* have them, even though it's normal."

"I'll get to that. But anyway, yes. In fact —" She gestured toward Cora, finding a hook to hang the edge of her absurd story upon. "— *that's* what I wanted to talk to Palpatine Malvern about! Do you remember?"

"You wanted to talk to him about having visions?"

"I thought I was going crazy. And you saw how he was; he's really psychic."

"So what did he tell you?"

Eila wasn't ready to tell that part of the story. She hesitated, ignoring Cora's question in favor of her original train of thought.

"One of the things I'd been dreaming of — and thinking of a lot even when I was awake, come to think of it — was this boy."

"A boy?"

Eila nodded. Finally, something Cora could relate to.

"Is he cute?" Cora asked.

Eila saw her opening and took it, knowing it would be worth spending a few seconds drooling over Levi for Cora's benefit. "Definitely. Black hair, really messy. But he's got bright-blue eyes that don't match his hair or complexion. Tall. A few years older than us, maybe eighteen or nineteen? I kept seeing him in this dark place, like he was a Doer — but one who worked somewhere filthy, away from the Ministries. Like, his face was always dirty, but there were raccoon circles around his eyes from goggles that he's never, ever — at least as I see him, anyway — actually wearing."

Cora was looking at Eila in the oddest way. Her confession should've been candy to Cora, but right now her face was creased with suspicion rather than intrigue.

"I met him, Cora. He's real. He led me to the Doer district — in my dreams, again — and to this big machine they call the Convenience, which handles our waste, like sewers and water and refuse, and I … " She hesitated. It was important to take baby steps, especially considering that outside of a few high-placed officials, Eila might be the only person in Alterra who knew this part. And she might *very* well be the only person who'd ever "cracked the seal," as Daw had said. "I went somewhere else with him, Cora, and he showed me something. What I learned is that the Building we do isn't inspired by the Aether …" she swallowed. "It comes from all of our own minds, because the Ministry is stealing people's dreams."

There was so, so much more, and she hadn't even reached the uncomfortable part. She paused to give Cora time to digest.

"You steal other people's thoughts," said Cora, her face still strangely conflicted.

"Their *dreams*. But the Builders don't know, you see. And the Dreamers — I'll explain them in a minute; they work on another half of the Blunderbuss that the Builders don't know about — have to *sort* those dreams. And Cora, I've seen what the Dreamers do. It's the worst sort of … "

Cora still looked suspicious. Something wasn't right. She should look afraid, worried, sympathetic, or any of a dozen other emotions. Her eyes shouldn't be so hard under angry, arched eyebrows.

"How do you steal thoughts?" she interrupted. "Like, could you steal mine?"

"Well, not just like that. And it's *dreams*, not plain thoughts. We're not psychics."

"But you went to *see* a psychic. *Because* of these dreams. So there must be some connection."

"Sure, but … "

"And you *are* taking thoughts. They're just nighttime thoughts. So you *can* just peep into the head of anyone you want, right? Is that what you do all day long?"

"No, we … "

"Did you ask Malvern about the boy?"

Eila blinked. She couldn't remember, or see why it mattered. Levi had only been a device to tell Cora this story — a hook to pique her interest. In the big picture of what Eila needed to tell, Levi didn't matter. She hadn't even gotten to the torture, the underground city, or the artifact she'd pulled from the Fog in her sleep. She hadn't told Cora about Daw, what he'd said about Crumble, or that she'd been asked to surrender her sanity in order to save them all.

"I don't know if I asked Malvern about him. He doesn't matter, really."

"He doesn't, does he?" Cora's face pinched. "What's his name, then, Eila? This mystery man who came to you 'out of nowhere'?"

"Levi. Levi Meade."

"Thin eyebrows?" Cora bit her lip. "And his build — is he lean like a stick?"

Eila shook her head. "*Thick* eyebrows. Bushy, but not bad on him at all. Built solid, like a machine cranker." She looked up at Cora, realizing too late that she'd stepped into a trap.

"You've been *prying,*" said Cora, the words leaving her mouth almost in a hiss. She stood from the table. "I knew it. I *told* you not to look, but you did. Because you're jealous."

Eila felt the world spinning. Something had happened, but she didn't know what. She was still sitting, but Cora had bolted to her feet fast enough to shake the table and nearly spill the cafei.

"Before the festival," said Cora. "When I wouldn't let you see in my sketchbook."

"Cora, I … "

But Cora was already tearing up with frustration — and with something that looked like a feeling of betrayal. Where had it come from? What had she done wrong? What had she said?

"But you know his name, too! So it's not *just* my sketches you snooped into, was it? You've been looking into my mind, haven't you Eila? Did Malvern help you? After he was done with me — after you sent me away so I wouldn't hear what you were doing — did he give you some sort of a key? A way to pick out little old Cora's brain from all the others, while you were at work with your army of spies?"

Eila blinked, still unable to stand. This didn't make sense. For some reason, somehow, against all reason and sanity, Cora had managed to personalize "dream theft." But why would she, if she didn't even know about or believe in dreams?

Levi. It's about Levi.

"It's not like that, Cora. Please. Sit down. There's a lot more I need to tell you."

"I suppose you know everything, though, don't you? Did you even *need* to peek at my sketches when you were over? Or could you see them in my thoughts? Can you read my mind right now?"

"Cora! What's gotten into you?" Whatever Cora was reacting to, her reaction was overblown. She'd leapt over belief as if it were barely a hurdle. Eila had somehow cut Cora deep; she'd said something that was truer than true inside Cora's mind, in her overly sensitive heart.

"Cora," said Eila. Then she hesitated, because she was about to say something absurd. "Do you *know* Levi?" Even saying it felt wrong. Levi had never been topside. How could she possibly know him?

Cora's eyes stared daggers. Eila felt herself pierced, ripped open. This was a one-way friendship now; to Cora, Eila had suddenly become the enemy. She shoved a hand deep into her bag. It came out with her familiar sketchbook, which she shoved at Eila's chest like a blade.

"Damn you, Eila!"

Frustrated tears of betrayal began to well in her eyes. She held her gaze, then turned on her toe and stalked off, leaving Eila at the small table with all four beverages and too many questions to count.

Eila caught her breath and looked around for Cora, but she had already disappeared into the early morning crowd, abandoning her most treasured possession.

Eila flipped open the sketchbook, knowing Cora would only leave it behind if she somehow saw it as tainted. She swallowed and began to leaf through it. She saw Cora's father, sitting in his chair, then herself at the solstice festival. She saw Cora's end of Rowley Row, lavender bushes rendered like purple clouds.

Then Eila reached a page that stopped her heart.

It showed Levi Meade, standing in front of the Convenience, his face dirty, a pair of workman's goggles dangling from his neck.

In the corner, Cora had drawn a heart and colored it pink.

Chapter Sixteen
The Guile

As days passed, Eila settled into a familiar routine of lies, deceit, and betrayal.

She spent each day in her room or at the Ministry, treading water, knowing that every creation came from theft and torture. The machine's waves stayed small and routine, making it easy to underproduce and seem insignificant despite Brampton's accusing stares and snide remarks about quotas.

She waited and bided her time, terrified of another Pianoforte.

What must it be like for the Dreamers during Pianoforte, when the rush of thoughts and dreams was so large? Vast skyships had been Built out of troughs in the Pianoforte waves. What nightmares must have accompanied them? Pianoforte was celebrated above. Was it the opposite below: a plague to be suffered through? Eila wouldn't be able to dog it and barely skate by if another Pianoforte arose. For Pianoforte to work — and for the resonance to remain strong and not break as it had before — she would need to fully engage or step out entirely. It would force her to make an impossible, polar decision: was Eila Doyle a knowing part of the problem, or was she willing to divorce herself from her own life (and, surely, her family) to become part of an impossible solution? She had no idea, and didn't want to find out.

After each shift, she phoned home and told Mother she'd be spending the evening with Cora, then raced down to the underground city. It would almost be a relief if Cora were to blow her cover. On some level, she even suspected she *wanted* to be caught; it would mean that Cora saw a need to fight and get it over with. But their relationship's main change wan't fighting; it was absence and nothingness. Cora kept her mouth shut, probably reluctant to admit a schism for fear of her mother and father's questions.

The rift was too deep even for fighting — a realization that gave Eila's chest a constant ache. She had no idea how Levi had entered Cora's mind and then her sketchbook — but given what she'd already confessed, how could she possibly convince Cora she hadn't been snooping and stealing?

And with everything else I've been given, how can I possibly find the energy to care?

That was the worst part of all. Of course she cared about what had happened with Cora, but it was at the bottom of an impossibly pressing list. Quarreling with Cora was hideous … but the fact that the need to solve the problem mostly annoyed her was so much worse. There was simply no room on her plate for thinking of Cora, whether that thinking took the form of caring or mourning.

The first time she went to visit Daw afterward, Eila showed the scientist Cora's sketches of Levi. Daw told her that Levi swam dreams to find people like Eila, and that every potential Dreamer cast a web around them. He *may* have visited Cora. If he'd moved to calling Eila instead, that meant that Cora didn't have the gift — but it might not mean that Cora, deep down, wouldn't somehow remember him.

Maybe she began dreaming about him on her own after Levi stopped visiting, Daw suggested. *The mind is a puzzle box.*

What can I do about it? Eila had asked, mainly because she felt she *had* to care, even though she didn't have the energy.

Ask Levi, said Daw.

But she couldn't.

A week passed. Another week.

Eila's routine went from familiar to boring. She left the Ministry each afternoon, changing into drab attire in the washroom beforehand. She took the same streetcar to the same stop, now familiar enough with the regular riders to nod as she boarded. The feeling grew into one of kinship, and Eila found herself feeling safer in the Doer district with every visit. These gritty, hardworking men and women knew the girl who rode their trolley, probably believing her to live near their neighborhood. If harm befell her, Eila felt certain, they would defend her as one of their own.

Every day, she would find the Convenience door, wondering each time if she was still the only one who'd used it. And once she reached Daw's home, every time, she'd ask. It became a game, or like a call sign necessary for entry into a nest of spies.

Has the Guile used the door?

They are not ready. The time has not come.

And she'd enter, feeling more and more at home with every passing day, just as she felt less and less at home in the Rose Belt.

She met the Guile.

The revolutionaries were ordinary Pavilion citizens, each with day jobs. Only one was a Dreamer. Eila found that odd at first (part of her had assumed that everyone in Pavilion Dreamed for the Ministry despite knowing better, and that Dreamers would be necessary on a team that wanted to straddle worlds), but Walker Burch, the Guile's de facto leader below Daw, explained that Dreamers were too often hollowed out to function. Thanks to what they did at the Ministry of Dreaming, they were usually sucked dry, missing the rebellious spirit membership in the Guile required.

It's not that Dreamers won't or can't seek change, darlin', Walker told her. *They just don't see a problem with how they live, and how they are.*

Somehow, this bothered Eila most of all.

The Guile was easy to like. There were six of them beyond Levi and Daw, each with a specialty:

Walker led them. He had an accent and a way of truncating words that was peculiar and of an unknown origin — to Eila, at least. He was in his thirties, tall and handsome with shoulder-length blond hair and what seemed like permanent stubble. His specialty was exploring the tunnels that were exactly where Eila's dream had placed them: behind a closet door in Daw's basement. Walker's most striking attribute was an overabundance of charm. He was good-looking and knew it. His constant almost-advances seemed to rankle the Guile's female contingent, all of whom Walker had given cute but clearly unwanted nicknames.

There was Genevieve Finley, a stunning raven-haired woman with exotic eyebrows and pale-green eyes, currently the Guile's sole conduit. Genevieve was bold in personality but soft-spoken in conversation, casual about her ability to receive confidential,

Ministry-insider secrets from an unknown mole on the surface level above. With the possible (and inferior) exception of Levi's dream-swimming ability, the Guile's information about Waldron's Gate all came from Genevieve's ability to see and receive. This made Daw nervous, because any scientist worth his salt (even a "dirty" one) hated to rely on a single source of information.

Genevieve struck Eila as flawlessly honest. What you saw was what you got. Her identity revolved around the Guile because her memory of herself extended only fifteen minutes prior to the moment she found herself standing on Daw's doorstep, fist raised to knock for reasons she didn't understand. Most mysteriously, Genevieve seemed to have memories of Waldron's Gate. Conduits always had such memories, she was told, but no one was sure if they'd ever actually lived topside, how they'd arrived in Pavilion, or what any of it meant.

Phoebe Horn was the Guile's lone Dreamer. She had black hair and looked like a walking thundercloud, her expression somehow unfathomably dark as if in wait of yet another awful disruption. She had dark eyes and wore darker black eye makeup and eye shadow — almost a parody of a Waldron's Gate woman, as none but the highest-society Pavilionites (such that there were any) bothered with cosmetics. Phoebe was plagued by constant nightmares even in her own, non-Ministry sleep. Eila still didn't understand the Ministry of Dreaming's operation and didn't know Phoebe well enough to ask, but from what Levi told her, Phoebe's condition was both an asset and a detriment to the lower half of the Blunderbuss. Because she was so plagued by darkness, she was an exceptionally talented filterer of disturbing mental imagery, and was often tasked to sort the streams of deviants. But conversely, her nightmares were so horrifying and constant that leaks from her end of the cradle array often ruined the Dream shift's harmony. Phoebe was moved from shift to shift, and other Dreamers were terrified of being placed beside her.

There was Willoughby Keys, the group's Tinker. The Guile had always had a Tinker and a conduit, Levi explained — even at its lowest point when it was just three members strong. Like others in the Guile, Willoughby was obsessed with learning from his predecessors, and was hampered by Pavilion's lack of a true written language or system of record-keeping. He took what sparse notes he could using the chicken-scratch the Guile had taught itself, and drew diagram after diagram to detail all he knew. More than anyone Eila had ever met, Willoughby both "Dreamed" and "Built" in the non-literal senses of both words. Without aid of a Blunderbuss, he'd created hundreds of devices and weapons of his own design. Although he was working with inferior tools, some of what he'd created was unlike anything Eila — as a professional Builder — had ever seen. More: They were unlike anything she'd ever *thought of.* The Ministry only Built extremely intricate variations on themes of steam and clockwork, but Willoughby's work incorporated electricity and other power sources that somehow employed no clockwork. The applications were small, but their significance wasn't lost on Eila. Where the Ministry had aggressively moved upward in their creations, Willoughby had moved *sideways*. She wondered what the Ministry might create with some of Willoughby's inventions as seeds — if the Blunderbuss were to begin with something he'd created, then moved upward in *that* new direction.

Finnegan Bennet was the oldest and loudest among the Guile. Like Genevieve, he seemed to have shown up in Pavilion inexplicably, with no memory before his arrival. Unlike Genevieve, he'd retained trauma from something beyond his mind's mental wall — something Finnegan described in his barking way as "a war I can't recall." Unlike the rest of the Guile, who were in their twenties and thirties, Finnegan was at least sixty. He was solid and strong, his body undecayed as testament to a life born in strife and discipline. According to Levi, Finnegan, who seemed so angry, was secretly a creative soul.

The way Levi described his efforts, Eila thought that Finnegan might have been a writer … had Pavilion boasted a language worth writing in. Instead, he "wrote" his stories in chalk and paint on the tunnel walls below the underground city, mostly in the mouth behind Daw's basement closet. Walker, knowing how angry Finnegan became when people gave him advice before his art was finished, often critiqued them loudly for kicks, then laughed as the old man chased him away.

And lastly, there was Savannah Welch, the group's impostor. Although Savannah — a buxom blonde with soft green eyes and long, straw-colored hair — had never been to the world she'd one day infiltrate with her wide red smile and substantial bodily charm, she'd spent most of her recent years training to do so. Savannah had been recruited and trained once Walker's tunnel explorations had reached surprising new depths, once Levi had learned to swim dreams, and once the information streaming through Genevieve had changed its flavor. It was only a matter of time, Daw seemed to feel, before the seal would be breached for good. When that happened — when the time came for the Guile to infiltrate the world above — a spy like Savannah would be necessary.

It took Eila a while to find the Guile's rhythm, but once she did, they became like a second family. It happened so quickly that it was almost a shock — and a betrayal, given the increasing discomfort she felt in her true home, among her true family. The underground malcontents, as strange and crass as they were, knew the truths she was forced to keep from her mother, father, sisters, brother, and friends. It was hard to feel close to people she couldn't confide in, and hard *not* to feel close those who knew her secrets.

Among Daw's motley group, Levi was the closest to Eila's age. Savannah was next, and Phoebe might have been the youngest of the rest. The others were old enough to seem alien, but all treated Eila as something between a friend and a daughter. And, strangely, Eila seemed to have a third role in the Guile: that of a leader in waiting.

She was the Dreamer who could Build. The Builder who could Dream. And one day, Daw implied, she'd take the reins and steer them where they needed to go.

At Willoughby's goading, Eila eventually brought the dragonstone from below and showed it to the Guile. She felt odd doing it, as if she'd written a poem and was being asked to recite it.

Daw was fascinated, and took the stone for analysis.

Willoughby wanted to know what "picking it up" inside the dream had felt like.

Genevieve seemed to doubt Eila's story — not as a deliberate lie, but a complicated mistake.

But then Phoebe, who'd been at the periphery, entered the circle and set her hand atop the stone, sharp black-painted fingernails catching the lamplight at the tunnels' mouth, and announced that *she*, for one, believed Eila. And Eila felt sure, watching her walk away, that she'd seen something light up in Phoebe's dark eyes as she'd touched the stone.

It was *recognition*, accompanied by a shiver.

Chapter Seventeen

Like Infection From a Wound

"You have doubles," Genevieve said.

Eila looked at her cards. They looked like flatboard beverage coasters — perfectly round, stiff, and each illustrated with an animal in the center. Ornate scrolling frilled the edges, different from card to card, though there seemed to be at least three or four "families" of similar marks. Eila couldn't tell, despite the fact that Finnegan had already explained the game's rules thrice, and louder each time.

Eila looked over at Finnegan, reluctant to ask what "doubles" meant for fear of an angry rebuke about how nobody ever listened to him. She shoved two of the cards that were face-up on the table into the center.

"Not those," said Genevieve. "I meant the beavers."

"Stop coaching her, Lips," Walker chided. Walker was probably angry about being behind in the game, but Eila wasn't sure. He seemed to have a tall stack of flat stones in front of him, and she thought those kept a player's score, which meant he'd be winning. And he'd been controlling play, which the winner was also supposed to do. Then again, maybe controlling play was a punishment. Eila had no idea.

"She's just learning," Genevieve said. "Now go ahead. Play your beavers."

Eila looked down at her cards. None had beavers. She saw two cats, three things that looked like dogs with an extra head, and a cornucopia of woodland creatures.

"I don't have any beavers."

"I meant those." Genevieve pointed to the cards in front of Walker.

"Oh, now she's gotta use *my* beavers?"

"Can it, Walker. Whose beavers would *you* play?"

"Yours!"

"Mine are reserved, idiot." She tapped a glass of Thunderclap straddling two of the cards. Eila had thought that Genevieve needed a coaster, but apparently the drink's placement had meaning in the game.

"Only because you got lucky."

"Doesn't change anything, does it?" Genevieve asked.

Eila, baffled, set her cards down to think. She wasn't sure what "playing Walker's beavers" even meant. Was she supposed to pull them into her pile? Her eyes flicked toward Finnegan, who seemed furious. Or rather, he seemed *about to be* furious. Then again, Eila had been coming down to Pavilion every afternoon for two weeks, and knew by now that it was how he usually looked.

"Oh, hell!" said Walker, throwing his head back as he watched Eila rest her cards on the table.

"You're sure you want to do that?" asked Savannah, who was shuffling her cards around in a way that Eila thought was either a strategic move or cheating. Savannah was wearing a tight, bright-red dress. It seemed so incredibly out of place in the basement with the tunnel door open to bare rock beside her, but Savannah always seemed to dress that way.

"What?" asked Eila.

Finnegan reached over. "She's played," he growled. "She wants to be a fool, that's her business." He flipped two of Eila's face-down cards over, then one of the face-up cards down, seemingly at random. A loud groan rolled around the table, most notably from Walker.

"Darlin, you sure you never played this before?"

"What did I do? Was it wrong?" Eila looked down. Finnegan was rapidly exchanging her cards with his own, then dragging stones from Eila's pile to his. Genevieve was busy stacking more cards under her glass of Thunderclap, muttering.

"You just quinced us."

"All of you?" Eila wasn't sure if she'd done something wrong.

"All but Finnegan. As if he needs more stones." Walker rolled his eyes, shaking his blond mane. "*Or* more beavers."

"You had your chance, Walker," said Finnegan, his eyes down, counting beavers.

Savannah reached out and smacked Finnegan's hand, then Walker's. Eila looked up at Savannah and each of the men, wondering what they'd done wrong to get chastised. They sighed as if caught and began shoveling cards toward her. They didn't send her any precious beavers, but Eila did see an elk and two things with cows' bodies and faces that looked strikingly like Prime Minister Morrison.

"Do I win?" Eila asked.

Finnegan looked at Eila like she was an idiot. "Phoebe won. Weren't you paying attention?"

Eila looked over at Phoebe, who seemed to be doing something with her nails using a file. Perhaps sharpening them.

"But she's not playing."

"Exactly." Finnegan turned his head. "Congratulations, Phoebe."

Walker groaned and began sweeping flat stones and round cards from the table, into a long, shallow box. Eila assumed this meant the game was over, but kept her seat just in case it was more gameplay she didn't understand.

The others stood from the table. Eila stood so that Finnegan could push the table aside. He left once the table was cleared, then entered the cave, grumbling.

Eila watched Finnegan, then looked over at Savannah. She was learning affection for all of the Guile, but felt closest to Savannah. When she wasn't playing vixen — which, admittedly, wasn't often — Savannah was a different person. It was as if Savannah had impostor mode and non-impostor mode, and dropped an obvious facade whenever she allowed herself to be the latter. But the front was mostly appearance (non-impostor Savannah wore slacks like a man and tied her shoulder-length hair with a band behind her head), and Eila, just a handful of years her junior, liked the girl in both of her guises.

"Why is he angry?" Eila asked. "I thought he did well in the game." She was thinking of Walker's comment about Finnegan's bounty of beavers and stones.

"He gets angry when he does well." Savannah laughed. "It's not unique to the game. Finnegan gets angry when most things happen. He's going into the tunnels to tell his stories." She gave Eila a small smile. It said that Savannah understood why Eila wouldn't get the rules of the game. She might, in fact, have been conveying an admission that the game didn't make much sense, despite the rest of the Guile acting otherwise.

Eila stepped closer, following the grizzled old man's angry mutterings as they echoed back from the tunnels, the stone walls sharpening his noises. Beyond a three-foot mini-passage, the tunnels opened into a wide area known as "the Mouth," off of which there were five branches — any one of which Finnegan might have vanished down.

"How deep have you gone in there?" she asked.

Savannah stood beside Eila, her profile strong and beautiful, wearing a light scent that somehow made the basement seem more civilized. If the Guile men hadn't been so used to Savannah, Eila suspected she would drive them nuts.

"Me?" She shook her head. "I don't go into the tunnels. They creep me out. Most aren't even mapped, because … well … it's complicated."

"I meant *any* of you," said Eila. "How deep has *the Guile* gone?"

"Walker's gone deepest. Ask him. All I know is that he's never found an end to any of them." Savannah pointed to each of the visible passageways off of the Mouth in turn. "All I'm willing to say, from my admittedly ill-informed position, is that *that* one goes under Pavilion. And *that* one goes under Pavilion. Oh, and that one? It goes … "

" … under Pavilion."

"And under *your* world. But don't tell anyone outside this house that, okay? The idea of there being anything 'above' us is as crazy to your average person as … well, as there being anything above Waldron's Gate would be to you."

Eila thought of her mother and her belief in The Crown. The Crown, said believers from Waldron's Gate all the way up to the church's seat in Thestic, ruled from the sky. Plenty out there sounded absurd that was still sometimes real. Eila was learning not to judge.

"So who dug the tunnels? Seriously."

Savannah shook her head. She looked like one of Juliette's pretty creations, but she spoke with confidence same as the men, and her voice held weight beyond her beauty. "No idea. It might even have been the Guile long ago; there's no way to be sure. Willoughby has this theory about there having been thirty-seven generations of us down here, but it's foggy at best because he's basing it on what he thinks of as a 'signature' on the prior Tinkers' inventions. A *style*, say. But whether it's been thirty-seven generations or not, we've been here a long time, and nobody's found a way to keep decent records until recently."

With this, Savannah nodded toward the box where Daw kept scribbled records of the Guile's activity — an archive barely worthy of a trash-basket in the Ministry.

"Who knows?" Savannah continued. "Previous leaders might have tried to keep their own records, only to have them destroyed. Or consciously erased. Or stolen."

"Isn't it strange to live without memory?" said Eila.

Savannah laughed. "Isn't it strange to live without dreams?" she countered. She turned and gave Eila a wide smile to cut any bite from the rebuke. "Not really. It's just how it is. If we didn't have Genevieve and Levi to tell us there was something else out there, we'd think nothing of it. Look at Genevieve. She has a patchwork history, and no idea which of her own memories are real."

"Sounds familiar," said Eila, thinking of the way she'd felt while visiting Malvern at the solstice festival.

"But you're getting used to it? Life without Crumble."

Eila shrugged. Even after two weeks, she was still on again, off again with Crumble. On any given day, she might feel the weight of the repugnant world around her and vow to never take the drug again, or she might rub half a block of the stuff over her gums with a helpless feeling of giving up. The way she was vacillating between euphoria and paranoia, her parents *had* to notice. She had survived so far by ducking in and out of her room, keeping to herself when not at the Ministry or in Pavilion — or "with Cora" as far as the Doyles knew. But sometimes she thought about how Father had seen through her lies that day at dinner and wondered if she was fooling them as much as she thought … or if she was being allowed her luxury of lies on purpose. Father had taught her to be disobedient, and Mother had shown her the Fog so that Eila might understand the box they were in rather than believing she was carelessly free. In her most Crumble-euphoric moments, both lessons teemed with hidden meaning.

"I suppose I'm getting by," she said. Then, watching Savannah's face as she looked down the tunnels, she had a thought. "Have you ever tried it? Crumble, I mean."

"We don't have it here," Savannah replied.

"Haven't you … ?" But she stopped, knowing the answer. It was easy to feel like the Guile came and went from Waldron's Gate as readily as Eila, but none had broached the Convenience door. Their entire knowledge of the surface world came from their conduit and dream-swimmer, and yet they spoke as if they had inhaled the warm scents of Waldron's Gate themselves. How strange it must be to know you're trapped, see the exit, and refuse to escape. Did the Guile see the gray sky for the rock face it was beneath the smoke and steam? Did they question the machines among them, knowing they processed waste for both worlds? They spoke as if they truly grasped the concepts of "sky," "outside," and "rain," but did they *really*? To Eila, it seemed like describing a color to someone who couldn't see.

"Walker explores the tunnels to find a way up," she said instead. "But there's a door just a short walk away; I've shown it to you. It's a long way up, but it's straightforward and sure. So why doesn't Walker simply climb the stairs instead of exploring tunnels with no ends?"

"Why don't you just jump off a cliff?"

Eila met her gaze, and again Savannah smiled.

"I didn't mean it like that. The short answer is that Daw feels things aren't yet aligned. Not ready for us to go up there. But the simpler answer — and don't tell Walker this, because he'll deny it — is that he's probably afraid. What made you come down to us? Weren't you scared?"

Eila thought back. As with Savannah's answer, her own reply could go two ways. The short answer was that there hadn't been an option *not* to go; she'd felt the pull and knew it to be choice between fear and insanity. But the simpler answer was that she hadn't thought it out. There had been no time or room for fear that first day. She'd come to the Convenience, then opened the door. There had been nothing more to it.

"I guess."

"Daw leads us for a reason," Savannah said. "He knows more about the engine and the twin worlds that anyone, I imagine. But mostly, it's because he's a *scientist.* Using equipment Willoughby's Tinkered for him, he's done all sorts of experiments I won't pretend to understand. We trust him to know what's best, and to create the plan." She nodded into the tunnels. "Walker's exploring. If he found a way out, he'd stop and talk to Daw. We'd plan together. You know our number, but I'm not sure you appreciate it. There are eight of us. *Eight.* That's not many people, Eila — not when the goal is to tilt the entire world. If we don't work together, we don't have a chance."

Eila had three siblings and two parents — six people who, until recently, had known everything that troubled and motivated her and all she'd ever hoped for. That was six people (already two-thirds of the Guile's total number in her own home) who'd do anything to help her, no matter what. That didn't count her friends, her parents' friends, her co-workers, or any of the innumerable others who could be summoned to struggle for a common goal. If Alterra fell victim to calamity, millions would rally after *that* goal, in search of solutions. And yet, down here, there were only eight people and one tiny chest of incomplete records. That was all that backed the Guile, or all that could — for now at least — even know what it faced.

The thought made Eila feel very alone all of a sudden. She wanted to go home, take her Crumble, and nuzzle between her parents while reading a book, but reality had made her mature without her permission, as if she'd been forcibly aged in a hurry. She felt lonely for Savannah and the others, yes, but mostly she felt it for herself. She had supporters and people who loved her, but she had no one to truly understand her. Not anywhere in the universe.

She turned away, a sudden cold sensation settling onto her shoulders. With her back to the tunnels it was easier to pretend that they were all above, in a nice home, under blue skies, without any cares.

She left Savannah and, aimless, began picking her way around until she reached the staircase. Eila had been encouraged to wander through Daw's home all she wanted, so she went upstairs, desperate for the Pavilion equivalent of fresh air, tired after living two lives for weeks. Desire for Crumble frothed inside her, stirring thoughts and stoking unease. She didn't like the ideas rising inside her. They were dark and discordant, and disobedient in the face of her lack of control.

Crumble would kill those ideas like infection from a wound. It seemed so cruel to refuse to take Crumble, and trap them inside to fester.

She went out onto Daw's porch, feeling claustrophobic. The day was bright for Pavilion, the many plumes marginally lighter as they puffed from their machines, more steam and less smoke. Eila stayed under the porch ceiling, keeping the sky out of sight. She felt the press of panic on her throat. If she remembered that the sky above was another world's floor and that it would take her at least fifteen minutes to surface into the sun (or moon — she wasn't sure of the time, and Pavilion's outdoors offered no clue), she'd suffocate for sure.

"I know how you feel," said a voice.

Eila turned her head as Levi walked through the doorway. She'd remained standing, gripping a post like a hug. He sat in a dark-wood rocking chair beside her, eyes innocently upward.

"No you don't," she said.

Her voice held an angry edge. Emotions were closer to the surface when she was off Crumble, especially the bad ones. She usually felt their claws before she saw them coming. Right now, she didn't want to talk to Levi. It was his fault she was here. If he'd never invaded her dreams — if he'd left her alone, up top and ignorant — her life now would be as it had. She'd go to work; she'd see Cora; she'd spend most evenings at home. One day she'd have taken over for her father, who was in turn due to supplant Brampton. One day, she'd have become Head Builder, and remained oblivious to her atrocities.

"I do, though. I've been inside your head." He sighed, seeming to vent a silent apology. "One of the side effects of what I do, swimming dreams, is that I absorb some of the personalities and mental states of the people whose dreams I swim through."

"You're an intruder. A violator."

"More like an empath," said Levi, unperturbed. He was rocking slowly, now looking out over the front lawn. "So yes, Eila. I know *exactly* how you feel."

"You *think* you do, but you don't. You grew up here. You *decided* to become what you are, to form this group. It happened slowly for you. Not me. I didn't get time to adjust. One day, I was doing my job — a job I'd wanted for years before I could have it. Then you showed up and ruined it all."

"I'm sorry."

"I don't know why I should have to do what you say," she said. "You have a door; you can go up. I'd offer to show it to you yet again, but hey … you know it because you met me there once upon a time, and watched me open it from the outside. But even if you didn't know where it was, you could pluck the thought from my mind whenever you wanted, couldn't you? Because you *know me.*"

"It doesn't work like that."

She spun to face him. "Then how *does* it work? What gave you the right to waltz into my mind and do whatever you wanted? And what gave you the right to visit Cora?"

"How do you know I visited her?" He shrugged. "Or tried to, anyway."

"Because she *dreamed* about you, Levi. Not in a way she can put a finger on, but she did it, all right. I could show you sketches she made of you, after you floated around inside her head, just below the surface. The likeness is amazing. She's quite an artist, my friend Cora. My *old* friend, Cora." She wilted behind her blossoming anger — the price of time spent off Crumble. "Turns out, maybe you don't know everything about us after all. Like how we still must dream, in our own way. How we somehow manage to hold onto pieces of what you steal."

Levi looked at her, his lips pressed together, unwilling to speak.

Coward.

"So," she said with a vicious sniff, "can you swim through dreams down here? Can you peek into Genevieve's head? How about Phoebe's? What about Savannah's?"

She drew the last name out, knowing it was preposterous to lay blame on the closest thing she had to a friend — to turn this little fit into a jealous spat — but was unable to help herself. Was this kind of emotional fragility what it was always like for people in Pavilion? How could they handle it? She felt out of control — a locomotive reaching its terminus, finding its brakes cut.

"No."

"Are your own dreams stolen? Do you have dreams *worth* stealing?"

"I hear it happens, but less overtly because we don't use Crumble," said Levi. "To minimize exposure of the Guile and our plans, we dump our heads out to Daw every night. We call it 'confession.' Daw says it's something the Ministry has researched about dreaming. Apparently, if the mind isn't burdened with unsettled information at the end of the day, it has less need to process what's inside it — through dreams — while sleeping. That plus our training and the mind's natural defenses seem to keep us protected. At least as far as we know."

Eila sagged against the post. Levi's straightforward, unemotional response was disarming — something he'd probably known in advance because he "knew her." She wanted to sit, but that felt too much like surrender. It was Atwell Doyle asserting himself through his daughter's blood: Eila didn't like to be predictable. There was rebellion in them both, and that rebellion was partly against being so known. So open and naked.

"It will get better," said Levi.

"You don't know that. You can't know what will happen. I don't even know the plan, or what I'm supposed to do. Do you know why? I've figured it out. Because there *is* no plan. Daw said I was supposed to help you get past the Fog. But how, exactly? Nobody has a clue. You don't have the Fog down here, but you're all just as afraid of it as we are."

"We have Genevieve to describe it. I've seen it." He hesitated, then added, "And we have Phoebe."

Eila shook her head, looking back out across the lawn. Phoebe was the perfect foil to Eila's feigned indifference. She'd had two weeks to get acquainted with Phoebe along with the rest of the Guile, but Eila hadn't wanted to get close to the Dreamer. Outwardly, Phoebe was quirky and interesting, even funny. But it was all too obvious that something damaged beyond imagining was squirming beneath. Especially on the nights that Phoebe, in her perpetually sleep-deprived way, accidentally fell asleep and screamed herself awake.

"You won't come topside because you can't topple the Ministry of Manifestation without causing big trouble. You can't do this halfway. If you shut down the operation from one end or the other, it will throw both worlds into panic. The people of Waldron's Gate would have to confront what we've done. The people of Pavilion, seeing sky, would have to confront the truth of the world, coming out of your box and facing whatever will follow. So you can't come up until you know how to deal with the Fog. But the problem is you're afraid, like we are. You won't just walk into it, then keep going until … "

She stopped, Daw's words returning.

You, Eila, must help us cross through the Fog and escape to the outside.

What *was* beyond the Fog? Was there an ocean, as she seemed to recall from her vision? If so, what lay beyond it? Would it simply stretch into infinity, as the ocean of Heaven?

Levi sighed, sparing her the need to finish the thought. "You're right. We don't know what to do. That's where you come in."

"How, exactly?"

"That's up to you."

"All up to me. No big deal. Let Eila decide. I'll take the front, and you brave people can march in the back while I do the impossible."

"It's not impossible."

"How can you know that? What would make you say something so absurd? Maybe the Fog really *is* thickening. Maybe it *is* getting larger and pressing in on us. Maybe there are things in it that want to eat us. But what makes you so sure we're not supposed to *sit here and die?*"

"There can't be a problem without a solution."

She turned her gaze on Levi. He was looking down, refusing to meet Eila's eyes.

Her fury returned. It sounded like something her mother would say. No answer, or plan of action. No strategy, or steps. Blind, vain hope. Worthless.

"Really."

"You'll see it. I promise."

"How can you promise something like that?"

"Look, I know it's tough, as you adjust. It's like you said, we had a lifetime to get used to the ways our minds work. Sometimes, they're dark. Sometimes, we don't know what we're doing; sometimes, we don't know why we're pulled in the directions we are; sometimes, we dream terrible things that seem like torment; sometimes, the worst means nothing. You haven't had time to build those defenses, but you will. It's like growing a muscle. Right now you feel like … "

"Stop telling me how I feel!"

Levi looked up, met Eila's eyes, then turned his eyes away. But as she stared him down, she found herself as mute as he was. She'd seized the upper hand, but held it with nothing to say.

Eila looked toward the front yard — to her world's entrance beckoning down those streets. She could go home right now, and never return. They'd never come up to chase her. She could go back on her Crumble, dose heavily, and wait for it all to fade into echoes of memory. Who knew? Maybe the Dreamers would even steal her conflicted thoughts away and help her to forget. Her problems could slither down here and become someone else's problems. Demons for another.

She thought of Phoebe. And Case, somewhere out in those mean streets.

Then, leaving Levi in his rocker, she walked back inside. She found an empty bedroom and sat with her legs hugged to her chest. She thought of her life above, knowing it was dead and gone forever.

She had to stay here. She had to do what she could. She had to be strong.

But because she was human, she stayed in the room a while longer, her face buried, and cried for no one to see or hear.

Chapter Eighteen

Very Real Decisions

"Try to focus."

Eila looked up. Daw's head was on the same beaver that had been on the game cards, floating atop a miniature pink cloud. His mustache was firmly in place, curled up at the ends, overly large. His eyes were giant, bigger than usual. And on the beaver's body was Daw's usual rumpled bow tie.

Eila looked down. She was wearing a plain blue dress, trimmed in white. Earlier there had been a mirror, so she'd been able to see the large blue bow in her hair. She felt ridiculous, but the mirror had dissolved in a puff when she'd wished it away, and now she had only the feeling of the bow … and, of course, this ridiculous beaver Daw.

"It's hard with you looking like that."

"The machine isn't making me look like anything. You're doing it. Same as you put yourself in that getup."

Eila looked down again. The dress did look suspiciously familiar. She looked like a character in a fable her mother had read her as a child. The beaver Daw? Well, that was another set of questions entirely.

"Look at the pair," Daw told her.

Eila looked away from the beaver thing, knowing she wasn't actually looking anywhere at all. In reality, she was lying in a device like a poor man's version of her cradle in the Ministry's array. Daw was speaking into a horn-type device farther along the giant clockwork monstrosity. The real Eila had her eyes closed, her mind in a trance very much like the one she used for Building. But now, instead of seeing her usual empty warehouse, she saw this meadow, with massive multicolored toadstools in the background. Daw's disembodied voice had become a beaver man at the ministrations of her quasi-dreaming mind. And Eila, herself, had become the exact opposite of how she actually wanted to be. She wanted to feel strong, perhaps dressed in black leather with buckles like one of the Dark Ladies above. Instead, she'd become a storybook damsel, seemingly ready to fret over porridge and spiders.

Eila saw two scenes in her construct: the "pair" Daw wanted her to consider. On the left was her family, having a picnic in the grass. And on the right was a fairy with gossamer wings.

"The fairy is real," she said.

Daw exhaled. "Don't screw around."

"Seriously. Stop making these so easy."

Everything snapped to black. Eila opened her eyes to see the top of what looked like half of an iron barrel. She was reclined in what seemed to be a trough into which Willoughby Keys had tossed a thick blanket for her to lie on. She pulled her head out of the barrel to see Daw on a stool beside her, dressed in his usual rumpled formalwear, the copper horn inches from his mouth. The machine's bulk was behind him, tied into Eila's makeshift cradle.

"Do you think this is a joke?"

"Yes. It's a joke. I know the difference between a fairy and my family."

"The sequence is progressive. They get harder."

"Please," said Eila, flashing her hands in mock terror. "Don't make them harder than that one."

"Do you have any idea how fragile the mind is? This is *conscious dreaming*, Miss Doyle. You are usually guided by your dreams, but we must teach *you* to control *them*. That means flipping input and response. Your mind is new to seeing dreams as they happen. We must teach it to process what it sees, then turn it around. Sure, you were able to manifest a dragonstone, but only after being stimulated to do so by the dream." He slapped his palm on the machine, which rattled as if about to fall apart. "I control the pairs now, Eila, but what if something had come for you? Would manifesting be so simple then?"

She sat fully upright. Daw was decades older than her and leader of this tribe, but two things had changed since she'd first come to visit: first, Eila had realized that they needed her more than she needed them, and second, she'd learned the pleasure of holding anger like a weapon behind her back.

"I'll make this easy for you," she said. "Manifesting wasn't 'simple' with the dragonstone. I don't know how I did it, and I certainly don't know now."

"You don't *need* to manifest now. The machine will do it for you." Again, he slapped it. "It's like a miniature Blunderbuss, basically stealing some of the energy the real Blunderbuss puts out to give us a means to test your ability."

"I see. So I'm supposed to wear this giant contraption on my back when I go out into the Fog to save the world?" She looked it over. The room was half-swallowed by its pistons and belching steam.

"We'll cross that bridge when our toes are at the edge. Best I can tell from my investigations at the Ministry, you were able to pick up the dragonstone because it was *given* to you, and you probably wouldn't have been able to make something you consciously needed in the moment. In short, *you were able to take it because you thought it was real at the time.* But do you see the problem with that?"

"It means … " Eila stalled. This part was so complicated.

"It *means*, Miss Doyle, that if you'd encountered a dragon instead of a dragon*stone*, it could have killed you. Instead of manifesting a stone for your pocket, you might have manifested a dragon biting you in half, thus making dreaming a rather dangerous proposition for your untrained mind. Your 'manifesting' the stone as real could have been deadly, because you'd lost all control."

Eila sighed. Daw shifted, moving into his all-too-common lecturing mode, preparing to impart yet another lesson. Or, as the case happened to be, to impart the *same* lesson yet again.

"We need you to Dream us a way into the Fog — to the far side, if there is such a thing," he said. "But that's *different* from actually crossing the Fog yourself. Do you see? It's like *you* are parting the waves for *us* so that *we* can walk through it for real. You will stay here and operate a machine like this one, safely in Pavilion. We, on the other hand, will walk your cleared path up top, through the actual Fog." He made his face serious. "*But* that requires two things to happen. For one, you must be able to Dream efficiently and lucidly enough to keep the true horrors from attacking us as we cross, by withdrawing your attention from the things you choose not to give full manifestation. And two —" Again, he slapped the machine for emphasis. "— *You must determine what is real and what is not,* so that you will not manifest out of fear and thus be killed yourself. Do you understand?"

"Yes." But that was a half-truth, because really she didn't understand at all.

"Shall we try again?"

Eila sighed. Instead of answering, she laid back into the makeshift cradle on the ersatz Blunderbuss that Willoughby had Tinkered together. It was ugly — almost profane — but using Eila's practiced Builder's mind, it was strangely effective at providing a genuine dreamspace in which to practice.

Eila focused.

Again she saw the meadow, but this time she was dressed normally, as in life. She didn't want to tempt fate by looking toward Daw's voice behind her, so Eila kept her dream eyes forward, looking at the fairy and the scene of her family.

"They're both fake."

"Technically, yes," said Daw's voice. "But let's stick with defining 'real' as something that has a corresponding object in life."

"How do you know there aren't fairies in life? Aren't they in the Fog, because they were once in someone's mind, and the Blunderbuss made them real?" Eila wanted to add that this clearly wasn't her family. Nicholas wasn't fighting with the girls, for one.

"'Real' inside the boundaries of Alterra. Inside the Fog."

Eila thought about protesting further but decided to play along. She wanted to see what would happen, but it all felt like splitting hairs. If she could Dream and Build, couldn't she make *anything* real? And once out in the Fog, wouldn't "real" be defined as "whatever surrounded them"? Eila had manifested the dragonstone from a dream, but if she'd been walking through the Fog, wouldn't a stone (or anything else) be there in front of her simply *because it was in front of her,* rendering the concept of "real" versus "not real" meaningless? Once out in the Fog, wasn't something "real" simply because it existed?

"My family is real," she said.

Outside the dream, Eila heard Daw turning a dial. Her scene changed into a huge troll standing beside a very ugly, very hairy man.

She said, "I don't see the point of this."

"I just told you the point. Now tell me which is real."

"The man."

"Which is the man?"

"On the left." She pointed. "That one."

Again, the scene changed. Eila found herself facing a horse and a centaur: half man, half horse.

"The horse."

Now she saw a tall sunflower, roots in the soil, and … another sunflower, same as the first.

"They're the same."

"Are you sure?"

Eila's mind prompted her forward, advancing her through the dreamspace. She touched the first flower's stalk and found it solid. If "real" was defined by touch, there was no question. She reached out for the second and its face turned, a mouth crammed with teeth snapping toward her. In a moment, two of its leaves were at her throat, trying to yank itself toward her. She fought it off and snapped the leaves in half. The monster sunflower whimpered and flinched, as if struck.

Eila backed away, heart pumping. Her real heart, in her real chest.

"The one that didn't try to eat me is real."

"Tricky, I know," said Daw. "But correct."

Another clacking sound. Eila found herself facing an empty meadow, with no objects to choose from. She turned without thinking, delighted to find that her mind, which had apparently learned a bit about discipline after turning Daw into a floating beaver thing on the first try, had finally presented him correctly. It felt like another small victory in her test: could her Crumble-depleted, increasingly untidy and undisciplined mind learn to see her instructor as he actually was?

Yes, it could. He was in a black suit, cut long to suit his long body. His hair was as greasy as it was in life, mashed flat as if recently missing his hat. He looked around his feet, as if searching for something. In the real world, Eila's eyes were closed, so she had no idea if he was doing something similar on the stool beside her or if this was part of the construct presented by Willoughby's Blunderbuss clone.

"Well," he said. "That was easier than I'd thought."

"That's it? Four tests? I could have flipped a coin and done as well. Are there really people who would have answered wrong?"

"Perhaps. Like those in Joffrey."

Eila felt a shiver, both in the dream and in her own head and shoulders. She'd been thinking about those poor souls more and more often. Half of the time she thought of them, she ran back to Crumble. Joffrey patients were always in her thoughts as Eila's shaking hands tried to get the pills or powder into her mouth seconds before — she always felt certain — her final straw snapped. Levi and the others had all suggested that her mind would strengthen like a muscle, and become better able to handle the chaos of thinking without Crumble. It hadn't happened. She kept expecting to wake up without fearing her mirror, to stare into nighttime shadows without imagining frightening beasts, or to stop having partial thoughts that her mind left hanging without finishing. She kept waiting for her constant doubts to quit their plaguing, and make a slow return to the confident control she was used to.

But none of that had happened, and one of Eila's constant anti-fantasies — one that her mental muscle still hadn't grown strong enough to fend off — was that one day she'd end up in the asylum, locked in a tower, howling at the moon like a lunatic.

"What about them?"

"Joffrey inmates would fail this test," said the Dream-Daw. "They wouldn't understand what was real and what wasn't."

"Could they even *take* this test?"

Dream-Daw shook his head. Again, for all Eila knew, he might be nodding outside of the construct. "No. Those poor souls don't have your advantage of a machine like this. They have to do this for real every day, seeing such conflicting objects apparently in front of their eyes. You merely have to *pretend* this is real. But now, since you've gone through it, if you encounter a troll and a hairy man on the street one day you can feel confident that you'll know which is real."

It took Eila a second to catch what he was saying because Daw's statement was strange, obtuse, and empty of sense. But the she realized: it was a cousin to the questions she'd already asked, about the meaning of the word "real."

"But if I'm out walking around and run into a man and a troll side-by-side, they'd *both* be real by definition. If I see both in life, I can't just choose one and make it go away."

"Technically, perhaps."

It was the same thing Daw had said earlier, when Eila had told him that both her family's projection and the fairy were fake. He was acting like the truth was arbitrary, and she was splitting hairs. "Tell you what. Let's try the next phase. This is where it gets tricky. Are you ready?"

"Um … "

Without waiting for an answer, Daw changed the scene. Everything became different. Eila was suddenly in her pajamas, sitting on the edge of her bed at home. Daw was in the chair behind her desk, also in pajamas — long, elegant, and bedecked with tiny pinstripes; the look made him appear even longer and taller than he already was — with one leg crossed over the other. Sheets were pooled around Eila's waist as if she'd only just woken.

"This is my bedroom," she said.

"Yes."

"How do you know what my bedroom looks like?" She felt somehow violated. *Levi.* This had to be Levi's doing — he with his damned ability to peer into her thoughts.

"Does it feel real?"

She bounced slightly, feeling the springs beneath her. She had thought she was in control of the construct, but she either wasn't or had been steered into doing something she wasn't aware of. Like a crazy person — someone who had no control of her thoughts, visions, or feelings.

"Yes."

"Is it real?"

"Of course not."

"How do you know?"

"Because I'm in Pavilion, lying in a machine. And because you're here." Eila tried to shift in the cradle, but could feel only the bed. It was an intense reality. She hadn't felt an imaginary world so tangibly since the nightmare in which she'd picked up the dragonstone. Her mind flitted back to Daw saying that Eila had Built the stone into reality because she'd believed in the world. Did the fact that everything seemed so real mean that she was failing?

"What convinces you that I'm not in Waldron's Gate, in your room, wearing pajamas across from you?"

"Because I know better."

"How?"

"I … " She trailed off, not knowing the answer.

"How do you know for sure that this world isn't real? What makes you so sure that *Pavilion* isn't the dream world?"

Without warning, Daw disappeared and Eila was left staring at an empty chair. His next words came deep inside her mind.

When you get right down to it, which seems more likely? You sitting in your room one ordinary night, or the idea that you've found an underground city of dream thieves and rebels — a place that doesn't exist for anyone other than you?

She wanted to reply, but it felt odd to speak. The house was quiet with Daw gone … if he'd ever been there in the first place. The mustached man across from Eila was already feeling like a Fog dream on waking. In her room's quiet, the idea that he'd been sitting in her chair a moment earlier seemed almost silly.

Which is real?

It was as if he'd snapped his fingers in front of her face. She almost jumped, coming out of one kind of trance inside another. The walls of her mind were apparently still too thin. She wasn't strong enough yet, and frightened that even the training might break her.

"Pavilion is real," she said around a swallow.

Her drapes fluttered open as if drawn back by an invisible hand then seemed to flutter in a nonexistent breeze. She stood and found herself looking out at the street, exactly as she had on the night she'd gathered the dragonstone — her awful first evening off Crumble. She'd been unsure, at the time, if the drug was a blessing or a curse. She thought the same thing now, wishing she were in her real room in the real world so that she could take one or six of the pills she had stashed all about. But was she really so sure she couldn't do that now? It all seemed so real.

She found herself confronting the same dark shadows outside the window.

She saw something long and snakelike sliding along in the gutter.

She saw the shapes of three impossibly tall, impossibly thin strangers with black cloaks standing in the garden across the street, their long fingers idly laced through the home's roses.

Her feet snagged on the rug as she shuffled backward, the backs of her legs striking the mattress and sending her onto her rear with a hammering heart.

She tried to breathe, but the dark room was too quiet.

She was there. *She was there.*

Are the things you see outside real?

Was there any reason to answer? The voice *itself* was barely real.

Are they REAL, Eila?

"No … they're not."

How do you know?

"Because I know where I am, and what's happening to my body."

Correct. As with the first round of tests. And now, as with the troll and the man, you'll be prepared. If you encounter those things on the street one day, you will know what is real and what is not. Knowing the difference will keep you out of Joffrey. Congratulations.

"I … "

Eila was about to protest that she *had* encountered those shadows in real life, and that at the time she hadn't been able to tell what was what. But then the scene changed, and she found herself back in her usual construct, the warehouse's white walls a few dozen yards around her in every direction. Blessedly, Daw was back — exactly as he looked on the stool in Pavilion, only this time her mind had given him a top hat. She squeezed her eyes shut, suddenly certain that it was vital to eliminate even that single erroneous detail.

She opened them again to find herself in control, the hat gone from his head.

"Which is real?" he said. Her eyes followed a gesture of his hand. In the middle of the warehouse, she saw two of her father.

"Neither."

"Oh, but one *must* be," he said. "Pretend this is real life."

But that felt like a trick, too. It was easy enough to pretend that the Build construct itself was real, but Eila's heart was still thumping from the previous scene. She'd very consciously wanted to keep that "reality" at arm's length. It had been all too easy to believe, and she knew she couldn't believe it, or be tempted to believe it. She wasn't strong enough to hold both views without breaking inside.

"Okay. Then both are."

"How could they be? You only have one father, don't you?"

She thought of the sunflowers. "Am I supposed to go over and poke them?"

It felt odd to say anything about the two Atwell Doyles. Both were staring at her in disbelief, four blue eyes waiting for Eila to decide what to do with them.

"No," said Daw. "You're supposed to decide another way."

Eila looked again. The men were the same, down to their dress. Then she looked harder and saw that the one on the right's face was dotted with stubble.

"There's a difference, but it doesn't tell me which of them is real." Even saying the words, she felt lost, as if swimming against an angry current.

"What is the difference?"

"The stubble. It's one of my father's quirks. When he's puzzling a problem, he stops shaving until it's solved."

"Ah."

She perked up, sensing a partially correct answer. "Is that it? What problem is the one with the stubble trying to solve?"

Daw, still across from her, leveled his gaze. He said, "Whether or not his daughter is a traitor."

Eila's head snapped around to stare at Daw. His saying such a thing was a violation, like the bedroom scene had been. She didn't like how casually Daw plunged his way into her mind — or sent others to do it for him.

"Which is real?" he repeated.

"I don't want to play anymore."

She wanted to find the edges of the cradle in the real world and push herself out of it, but the simulation was too complete. For now was here, in this empty warehouse. Out of control and in the hands of a madman.

"What about this one?" Daw's hands didn't move, but she heard the dial turning. She turned to see that two copies of her mother had replaced the Atwells. "One of them loves you. The other does not."

Eila's breath caught in her throat. She spun. She wanted to leap at Daw and throttle him.

She heard the dial again. Now there were two mirrors before her. One mirror showed Eila's reflection as she'd always known it and the other showed the Eila she'd been seeing in her mind while lying to hide her lack of addiction. That Eila looked bedraggled — hair unkempt, body too thin, eyes hollow as deep pits devoid of emotion. She'd stared into plenty of mirrors, both at home and in Pavilion, to ensure she didn't actually resemble the monster she saw in her mind.

"Which is real?" said Daw.

Fuming, Eila pointed at the normal-looking reflection. "That one."

"Are you sure?"

"I'm sure." The words came out sharp, as if Eila had bitten off their ends.

"Haven't you ever seen anyone who you found unattractive, but who thought themselves beautiful? Haven't you ever known someone who thought themselves important and proud, but whose accomplishments you knew to be the work of others … like Rabbit Brampton?"

Eila said nothing.

Daw's eyebrows raised. A small, maddeningly smug smile tugged his lips at the corner.

"All right, one last pair," he said, giving up on her unwillingness to play.

"I want to stop," said Eila. "I'm finished."

"You haven't even been trying."

"Because it's meaningless! Because you're toying with me!"

"Am I?"

She wanted to scream. Daw wasn't just toying with her; he was doing it in the most obnoxious, mocking way. This was a joke. He had no plan; they were all trapped down here forever, cursed to know their fate and do nothing to change it. Daw was a coward who made the Guile do his work, and Levi was a lily liver who swam through the dreams of others but never suffered the same intrusion. Even members of the Guile, who claimed to believe the tunnels would be the means of their escape, had yet to reach their ends. How hard could it be to keep walking? Did a tunnel present the same insurmountable difficulty for them as climbing the spiral staircase seemed to? Why was *she* the one being tested? Why weren't *they* on the scales, their own mettle weighed?

The scene changed. Eila saw two copies of herself, as she actually looked, both sitting on wooden chairs so bright white they nearly vanished against the walls and floor behind them. Both Eilas were identically dressed, knees pressed together, palms on their thighs. Both were looking straight forward, past Eila and Daw.

"I've already faced me," she said.

"Not like this," Daw said.

"I'm done. I want out."

"You can't get out. You have this one final pair to decide on. Your inability to choose the proper option — to tell what is real and what is not — in prior tests won't matter if you get this one correct."

"You didn't give me a chance to pick the last ones before … "

"But if you *can't* choose correctly here, I'm afraid that bodes poorly for you as a whole. This is the big one. The only test that truly matters."

She sighed.

Daw pointed at the Eilas and said, "One has broken inside, and the other is whole. One can control her mind; the other cannot."

Eila stared the scientist in his unflinching eyes.

"Stop it. This isn't fair."

"One of them," he continued, "believes that fairness is a real concept, and that it matters."

"Let me out. Now."

Daw leaned closer, his words coming faster and gaining the weight of importance. "You need to know this one, Eila. You must make a choice. Choose correctly, and you're telling your mind what to do and believe. The wrong choice will take away your chance. You are at a crossroads, still trying to keep your feet in two worlds, *and* two lives. You won't embrace who your destiny is leading you to become, but also you won't allow the fantasy to end and curl back into who you used to be. You go on and off Crumble, unable to commit. You worry when you're off of it, and feel guilty when you're on. When you Build … "

"How could you know what I think when I Build?"

"I know!" Daw pointed. "Choose, Eila! Whether you choose correctly or not, we must know where you stand. The seal has been breached, but we cannot move forward. We have tunnels but cannot go through them. We found whom we sought, but it seems she is not what she *herself* was looking for!"

"But I don't know! There's no answer!"

"One of those girls believes there is an answer. The other does not."

"I can't do what you need me to do, Daw! Give me time!"

"One believes she needs time. The other knows that the hours are already gone."

"Stop speaking in riddles!"

Eila felt herself cowering, shriveling up. Daw was already tall and now seemed taller, moving over her. "One knows what awaits her in the Fog and is prepared, while the other does not and is afraid. One feels confident; the other is timid. One could look at any pairing and choose between them, while the other feels there is no correct choice. So which is real, Eila? Who do you want to be?"

"The confident one, okay! Just show me how to do what I need to do!"

"One needs to be shown. The other already knows."

"What do you want me to do?" she screamed.

"I want you to choose! I want you to pick the correct option and discard the other! I want you to see the choices and *tell me what is real!"*

The weight of the past weeks settled on Eila's back all at once, and she felt her will crack like a twig over someone's knee. She'd thought she was getting stronger, but she realized now that it wasn't true. She'd thought she was maturing, but saw that she was still too young and naive. She thought she'd begun to make her peace with Pavilion, but it was still alien and angry and wanted her no more than Waldron's Gate. She'd begun to feel at home, but it seemed she was not.

Her family was no longer home, either, and Cora was no longer home. She was alone, crushed, and unsure. Out of control and broken.

"I can't." She sagged, wanting to fall but somehow staying upright. She looked at the two Eilas, both now vacantly staring at her. "There's no right answer."

The room clicked away, as if someone had snapped their fingers, and Eila found herself staring at the inside of an iron drum. Beneath her was a folded blanket. Her body felt stiff. And for what felt like the tenth time in just a few days, her face was wet.

She thought she'd been growing strong, but it had turned out to be just self-deception.

Daw was on his stool, the screen on the faux-Blunderbuss dimming as it powered down. He looked like he was trying to keep a straight face but was mostly failing. What Eila saw beneath the man's mustache and his usually somewhat wild-eyed expression looked like disappointment.

"We'll try again tomorrow," he said.

Chapter Nineteen

In Brampton's Office

THE NEXT WEEKS PASSED LIKE a belt running on a loop.

Every day, Eila would wake up, head to the Ministry, and Build in a daze. She felt like an impostor, a criminal, and a slave-driver wielding a whip. She Built with only half a mind, saving the other half to flog herself.

She was lying to her parents and hadn't reconciled with Cora. It seemed unlikely that she would. She lived a decadent life, and was now too aware that it came at the expense of an underclass living below the city's streets.

While on Crumble, Eila was dumping her dreams into Pavilion Dreamers — perhaps right into Phoebe Horn. When off Crumble, she kept her dreams to herself and felt unsettled by an ever-shifting reality.

And on top of everything, she wasn't Building well. Her production rate slipped, and her Builds had a climbing number of faults. It was only a matter of time before Brampton came yelling.

After showing one false face to her family and another to the Ministry, Eila boarded the streetcar every afternoon and rode to the Doer district, where she disembarked and walked in a daze to the Convenience door with neither joy nor duty. She was numb, going through the motions because she didn't know what else to do.

Each day, she descended the spiral staircase, always pausing to glance at Atlas with the world on his back. Sometimes, she wondered how she knew who Atlas was and who had conceived the world as a giant ball. Other times, she wondered about the rooms on each floor. Mostly she walked, not really caring. She went to Daw's. She spoke to a few in the Guile, and then Daw hooked her to the machine where she went through the sorting exercise again and again, her parameters and visions different every time.

Each day, she faced things she'd seen in life that Daw implied were false, and each day she faced fantastical things that he seemed to suggest were quite real indeed. Each day, as her final test, she was to make a choice. Sometimes, she had to choose between versions of herself like she had that first day. Sometimes, she had make a choice of action — which of two beings she would choose to kill if the Fog hurled them her way.

Each day she was unable to choose. Options were even, with no obvious answer.

Each day, she failed.

Eila felt beaten and stomped upon. Not long ago she'd felt confident; now she felt empty. The Guile members tried to be friendly, but none of them really knew her. None knew who she'd once been, or how happy she'd been in her ignorance. None knew what it was like to live on the surface, under the sun, going to festivals with former best friends and watching their mothers fret over the arrangement of roses lining the walk. None knew what it was like to hope — to look into a beautiful future — only to have that hope yanked away.

Pavilion's people didn't know they could want more, because they didn't know there *was* more. The Guile members knew, but they'd been raised with no hope.

None knew how lost Eila felt. None knew what it was like to be so … so *sure* … about things, only to have that certainty snatched away time and time again.

Each day, the hangover of Daw's tests followed Eila into morning. She woke up exhausted, her neck limp, gaze low, and feet plodding. Sometimes, she sneaked Crumble to dull the edge, but it hardly made a difference. Daw yelled if she took too much. She practiced her smile in the mirror each morning before heading downstairs, then studied her father's face when she encountered him in his study, packing the worn leather work bag he'd owned since the day of her birth, looking for telltale stubble on his face. She forced her smile higher, telling Mother that she'd be going to Cora's after work … then felt the stab in her heart every time.

Cora hadn't blown Eila's cover. Maybe (probably) because Cora had stopped caring.

On the weekends, when Eila didn't need to work at the Ministry, Daw let her stay home. Mother asked why she didn't see Cora on the weekends, but Eila was always an excuse away from the truth. She offered to call Belinda so that both families could head downtown together for lunch. The mothers had been close since before they were mothers, and had remained close despite Juliette's higher standing as the wife of a Ministry Builder. Eila said she was sick, and Juliette went alone. Upon her return, she reported that Cora had been sick as well.

On weekends, Eila dosed as heavily as she dared. There were no nightmares, nor did she wonder at every shadow and uncertain thought. But there was no euphoria either. No joy. Nothing at all.

Atwell grew stubble. Shaved. Grew stubble, and shaved again.

Eila avoided him, terrified that he'd see right through her. Daw had been right. She wasn't fully in either world, and that made her a traitor to both. While she remained part of the upper world, she worked to worsen existence for Pavilion's Dreamers. And when she was below in Pavilion, she undermined her father's work. She betrayed the Ministry, risked her family's existence, and empowered a group who threatened to topple life as Alterra knew it. And yet that toppling was, out of all the gray and halfway things in her life, what Eila strove for most.

Successful tests on Daw's machine continued to elude her. Frustration mounted.

One day, Eila sat up in her Ministry cradle to find Rabbit Brampton standing above her, his white hair frozen in place as always. He was wearing a gray suit, immaculately cut and pressed, and a dull-blue tie, its fabric matte and free of shine. The tie's end was tucked into his buttoned coat, and as he leaned forward it didn't flap out. Eila wondered how it was possible, and almost laughed inappropriately at the thought that its end might be tucked into his belt. It seemed like a such a Rabbit Brampton thing to do.

"Miss Doyle," he said.

"Mr. Brampton."

"I'd like to see you in my office, if you would."

He didn't wait for a reply or for Eila to follow. He walked down the gantry, one hand behind his back, the other brushing the railing.

Eila neither dawdled nor hurried. By the time she made it to Brampton's office, he was sitting behind his desk, leaned back, feet on the blotter. She got the distinct impression that he'd rushed to arrange himself before she walked through the door for her berating.

"Have a seat," he said. Then he added, "On second thought, don't. You look like you're about to fall asleep."

"I had a tough night."

Eila felt a thousand years old. Of the two of them, Brampton seemed like the young one.

"Who has tough nights? Especially as a Builder. You sleep all day."

Brampton was a scientist. He wasn't a Builder, and never had been. Still, there was no question that he knew the difference between a Build trance and sleeping. Or did he? *Someone* at the top of the Ministry had to know the engine had a bottom. *Someone* had to know about the Dreamers. Otherwise, how could it all work? And didn't it make sense that such knowledge would be held by the Head Scientist?

"I'm sorry."

"Oh for Crown's sake. Sit down. I was kidding. You look like you're going to fall over. How old are you, Doyle? Sixteen?"

Of course, he knew the answer. She'd barely worked at the Ministry two months, and her father had petitioned for early occupation a full year before that. They'd repeatedly denied her, insisting that Builders be fifteen, at least. Most of those denials had been stamped at Brampton's desk.

Eila sat, saying nothing of her age. She forced herself not to slump, and tried pushing her face into a pleasant expression. She looked around the office, in search of distraction. One wall contained a viewbox showing the engine's status, gauges, dials with jittering needles, and a rolling display of white number cards that flicked over every few seconds with a click. Behind Brampton were rows of pneumatic tubes, some with filled carriers sitting in their bottoms. Eila wondered if he was ignoring his messages or had yet to notice them. She wanted to point them out, just to see what he'd say.

"I've tried not to call you in," said Brampton, his leaned-back chair squeaking, "because your father is helping me with something up on Enigma. Don't get me wrong; it's his *job* to help me. But he can help and he can *help*, if you catch the difference, and I need this quickly. We've sparred about you before, and … "

Eila sat forward. "About me?"

Brampton looked annoyed. "Yes, you. And … "

"What about me?"

"Frankly," said Brampton, "I think last month's Pianoforte collapse was your fault."

Eila blinked. Father had implied that he suspected Eila's involvement in the incident, but she'd assumed he'd reached the conclusion on his own and had kept it to himself. Now it looked like either Atwell had told Brampton, or Brampton had raised the issue to Atwell. Neither scenario was good, but one seemed much worse, and she found herself again wondering at her place in the world, or worlds. Suddenly, Eila was quite sure that of all places, the Ministry of Manifestation wasn't where she belonged.

"Oh."

"You don't seem upset. You're a teenager. Aren't you supposed to be outraged by my accusation? Aren't you supposed to tell me that I don't know you? It's what my daughter would do."

Eila hadn't known Brampton had a teenage daughter. She also hadn't thought of him as the kind of man who'd have a family. Or as a human.

"Regardless. You screwed up. It's what kids do, whatever. So you cost the Ministry untold millions in development, and … "

"Do you sell what we make?"

"Excuse me?"

"Do you sell it." An enunciated re-statement, not a question. "To Stensue, for instance. Or are our Builds government property, so various districts simply receive what they need?"

"I don't see how that could possibly have any bearing on … "

"I just wondered what kind of theft this is. Is it pilfering, or is there financial gain?"

She met Brampton's eyes — steely, but not on fire like they should be. No one spoke to Rabbit Brampton that way. He was a spiteful little man who never gave anyone the dignity of a real response.

"I guess you're a teenager after all."

"Do you dream? Or do you take Crumble like the rest of us?"

"What are you talking about, Doyle?"

Brampton's voice had a warning edge. Eila couldn't tell if she was hitting the mark or not, but found she didn't care. She'd spent the past few weeks feeling powerless. Hurting someone — even someone as reprehensible as Brampton — felt empowering. It was a cruel feeling, but Eila didn't care. At least this was a decision she could make, unlike what Daw spent each workday beating into her head.

"Nothing." She felt a small smile cross her lips.

Brampton paused, studying Eila. In the quiet moment, a carrier dropped from one of the tubes behind his desk. The numbers on the rolling card display flipped to the next digit.

"What did you want to see me about, Mr. Brampton?"

Another assessing look. Then, "Your production is way down. It's getting sloppy."

"It's probably my lack of focus."

Brampton seemed annoyed that Eila was beating him to the punch. This was no fun when the employee berated herself.

"That's what I told your father. About now, and about the Pianoforte."

"Yes. I was unfocused during the Pianoforte. Perhaps a dream escaped me."

Brampton ignored the dream mention, again, and Eila couldn't tell if it had registered. She was endangering both herself and her father, but simply didn't care.

"We're seeing all sorts of anomalies in your Builds. It's like you're not even paying attention. And you look tired as hell. Like you haven't been sleeping. Frankly, after going through the data, I have questions about your mental state."

Eila noticed how he'd said "questions" rather than "concerns." A normal person would have "concerns" about someone's mental state. Not Brampton.

"Maybe I'm losing my mind."

His feet left the desk's blotter. "Do you think this is a joke?"

"Not at all."

"Do you understand that I can relieve you of your position, legacy or no legacy? Do you have any doubts about what will happen if you don't start … "

"What's the longest you've ever been off Crumble, Mr. Brampton?"

"'Off Crumble'?" He said it like he didn't understand the expression.

"I've been wondering something. If a person is allowed to dream, and those dreams can't be stolen, that's one thing. But if that same person is a Builder, would it affect her ability to Build? I know Building is like dreaming, but how *much* like it, Mr. Brampton? Would dreaming — a true dream state — create a fault on the array? Or would it create Built objects the Ministry doesn't understand, even if they might be works of genius?"

He blinked. "Are you intoxicated? Are you on something?"

"On. Or off."

"You aren't serious about Crumble." His expression was turning from its usual cockiness to something like alarm, or perhaps concern. "You aren't taking less than you should, are you?"

"What if I was?"

"Oh, wow. Oh no." He stood. "How long have you been on-shift today?"

"*Just* today, or since I stopped taking my good-girl drugs?"

"Hell. You're kidding, right? Tell me you're kidding." His eyes flicked between Eila and the readout. There was a brass horn, not unlike Daw's, beside the readout, and he kept looking at it as if he wanted to yell into its mouth. He could probably stop the machine — shut the entire place down, as it were — but what would it cost the Ministry? What would it cost Waldron's Gate and Alterra? Would it cost Brampton his job, or would he be praised for acting in the engine's best interest? Eila didn't entirely understand the look on Brampton's face (did he think her mind had somehow damaged the array?), but she liked it. At least she'd broken the stalemate. She doubted what came of this reckless little encounter would be good — and in fact, the aftermath to her, Father, and her family would likely be awful — but at least she no longer felt stuck.

"Okay, I'm kidding," she said.

He looked back at Eila. "You're not kidding. Stay there. Okay?"

Brampton pressed something on the Blunderbuss readout, then leaned close to the brass horn and whispered into it. She couldn't make out what he said, but was content to stay as ordered.

"*If* I wasn't kidding," she said. "What would it mean? To be off Crumble and work the Blunderbuss?"

Brampton took another look at Eila and fled his office. She watched him go, seeing with an odd sense of satisfaction that his suit coat had come unbuttoned and that his tie was flapping. He took a few running strides, then turned and sprinted back to the door, momentum throwing him into its glass front. He fumbled for something in his pocket, and then there was a click as he locked the door. His wide eyes bugged out at Eila for a split second before he turned again and ran off onto the Build floor.

Eila stood, then placed her hand on the door handle.

There was a click, and the lock opened.

She left Brampton's office, strolled calmly to the main doors, and slipped out of the Ministry.

Chapter Twenty

In the Treehouse

Eila knocked three times on the wooden door.

A single knock came in return.

Another two knocks, then a pair from inside.

Eila knocked five more times. Then there was a click, and the door opened.

The room inside the treehouse seemed tiny. Eila hadn't been here since she was eleven years old, and looked on the space now with the peculiar sense of broken recognition that always comes with revisiting a childhood memory after a few years. She was sure she'd been eleven that last time, because it had been the day before Mother had taken her to see the Fog on the outskirts of Waldron's Gate. After seeing the Fog, Eila decided that she never wanted to sleep outside again. Not until today, when she found herself with nowhere to go.

Before entering, Eila looked at Cora's angelic, blonde-framed face to read her mood. Cora had gone to the treehouse in the orchard after getting Eila's message — that had to be a good sign — but there had been weeks of absence between them, and plenty of tension before that. Still, they'd known each other their entire lives. The question was, did the new Eila still fit into that life? Or was she someone — or some*thing* — else now?

"I don't think the knock was necessary," Cora said. "I could see you coming through the orchard."

"I wanted to see if I remembered it."

"What would you have done if you'd forgotten, and I refused to open for you?"

Eila chuckled at Cora's playfulness, relieved that her friend was stronger and nobler than she was, and that she was willing to forgive and forget something that had been entirely Eila's disinterested, distracted fault.

Her mind returned to Brampton's office, maybe to remind her that some of this was *nobody's* fault. The world — and Eila — had changed underfoot. Brampton had tried to keep her from leaving. She hadn't even considered getting caught; the way out had been as plain to her then as it had been that first time at the Convenience, when she'd manifested a door to break the seal.

"Something tells me the treehouse lock wouldn't stop me."

Cora didn't ask what it meant. She shuffled aside to allow Eila entry, then closed the door behind her. The room had been huge when the girls were smaller. But although it seemed to have shrunk, there was still adequate room for them to lie down and sleep.

"I'm … "

Cora stopped Eila by pulling her into a hug. Her gesture was unashamed, unabashed, and fearless. Its vulnerability made Eila want to cry.

"I'm sorry," Eila said, finally pulling away from the hug.

"It's okay."

"I was selfish."

Cora smiled. "You always were."

"It's not like you said earlier. I didn't sneak into your mind. It's … "

"It's okay." Cora patted the blankets and pillows she'd lugged to the treehouse, probably after telling her mother that she was going to sleep over at Eila's … and, if Eila knew Cora, she'd probably also called Juliette to explain that *Eila* would be staying over at *her* house. Eila had no idea if Cora's excuse would be enough. It seemed impossible that Brampton's word *wouldn't* reach Atwell, but there was always a chance. Not enough to sleep at home or at Cora's, but a *chance.*

"You're not mad?"

"I was. But it's okay."

"You didn't tell anyone that … "

"I didn't tell anyone, Eila." A small, sly smile creased the corner of Cora's lips. A devious look, odd but flattering.

Eila wanted to play along, but she felt too beaten. It was tempting to pretend that they were in the playhouse just to relive old times or chat away from prying ears, but the truth was heavy on her shoulders. Eila's admission at the Ministry had been one level of bad, and her taunting Brampton a layer atop it. She'd be fired for sure, even if she'd done nothing wrong. Her recklessness had felt good because she'd been in charge for a moment, but the hangover was agony. She'd wanted to be a Builder since she'd understood the concept. At age nine she'd appropriated her brother's magic set because making things appear through trickery was her preferred mode of make-believe. Now that was over. She'd lost her job, and her future. And, for good measure, she may have cost her father his.

"Thanks."

Cora touched her hand. "Of course."

Eila met her eyes for the single second she could stand, then blinked and looked around the room. "You brought blankets and pillows."

Cora nodded. "You said it was a sleepover."

"I mean, you brought enough for both of us."

"I'm no Palpatine Malvern, but I'm psychic enough to know you weren't wanting to play dolls. You sounded half panicked. I figured you probably couldn't bring your own."

Eila wanted to say something, but didn't know what.

Cora continued. "I caught a broadcast while I was waiting." She tapped the small, old wave receiver. "I guess the Ministry of Manifestation is on temporary lockdown. They claim it's nothing, but rumor says there was a break-in. Someone unauthorized came in and … well, toyed with something they shouldn't have."

"I don't know anything about that," Eila said sarcastically, playing along. Cora had come this far. She might be, quite literally, the only person Eila could trust. The only person who would harbor her secrets and want nothing from her in return. Now more than ever, Eila felt desperate to tell those secrets.

"I'm sure."

"It's real, Cora. The things I told you earlier. I didn't sneak into your head, your room, or your sketchbook. It's … " She hesitated, not wanting to set her last friend off like before. "Well, it's … *Levi* … himself. He's a kind of … Oh, I don't know how to explain it in a way that won't sound crazy."

"Then explain it in your crazy way."

"He can move into minds, Cora. Mine. *Yours*. You might even be having dreams without knowing it." She paused. There was no way to start the discussion. They had no common ground, and every step felt sensitive. How could she explain what Levi did with dreams, when the word meant nothing to Cora beyond what Eila explained over cafei? "It's true. I swear."

"I don't know if it's true," said Cora, "but I believe you're not lying."

"So I might just be crazy."

Cora shrugged. "How would I know the difference?"

Eila thought back to Daw's dream machine and his warning about Joffrey Columns — the place you went when you were unable to tell dreams from reality.

"I could show you. I *can* show you. Tomorrow." A desperate hope pierced the clouds over Eila. She grasped Cora's hand in both of hers. "Come with me! I'll show you in person. I'll show you around Pavilion. I'll introduce you to Levi. The *real* Levi."

Cora slowly pulled her hand from Eila's grip. It was a move of hesitation, not rejection. Eila could smell her own desperation and knew that Cora could smell it, too. A drowning girl would grasp at anything — or any*one* — to save herself.

"Why don't you just tell me, to start."

So Eila did. As evening fell into nighttime and the orchard grew darker, Eila told her oldest friend all she'd seen and done with nothing held back. She explained what Palpatine Malvern had said about the visions, down to his dire prediction; she explained what Pianoforte was and how she had fallen asleep during the latest one — then managed to shut down the system after Levi had led her through a crumbling path in her mind. She told Cora about that first visit to Pavilion, about Daw, his mustache and his bright-green drink, and about the second half of the Blunderbuss in the city underground. She told Cora about Crumble, the lying she'd done, the way she'd scampered around her family and hidden her face, the nightmare, the dwarf on the beach, the tunnels, the Guile — even the way she'd been terrified of her own reflection. She told Cora about Daw's training and how it seemed to mean nothing more than frustration and failure.

Lastly, Eila told her about Brampton: the way she'd baited him for a reason she didn't fully understand, and how he'd scampered out to sound an alarm dire enough to shut the Ministry down for the first time that either of them had ever heard.

Once done, Eila looked up from her confession to see Cora's gazed fixed to the corner, her face unreadable. When she looked back, Eila still couldn't tell what Cora was thinking. Did she think that her friend had snapped, become a deviant and a criminal, did she think her a liar? Or had she held her faith in Eila's truth … and decided that the only explanation was her best friend's insanity?

Before Cora spoke, Eila heard Daw in her head: *Sanity is a matter of opinion.*

Never before had that seemed so true. Eila herself had lost the trails inside her convoluted tale. What was the real world, and what was in her mind? All was memory, and in hindsight, the distinction between real-life and dream memories seemed almost arbitrary. She'd held an unreal artifact in her hand, and had been seeing the real world through a blur for days.

Who was to say what was true and what was not?

She didn't know, or care. For her entire life, Eila had always been given questions with black-and-white answers. She'd been given objects to Build rather than needing to Tinker like Willoughby Keys. There had always been a right and a left, an up and a down, a real and an unreal. Now there was only a miasma of memory where everything blended together. Now almost nothing was black and white. Yet, for the first time in weeks, Eila found herself no longer bothered by the uncertainty.

Cora said, "That's quite a tale."

"Do you believe it?"

"I believe that you did something the Ministry didn't like. And I believe you need a place to sleep. That's enough for now."

"But *do you believe it,* Cora?"

That seemed important. So far, the only people other than Eila who believed her story were Daw, Levi, and the Guile, but their votes didn't count because they were part of the story. If this was a cosmic joke on young Eila Doyle and Cora thought her crazy, she'd have no supporters at all.

"I'll try."

Eila found herself wanting to be angry at Cora's non-answer, but a firm voice spoke inside her.

You are not allowed to be righteous. Not here. Not now. Not with Cora.

She stuffed it down with tremendous effort, and after a few quiet moments as the day's last light bled from the sky, Eila turned the conversation toward the things Cora fussed over most. She asked about Cora's work, such that Cora cared about it. She asked about her sketches, returning the sketchbook she still had stowed in her pack. She asked about the solstice festival's closing night, as if her failure to attend had come from illness rather than ego. Delicately, Eila asked about the mercantile, ferry shaws, and ruddermouths. Cora had gone alone, but had run into several of the girls they'd gone to school with. Eila found her heart hurting through the stories. Cora had had fun without her, living a carefree life she might never know again.

In the orchard's dark, Cora reached up and snuffed the lantern. She hung it on a hook so neither of them would kick it, then lay beside Eila on the wooden planks padded with a single blanket, their heads on Cora's pillows.

Strangely, it was the most comfortable Eila had been in a month.

Just as she thought Cora had drifted to sleep, a voice warmed the darkness.

"Eila?"

"Yeah?"

"Did you really stop taking Crumble?"

Eila hesitated. They'd grown up together and shared most of the same beliefs and stories. She didn't have to ask Cora extra questions to know what she thought about Crumble and those who eschewed it, because it was what she herself had so recently believed.

"Yes."

"Totally?"

"Mostly. I slip now and then."

"You slip and forget to take it?"

Eila almost laughed. There was so much in that sentence.

"I slip and *take* it," she said.

"Oh."

There was a long moment of quiet. In the dark, she couldn't see Cora's face. *Oh* could mean anything. She had said it in almost a whisper, as if in surrender. As if she'd realized there was no use arguing with someone so far off the deep end.

"Why? If that guy told you that you don't need it and you can live without it —" Eila could hear the doubt in Cora's voice. "— then why would you go back on it?"

"Because sometimes I'm scared."

"Why?"

"Because without it, I see things. My brain gets jumbled. Sometimes I get paranoid."

"'Paranoid?'"

"It's a Pavilion word. It means that you think a bad thing is true when it's not."

"Oh." Again, she heard Cora's latent concern. She thought of the oddity in her own words. Going off Crumble made her see things and lose her mind, and yet she needed to give it up? No wonder Cora didn't understand.

"If you get scared, why do you stay off it?"

"Because I need to dream. To *really* dream."

"Why?"

Eila wanted to answer, but found herself unsure what to say. The truth had only earned her more fear and uncertainty. Doubt, paranoia, and nerves to coat her sour stomach. Disorderly thoughts diluting her focus. She'd manifested her way out of Brampton's office, but she'd done something more impressive the first time she'd visited the Convenience while fully addicted to Crumble. The only real improvement now was her ability to operate Daw's Blunderbuss clone, but even that had offered more questions than answers.

More failure, uncertainty, and fear. Less reason to hope.

Eila sighed, more in exasperation with herself than with Cora. "I don't know."

"Oh."

More minutes passed. Eila stared at the treehouse ceiling, where a sliver of moonlight outlined a space between the boards. At first, she was just waiting out an uncomfortable moment between them, but by the end she again assumed that Cora was out, dreaming thoughts of the dreamless.

"Eila?" she said.

"Yeah, Cora?"

"If — just *if* — what we've always believed about Crumble were true — and I'm not saying it is; just asking — how would you know if you … I don't know … crossed a line?"

"You mean, how would I know if I'd gone crazy?"

A beat of quiet.

"Well, yeah."

Eila rolled to the side, avoiding the scrutiny of even Cora's dark outline. She wanted to answer the question head-on — to hit it like a locomotive striking an obstruction — but the exact same concern plagued Eila every day. Still, if she left Cora with anything less than a confident response, her friend would worry. So rather than admit the truth (that she was *quite* worried about that exact thing), she found herself repeating something Daw said every time she raised the topic.

"'Crazy' is just a word for what happens when you start to believe."

She waited for Cora's response in the darkness. The second she repeated Daw's phrase, she wondered if it had been a wise thing to do. When the topic was madness itself, perhaps the words of a madman weren't the best source of authority.

But this time, Cora didn't give her a soft, concerned, single-word answer. Eila imagined her staring upward, waiting for Eila to continue — to reassure Cora about her sanity in the way that Eila had hoped Cora would have reassured her. But here and now — in the dark, off Crumble, and on the run — she didn't feel capable of telling Cora that everything would be all right.

Eila couldn't say it either, because maybe things *wouldn't* be all right.

She didn't remember falling asleep as the quiet seconds grew into minutes.

And then the dreams came.

Chapter Twenty-One

Sleep's Stickiest Webs

Eila stood beside Levi in the center of the stone arena.

The Citadel looked new rather than crumbling (hadn't she seen it falling apart sometime in the past?), but it was vacant — the king and queen away, the gladiators gone, the cheering crowds absent from the long stone bleachers. Now it was just Eila and Levi. The sky overhead was open and blue rather than overcast as it had been once before.

A strange place to meet.

You shouldn't be here, said Levi's voice.

Eila looked over at Levi. She'd seen him a handful of days ago, in what had to be a rather mundane dream. In that dream, they'd had a fight. They'd been standing on Daw's porch, where she'd confronted him about swimming through Cora's mind in addition to hers. He'd been nothing but sympathetic; that had been the most maddening thing about the conversation. But that's how dreams were; they went in circles, spinning wheels of frustration. Eila was getting used to it. She'd had a dream about reuniting with Cora recently too, and that one had been equally frustrating. In *that* dream, they'd met in the old treehouse. Eila had spilled her guts, but in the end there had been no way to convince Cora that she wasn't crazy.

I have every right to be here.

She felt annoyed for a reason she didn't entirely understand. Levi was always telling her what she should and shouldn't do, what she did and didn't feel. He told her that things would work out when clearly they wouldn't.

Levi disappeared, leaving Rabbit Brampton in his place. Brampton was wearing a bright white suit, a white shirt, a white tie, and white shoes and socks. On his head of white hair was a bright white top hat.

Don't snap at me, Miss Doyle. You're *the bad guy here.* You *opened the doors.* You *failed your tests.* You *are unfit to work with the others. Nobody else has your problems. Are you really so arrogant as to think that your way of looking at things is the right one? The entire Ministry disagrees, and yet you feel you know better? How can you possibly be so arrogant and blind?*

Eila found herself taken off guard. If she was willing to push Levi, she was certainly willing to push Brampton. But her tongue was tied. Something in what he'd said made sense to her, even though protest was her knee-jerk reaction.

She realized the stands were no longer empty above them. Seven pitch-black, winged demons glared down in a row from the stone bleachers, each clutching a flat stone in one claw. All had eyes as yellow as the midday sun, and even from where Eila was standing in the arena's center she could see their pupils — elongated black ellipses, like capsules on their sides.

Who are you to say what is right? Brampton continued, seeming not to notice the fourteen yellow eyes staring at them from the stands. *You are* one *Builder on an array. Yours is* one *array in the department, and the department is only* one *of many departments using the engine each day. The Blunderbuss and its Builders have created everything Alterra has today, as they've done for over a thousand years. You are a single, hot-tempered, emotional little girl. You have been at the Ministry for under two months and are our most junior employee. Do you really think that your single, dissenting point of view is correct? Have you honestly never considered that* you *might be wrong? That* you, *Miss Doyle, are the person who is incorrect? Think about this for a second, if you can bring yourself down from your high horse to do it. What is more logical: that for a thousand years, Alterra has been divided in two without either half knowing of the other … or that you have simply lost your mind?*

Eila turned toward movement in the stands and saw the king arise from the staircase behind his plinth. He was wearing robes as described by Eila's father when he'd read her the stories as a child: red trimmed in white, snow-colored fur bedecked with ebony spots. His golden crown held a jewel in the center and his small beard dipped down to an angry point. His eyes were malicious, mad with power.

He placed his hands on the stone wall and watched the arena's scene unfold.

You dream of rebellions, like any desperate child. You dream of a handsome suitor come to save you from mediocrity. And yet the world is wrong, and you *are right?* Brampton gave a condescending shake of his head. *You stand in the middle of a stone arena that doesn't exist … and believe that* you *must be correct, while everyone else is wrong?*

I've seen Pavilion, Eila said with less strength than she'd hoped.

You've stopped taking Crumble. You know it's made you see things. You jump at shadows. You get confused. You come into my office and berate me? Another shake of his head, this time with a roll of his eyes. *Your impudence has put us all in danger, Miss Doyle.*

The accusation made Eila angry. She suspected her rage was a defense for having nothing left inside her, but shoved the thought aside to face him.

How? How have I put us in danger, even if I'm wrong. Even if I'm ready for straightjackets and shock treatments? According to you I'm one crazy girl with a lunatic's opinion. How could I have put anything *in danger?*

Such arrogance. Such misplaced confidence. I should have seen it coming. The flair you gave your Builds. The ways you took liberties. It was like you thought you knew better than the Aether. I spoke to your father, but he said you were young, and that you'd grow to know your place. I should never have listened, because you are exactly like him. Always breaking rules when you think you know best. Always so cocksure. As with your father. As with your father's father.

What about him?

Eila had barely known her grandfather, and those memories were mostly mist.

Brampton looked up. Eila followed his gaze to a dragon-filled sky.

Now look what you've done, he said.

Eila looked over at the king. He shook his fist in anger, then turned it upside-down, thumb protruding from the bottom — the sign, in the old books, that the king was declaring a death sentence to the arena's condemned. She looked to the rear doors, where the beasts would be kept, and saw that they were already open.

The great dragons she'd so feared as a child had been released and were circling above, their breath curling with fire.

She began walking backward, away from the king and Rabbit Brampton's accusing eyes. Brampton had been in the arena's center with Eila. It was his death sentence too. It belonged to them all.

Eila pressed into something as she backpedaled, and found a hand on her arm. She looked up before she could scream and saw Mother standing in her way. *Another* person in the arena. *Another* sacrifice for the king's dragons. Eila glanced up as they started to dive, swooping lower and lower. This was where the crowd would be cheering, knowing how the dragons liked to rouse the crowd with a show before coming in for the kill.

It's okay, said Juliette.

Eila tried clinging to her mother, but instead of hugging her close, Juliette gave her a shove. A strange emotion flitted through her mind. Was it okay, or wasn't it? Did Mother want Eila with her, or did she want her gone? Was she greeting the prodigal daughter or casting her out?

Again she approached Juliette, but again she pushed Eila away. This time the shove was hard enough to tangle Eila's feet beneath her. She fell to the dirt, looking up, aghast.

You are here by grace. By Providence, she said. *You must appreciate the life you have, because the worst trap is one you refuse to acknowledge.*

Eila stood. This time, Juliette was the one who came forward. She shoved again. Eila barely held her footing.

What do you want from me? Eila said. Behind them, a dragon swooped just inches from Brampton, knocking his top hat to the dirt. He stood frozen, arms crossed, accusing eyes boring into Eila.

Acknowledge the trap, said Juliette.

Eila turned. The door to the outside was closed.

I acknowledge that I'm trapped in this arena!

Mother shook her head slowly, disappointed. Eila's answer was wrong.

What do you want me to … ?

But before she could finish, another dragon dove low enough to snatch Juliette around the waist. Panicking, Eila turned and ran, her heart thumping a murderous rhythm. She glanced up just a moment later, but already the dragon that had taken her mother was gone.

You always think you know best! yelled Brampton. *Only looking for the way out for yourself — running before looking after your own mother! Always seeking what's best for you! What's …*

A line of flame shot down from the sky, charring the dirt and striking Brampton mid-shout, setting him aflame.

Eila ran to the door as more dragons began to swoop and dive. She hammered against it, then hammered harder. There was no latch. No way out.

The door vanished under Eila's banging fist, and then suddenly there was.

She ran. Out into the world, away from the king and the dragons. Heedless of whether Brampton burned to death or not. He was done for. Eila could only save herself.

But Brampton, now fully aflame, hadn't yet said his piece. As she darted through the arena door and into the surrounding field with a dragon behind her, bearing down behind her with its spark churning, he continued to shout from her rear.

Who are you to say what is right? he bellowed as the dragon cleared its throat, its massive leathery wings pushing waves through the air toward her. *Who are you to say what is real and what is not? Real is real, Miss Doyle! Real is …*

" … real!"

The hand on Eila's arm was shaking her so hard that at first she thought the ground had come unseated from the world's spindle. She jolted out of the dream in an instant, heart still thudding with thunder, breath rapid and shallow, eyes snapping open in sudden, unexplainable fear.

"It's real, Eila! Wake up! They're swearing it!"

The treehouse dragged Eila into reality.

It was only a dream. And with morning sun already streaming through the cracks between boards, the terrifying imagery was breaking apart like tissue in water. Within ten seconds, her fears of the dragon were already starting to feel foolish. Even the memory of her mother being carried away, though haunting, was slipping away.

"Crown, Cora! You scared me to death! What's the matter with you?"

"You have to see, Eila! You have to come and see!" The door was open behind her. She'd obviously peeked out, probably to get them something to eat or drink, while Eila was still sleeping. Something shake-worthy had grabbed her attention.

Eila looked around the treehouse, still fighting sleep's stickiest webs. She remembered the comforting wake-up that had always come with her Crumble: the feeling of opening her eyes to a world without conflict, because the waking world was the only one she'd known. Waking to a day without Crumble — especially suddenly — was jarring by comparison. Her brain was one place in one moment, then thrust into another the next. It felt like jumping from a springboard into a freezing cold pond.

"See what?"

"You have to come to my house. You have to see the broadcast. Hurry, Eila!"

"I can't go to your house." She shook her head, wondering how Cora could be so obtuse. "How could I *possibly* go to your house?"

Cora made a shooing motion, presumably meant to indicate that what they'd discussed the prior night no longer mattered. So what if Eila had mouthed off at the Ministry? So what if she had delusions about an underground world? Those were girlish flights of fancy compared to whatever pressed her now.

"Just come! Nobody will stop you. Not now, they won't!"

"What's so important, Cora? Just tell me! What's so special and amazing that I can just run home in spite of everything and … "

With a heavy sigh and a roll of her eyes, Cora thrust a newspaper at Eila. Eila had known Cora long enough to understand both the sound and gesture. Cora had wanted a proper dramatic reveal and resented having to come out and say what was on her mind — or, apparently, to show her the newspaper version — but as usual, Eila's obstinance was drowning their fun.

She gave Eila a moment to look at the front page, read the headline, and absorb the photograph. Her eyes flicked up to see Cora still kneeling in the threshold, door open, hand out, beckoning.

"I thought it was a joke or a scam, but it's real. It's on all of the broadcast channels. You should see the store where I got the paper. We have to go, Eila. Now! Come on!"

Eila looked back down at the paper, sure she'd seen the wrong things in the plain-as-day photograph, or read the headline incorrectly.

The photo had been taken from above, probably from a balloon or a news dirigible. It showed an enormous dark form in a field at the end of a long furrow, as if it had crashed with tremendous speed and force.

The headline read, *SUPPOSED "DRAGON" SHOT DOWN OUTSIDE WALDRON'S GATE.*

Chapter Twenty-Two

Food. Fuel. Safety.

Eila ran behind Cora, their hard-soled shoes clacking on cobblestones.

The orchard was on the city's outskirts, on the side blessedly farther from the Fog, on Cora's grandmother's property. Getting to the treehouse without her parents' vehicle would have required Eila to ride two different streetcars with a large armful of bedding. That had seemed a humorous image last night, but now nothing was funny.

The small country town was alive with too much activity for a weekday morning. Merchants seemed to be guarding their stands more than tending them, waving short-barreled derringers and ancient muskets at customers feverishly grabbing for supplies. Tension was high, and Eila wondered what might happen in an altercation — if the grabbing and running at the stands would turn to looting and chaos. Firearms were common in the outskirts but were family heirlooms or meant for hunting. If shooting began, those who pulled the triggers would find their fingers blown off, or targets would splatter to paste in front of the large-bore antiques.

Cora was sprinting for the streetcar, her dress swishing. Eila fought her fleeing sense of reality. The last time she'd truly seen Cora run, they'd been so much younger. Now she was making haste in a corset.

"Hurry, Eila!"

Eila didn't move. "You wanted me to see the broadcast."

She had slowed in front of a Tinker's window. One of the items on display was a modified viewbox, showing choppy video of the downed dragon. It was a dull green, its head bent almost beneath it from the impact. One wing was folded and seemed broken. The other was wide, as if spread for takeoff. It sent a chill down Eila's spine. There was no question. It was the dragon that had taken her mother.

The land around the beast was singed black, as if it had gone down trying to kill as many of its murderers as it could before impact. A huge swatch of forest, emerging from the Fog on one side and extending into it on the other, was aflame. Eila couldn't see the fire's extent; it sprawled past the screen and the camera's span. She wanted to wait until the shot pulled back farther, but it was back fairly far already. How many square miles of wood had been swallowed by flame? Tongues of fire were jutting impossibly far skyward. How would they ever put it out without igniting the zeppelins? Would they co-opt shaws to deliver water? What about the Fog? Eila could tell that the fire extended into it, but how far? And how could *that* be extinguished? It was impossible; the Fog would burn until it was done — the only way, in Eila's mind, to make the wall of horrors more terrifying. More *personal.*

Cora grabbed her arm and tugged, still pulling Eila toward the trolley stop. "We can see the broadcast from my house! Come on!"

Three men rushed past them, knocking Cora's arm away from Eila. They were carrying a small horde of supplies, their eyes darting around. Eila felt the brush of metal as they scraped by and realized that she'd been rubbed with the dull edge of a wheat-cutting blade clasped amid the wares. If the man had happened to be holding it the other way, she'd have been sliced to the bone.

"I want to see this."

"We're going to be trampled, Eila!"

Eila's eyes stayed glued to the screen. Words appeared at the bottom: *ARTILLERY STRUCK "LUCKY SHOT" ACCORDING TO REPORTS.*

"Eila!" The hand was back, pulling. Shouting erupted across the square. A cart filled with green apples crashed to the stones, and both girls turned to watch them spill. Shame vanished with the rolling apples, and panicked people rushed forward, grabbing what they could and shoving for more.

Cora pulled again, and Eila felt herself toddling behind her. They were rolling along on the trolley before she could think. The car was mostly empty. The crowds in the rural square, it seemed, didn't want to go into the city toward the Fog, and the dragon.

But as Eila's mind began to process, she realized that the city's center was where *she*, for one, very much needed to go. She could switch to another trolley there and head to the Doer district — the only place where she might find answers.

Cora exhaled, trying to make herself comfortable and failing. The car's rocking made her shake and bounce on the bench.

"It's okay," said Cora. "We'll be home soon."

"It's not," said Eila.

It was the kind of thing Daw would say. Eila could Dream and Build, but she'd lost control last night and now nothing was okay at all. She hadn't just manifested an ordinary catastrophe. She hadn't made a zeppelin crash or caused a sinkhole to form. She'd drawn something from the Fog into Alterra's heart — something that shouldn't exist, and that nobody would understand. Somehow, artillery had brought the dragon down, but the damage had already been done. Everyone knew what dragons were, but they were superstitious legends and folk tales. They weren't supposed to be real.

"This changes everything, Cora."

"We just have to get home." Cora was breathing shallow, her eyes wide.

Eila looked over and considered saying more, but there wasn't a point. Cora's knuckles were white as she grasped the trolley bar. She stared straight forward and down, seemingly through the floor boards, watching the street pass and thinking of home. It didn't matter that going home would solve nothing, and it didn't matter that the actual threat from the Fog was almost surely over. What the dragon had begun, the citizens would perpetuate. When chaos erupted, people fought and looted over resources as if they were suddenly sparse. And when the world inverted, home seemed the safest place to go — except for Eila, who had another destination in mind.

They rode in stillness. There were a few other people in the car, as vacant-looking as Cora. No work would get done today, or tomorrow. If farmers tended fields, they'd do it only to occupy their minds. If they fed their animals, they'd keep their eyes on the sky

— waiting for it to fall as if it were rock, as if they were trapped in a collapsing cave.

"What do you think it was, Eila?"

Cora spoke from the blue, venting the most useless possible question. It couldn't be plainer what "it" was, on the broadcast screens. *It was a dragon.* Cora just didn't want to believe.

"I don't know, Cora." She knew plenty, but didn't want Cora to snap. She knew where it had come from, too, and that there were more horrors waiting at Alterra's border.

"It can't be a … what they say. It must be an experiment. Something Stensue is working on for air defense." She breathed deeper, her head starting to nod. "It must be clockwork, right? They can do such things?"

"I don't know."

"At the Ministry," she said — a statement apparently supposed to make sense on its own. "You could do that. At the Ministry."

"Do what, Cora?"

"You could make a clockwork … something like that. Right?"

Eila didn't know. Certainly no Builder could Build a clockwork dragon, but they could Build it in pieces for later assembly. There were even rumors of a secret government project, for which all in Enigma had likely Built pieces. It was referred to as "The Implement," but this wasn't it. This beast, ironically, Eila had Built on her own.

"Sure."

"That must be it. It got out. There was a pilot that escaped from the wreckage before anyone saw him. Or perhaps he was thrown clear when it crashed, or was killed in the fire."

Eila said nothing, thinking of the burning trees she'd seen on the broadcast, of the way the fire's scourge had extended into the Fog itself. She didn't want to indulge self-deceptive fantasies. She'd remain mute until Cora demanded more.

They got off the trolley and stepped into chaos.

The rural market had been busy with frenzy and panic, but the city was the Pit itself. The close proximity of people had turned them to fighting for supplies, as if a few gallons of fuel or loaves of bread would protect them from dragons tomorrow — as if more demons were descending upon them right now. Part of Eila's mind had gone curiously still on the trolley ride over, and that part wondered at the behavior. In a way, it made sense: when confronted with something they didn't understand, people clung to what they knew.

Food. Fuel. Safety.

The day had grown overcast, and there was a strange pall over the city's central trolley switching station and the surrounding buildings. It was as if night had fallen early, and people were darting around through daytime shadows, their fists full of whatever they could find. Plenty had goods; some had weapons. Everyone's eyes were wide, and most were running. Mothers scuttled behind children, pushing them from behind or dragging them by the hands.

Cora looked around, her eyes like saucers. She'd been cool and collected back in the orchard and had had the strong hand when Eila was hypnotized by the beast and flaming forest on the viewbox, but she'd used up all she had. She looked exhausted and terrified. Eila could sympathize. Neither had ever seen something this bad in their lives, and only Eila had had the practice of seeing worse in dreams. *And*, her mind insisted, *in training*.

"Why are they doing this?" Cora blurted. "Do you think there was another dragon here?" She looked up. "Do you think there are a lot of them? Has someone come to take us over? To burn Alterra down?"

"Come on, Cora. There's the trolley to Rowley Row. If we hurry, we can catch it. I don't want to wait here for the next one." There was a conversation in screams somewhere behind them.

"What if there *are* more? Oh, Eila, I'd assumed that was the only one! What if it's not clockwork? What if it's a real dragon? What if the legends and stories were all just …" Cora didn't finish the sentence, scooting back on her seat instead, trying to hide as if the trolley's roof would protect her.

Eila's eyes kept flicking up. The others would run and scream, but she might be able to help. She'd abandoned Cora too many times and would never do it again. Cora first, Eila and the rest of the world second.

She reached in, grabbed Cora's hand, and pulled hard.

Cora yanked her hand away. "No. I'm not going out there. Look at these people!"

She didn't need to look. Eila could feel them shoving past her as she stood just off the trolley from the rural district with her hands reaching in for Cora; she could hear them shouting; she'd heard a small bang a few seconds earlier and knew that someone was shooting or that an incendiary had blown. There was a reddish glow toward the station's edge that Eila thought might be fire. Because *that* made sense. Dragons are real, and dragons might kill them all, so the logical thing was to burn what others had.

"Cora! *There is no time!*"

As if adding an exclamation to her sentence, there was a squeal as the Rowley Row trolley across the lot inched forward. Eila shouted for it to wait, but the driver, at the far end, wouldn't hear her in the tumult.

"Why are they doing this, Eila?"

"Because they don't know what else to do, Cora. Something bad happened in a place where nothing bad happens, and they don't know how to handle it, so they're doing stupid, pointless, destructive things like resisting and hiding in a trolley while their friends are trying to save their lives. Now move!"

This time, she wasn't gentle. Eila planted a foot against the trolley's edge step and pushed after she'd again gotten hold of Cora's arm. She didn't care if she dislocated her shoulder or pulled Cora's entire arm off. She'd knock her out and drag her over if she had to.

Eila was thin, but Cora was thinner. She wasn't prepared for the pull and came unseated, stumbling out and barely keeping her feet. She wasn't prepared for the car's edge and took it at a shambling run, landing awkwardly and coming to one knee.

Cora stood, her skin scraped and bloody. She looked up at Eila, shocked. "You … you …"

"Yes, and I'll do it again. Now go!"

Half shoving and half dragging, she steered Cora past a group of arguing men with machetes, dodging spilled goods and the shambles of a popcorn cart that seemed to have met its end some time ago. The trolley hadn't moved farther, and as they closed the distance Eila could see why. A line of people — orderly, not rioting for a pleasant change — had formed in front of a bakery not unlike her childhood favorite on Drury Lane. The line was blocking the tracks. The city was about to erupt into anarchy, and they were queuing up to buy fine baked goods.

The driver was shouting at the line. These men and women were the opposite of those who were shouting, running, and looting. They appeared impatient, tapping their collective feet as if the bakery's clerks were simply taking too long. It was another group of people doing what they knew, heads in the sand, pretending all was well.

A big man with a broad back — apparently a clear-headed trolley rider — was shooing the line away as the girls reached the car. Eila motioned for Cora to get in first, then watched the broad-backed man re-board with a nod of thanks from the driver. Cora sat, then looked down to see Eila still standing on the street below the step.

"Come on," she said. The words were meek, almost helpless.

"I'm not going with you, Cora."

"What do you mean? You have to come!"

"I have something to do. You'll be fine."

Cora started to stand. "Then I'm coming with you."

Eila felt something inside her snap. She was trying to do right by Cora, but could feel precious seconds ticking away. Terror and confusion was rolling across Alterra and would surely continue to do so. The Fog burned with dragonfire. The Guile surely waited, Daw with his hand on the switch of a machine, whether Eila was ready or not.

"No you're *not!*"

"You have to stay with me, Eila!" Cora was pleading, eyes wetting. She looked like a little child. Hating herself, Eila found herself wondering if they'd grown too far apart to fit. Why did she have to be the responsible one? Why did she have to do all the saving?

But last night, Cora had saved *her*. Last night, Cora had been *Eila's* rock.

Her frustration dulled, less of a yoke to bear and more of a problem to solve.

"I'll see her home, Miss," said a deep male voice.

Eila looked past Cora to see the man who'd cleared the line in front of the trolley standing behind her.

"I swear, Miss." He fumbled in his pocket, then drew a battered wallet from inside. He opened it to the center and showed her a well-worn photo of himself with four children: three girls and a boy. Just like her own family, in the home she used to have. "You can count on Edgar. I got a family of my own. On Bourgeon Place. Number fifteen, if ya wanna come visit for tea."

Eila looked from the man to Cora, from Cora to the man. The trolley was inching forward, and Cora still had Eila by the wrist. The driver was supposed to check his mirrors before moving, but urgency had rushed his protocol. Her options were drying up, but something in the man's big face — along with the way he'd gently cleared the line so everyone on the car could go home — urged her to trust him.

"Rowley Row," Eila said. "Two stops before yours at Bourgeon."

"Sure thing, Miss." He looked at Cora. "I'll keep ya company. What's your name?"

When Cora said nothing, Eila, now pacing the car as it shoved through a new crowd, answered for her. "Cora." Looking around at the chaos, she added, "Keep her safe. Swear it."

Edgar chuckled and held out an arm, big as a ham. "Sure thing. I swear it on The Crown."

Cora's eyes pleaded with Eila to come, but Edgar placed one of his big hands around Cora's wrist and pulled them apart. The gesture was gentle, fatherly. Cora let it happen, but her eyes still held Eila until the crowd swallowed the car.

With the car departed, Eila found a talkbox and called Cora's home, then told her father that Cora would be arriving by trolley and that he should meet her at the stop. She'd be with a big man named Edgar. A big man Eila hoped she could trust — a commodity that, like fuel and bread, was about to be in short supply.

Before she hung up, Jerome asked her if it was true — what Atwell had said about Eila leaving the Ministry. He asked if she was okay. He'd heard she'd run off, and her parents were worried.

Eila didn't answer. She stuffed down the strange mishmash of emotion threatening to bubble up inside her, disconnected, and turned to board the trolley to the Doer district.

She had all the conflicting emotions she could handle without considering any of that.

Chapter Twenty-Three
Into the Tunnel's Mouth

EILA ARRIVED AT DAW'S DOOR to find him finishing her thought almost before she had it.

"I—"

"Lost control? Gave the world a beast that shouldn't, by any rights, exist, thus inciting panic? Caused a commotion at the top-side Ministry? Yes, I know. Genevieve told me most of it, and Levi covered the rest. Oh, you've created quite a challenge for both worlds today, Miss Doyle. I would barely need my conduit or dream-swimmer to tell me a thing. You can practically read the truth in the thick black smoke coming off the Blunderbuss as it processes the 'daymares' from millions of topsiders."

Eila looked at Daw for a long moment, then spun on her heel and trudged back up the walkway toward the street.

"Running away?" Daw called after her. "Misunderstood and put-upon, are we? Have some dignity, little girl. You won't leave for good, so don't make me call you back because you're proud. And don't make me close the door, leaving you to pout until you realize that coming inside is all you can do."

Eila took another few steps before stopping, then a few furious breaths before peeking back over her shoulder. She wanted to run and rant and rage, but deep down, her logical part knew Daw was right. She had to be here; there was nowhere else to go. Eila could allow Daw to berate her now for her lack of control, or huff, waste time, then come slinking back later when the damage might be worse.

Still, she looked at Daw's long, tall figure in the doorframe and felt she had to say *something* to claim what little dignity she still had. Her first thought was to insult him — to say, for instance, that he dressed like a circus ringmaster — but her second choice was more reserved.

She came closer. "You need me."

"Yes." Daw stepped aside, making room for Eila as he held the door. "So hurry inside."

Eila watched him, irritated that he wanted no quarrel. She'd go along and do as he said, but she'd been his doormat for weeks and wanted to fight.

Daw closed the door and turned in the foyer rather than leading her downstairs, disarming Eila with a kind hand on her shoulder. Anger drained as she looked up at Daw's mustache, big as ever, curled into that preposterous loop at the end. Somehow, his gaze had grown familiar. Perhaps welcome.

"This has been hard," he said.

She still felt defensive. "It's no picnic for me, either."

"I *meant* for you. But you're not yet seeing the full picture. Things have accelerated due to … to today's events. That's unfortunate, but maybe you will still come to understand. I can only hope your training has been enough. Come."

Daw turned, leading Eila into the Guile's basement lair. She wanted to comment on her so-called training and just how effective *she* thought it had been, but Daw's departing back gave her no time. The weeks had been more than *difficult*; they'd been utter *failures*. Not a single lesson could help Eila now. Beyond differentiating a troll from a hairy man and a fairy from a scene of her family, she hadn't managed to get a single trial right. Most of the time, she could see no difference between the "real" item in the pairing and the one that was fantasy. She'd guessed without thought a few times, just to see what happened when she chose truth at random. But thus far, she had answered wrong *every time,* as if cursed.

Eila arrived in the Guile lair and saw them all at work. Finnegan was making notes on paper, using the strange Guile language. Genevieve was sitting in a corner with her eyes closed, possibly doing whatever she did as a conduit. Willoughby, a small brown hat perched on his head, was helping Walker strap an odd contraption onto his back. Levi was standing beside them, shrugging on a jacket. In the moment before the jacket settled, she saw a flash of metal on his back, indicating he was wearing something similar. Phoebe and Savannah were poring over scrolls of paper, muttering at Walker. Every few seconds, he'd make a snappy comment back, usually employing one of his unwelcome nicknames. Savannah was "Blondie." Phoebe, dressed in black and looking even more dour and nightmarish than usual, was "Sunshine."

Eila stopped, leaving Daw to march toward the back room and the Tinkered Blunderbuss clone.

"What is this?" she asked. "What's going on?"

Walker turned, long blond hair brushing his brown leather jacket.

"Well, look who came back! You gonna ride the lightning for us, Tinkerbell?"

Levi sat on a wooden chair and began lacing up a set of tall black boots. She'd never seen them worn, though she'd noticed them outside the closet door that led to the tunnels. Walker was already wearing a pair. Both had their pants tucked into the boots, as if anticipating a wade through deep water.

"What are you doing?" she asked. "What are those things on your backs? Are you going somewhere?"

Levi nodded and gave Eila a tired smile. "Yes. We'll head out shortly."

"Where?"

He tipped his head toward the tunnels.

"You're going exploring? *Now?*"

"Not exploring, Tink," Walker said. "Goin' to battle."

"Not battle," said Levi.

"Yes, *battle*." Walker looked at Levi before turning to Eila. "Ain't no Sunday stroll. You think we're gonna find anything up there doesn't wanna tussle, maybe you should have Willoughby unstrap you. Leave your machete and blades, and your impeller. Take a handful of daisies instead."

Eila didn't know where to start asking questions. Her heart thumped, but she wasn't sure why. They hadn't said *she* was going, after all. "Impeller?"

Willoughby didn't look up from adjusting something under the edge of Walker's coat as he answered. "It's a projectile weapon I designed. Works through the movement of water. Like pneumatics, but … ”

"Just say it's a weapon." Walker rolled his eyes.

"What do you need weapons for?"

"Battle." This time, Walker rolled his eyes right at Eila.

Savannah came over and, as if offering support, lightly clasped Eila's arm. "They're going topside."

"Through the tunnels? But I thought you didn't know where they came out?"

"Sorta," said Walker. "Do we have a good reason to believe we know exactly where some of them go and where they surface? Yeah, we do. But have we ever gone half that far ourselves?" He grabbed an apple from the table, took a bite, then spoke with his mouth full of pulp. "Not a chance."

"Why?"

"Something with the air," said Levi. "It's poisoned somehow. Willoughby has breathers, but it's … I don't know how to explain it. It's more than that."

"They're haunted," Walker said around a mouthful of apple, as casually and helpfully as most people would say, "Turn left."

"Not haunted," said Levi.

"They move and change," said Walker. "See those maps the girls are pretending to understand?" He jerked his chin toward them. "Might as well be doodles. I drew a few myself, even taking one of Willoughby's trackers to be sure I got it right. Went as far as I could, until I started seeing lights in the dark ahead. That's when this big brave man decided he'd had enough and ran chicken. Retraced my steps, using my spankin' new map. But it wasn't the same on the way back. I got lost."

"You took a wrong turn," said Savannah, smoothing the maps.

"Wasn't no simple wrong turn, Blondie!" he snapped. His eyes met Eila's, and she felt a strange sense of kinship. Walker was maybe twice her age, but there was no mistaking the way he was addressing her as an equal. Softer, he said, "Took me a day to get out. They were practically making my tombstone when I got back. Hungry. Thirsty. There are normally springs inside, either cut by whoever made the tunnels or natural, from the ground. We have 'em mapped, too. But the springs were gone from where they should've been. Almost as if the tunnels were trying to teach me a lesson: don't come in here unless we *want* you inside, or else you'll never leave."

"And you're going in? Now?" Eila was shocked. She'd always figured the tunnels factored into the Guile's larger plans, but after hearing Walker's story, the Convenience staircase seemed so much wiser.

Levi nodded. "Something has changed. Since this morning, when … you know."

"What changed?"

Walker again nodded toward the tunnel entrance. "Now it *wants* us inside."

Daw might have been behind Eila the entire time, but only now, as he came around to sit at the map table, did she remember he was there. "You've forced our hand, I'm afraid. I won't bore you with details, but the instruments I use to monitor what you call the Aether — as well as some measurements of a medium above it that I call the 'true Aether' — have indicated a … a substantial shift in polarity. Meaning there now *is* polarity."

"Polarity…" Eila couldn't grasp the idea at the edge of her mind.

Phoebe said, "You would call it 'Pianoforte.' It's when everything in the dreamscape seems to line up, as if everyone is thinking the same thing. Like they're all preoccupied. Synced somehow. We see it down on the Dreamers' end of the engine, just like you do."

"Is it … " Eila began. She made a pained face, thinking of her earlier questions about Dreamers' experience of Pianoforte.

"We're used to it," said Phoebe.

Eila watched her, feeling like she should apologize on behalf of all of Alterra. But Daw's interruption erased the awkward moment.

He said, "As far as we can tell, the tunnels respond to that resonance, same as the dream engine. If there's a time to go through them, Pianoforte is probably it. We have little tunnel-crawling machines in there. They report back when there's no interference, which tells us a tunnel has opened. A big one. Sometimes they go right, and sometimes left. I have a theory: If we followed those tunnels, I think they would take us to something the tunnels themselves want us to see. Or perhaps it's the Blunderbuss that wants it. But we never know when a Pianoforte will end, and—"

“So why are you going now?” Eila was still watching Levi and Walker dressing for battle. She’d noticed weapons sheaths inside both jackets, at their waists, and down each arm. There was gear to be taken, stacked in the corner. What were they planning to face? Eila’s heart galloped as if she were going along.

Walker said, “Now the tunnel’s so clear and wide, it’s practically a thruway. According to the crawlers, anyway.”

Something dawned on Eila. “You think it goes to the dragon.”

“It responds to Alterra’s resonant thought,” said Daw. “And right now, the dragon is what everyone is thinking about. It’s what everyone fears. And fear, Miss Doyle —” He paused to sigh in the room’s heavy air. “— isn’t something your people have much experience facing.”

Eila’s mind responded to the word *fear* as if Daw had pressed a button. She saw the burning field in her mind. The burning trees. The charred ground and the great dead beast at the end of the long crash furrow. There would be Parliament Guards tending to the dragon’s removal. The Fog itself was on fire, flames licking gray haze, churning like thick dyes slowly mixing in water.

“Don’t go,” she pled. “Stay. You said you weren’t ready. You said you needed time.” Eila felt her reversal as if it were physical. She’d called them cowards for their refusal to do what had to be done, and now she was holding them back.

“We wanted to take more time,” Levi said, “but we’re out of time. If we don’t go now … ”

Eila looked at Daw as Levi trailed off.

“The Blunderbuss, across town,” said the scientist, answering Eila’s unasked question, “is thick with blue-sky daydreams to blacken your soul. Do you know what true panic feels like?”

Eila nodded. She’d felt it the moment Cora had gone, safely in Edgar’s hands. Once she had no one to look after, her mind seemed to shake loose in an instant like a poorly bolted machine. She’d wanted to run and loot, to fight for bread and fuel. It had taken every ounce of strength in her still-unmuscled mind to get her on the trolley to the Doer district. It had taken all she had to keep putting one foot in front of the other. If she’d had her Crumble, she would have taken it to shutter the horror.

“Well, now imagine being a Dreamer and experiencing millions of people's panic at once. Dreamers can't process that kind of flood fast enough, but that's the kind of seething fright that's now topside. Thanks to Alterra's broadcasts, everyone with eyes and ears knows what happened. Something terrible — something that shouldn't exist — has appeared among them. It's as unseating a revelation as finding out that you live underground, with another world above you." He looked up, through the house, at Pavilion's rock sky. "It's a Pianoforte, but it's a forced one — thrust upon us all, rather than natural."

"I still don't see why—"

Daw cut her off. "Right now, it's daytime. But can you imagine what will happen once night falls?"

Again Eila looked at Walker and Levi. Her panic was returning, and she didn't know why.

"Dreams," she said.

"Dreams. *Nightmares.* Crumble is manufactured to suit Alterra as it exists, with its current mental needs. But as people go to sleep tonight — if they *can* sleep — they *will* dream because the drug will not be strong enough to release what stems from an imagination reawakened by terror. People will wonder at things they've taken for granted, like safety and their own conviction that 'legends' are just frivolous tales meant for storybooks. The Blunderbuss will be unable to keep up with what comes. Dreams will leak topside. Our Dreamers will filter all they can into the Fog, which will continue to thicken and grow. But the Dreamers will be overwhelmed too, and nightmares won't be sufficiently swept from the stream. What drains upward through the Blunderbuss will not be totally clean and will contain some dark impurities. Do you know what that would mean?"

A chill ran through Eila. "They'll be Built."

Daw nodded, then pointed to the tunnel's mouth.

"Given the current resonance," he said, "that tunnel should be straight and true. If the crawler reports are accurate, it'll be a mile or so, heading up at a gentle incline, through a tube as clear as a vehicle tunnel. But it will only grow larger if we wait. Straighter. Maybe *shorter*."

"Easier to reach the Fog when you are prepared," Eila said, shaking. "When you *are* finally ready."

"You don't understand, darlin'." Walker shook his head. "If we wait until people start dreaming and that tunnel gets any bigger, what's in the Fog will almost certainly come to us."

Chapter Twenty-Four

No Time for Blame or Pity

Eila nestled into the makeshift cradle on Willoughby's Tinkered Blunderbuss clone and felt the last emotion she would have expected: *relief.*

"Are you comfortable?" Willoughby asked, sitting on Daw's usual stool. Eila could see him from the corner of her eye, brown hat still perched atop his head. He had small spectacles, a petite black beard, and a trim little mustache. He was the only Pavilion Tinker she'd ever met, but he set the standard perfectly. If there was a definable look that accompanied a man who crafted impossible things with no help from an engine, Willoughby had it. It was a lie that Eila was the only person who could Dream and Build. Willoughby did the same thing, and left his evidence in the lair's every corner.

"Surprisingly, yes," said Eila.

"Surprisingly?"

"I should be afraid, shouldn't I?" she wondered aloud. "I should be nervous for Walker and Levi, going up the tunnel. I should be nervous for myself. I should feel guilty, maybe, about the dragon, and the way this is all my fault."

"It's not your fault. It's just that … "

"And I *am* afraid, I guess, but it's different. I feel like … I don't know."

"Like something fell apart, and you picked up a screwdriver?"

Eila sat up. "What's a screwdriver?"

A small smile creased the Tinker's lips. "Something fell apart. Something made a mess. But as long as you only stood around feeling bad, you were helpless. But the minute you pick up a … a *broom*, say … that feeling changes, even if the mess is still hopeless. Because you're no longer standing by fretting. Instead, you're doing what you can to fix it."

Eila nodded. She wouldn't have been able to articulate what Willoughby had just said, but he worked with his mind all day, every day. Despite training her entire life to be what Alterran society called a "mind worker," she was still new to the experience.

"Just do your best," he told her.

"Wield the broom as best I can."

"Something like that. Do you understand what you must do? Did Daw's training prepare you enough?"

Those were separate questions, and they had opposite answers. But Eila had no time for self-indulgent blame or pity, so she answered his first query. If the second was a problem, at least this would all end with a broom in her hand, doing what she could.

"You'll siphon off the Blunderbuss … whatever …"

"Its Aether feed. Yes. It's what powers this machine remotely."

" … and you'll give it to me in here, so I can part the way for Walker and Levi."

"Like in training." Willoughby nodded. "In one sense, everything up there is real, and will exist in front of them. But in another sense — the sense that amounts to you lying in a large tin can and imagining it all — *none* of it is real. I can broadcast from this machine, same as I can steal the Aether feed, but the outbound signal piggybacks on the waste discharge from the Blunderbuss. While it's busy dumping new horrors into the Fog to try and keep surface minds clean, you'll be able to spit out what we call 'corroborating corporeality.'"

Eila shook her head.

Willoughby chuckled. "Daw likes big words. It just means you can choose what to make *more real* for Walker and Levi, and what to make *less real.*"

It was too much information. She had trained, but not for this.

"So what do I do?"

"Dream them a path," Willoughby said. "In your shoes, that's the way I'd think about it."

Eila felt her eyes roll up, her brain processing.

She laid back, feeling the cradle's metal edges around her as she closed her eyes and the Build construct started taking shape in her mind.

"Are you ready?" Willoughby's voice was still coming from outside.

"Almost." She focused more and at the last minute decided to eschew her usual practice construct — the grassy meadow, where a Beaver Daw had once floated on a pink cloud — for the more familiar white warehouse she used at the Ministry. Then she settled in, and found herself strangely comfortable. Without the meadow or Daw's voice at the helm, her memories of failures felt lighter.

I can do this.

"Ready," she said.

"Starting feed."

Eila's eyes snapped open. She sat up. "Wait."

Willoughby looked over mildly, as if they had all the time in the world. Right now, if the crawlers' estimates of the tunnels' length were correct, Levi and Walker would be entering Eila's world for the first time. She should hurry, but was captivated by that image. She was down here, making pictures in her head. They were up there for real, waiting. Would they be looking up at the huge blue sky? Or would they be more bothered by the nearby dragon and the fire, ducking to stay far from the Parliament Guards tending to both?

"Yes?" he said.

"What if they get trapped?"

"Don't *let* them get trapped." He didn't say what came next, but Eila heard it just the same: *Whether or not they get trapped in the Fog is up to you.*

"But Daw wants them to go *through* the Fog, right?"

Willoughby nodded.

"What if there isn't a way? And how does getting through it solve the problem?"

"Whenever I ask, he says he's sure there's no solution inside the borders."

"But if there's nothing *beyond* the borders, or if the Fog is too thick … "

Willoughby gave Eila a helpless shrug. He could fake an answer, but it would only be more of the same. Sometimes, there was no pleasant response. When Daw first told Eila that she had to break her addiction to Crumble, she'd begged him to tell her that everything would be okay in the end. He'd refused her false assurances then, and Willoughby would offer none now.

She laid back down. Closed her eyes. Saw the construct.

"Ready?"

She breathed deeply, forcing herself to calm. Peace came surprisingly easy, given the situation's weight and her own responsibility. She'd spent years training her mind to Build, and the construct was as much her home — was as *real* — as any place she'd ever known.

"Ready."

"Just make a path," said Willoughby's voice. "That's all you need to do."

Another long, slow breath. "Okay."

The room began to darken, and Eila could see the first shadows of burning trees.

"Then let's begin."

Chapter Twenty-Five

Into the Fog

Eila looked down, unsurprised to find her feet bare, soles kissed by dark soil and rotted leaves. Ahead of her were two men, one wearing a brown leather jacket. The other was in black, an oily glint of metal appearing at his belt as he walked. That metal, as she'd seen it in life, cast a blinding reflection. But here in the Fog, the only reflection belonged to the fire. It was black, then red. Then nothing at all.

Eila was wearing a simple white nightdress — a token Daw had suggested seeing herself in after their first few sessions to remind herself that she was somewhere else, in a version of sleep. It wasn't quite like a dream due to the Aether feed's boosting energy, but it wasn't quite like a normal Build session either. When Eila worked the Blunderbuss, she saw the objects in her warehouse as if she was holding them with invisible hands. When she turned them over, shaped them, added her touches, and turned vague ideas into manifestations, it *felt* like she was holding them, and could rotate them this way and that. She could normally sense and feel parts of a Build object — but she could feel *everything* right now. It was an ultra-real dream, as if she were right behind Walker and Levi as they tromped through the woods. As if she herself had breached the Fog with them.

It's not real. None of it is real.

She wanted to curse Daw. Why hadn't he put her into any useful simulations to prepare her? Every training session had been comprised of two objects inside a safe construct, usually indistinguishable, frequently vague. Eila on the left versus Eila on the right, one thinking X while the other thought Y. How could she possibly tell, and why did it even matter? Couldn't she think one thing or the other equally? And, by facing two Eilas, wasn't she doing exactly that — proving *both* to be equally real … while at the same time knowing full well that *neither* was?

The world she found herself in now was entirely different. There weren't two simple objects; there was a *forest* of objects. Despite knowing the sun was out, the world around her was mostly dark. There was the fire, both off to one side and ahead. She had a moment of panic (what would happen if the fire ate them?), then forced herself to look down, see her nightdress, and remember where she truly was.

Eila looked ahead, at the mens' backs. She wanted them to turn so she could see their faces and feel them as close — to feel like *they* were *her* protectors, instead of the truth — but that line of thought was filled with folly. They wouldn't even see her because she wasn't actually there. She'd stayed behind, safe in Pavilion, while they risked their lives to clean up the mess she'd made of the world.

Without warning, a small creature, more hair and teeth than flesh or bone, ran from the brush to the right. It had enormous fangs and, as far as she could see, no eyes or legs. It was a mass, making for Walker's ankle. It dove up and sank two fangs into the man's calf, which spurted blood.

"Get it!" Walker shouted. "Get it off me!"

He fumbled for something in his coat, but the thing's bite had surprised him into dropping his blade. Levi had a knife, but as he turned toward Walker and the creature, he seemed to forget it. Walker kicked out with his foot, trying to knock it away.

Eila's heart doubled its beat.

She'd thought they were standing in a clearing, but now she realized that something in her mind had been holding the Fog at bay until just now. As she watched Walker thrash and watched Levi kick out at the thing, the clearing seemed to be shrinking. The Fog's borders were closer on all sides. A moment ago, Eila had been able to see the outside world — the open sky of Alterra, where they'd entered — behind her. It had been her only anchor point, the only way she could tell where to go. Now that glimpse of sun and green grass was being eclipsed, like an iris narrowing to a point. The air wrinkled into darkness as the crackling snap of fire closed in around them.

"Eila!" Walker yelled. "You here, girl? You payin' attention?"

She still heard the fire, but the popping grew thinner.

Make them a path.

It wasn't about what was real and what wasn't. It was about what Eila chose to give reality and what she chose to steal reality from. Everything in the Fog was there because someone had dreamed it, before being discarded by Dreamers. Everything around Eila existed because someone had believed in it first.

It was her decision whether she, as a Builder, believed in it too.

She pushed. The feeling was distinct, like shoving against a stubborn door. She saw the creature of hair and fur as if it was in front of her, in her Builder's hands, being turned over and weighed. It was an unworthy discard. Builders at the Ministry didn't discard; they Built whatever they were given. But Eila was a Dreamer, too.

She could decide, and did.

The clearing widened. The thing on Walker's leg didn't vanish, but it did stop moving. It remained on his leg, its fangs impaling him — but now, rather than being attacked, it was as if he'd tripped and fallen on something inert, like a sharp garden rake.

He looked down, seemingly mystified, then shook his leg. The thing dislodged and fell to the leaves, its magnified mouth like a spider's open to enormous fangs. Walker raised his wounded leg and stepped on it hard, eliciting a satisfying crack. He retrieved his machete and swung it down on the creature, cracking the air as he split it in two. Rather than spilling blood, green fluid gushed like a bug's guts.

Walker looked at Levi, both of them frozen. He glanced over his shoulder, toward Eila. He never quite saw her but he moved his head around, as if searching.

"Thanks?" he said.

Levi looked at Walker. "Was that her? Did she do that?"

"Either that, or this thing just got bored." Walker kicked half of the creature away, as if telling its right and left sides to break it up and go to their separate corners.

"Can you walk?" Levi looked at the wound.

Walker tried a step, then another. There was a slight hitch to his gait. "I'll live."

Levi looked back, directly through Eila. He consulted something on his wrist (probably some sort of compass, knowing Willoughby), then looked forward with an expression like regret. Eila could feel the same thing inside herself. She'd have to follow them. And although that particular monster had gone after Walker, she felt sure similar things would pursue her in time. This was a nightmare, after all, and everything in here would be looking to her as the Dreamer, eager for her belief to make them stronger.

All at once, Eila felt the enormity of what lay before them. The focus required to push the Fog away was immense. As they went deeper, she'd surely lose some of her concentration. She'd want to sleep, then believe what her senses insisted were true.

Levi began to move. Walker followed a step behind and to his side, a slight limp in his stride.

Eila slowly followed, suddenly aware that the men in front of her had spent a lifetime amongst their own dreams. They'd never been topside or into the Fog, but each day they'd confronted worries and mental fragmentation that Eila, until recently, never had. Each night, Walker and Levi faced their fears. At first, when Daw had talked to Eila about nightmares, she'd thought they sounded like a cruel joke. Even now, today, as she fought her Crumble, it seemed impossible to believe that nightmares could be natural. Why would a healthy person's mind betray them in such a horrible way?

Looking around, trying to cast her cone of negative belief, she felt hideously unprepared. Walker and Levi seemed frightened, but they were still going forward, each armed both on the outsides of their bodies and in their own heads. *They* hadn't had to be strapped to an engine to train their weak minds. *They* hadn't failed their training, over and over and over.

Eila turned. She could still see the green spot behind her. Out there somewhere (hidden, she hoped) was the tunnel's open mouth and her safe world, where bad things were kept away. Out there was the family she'd abandoned. Out there was sun and sky. And the dragon.

An invisible hand seemed to be keeping her head turned toward the way in — now the only way out — and away from those she was supposed to protect. In the sun, visible through an eye-shaped ellipse in the mist, she could see one of the Parliament Guards on patrol. The Guard was standing at the Fog's edge, facing it, peering in, as she had once done at her mother's side. Perhaps the Guard, taking a break from trying to solve the dragon's puzzle, was contemplating the Fog as she had. Perhaps he was seeing the walls of his prison to know the nature of his trap.

Eila.

She could almost hear the Guard calling to her. It was the siren song of the outside world. The *safe* world. She'd stepped away from Crumble's sanity and had allowed the demons to advance. She thought, *Just look where giving up Crumble has gotten me.* She had wanted to warn the Guard to stay away, forgetting that her true body was still underground.

Eila.

Behind her somewhere, Walker yelled again, his voice concerned. "Eila?"

She blinked. Her dream head turned, followed by her dream eyes. She needed to feel the world as fact to sift it, not unlike a Dreamer working the Blunderbuss. But she didn't want to. She wanted to go home, into the outside world. She wanted to sleep, and dream a dreamless sleep.

Something slapped her, waking her from self-pity. She wasn't here, so nothing could hurt her — but those terrible things *could* hurt her if she kept losing her focus. And more than anything, they could hurt the men she was supposed to be protecting.

She took one final look at the Guard beyond the Fog's border. He was wearing a suit, rather than a Guard's uniform. Probably not a Guard, then. It was a reporter, interested in mysteries. Curious about the dragon's true nature, perhaps wondering if it had come from the Fog … and, therefore, if more lived inside.

What would it mean if the broadcasts shared *that* theory? Alterra was panicking right now due to a single beast. What would the country do if they learned that all of their fears, in all of their forms, were waiting in the haunted woods?

As Eila turned, the Guard/reporter set down a bag he'd been carrying and raised his empty hand, palm forward, as if beckoning her.

Closing her dream eyes, she turned away. It was too much. She wouldn't be tempted. She had a job to do.

She scampered to catch up with Levi and Walker, quickly closing the distance. As she found their twin backs, still moving slowly, the air cleared around them. In the brush ahead, something scampered back. It half purred, half hissed, angry at being denied its chance to strike.

The men looked back briefly at her arrival, then looked forward again.

They continued on, the Fog's opacity eclipsing everything. The sun's oval vanished behind them. Eila felt vertigo and had to keep her eyes forward lest her dream feet stumble. There was no way to see forward because there was no way to see the path out. Every direction promised a misty darkness outside of the slightly clearer area she kept open around them. The clear air was somehow illuminated, but beyond it were indistinct shadows. Trees had become arms with broken fingers. There seemed to be great holes in the dirt at the circle's edges. Between them were smaller holes in clusters like lotus blossoms in the soil, each hole the size of her fist. What lived in them? As she wondered, the Fog tried to show her. It took her interest as belief, and tried to push the circle tighter around them.

I shouldn't wonder about the things in here because they're not real. And if I make *them real, we'll pay.*

But they *were* real, weren't they? Her logical brain — the part that had been trained by a father who worked the Ministry's Enigma Floor, where creations were mathematical and precise — kept on insisting they were. That was one of the reasons she kept failing Daw's tests. She was supposed to decide what was real and what wasn't, but hadn't Daw himself explained that Dreamers sorted garbage from nightmares — and that those nightmares became real in the Fog?

How could she make an artificial distinction about that reality? It was what it was, and her opinion would change nothing.

She imagined her father's response. To him, even the most frustrating, most devastating, and most frightening things could be deciphered through logic. Even her mother's occasional emotional meltdowns, when something inside her mounted and spilled over behind carefully closed doors, could be practically explained by

Atwell.

She thought of what Cora's father had said on the talkbox. *Had Eila really left the Ministry?* Atwell had told him that. Her father knew, of course. He *knew* she'd lied, just as she'd known he would.

Father wouldn't be angry; that was almost the worst thing. He wouldn't blame Eila. He'd feel bad for her, then try to figure out where she'd gone wrong. Even if he only *suspected* she'd been neglecting the drug that everyone in Alterra knew kept them sane, he'd investigate rather than confronting her. He'd only face Eila with indisputable facts once his evidence was in order, and impossible to refute. He wasn't easy to argue with, and harder to fool. Eila thought back to that night in the study after she'd freaked out at dinner. Father had known she'd ruined the Pianoforte even before Brampton.

In front of her, Walker stopped, then almost fell over. It took Levi a second to see why, and took Eila another second after that. She felt cold, her limbs paralyzed. There was something ahead, pitch black, its shape darker than the rest of the shadows. Whatever was in front of them was standing on two feet, its height easily twice that of Walker. Eila could only see its outline; the creature seemed to be made of blackness itself. It had broad shoulders and feet long enough and high enough to look like backward-bending knees. She could make out two red eyes that, at first blush, seemed more like large round insects hovering far above. The behemoth was watching, unconcerned, and in no hurry.

The clearing around them began to shrink as the shadow beast took a step forward.

Eila closed her dream eyes, forcing herself to focus.

I'm not here. This is a dream. Nothing here is real except for Levi and Walker.

Her father's voice in her head, more disappointed than angry: *This is what happens when you don't take Crumble.*

I'm lying in a cradle. Willoughby is beside me. I could be asleep, safe in my bed. It's a dream. A dream. A dream.

Again she thought of Father, his suspicions of Eila's lies confirmed as Brampton broke the news. Brampton would of course have told Atwell exactly what his daughter had confessed — that she'd been failing to take her Crumble, and working the Blunderbuss impaired.

Atwell would have done what the Ministry required, because it would be his highest logical priority, then start deducing, perhaps getting other Enigma workers to help him. What happened when you worked the Blunderbuss without Crumble's protection? Eila had asked Brampton, and he'd fled in a panic.

The great dark thing ahead of them sat down on something titanic, its body language like a patient waiting for the doctor. She thought for an insane moment that it might cross its legs — maybe sip some impish cafei — but instead it sat and watched, patiently waiting to taste their fresh meat.

What happens when you go off Crumble, Daddy?

You lose the ability to keep order in your mind. Then the asylum comes to take you away.

What happens when you use the engine off Crumble, Daddy?

I don't know, Eila. She saw him as he'd been that day on the Enigma Floor, turning a wrench like a lowly assembler. *But I promise to find out.*

"Oh no," she felt herself say aloud. "No. No. No … "

She heard a new voice. It was Willoughby, speaking into the horn Daw used to talk to her during training.

"Eila? What is it?"

"You have to send someone. Up the tunnel. You have to help!" She felt panic creep into her voice. Her focus wavered; the clearing shimmered as if it were a projection intermittently blocked by a waving hand. She felt the dream world thrumming — in and out of focus, lit and unlit — as if someone were beating an oversized drum. The rhythm synced with her beating heart as both gathered speed. Her eyes watered, both in the dreamscape and in the machine. Eila felt the cradle around her, but that wasn't good; she was supposed to be immersed and unable to feel anything in the so-called "real world" around her. Inside the dream Fog, the great black creature seemed to lean forward, as if interested in the two approaching humans and the ghost of a girl in her nightdress. Somewhere — now sounding distant — Levi and Walker began to shout in surprise, then fear.

"What, Eila?" said Willoughby's voice, urgent. "Help *what?*"

She opened her eyes to find him standing in front of her half-there, like a double exposure. She could see the white warehouse construct, Willoughby, the cradle's edge, and the twelve-foot demon all at once. The giant dark thing was coming to its toes, goat legs flexing, ready to move when the clearing collapsed and the darkness returned. Eila felt herself panic. The worst had happened, and she had no way to filter reality from fiction.

She heard Walker shout. Then her eyes came the rest of the way open and she heard nothing at all, save the hum of the Blunderbuss clone.

"Eila!" Willoughby yelled, now furiously pulling levers and turning dials. "They're defenseless!"

But Eila couldn't think about that. She had no room in her mind for it. Where she'd been had been false, just a dream.

But the brown leather bag set down by the man at the Fog's edge — *that* had been real. Father had carried that bag to the Ministry every day for years. It was his superstitious token, bought the day his eldest daughter was born. He'd carry it until it was nothing but buckles and scraps. A strange ritual for a logical man.

"You have to send someone up the tunnel!" Eila shouted at Willoughby. "My father! My father is going into the Fog!"

Something in Willoughby's face shifted, and despite the situation's urgency he seemed to relax. "It was part of the Fog, Eila. It's not real."

"It was *outside* the Fog! I saw him! I *heard* him!"

"You're not making sense."

But she *was* making sense; there was no question. She hadn't been sure of her decision to train with Daw; she hadn't been sure of herself today at the trolley station amidst the chaos; she hadn't been sure Cora would make it home safely or if she should have stopped taking Crumble. But this was different. *This* was sharp in her mind, like a blade.

Her father was head of Enigma. He was a deducer and a problem-solver. If he hadn't already known she was lying (which he surely had), he'd known once Brampton ran upstairs to tell him. But Atwell Doyle wasn't the kind to despair and wallow when he learned about a problem; his mind immediately turned to solve it. He wouldn't cry with his head between his knees, bemoaning Eila's plight. No. He'd try to puzzle it out, to find the solution that logically had to be there. And thanks to his access to her Ministry of Manifestation's records, he'd have everything — straight from Eila's mind — that he needed to solve it.

He'd put it all together. He knew how delusional she'd been lately, and how she'd been hiding her lack of addiction. He knew, of course, how much the Fog had plagued her mind following her visit at age eleven. He'd told Eila himself that the only way to conquer your fears — the kinds of fears that a lack of Crumble would make especially vivid — was to boldly confront them.

He'd known she'd go to the Fog. So of course he'd gone there to save her.

"He's up there, Willoughby! I don't have time to argue. Just go! Just send someone!"

Willoughby tapped something on the machine, then swiveled a screen to show Eila. "This picture is coming from one of the crawlers at the top of the tunnel. See? There's nobody there."

"I see footprints!" She jabbed her finger at the screen. "There! Where the grass is trampled. He's gone in!" Helpless tears spilled from her eyes. Not only was this all going wrong; it was all her fault. Eila had lied, and now Father would pay for her deceit.

"Those could have been made by anyone."

Eila began climbing out of the machine's cradle, aware in a distant part of her mind that she was doing something both foolish and painfully selfish. But it didn't matter. It was all she had.

"Eila! You need to lie down! They're unprotected in there!"

"I'm going. I'm going up to find him."

"You are *not!* We need you!" Willoughby's voice was ringing with the same panic that Eila felt coursing inside her. "Eila! Get back in there! Think for a moment! What did you see? What was around them? You yelled out earlier; did something try to get at them? *You are all that is keeping them safe from every demon Alterra has ever dreamed! You can't just leave them to die!*"

A cold and pacifying rain spilled over Eila. Suddenly, something clicked into place.

"What does this machine do, Willoughby?"

"Eila, please!"

"What does it *really* do? You've never seen someone who can both Dream and Build, so you couldn't have made this for me. You've had it for a while. I pulled a dragonstone from the Fog while home in my bed. So why do I need to be hooked to it? Why does it matter?"

Willoughby appeared lost. She'd never seen the Tinker panic, and it seemed undignified on him. His hat was askew. His goatee looked ridiculous on a quivering lip, instead of intelligent. "The Fog is closing on them! For the love of The Crown, Eila, get back in there! They won't survive long without any protection!"

Cooly, she replied: "Then answer me quickly."

His words tumbled out in a rush. "It's no different from any cradle, okay? Except that it piggybacks atop the Aether's Blunderbuss feed. It allows a lucid Dreamer some measure of control over a projection."

"You mean it allows me to do what I can do on my own."

"Yes, but … "

"You don't need me here, Willoughby." She stood and quickly slipped on a spare pair of the big black boots. She donned a jacket for the chill, but passed the stash of weapons. If her instincts could be trusted, she could surely make her own.

Willoughby, with a glance at the screen, rushed over and took Eila by the shoulders. He wasn't nearly as tall as Walker, and Eila found she could look him in the eye nearly without tilting her head.

"Eila. Please. Just listen to me. The buffered focus you gave to that little clearing around them in your construct will run out in seconds. When it's gone, *they will die*. Do you understand me? We weren't ready for this. We know you're important, but we expected more time to figure out how to use you, how to cross the Fog to see if there's another side. We don't know, but we *do* know you're the most powerful person we have. Our men need protection, and we know that without you they don't stand a chance."

A shadow entered her peripheral vision. Eila turned to see Phoebe standing beside them. Her dark-rimmed brown eyes turned to Eila.

"I've seen your father's dreams," she said. "And I believe you."

Phoebe turned to Willoughby.

"Any lucid dreamer can hold the opening," she said. "So strap me in."

Chapter Twenty-Six
Thank the Crown

Through the door, into the tunnels, into the anteroom where the tunnels split.

Eila didn't need to wonder about the right way to go. The central tunnel, dead ahead, was wide enough for two trolley cars side by side. Despite the need to hurry, she couldn't help pausing for a moment to stare straight up its bore, focusing dead ahead, seeing how the passage was slowly expanding before her eyes.

She ran.

The tunnel seemed both short and impossibly long. She'd played games when she'd been younger, but had deferred to more dignified, more adult activities over the past few years. Still, she felt able to run without fatigue like she had as a child, her boot-clad feet smacking the fractured stone with echoes like gunshots. Her heart was hammering — now thankfully in her chest where it belonged, rather than miles away from her mind like earlier.

She wasn't tired, wasn't tired, *wasn't tired.* And still, the run through the tunnel seemed an eternity.

Less than ten minutes later, she found herself facing a thick clutch of trees. She stepped out, then looked back. The tunnel's entrance was plainly visible in what looked like an out-of-place hillside, but one that wouldn't be at all obvious to anyone not in that particular grove.

She shambled forward, feeling the vice of time. If Phoebe was right and if Willoughby had told them the truth, the Dreamer would be able to keep her foot in the Fog's door, holding it open enough for Walker and Levi to pass. But who was protecting Atwell? And what effect would Phoebe's mind have on the Fog around those she was supposed to be protecting? She might be able to prop it open, but Eila's mind showed her an image of an upturned glass shoved into a box of snakes. The inside of that glass would be protected, but the horrors plastered against its outsides, with Phoebe feeding the Fog's reality, would be terrible.

Eila exited the trees and found herself at the edge of a clearing. To the right, not far off, was the dragon's body. There were scores or possibly hundreds of workers around it, most still milling, some starting to offload heavy equipment from military skyships docked around the clearing's edge. She could see a news zeppelin far above and picked the brighter clothing of reporters from the sober attire of Parliament Guards. What were they reporting? Would they watch as crews cut the beast into pieces for transport? Were people watching from their viewboxes, bunkered in with candles and kitchen knives for protection, terrified of their own shadows? Was there rioting? Were cities burning — or had people finally retreated, having stolen what they felt they needed to survive the night?

Eila thought of the Blunderbuss and what Daw had said, about how it would never be able to keep up with tonight's terrors. The tunnels responded to what the Ministry called Pianoforte, but they'd formed a double-wide tunnel while the sun was shining. What would happen when heads were laid down to dream? Nightmares would leak. Eila could imagine her co-workers on the Build floor, reluctantly Building the terrible things that leaked through in the deluge. Somewhere in the Ministry those things would take shape and begin to roam. She could picture the Ministry like an animal with a fire in its belly, being eaten from the inside out.

Fire.

Eila came forward, approaching the Fog's sharp demarcation with steeled nerves. She had to plunge like a swimmer into cold water. Otherwise, she'd lose the urgency she had, and wallow in the self-doubt that Crumble no longer protected her from. The workers around the dragon hadn't managed to extinguish the fire — not even close. Near the beast, a second swatch of forest was being licked by the flames, tree tips black, soot wafting into the updraft. Firefighting craft were attempting to douse the flames, but they wouldn't approach the Fog, in which Eila could see fire shapes teeming like serpents.

Was she seeing the Fog's trees, aflame like the rest? Or was she seeing Phoebe's nightmare contributions to the obscene carnival — her own way of holding the clearing by making the rest of the Fog bleaker?

She stood at the Fog's border, where Atwell's footprints bent the grass. She reached out, sliding her wrist through the sharp wall of mist she remembered as a child. She'd been inside the Fog in her dreams, but this was different.

Now, she had to enter by choice.

She thought of Father, standing at the edge moments ago as she was now, Atwell knowing his daughter was inside. He'd been right — and simultaneously wrong. Now Phoebe Horn was steering the ship around them — the Dreamer whose visions were so dark and so violent that others at the Ministry of Dreaming rearranged shifts to avoid her.

Eila stepped inside and was shrouded by an angry mist.

Only once she was deep enough to have lost sight of the field behind her did Eila realize she had no clue where to go. She'd already spun several times to listen for sounds and look for sights, but the movements had only caused her to lose direction. In her vision — even that very first dream, when she had yet to create a safe bubble — the Fog hadn't been this thick.

Had that been her mind trying to protect her back then? Or was it actually worse now, thanks to Phoebe?

Something slinked by to Eila's right. It had the shape of a panther and moved like a cat. She watched it curl into a ball, then become a tall man with arms that touched the ground, and finally morph into a large bird like an eagle. The eagle shape flew to the shadow of a tree amid the pale to watch her before draining beneath the branch and hanging like a wasp's nest, its surface unsettled and shifting with lumps.

She clenched her fists and closed her eyes.

I'm in a bubble.

She opened her eyes and found that her mind had obeyed. But the resulting bubble was disturbingly literal; she was in the middle of a perfectly clear domed area that looked like a ten-foot-wide glass snow globe. She flinched at a series of thumping noises and looked up to see an entire section filling with massive black insects pressed against the border as if it actually were solid glass, their jointed limbs thrashing and mandibles clicking, seething to get inside and bite.

Where were Walker and Levi? Were they ahead? Behind? To the left or right?

There was no way to tell. The mist was almost opaque, leaving Eila with only the vaguest notion of what lay just ten feet away from her bubble's edge. She had no idea which direction led to the clearing and the dragon, versus which led into the Fog's heart. Would she even feel the flaming trees before being surrounded by them? She felt a hot moment of panic. Maybe she wouldn't. But at the same time, there was a satisfied spark inside her imagination as she pictured the insects plastered to her protective dome meeting the flames and popping like corn.

And where was her father? She'd been so sure that this was the way to find him — to rush inside the Fog and pull him out. He wouldn't come out unless she was the one to find him, because he had to see that she was safe. She'd been sure that she could part the Fog without Willoughby's machine and had been right, but she hadn't thought of how she'd find Atwell once inside.

"Father!" she shouted.

Her word held no echo; it was swallowed as if she'd shouted into a pile of velvet. A mocking sort of chuckle came back instead, as if something in the dark found Eila's plight amusing, and wanted to play with her before committing murder.

"Father!"

Father! Father! a voice mocked inside her head. *We've got him, don't you worry. Well …* parts *of him, anyway.*

Again, Eila closed her eyes. *Fear.* It was only fear. Fear meant nothing. Wasn't that what Daw had been trying to make her understand? That perceptions meant nothing? She felt herself trying to understand, still not quite grasping her lessons. She could almost see the scientist shaking his head.

But what she saw now couldn't hurt her. Alterra had dreamed the things around her, but they were not her nightmares unless she allowed them to be.

Their fears don't have to be mine.

The forest erupted in fire around her. The bubble held, but Eila could feel the searing heat, baking her like a casserole. The dark insects squealed, batting shiny legs against invisible glass as they flailed. She watched as they began to erupt, draining viscous liquid that ran down the bubble's edge. Flames rolled around the clear dome, licking as if trying to come inside. Everything became red and black shadow, the fire casting bright light that seemed scant amidst all the darkness. Eila watched a madcap carnival of horrors dance around her feet as her shadow leapt from side to side, shortening and lengthening with the shifting flames.

Carlo. The bakery.

All at once, the bubble was gone.

Instead of standing in the forest, she found herself on a white-and-black tile floor, its surface cracked from immense heat. Warmth puffed up through the soles of her black boots, and when she looked down she could see their edges beginning to melt and distort. All around her, Eila saw a parody of a baking kitchen, mixing devices and pressure machines turning black from soot and smoke. She couldn't breathe — but not just from smoke; the superheated air was oppressive, and Eila could feel it burning her insides as she inhaled. Her chest felt constricted. She wanted to drop to the white-hot tiles, but couldn't. The air would bake her, but the floor would fry her like a crepe.

There was a body on the floor beside her, its white uniform aflame. It was Carlo — the kind baker who'd sold her and her mother sweet treats before his shop had burned with him inside. Eila wanted to run, knowing what was coming, but the dead man opened his bloodshot eyes before she could flee.

"Why did you do this?" he said.

She couldn't respond. She was in too much pain, and too much horror. Flames were closing in around her. She was going to die in a kitchen, smelling an ironic aroma of burnt plaster and freshly baked bread.

"Why did you do this to me, Eila? I was good to you. I gave you pastries. You *and* your mother."

Eila didn't do it. *He'd* done it. It was his fault. Or rather, it was nobody's fault. An accident.

"Why, Eila? Why do you keep me alive in here?"

Then she saw the truth: this was *her* dream. This was *Eila's* nightmare. She had dreamed of the bakery fire before, probably again and again over the years, without even knowing it. Many nights she'd woke up uneasy, not knowing why she felt so unsettled as her subconscious mind grasped for a nightmare. But the nightmare was already gone, because it had been taken away. It had been brought here, and made real.

Daw's voice in her head, sub-audible but more real than Carlo's: *Which is real, Eila? Is it the dying baker in his fire, or is it you?*

Focus. Fists clenched. She didn't need the machine. *She was the Dreamer.*

She opened her eyes, but the bakery was still there.

Carlo crawled closer, his hands sizzling as they pawed the tiles.

Which is real? Is it Eila the coward, or Eila the courageous?

She was supposed to know that the real Eila was the one with the strength to stifle her terrors and see only good thoughts. But as she watched Carlo, his mouth still forming whys as he came closer, something cleared inside her mind. And she knew the answer.

Both. Neither.

Which is real? Daw's voice asked. *Eila the sane or Eila the insane?*

Neither. And both.

All at once, the bakery's flaming ceiling collapsed. She curled up, squatting low, some primal part of her keeping her hands and arms up and away from the sizzling tiles. She waited for plaster, iron, and wood to crush her, but after seconds of nothing she opened her eyes to find herself back in the dark woods with damp leaves underfoot.

I'm insane. I've lost my mind.

It was true. She could feel the truth with her entire being, as indisputable as the boots on her unburned feet.

"Eila?"

At first she though the voice was Carlo the baker, but of course it wasn't. It belonged to a tall man with piercing-blue eyes — eyes that, when he concentrated very hard, blurred at the edges and turned slate gray.

"Daddy?"

Atwell's face flinched, then softened. He rushed forward and clenched Eila in a bone-crushing hug. Her feet left the ground, swept just inches up but still feeling high, as if she were a little girl again. And to think she'd thought *she* was the hero.

"Thank The Crown. I was beginning to think I'd never find you."

Tears came too readily. Emotions swirled. Eila didn't know if she was crying from the joy of finding her father, weeping at fear for them both, sobbing for her lies, or because one way or another, life as she knew it was over forever.

"Oh, Daddy. I'm so sorry. I'm so sorry for all of this."

There was a terrible roar. Eila looked up to see a plume of flame in the mist and realized a dragon was coming to set them ablaze. And much closer, she saw a group of five beings standing stock still, staring at them. The things were paper white from head to foot, roughly man-shaped, with ebony eyes that were all pupils, as big around as the palms of their two-fingered hands. As she watched, all five opened their mouths in unison. Their mouths were on their necks — ochre openings crammed with teeth.

There was a distant sucking sound as tree limbs bowed, bent from their anchors as the dragon inhaled. Eila could feel the suction's tugging, and could see how Atwell's shirt fluttered toward those beckoning mouths.

"Eila," her father said, his voice strangely calm. "Build us a safe place."

"But … "

"Just do it," he said.

So she did.

Chapter Twenty-Seven

The Meaning of Blue

EILA BLINKED. THE WORLD SEEMED to change in that fractional second.

The white beings were gone. The disembodied dragon's breath was gone. It was just Eila and her father, sitting at an iron-and-glass table in two padded wrought iron chairs, cups in saucers before them as if they were having tea at a cafe. But they weren't at a cafe. They were in the precise center of the Citadel's arena, the bleachers above full of strange things that were curiously quiet, as if watching and listening, their demeanor polite.

"Strange place to choose," Father said. "Is it because you want to remember you're in the Fog, and not be fooled into thinking we've escaped?"

She looked around. There had been no conscious choice about what had just happened. He'd told Eila to act. She'd acted. Command and move to obey — nothing more.

"You know about what I can do," she said.

"Of course I know."

"*What* do you know?" She didn't want to believe it. She *couldn't* believe it.

"I'm head of Enigma, Eila. Did you really think I wouldn't put it all together when I saw your off-Crumble metrics? It's my work to solve puzzles." He looked at the cup in front of him and, with an amused chuckle, picked it up to sip. "Well. It *was* my job, anyway."

"*Was?*"

"It's not important. You can Build us protection. You can Build us a way out. We'll deal with the rest once we're out."

"Are you in trouble?"

"*You* are the one who's in trouble, Eila. Don't let the fact that you came in here to save me deceive you."

It was a strange thing to say. *He'd* come in to save *her*; *he* had, as far as she knew, found *her* in a pile on the ground in the place they'd been a few seconds ago. Who had saved whom? It was a circle, with no correct answer.

"I meant, did … "

"Not important."

"Father, did I … "

"I'm not bothered by any of that. Not as much as I'm bothered that you didn't feel you could come to me. Why didn't you think you could tell me your mind?"

Because my mind has been absent, she thought. But she answered more directly: "I didn't think you'd approve."

"Eila," he said, and she could see the effort it was taking him to keep himself calm and logical and rational, as he always was, "what does that say to you, that I wouldn't approve? I raised you to think critically. To always look before you leap. It's your mother who believes in flights of fancy — in The Crown and Jonah and superstitions she can't see or hear or touch — but you've never been like that. You don't care for Decorum; you care for reality." He knocked the table for emphasis. Around them, the audience of dark creatures leaned forward, as if riveted by their discussion. "If you'd thought out an action enough to know I wouldn't approve, why didn't you think it out the rest of the way and not do it? Did you think you knew better than me?"

A chorus of jeers erupted from the demons and specters circling the Citadel's edges, chiding her.

"It wasn't that."

"Then what was it?" He reached across the table's cool glass surface and took her hand. It wasn't a natural gesture for him, and she immediately saw his intent. If he continued, he'd end up chiding her. He wanted to understand, not lecture. She could see the reason in his eyes, and it broke her heart. He wanted to understand why his own daughter had lied, betrayed him, and broken his confidence. He wanted to know why she'd cut him so deep — how she'd managed to hurt Atwell Doyle, a man whose life marched behind logic.

"I needed to know," she said.

"To know what?"

"I needed to know what I was seeing. I was having … "

Atwell nodded. "Visions? I suspected. Remember that night at dinner, when we spoke in the study?"

"Yes."

"Why didn't you tell me, Eila? It happens — Depth Syndrome, or maybe just scattered focus. You're fifteen. I had to get special permission to get you a Build position so young. Brampton fought it, and maybe this is all my fault." He sighed, and Eila's heart ached, heavy with regret. "You're going through changes. Sometimes, in Builders … " he trailed off, shaking his head.

"It wasn't Depth Syndrome, Father. I just … "

"You had to go off Crumble to find out for sure? You *knew* I wouldn't approve. You could have talked to me. I could have helped you through it. Sometimes, Builders have errant visions. Even Enigma workers have them, but it's especially true with Aether Forefront Builders, due to the highly creative nature of their work. I don't understand, Eila. I've never given you any reason not to confide in me. I've never judged you. I've always respected your decisions as I would any adult's, and I've never invaded your privacy. So when I realized you were experimenting with your Crumble dose, I let it go and tried to show you a better way. Should I have intruded earlier? Should I have acted as an authority, as your father, and commanded you to do as I said? Would that have prevented all of this?"

She couldn't meet his eyes. All of a sudden, that felt impossible. Eila thought of all she'd done. The lying. The sneaking around. Avoiding her family and Cora; fraternizing with strange men and women with disruptive plans. Why *hadn't* she told him? He would have disapproved, but did that excuse it? She looked up when he looked away, and saw something terrible on his lean features. He was *disappointed*, not angry. That was so much worse.

Around the arena, gargoyles and nightmares began to gibber, discussing among themselves. One shouted, but Eila barely heard it. She was in the Fog, surrounded by the world's terrors, but felt only sadness.

"No, it wouldn't have prevented anything." She stared at her lap.

"How long have you been off? *Totally* off Crumble?"

"A few days. But *mostly* off for weeks. Two. Three." She sighed and shook her head, eyes still down. She was wearing telltale black boots, but otherwise her view could have placed them anywhere other than where they were.

"Oh, Eila." He took her hand again. "Oh, my darling little girl. Why did you do this?" His voice cracked. When Eila looked up, she saw tears in his eyes.

"What is it?" she said. "What's wrong?"

"What you've done could be permanent. You might not be able to reverse the damage."

A blue streak of panic. She recalled the snap she'd felt earlier, as the bakery had disappeared. There was no right answer. It didn't matter. *Sane. Insane.* She no longer cared which was true.

"What do you mean?"

"Do you still crave it? Crumble?"

Eila realized the strangest thing: her craving was gone. She no longer wanted to dose. She was a citizen of Pavilion, her mind naked and open. She was a box of loose cards, none in order. She couldn't have cared if she'd wanted to.

"No."

Despite not caring about her disordered mind, what Eila saw from Atwell disturbed her plenty. He looked like he was the one coming apart. The always-in-charge, always-with-a-plan man she'd grown up with, rattling loose at the threat of her failing mind.

"Oh, Eila."

"What?"

"We need a way out. A way to get home. Maybe a doctor can help you." Atwell looked away, his calculating mind knowing the odds were against him. "Maybe it's not too late."

"Not too late for what?"

"Once off Crumble, it can be hard to resume. It's meant to hold tight to a mind that's mostly in balance. If you no longer crave it … "

"What, Father?"

He sighed. "It might mean your mind has surrendered."

She thought of Daw, earlier, telling her about Crumble's inability to cope with the flood of dreams that was sure to follow the dragon's rampage. She thought of the snap in her mind and the way she no longer cared which answer was correct. The way she might finally pass Daw's stupid tests through a loophole, refusing to choose one object as being more real than the other. But as Eila watched Atwell, she felt his concern mingling with her respect. He was the Ministry's best Builder, and smartest man. Right now he was worried, and her certainty mattered less.

"What do you want to do?" she asked.

"Maybe they can give you a higher strength. Try to get things back in order." He looked away, stole a breath. "Try to shut the door to madness."

"Madness?"

"Look around you, Eila! I can see what you've Built for us! We're in an arena, surrounded by monsters, drinking tea. You Built the world a dragon! How is any of this normal? How is any of this *sane?* How can you possibly think that this *isn't* the road to insanity?"

The stands began to fill with boos and hissing.

"But nobody in … " She stopped, unsure if she should mention Pavilion. "There are people who don't take Crumble. Maybe it's the mind's natural state."

"The natural state is madness? Dragons and fire and death and confusion? Haven't you been confused since quitting your Crumble? Hasn't your logic grown fuzzy?"

"I seem to be adjusting. It's getting better."

Atwell looked up, blinking. "Did you really think you knew better than all of Alterra? Just *you?* Didn't it dawn on you that you were the only person out of millions who saw Crumble as bad? Eila Doyle, outthinking our entire society all by herself while the rest of us stumbled dumbly, fooled by a lie?"

Shocked, Eila said, "I … "

"Look what's happened! And look what will happen next, now that it's probably all over! I was your age once, too. I thought I could make a better home for myself than my parents, so I ran away. But do you know what, Eila? It only took one night for me to see that food wasn't free, that shelter didn't come easy, and that all I thought I'd known better was actually just the result of not knowing the whole story. But not you, right? You *knew* that I was wrong. That the

Ministry was wrong. That everyone who doses with Crumble every day is wrong. Rather than seeking help for your visions, you believed you knew better, and you knew that for you — and you alone — those visions were a *good* thing. The doctors in Joffrey Columns were wrong when they said that a mind free of Crumble is fit to join them, right? Inmates rant and rave at the moon, but it would be different for you, wouldn't it? You could do what they did, but be rewarded with an enlightened existence rather than a padded cell. *You* wouldn't lose your mind. Because the rules of life are different for you, and —"

"Father, I didn't think that … "

"That's exactly right. You didn't. You *didn't* think. Instead, you 'thought' like an Aether Forefront Builder. Like a thought artist, instead of someone with a head on her shoulders."

Eila blinked, feeling slapped. Father had never hit her before — with his hand *or* with his words.

"You don't mean that."

Creatures began to stand and jump around the arena, shocked by Eila's defiance. By her daring to speak back to her father.

"I swear, Eila. I taught you better. I taught you to think, not simply react like a child. I suppose I can blame some of your impudence on your mother, but there's a streak in you that refuses to lie quiet, like an errant lock of hair that won't obey a braid. I don't want to impose on you; I've always tried to respect you as a person, capable of thinking for yourself. But sometimes, you just can't. You could never be in Enigma. You'd fall apart. It's why I never pushed it. It's why I allowed you be in Forefront instead."

Eila felt the world go still around her. She forgot about the Fog. She forgot about Levi and Walker, out there somewhere in Phoebe's carnival of nightmares — or possibly dead. She forgot about the tunnels, Daw, the Citadel, and the creatures watching and waiting. There was only Eila and her father. Or maybe not even that.

"You always wanted me to work in Enigma," she said.

"Of course," he snapped. "You have a great mind. You could have Built engines that moved the world instead of creating comforts. You could have made clockwork armadas. Steamships. You could have made thinking engines to rival the Blunderbuss. Machines for Stensue, or for attempting to pierce the Fog. You could have made the air cleaner, the water better, the crop yields more abundant. Stronger bridges. Better homes. Instead, your talents are spent on flights of fancy like your foolhardy decision to go off Crumble. But it can be fixed, if we hurry. It can … "

"You're disappointed in me," Eila interrupted. "In my decision not to follow you, and my decision to make mental art rather than things you feel are of value. Despite the fact that *we* make engines, too, and things that help Alterra run."

"*Faster* trains. *Prettier* tube systems. But you chose delights at the expense of efficiency. And to think … "

"You're not my father."

Atwell looked up at her for a long, quiet moment, his eyes wide and aghast. Father could be compassionate and caring — but his best emotion, when used like the weapon it was, was condescension. He looked at her that way now, unable to fathom her juvenile stupidity.

"You're not my father," she repeated. She stood, then stepped closer, now standing over Atwell. "You're a dream."

"I'm a *dream?* Will you *listen* to yourself?"

"A nightmare. Something I dreamed, sorted from the stream and sent here to haunt me." Something else clicked — something she'd heard piecemeal since discovering Pavilion behind the Convenience's door. "Phoebe said she'd seen you in … "

"Oh, *Phoebe* said? The maddest of them all? She with her darkness and gloom … "

"My father doesn't know Phoebe." She put her hand on his shoulder. "And my father is proud of me, no matter what I've chosen."

"Eila," he blustered, "if you don't come back with me, and if we don't get you back on a Crumble drip *immediately*, you'll forever be —"

"You're a horror I once had, during a time when I was on the drug I'll never take again. You're my mind's dirt working upward. It would have hurt to see you one night if you hadn't been sent here instead, but I wish I had, because I've learned something, 'Father.' I've learned that our wounds make us who we're supposed to be. And I finally understand what Daw needed me to learn."

"Daw?"

Father's face was scrunched, furious. He was just another demon

— a bogeyman sent to scare her. But Eila wasn't afraid, because she finally understood.

"I see now that sometimes there is no right choice. That sometimes, it's okay to be afraid, even if what you fear isn't real." Eila met his eyes. "And I've learned that if anyone is to be truly sane, they must learn to be a little crazy."

"Eila," he blubbered. "If you don't stop this nonsense and come with me immediately, you'll … "

"It's okay that I never met you in my dreams. I've dreamed about you now." She leaned in, surer than she'd been even in her days of addiction. "Now I'm not walking around with my eyes closed, believing I can see the world with my hands." Her other hand found Atwell's opposite shoulder, their faces just inches away.

"Now," she whispered, "I know the meaning of blue."

Atwell evaporated under her hands like smoke, twirling up into the waiting Fog. The Citadel arena faded away like a developing photograph bleaching in sun. Even the Fog around her vanished, and soon she was in a bright-white space, like her Build warehouse but infinitely larger. She heard a great thrumming behind her and turned to see the great, bell-ended dream engine, its visible wheels turning, chrome and brass gears intermeshing. She could see the entire machine, top and bottom, as if the ground itself had vanished. White steam plumed from both ends, its clamor hypnotic.

Eila closed her eyes within the vision, and watched as a ratcheting arm inside her mind's clockwork caught a cam, pulled it back, and made two halves into something whole.

Build and Dream.

Dream and Build.

She opened her eyes and looked at the Blunderbuss.

And she knew how to use it.

Chapter Twenty-Eight

The Water's Edge

EILA FELT A HAND IN hers, then looked down to see that Levi had taken it.

It didn't seem to be an affectionate gesture. It was a higher kind of comfort — one human finding another in a desolate land. He was supposed to be the big, strong one, but that wasn't the case. Eila smiled. She could let him feel big and strong. There was no longer any reason to be right, or to be certain of anything.

"I've never seen anything like it," he said.

Eila looked out across the vast expanse of water, seeing how the slight wind gave white tips to the waves. The lulling sound was somehow enormous, as if there was nothing left in the world. In a way, there wasn't. But in another, the world had only begun.

"I have," said Eila. "In a dream."

Walker had strolled to the water's edge. There were shells and rocks on the sand, and he was looking at each one, curious. There were similar things around bodies of water inside Alterra, but they were poor by comparison. The water promised innumerable unknowns, and unfathomable depths.

"I smell salt." Walker touched the water lapping his boots then, with a glance and a *why-not* toss of his head, licked the wet finger. "Taste it, too. You want a drink, best head home to get one." He sighed. "Wish I'd thought to pack a water bottle."

Levi looked behind them, at the corridor Eila had cut through the Fog — as wide as the tunnel she'd taken to come topside, its walls sharp and firm. Nightmares capered at the edges, long teeth and sharp claws scratching, as if on glass. But those things couldn't hurt them now.

"I don't want to go in there again." He sighed. "Not yet anyway. I'm still dealing with a near-death experience."

Eila gave Levi the light laughter he seemed to want. They'd never really been in danger. Not once she'd seen how manifestation truly worked when so completely surrounded by her denials. Alterra's waste, strangely enough, had allowed her to Build better than she ever had on the Ministry array. Eila doubted she'd always have access to that little internal Blunderbuss, but once she'd seen it, finding the men had been simple. The Fog had cut like butter. There was no reason to think that going back would be harder, but the real question was what came next. She'd once accused Daw of not having a plan, and still didn't think he had one. Getting through the Fog, of course, had truly solved nothing. Alterra was still asleep. They were all as addicted and self-denying as she'd once been. They were all still afraid, still unequipped to handle that fear. What had Daw thought — that she'd find a way through and lead millions of people into Jonah's ocean of Heaven? It sounded like ritual suicide to Eila.

Eila smiled at Walker. "I could probably go in there and *make* you a bottle of water."

He shook his head. "Hell naw. Anything you find yonder would probably have little demon fish swimming around in it. Thanks but no thanks." He picked up a flat rock and threw it sideways at the water. The rock bounced six times before finally sinking, and she wondered for the first time if they had lakes in Pavilion. One of the millions of things she'd yet to learn … or might never know.

"What next?" Levi looked at Eila as he said it. He was older than her, and Walker had to be near thirty, but after Levi spoke they both waited for her answer. But nobody knew that answer, so they'd just move on and see what happened. There was no way to know if they'd succeeded or failed, if they'd done something good or bad. Answers were up for grabs, and that was the point. Little by little, it was what the people still inside would need to learn.

"Now we take a walk, I guess," she said.

The landscape was different than she'd seen in her dream of the dwarf and his bone-finger pipe, the memories of the departed vision now slowly returning. She didn't see the same jut of land, or the same small town. She didn't know if that had been a real place or not, but there was only one way to find out.

The beach to the right ended, folding into the Fog so that the wall of mist draped the water like a curtain. In time, maybe they'd find the courage to swim, but not yet.

"That way," she said, pointing left.

"Can't swim anyway," said Walker, looking at the water.

They walked slowly, and it only took a few minutes before Eila found herself forgetting that the white wall on their left was a place of nightmares rather than some sort of natural barrier. To the right, the ocean was endless. The light breeze blew on them, making them taste salt on the back of their throats. It was a leisurely stroll where nobody had been, looking for a place with no right to exist.

They reached a peak where beach and Fog both jutted out and then doubled back like a corner. They walked around it, climbing on slippery rocks, and managed five or six steps onto a new patch of sand before they stopped.

Levi looked up.

Walker looked up, his mouth hanging open.

And Eila looked up, suddenly finding herself facing an insanity that even her newly elasticized mind wasn't prepared for.

The beach and the Fog stretched away in front of them, continuing as it had for the first part of their stroll. A slight breeze stirred the air. Waves lapped the shoreline.

To their right, a sleek metal skyship the size of a city was floating just above the water, its breadth beyond comprehension.

Chapter Twenty-Nine
When You Start to Believe

Six Days Later

CORA SAT ON THE STOOP of 13 Rowley Row, her eyes watching the small movements of the lavender bushes lining the walkway as they riffled in the breeze. Mother had come out earlier, and Father a while later. They were both concerned, but had let her be.

Cora's parents were strangely intuitive that way, and their delicacy had almost surprised her. She'd expected them both to be overbearing, to push her to come inside and have dinner with the family. But that would have been wrong, just as not checking on her would have been wrong. She wanted assurance that someone cared, now that Eila was no longer around. But she didn't really want to talk. Not yet anyway.

Alterra had been through a lot over the previous week, and Cora's empathetic nature told her that while so many were anxious and sleepless, it would be indulgent to feel what seemed to be percolating inside her. Specifically, Cora wanted to mope, and not help her mother clean the dishes. She wanted to sit in her room, or out on the stoop. She wanted to stare at the lavender bushes, without really seeing them. She wanted to walk the neighborhood, indulging in an odd variety of hurt as she passed Eila's house in the Rose Belt. And Cora wanted to do it all without anyone worrying about her.

She would be okay. She hoped.

Cora stood as the sun inched toward the horizon, backlighting the lavender and making it somehow more beautiful. What had been purple and blue was now tinged with red, orange, slight hints of yellow. She'd never noticed it before. It had been like that a lot recently: noticing things that had always been there as if they were new. Was her week of chaos responsible? The Ministries and police had certainly scrambled to assuage the chaos felt by most people, going so far as that exposé on the military's clockwork "dragon" experiment, showing its every gear and cog. It had been a false alarm after all, but she'd known that, hadn't she? She'd even proposed it to Eila on the trolley that last day — the day the dragon machine had been found and thought real — and Eila had agreed.

Everything was okay. So why did she feel like it wasn't?

Eila. Eila was why.

Eila had been strange that last day. She'd seemed terrified yet confident, and while she'd been shoving Cora away, Cora had seen her calculating, preparing to do *something*. She'd known Eila all of their lives, and was fluent in her looks. She'd been about to do something foolish — probably arrogance in pursuit of the greater good, because Eila believed she was smart enough to know better than most. But what had she done? And where had she gone? Was she dead? Had she gotten herself thrown into Joffrey Columns, per one neighborhood rumor? Or had she run away with a boy — maybe even the mysterious Levi — per another?

Everyone had made their decisions, it seemed. Even Eila's mother seemed back to normal, nothing exposed above her thick, cool exterior. But Cora had yet to see Atwell. He, who was supposed to be the family's most logical voice and yet was a softy below the surface. Cora doubted Atwell believed any of the rumors, and might even know the truth of whatever had happened. Either way, he'd be despondent but plotting. *Planning*. Trying to solve the puzzle of Eila's disappearance all day every day, now that another neighborhood rumor said he'd been barred from the Ministry of Manifestation.

What happened to Eila?

She ran away. She was sent to the asylum.

Cora didn't know why, but she didn't believe it. She'd always thought her parents and the authorities told the truth. She'd always trusted them implicitly, but this was different. This was…

… *paranoid,* Eila's voice said inside her head. *It's a Pavilion word. It means that you think a bad thing is true when it's not.*

Pavilion. The city under the city. The mythical place Eila had told her about, during that confusing night. At the time, Cora had thought her friend was spewing crazy talk, but it had tickled the back of her brain ever since. Eila hadn't given her all the details on how to find the place, but Cora hadn't tried, because at first she'd known for a fact that the mythical "Pavilion" wasn't where Eila had gone. She'd gone to Joffrey Columns, or she'd run away.

Six days later, Cora wasn't so sure.

She stood and turned to go inside the house, wondering at the strange swell of emotion she'd felt since that day, wondering why her ponderings wouldn't lie down and be still. Twice now, she'd had nighttime thoughts of the mysterious boy — of Levi, who she'd thought she'd conjured herself. But these hadn't been thoughts; they'd been *visions*. Visions like Eila had had before she'd cracked up or run off. Visions of Levi, standing in front of Cora as if in life, beckoning, drawing her closer. Visions that were like going somewhere else, except that she never went anywhere at all.

Cora found the living room deserted, her family blessedly tucked into their own little corners for the evening. She thought about doing the same, but the lure of the strangely quiet living room was too much to resist. She didn't have to have more of these disorderly thoughts for at least a little while longer. She didn't have to go to bed yet, equally worried and excited that Levi would appear to her once her eyes were closed.

She turned on the viewbox. Prime Minister Morrison was announcing changes to parliamentary procedure. Perfect. Cora had no interest whatsoever in politics, and Morrison's voice, though nasal, always degenerated into a boring drone. She didn't need to worry about trying to sleep. The box would do it for her.

Ten minutes later, Cora was preparing to turn off the set and go to bed (it was too boring even for an evening that was begging for boredom) when the screen flickered just as she was about to stand.

She saw Eila on the screen.

Cora stood. Sat. Stood. Sat.

She wasn't asleep. This wasn't a vision . This was real. But the appearance of her friend on the box didn't excite her so much as surprise her, and so she sat on the edge of her chair, knees together, hands folded atop them, leaning slightly forward.

Was it a news story? Had they found the lost girl from Rowley

Row — daughter of Enigma Head Atwell Doyle — somewhere wandering the country? Was she being committed to Joffrey publicly rather than quietly? Had she been arrested?

For a few seconds, the image of Eila did nothing. She wasn't surrounded by police or medics, and whatever she was doing appeared to be happening live. The camera was unsteady; the sound was almost terrible. She was standing somewhere with a horrible echo, a giant wall of dials and tiny lights behind her. It was like no place Cora had ever seen or even heard of. Was Eila at the Ministry? Some sort of secret department?

Eila began to speak, peering into the camera.

"My name is Eila Doyle," she said. "Many of you won't know who I am, and most of those who don't would never care. If you search the records, you may find hints. I was declared missing four days ago, two days after the dragon was knocked from the sky at the border of the Fog near Waldron's Gate. I'm told that the Guard and police searched for two days, talked to my family, then gave up. I imagine there are rumors about me and my whereabouts, because before I disappeared, I did something that nobody seems to have ever done without being locked away. I went off Crumble, and let the wild things inside.

"Many of you are already dismissing me — and right now, I imagine there are Ministries tracking this transmission. It's fine. I won't stay long. If you want to turn off your set and walk away, to tell yourself it was all a bad dream and that everything is okay and selling yourself the same lie you've been using your entire life, I encourage you to do so. If that desire is real, then you aren't ready to hear what I'm about to say.

"But if you bristled at the word 'dream' — a kind of deep recognition like dejavoo that tells you that you may have heard it before, though you don't know where — I'd like to suggest something. You may think me crazy for doing what I did and for saying what I'm about to say, but before you dismiss me, ask yourself if you've felt something change in these past few days. Ask yourself if you're doubting what you've always taken for granted, or if you seem to see things that simply couldn't be possible. Ask yourself if you ever know things you shouldn't, as if you have stolen memories inside you. Ask yourself if you've ever had visions. If certain things around you seem brighter, or darker, or more interesting. Ask yourself if, over the week since the world was shaken by a dragon that was quickly sold as a farce, you've noticed something in the air, as if the Aether the Ministry uses to Build were accessible to you. As if those things are close, every night when you close your eyes.

"If you feel that way — and it may only be a few of you, but I know you are out there — I'd like to ask you to do something: tonight, skip your Crumble and ride out the night until morning. You will be frightened, but that's okay. Accept that you will feel like you need to gather what you've spilled lest you lose it forever. *Resist.* Hold out for one night, because you owe it to yourself to know for sure. If you don't at least open the box to peer inside, you will never know what your feelings mean."

Cora sat forward, wanting to touch the screen. On the viewbox, Eila looked to one side, then the other. Behind her, the metal wall of buttons and lights shifted, many of the lights turning green.

"If you like what you discover in the morning — if you feel that finding your lost mind is not the same thing as losing it — then stay off Crumble. Hide what you're doing, and remain hidden. If you do that, I promise that we will find you."

Again, Eila looked to the side of the screen. Someone beside her started to say something, but the broadcast cut off. The set returned to the political program as if nothing had happened.

After a long moment, Cora reached down and turned the box off.

She sat in her dark living room, shocked, then went to the window, wanting to reassure herself that the world was still there and was still real. At first, she flinched away when she saw shadows in the gutters she'd never noticed before. Then they were gone, and there were only the other houses across the Row and to each side, their living rooms suddenly alight, the shadows of agitated occupants moving frantically about as if they'd just heard something terrible.

Cora turned from the window, went to her room, and grabbed a vial filled with her own store of Crumble — the same Crumble, in fact, that she'd been trying and failing to use over the last week to quiet her thoughts of Eila, her thoughts of Levi, and her fears about the visions that were all of a sudden haunting her nights.

She walked to the bathroom, poured herself a glass of water, and emptied the contents of the vial into her hand. She stared at the pills, watching the way they rolled around in her palm, the glass of water in her other hand.

Cora looked into the mirror, peering deep into her own eyes, trying to see the soul behind them. She was looking in, but who was looking out?

She tipped the pills from her hand into the toilet, then flushed.

"Crazy," she whispered to her reflection, "is what happens when you start to believe."

Want to Know What Happens Next?

WOULD YOU LIKE TO KNOW what happens to Eila, the Guile, and all of Alterra? Be first to know when the next book in *The Dream Engine* series is coming out!
(And get plenty of freebies and FUN STUFF!)

SterlingAndStone.net/RealmAndSands

Author's Note

As I (Johnny) write this, there are well over 2 million published words out there with my name on them. And yet, right here and now, the book you're holding is my favorite out of everything I've written.

Now, that's different from saying that this is our *best* book or our *grandest* book or our *most popular* book (I'm not willing to commit either way on any of those), because *favorite* is something different. Here, today, I *like* this book best. And given the volume of work I've authored or co-authored, that's saying a lot.

To explain why, let me tell you about the creation of *The Dream Engine* — the story behind the story, as it were — in brief.

In early 2014, Sean and I (along with our third business partner, David Wright) got this bug to do something grand, and to find a writing project worthy of crowdfunding on Kickstarter. By March, Sean and I had narrowed that vague idea down to "let's write a book live, and let everyone watch!" (complete with exclamation point; Sean and I use a lot of them in real life) and Dave had run away to hide, because that notion was way too crazy for his blood.

By the time we launched that "crazy" project — something we called *Fiction Unboxed,* now a permanent fixture in our online archive — we'd expanded it and fleshed it out, making it even crazier. We decided that not only would we write a book in front of anyone who wanted to watch (posting each day's new rough-draft words immediately after they were written, recording and airing all of our story meetings, publishing every stage of the draft, and sharing all of our story-related emails and texts), but we'd also create a "story world" big enough for other writers to tell their own stories in.

Oh, and we also decided to do it in 30 days, starting from *nothing* on Day 1. That meant we'd actually begin the project *without any clue* as to what the story would be, who the characters would be, what the "world" might be like, who the ideal age group of readers would be, what genre it would fall into, or anything at all.

We could have ended up writing a dark horror tale about serial killers who breed sheep.

Or, we could have ended up writing a young adult steampunk novel about a girl who discovers a hidden world beneath her own, and can manifest objects with her mind.

Whether you're a writer or not, I hope you can appreciate just how crazy a scenario that was. *Fiction Unboxed* began on June 1st of 2014, and on that day we had a thousand people peering over our shoulders, waiting eagerly to watch us write a book, from start to publishable final version, in 30 days. We had just a month to deliver a book of around 100,000 words, fully revised and edited, with a beautiful cover, that was not only good and compelling … but which also opened a rich story world that others could write in.

And on that first day, with the 30-day clock already ticking, we had *absolutely no idea* what we were supposed to be writing.

Well, you know the ending of the story, because you're holding it in your hands. Within four days Sean had created a very rough outline for *The Dream Engine,* and within five I was able to sit down and begin writing it. At the time, the book-to-be had only the vaguest story arc and didn't even have a name. It had the working title of *Blunderbuss* because we needed *something* to call it, and in those first days the lead girl's name was "Ila Steward." (Eila had another last name before Doyle, too, but neither of us remember it.) Then, when the Blunderbuss engine actually showed up in Sean's story outline, I did a little cheer. Because that's how we always give birth to our stories: they're magical without being magical at all, and many things we use in them are just recycled elements of our own lives that we found amusing.

Why was the machine called Blunderbuss? Because it was a silly word we'd used to refer to the book before it had a name. And why is the forbidden drink called Thunderclap? Well, that's another story.

I think *The Dream Engine* is my current favorite because it was born to such adversity, yet triumphed above and beyond — not in spite of the project's limitations, but *because* of them. Sean and I both believe that fences make great art, and the notion that adversity is usually an ally rather than a foe is a common theme in our fiction. In one of my favorite novels, Frank Herbert's *Dune*, the Fremen are such amazing warriors because they've lived their whole lives in the brutal Arakeen desert, unable to even count on water as a given. That's how I feel about *The Dream Engine*: it was forced to bloom from harsh soil, and became amazing *because it had no choice.*

We wrote this book while a thousand people watched (a number that continues to grow as more people find *Fiction Unboxed* and watch the process non-live), knowing that if we screwed up, we'd look like fools. That meant we couldn't *couldn't* screw up. Like the book itself, we *had* to be amazing.

Whether you agree that our improv book is amazing or not — though I certainly hope you do; you made it this far — there's no way we could *not* feel deep affection for it. We didn't just write it *in front of* our audience of "Unboxers"; in a non-literal but very real way, we kind of wrote it *with* them. They were our cheering section. They were almost as vested in the project as we were. They watched the characters be born; they watched us tie the story in knots and hold emergency story meetings to untie them. They watched us flail in a marathon meeting at the very end, after we realized we'd slated an obnoxious "serial-style" ending for a book that was intended to be complete as the first book in a series. Reading along as we wrote, they watched as major reveals at the end of the manuscript occurred … and only *then* watched us go back and add the steps leading up to those reveals.

Our fans watched *The Dream Engine* be written backward, upside-down, and inside-out. They watched it unfold like one of the blooming roses lining Eila's home on Rowley Row, becoming the first novel in a series we absolutely can't wait to continue. On one level, it was thrilling to write a complete book in front of a live audience in 30 days, because to our knowledge it had never been done before. But on another level — a much better, much higher, much more gratifying level — it's so much more amazing to have written *a book we love* given the restrictions.

We spent 30 days in the world of Alterra, watching Eila grow and become who she was meant to be. We spent 30 days poring over the motives of Daw Blackburn and the Guile (including and especially Walker Burch, who was born behind the scenes as "Coyote Sawyer") and learning the true nature of the Blunderbuss. We spent a full month on display, with a crowd eagerly urging us on, cheering for us, marveling at the world's development and eager to lend their own voices to it in projects of their own. It wasn't just creatively exciting. It was creatively *immersive.*

Three days ago as I write this, Sean and I began work on our next project — a more literary, more adult book with the working title of *Axis*. It's amazing and gratifying to delve into that new world, given the fact that we'd put it off for *Fiction Unboxed* and *The Dream Engine*, but most of all it's *different.* Most of all, it's *quiet.* Because we're alone again, and we'll have to wait for our readers to receive that book, then hopefully to cheer again.

Just yesterday, Sean and I were arguing about a fine point in the evolution of our way of telling stories. Sean says he's grateful for *The Dream Engine* because it was a turning point, allowing *Axis* to be the first step in our next phase. But I kept fighting back, saying that he's wrong. It was *The Dream Engine* that was first in that next phase, because it taught us how to think outside the box specifically because we'd been confined *inside* a box.

Either way our argument tips, we think that you, our dear reader, are the one who wins.

We hope you enjoyed our story, and will keep in touch as Eila's journey continues.

Johnny B. Truant
(and Sean Platt)
July 4, 2014

Please Help Alterra Grow!!!

If you enjoyed this glimpse of Alterra and the world of the Blunderbuss, the best thing you can do to help it grow (and get more awesome books written) is to tell a friend — or friends — about The Dream Engine, or leave a review.

Thank you so much for supporting our work!

About the Authors

Johnny B. Truant is an author, podcaster, and co-founder of Realm & Sands who, like the Ramones, was long denied induction into the Rock and Roll Hall of Fame despite having a large cult following. He makes his online home at Sterling and Stone and is the co-author of *Unicorn Western, The Beam, Robot Proletariat, Cursed, Namaste, LOL,* and *The Dream Engine,* as well as author of *Fat Vampire* and *The Bialy Pimps.* You can connect with Johnny on Twitter at @JohnnyBTruant, and should totally send him an email at johnny@johnnybtruant.com if the mood strikes you.

Sean Platt is speaker, author, and co-founder of Realm & Sands and Collective Inkwell. At Realm & Sands Sean is co-author of *Unicorn Western, The Beam, Robot Proletariat, Cursed, Namaste, LOL,* and *The Dream Engine* with Johnny. He has also co-authored the indie hits *Yesterdays's Gone, WhiteSpace, and Available Darkness*, with David Wright at the Collective Inkwell. You can find Sean (along with Johnny and Dave) at Sterling & Stone. Follow him on Twitter at @SeanPlatt, or email him at seanmichaelplatt@gmail.com.

Johnny and Sean, along with David Wright (the guy whose curmudgeony stance on western research inspired the Unicorn Western series) host two podcasts: the horror/comedy show Better Off Undead and The Self-Publishing Podcast. Sean hosts the Indie Fiction Podcast where he reads final drafts of Sterling & Stone projects out loud before they are published. All three podcasts are available on iTunes and the other podcast directories, as well as on Stitcher Radio, and are for mature audiences only.

Thank You!

These People Helped Change the World With a Story …

A. P. Jensen, A.J. McWain, Aaro Blake, Aaron Tyrrell, Abby Weeks, Abe Cedarian, ABF, Adam Causton, Adam Di Stefano, Adam Haviaras, Adam Mackay, Adam Poe, Adam Shopis, Adrian, Adrian Faulkner, Adrian J. Mayer, Adrianne Kennedy, Afzal Mawji, AJ Lemke, Alan Carr — Copywriter, Alec Yeoman, Alex Albrinck, Alex Gairey, Alex Maven, Alex S Girard, Alexander Löffler, Alexandra Amor, Ali Cross, Alinka Rutkowska, Allan Körbes, Alyne de Winter, Alyssa Archer, Amanda L. Mitchell, Amanda Rosko, Amanda St. Germain, Amante Reale, Amber, Amy Allen, Amy Lamont, Amy T. Schubert, Anael Verdier, Anderson Crispim, Andrew "The Lava King" Hill, Andrew Couch, Andrew Griffith, Andrew Lakin, Andrew Montgomery-Hurrell, Andrew Nicolle, Andrew Norton, Andrew Perkins, Andy Bald, Andy Conway, Angel R. Suarez, Angela Bardot, Angela McConnell, Angela Williams Stillwell, Anita Soelver, Anma Natsu, Ann, Anne Samoilov, Annie Bellet, Anonymous, Anonymous Person #531, Anthony Erdmann, Anthony J Melchiorri, Anthony Kentuck, Antra Celmina, Appu Ruby, April Dawn Duncan, Archer Caldwell, Ari Lessiers, Ashley B. Coombe, Ashley Marie Callahan, August Gardiner, Autumn Anderson, Autumn Kalquist, Autumn Miller, Axie Barclay, Ayla Dawn Kane, B J Brafford, BarbF, Barry J McDonald, Barry Skelhorn, Bart Simpson, Becky Stodola, Bekkah Smith, Ben Faroe, Ben Wilson, Ben Zackheim, Beth Farrar, Beth Robins, Betsy Cameron, Betsy Horvath, Betsy Talbot, Bill Dowis,

Bill Meeks, Bill Morefield, Blaine Moore, Brad Hendricks, Brad Johnson, Brad Power, Bree Dahlia, Bregmann Roche, Brett Sobol, Brian, Brian Alex Clark & Madelyn Ember, Brian J. Jarrett, Brian Meeks, Brian Sacan, Brian Schwimmer, Brian Shea, Bruce Balsinde, Bruno, Bryan Cohen, Buddy Gott, C. Christian Scott, C. Fox, C. G. Cooper, C. R. Reaves, C. Thomas Smith, C.M. Riordan, C.S. Madison, Cache Hamilton, Calishat, Cara Tegel, CarlB from Austin, Carmen Jessee, Caro Bégin, Carol Scarr, Carol Zombo, Carolyn Armstrong Horn, Casey Dickson, Cassie Jeon, Cassie Rauk, Cate Morgan, Catherine Walker McKinney, Cathy Pelham, Cathy Stucker, Caylie Marcoe, Celeste Lau, Charlene Holsendorff, Charles Scott Link, Charmain Marie Mitchell, Cheri Baker, Cheynne Edmonston, Chip S Paschal, Chris Huddleston, Chris Lawton, Chris McCullough, Chris Scott, Chris Thompson, Chris Zydel - Wild Heart Queen, Christian Horrell, Christie Speich, Christine LaBrie, Christine Livingston, Christine Royse Niles, Christoph Hehemann, Christopher Macy, Christy Zigweid, Chuck Smith, Ciara Darren, Cindy, Cindy Powers, Clarissa Reyes, Clark Chamberlain, Claudie Muchindu, Clyde Adams III, Colin Mobey, Colin YJ Chung, Connie Myres, Conrad Thonger, Courtney B Davis, Craig A, Craig Anthony Puckett, Crissy Moss, CrowdfundingHeroes.com, Crystal Bulmahn, Crystal L Maxwell, Curt Hanson, Cyndi Rodriguez-Anthony, Cyril Vallée, D. Marie Prokop, D. Robert Pease, Dahlia West, Damon Carpenter, Damon J Courtney, Dan Harris, Dan Paradise, Dan Radke, Dan Ronquillo, Dan S Ziegler, Dane Laughlin, Daniel and Laura Martone, Daniel Fleming, Daniel Gardina, Daniel N. Gullotta, Daniel Rose, Danny Corona, Darcy Prince, Daren Bush, Darin Ramsey, Darkwing Duck, Darren Wearmouth, Dave Cornford, Dave Eberhart, Dave Higgins, Dave Konig, Dave Lockwood, Dave Lundgren, Dave Marshall, Dave Versace, David Anson, David Bain, David Bates, David Bernstein MD, David Blake, David Britland, David Bruns, David Ellis Dickerson, David Hadley, David J. Diaz, David Mark Brown, David Masters, David Peralty, David Peterson, David W, David W. Dellinger, David Wynn, Davie B, Dawn Oshima, Dayne Edmondson, Dean Dibling, Dean Evans, Dean McAtee, Debbie QVCUK Flint, Debbie Spurlock, Deborah Conner Mascot, Debra Brown, Debra Hilton, Debra Lang, Debs Nock, Dede Nesbitt

— Writer, Delia Strange, Demelza Carlton, Denise Wakeman, Denise Yoko Berndt, Derek Alan Siddoway, Derek Walker, Desiree Moodie, Diane Patterson, Director Morris, Major Secret Agency, Don Culley Hopkins, Don Iksé, Donovan Scherer, Dori Etter, Doug Johnson, Doug Peffer, Douglas Dorow, Douglas E Wright, Douglas Pierce, Dpn Hodge, D-Rock, DS Boggs, E. Toussaint, E.S. Wong, E.W. Pierce, edavis10, Eddie Schodowski, Eden Hudson, El Edwards, Elizabeth Chen, Elle Naumant, Ellie Di Julio, Ellyn Davis, Elton Jones, Emerson Hammonds, Emily Craven, Ephraim Mallery, Eric D Vincent, Eric Glaser, Eric Guindon, Eric John Kurt, Eric O'Brien, Eric Silva, Erica Converso, Erin M. Klitzke, Esly Regina Carvalho, Ph.D., Eva Hudson, F. Lewis Miller, Fan of Self Publishing Podcast, Faye Keegan, Felicia Beasley, Felicia Fredlund, Fictiongal, Flying Kraken...release the imagined!, Frances M. Thompson, Frank Carey, Franklin Kendrick, Garrett Robinson, Gary MacLeod, Gary Speer, Gary Taylor, Gary V. Vaughan, Gemma-Louise Carver, Geoff Ogle, Geoff Rip, Geoffrey Allan Plauché, George Donnelly, Gerald Davis, Gerald Hornsby, Graham Davidson, Greg Dessau, Gregory Lynn, Gregory Miranda, Gregory Roll, Gregory Wilson, H R Baker, Hal and Sarah Leonard and Family, Haley Kunkel, Harlow Quill, Heather Dixon, Heather Goldsby, Héctor Manuel Elías Oliver, Hedonist Six, Heiner Klussmann, Helen J Martin, Holiday Mathis, Honorée Corder, Horace Garry, Howard D Aitken III, Ian J Harkin, Ilona Tonnaer, Inglath Cooper, Ingrid K. V. Hardy, Ioa Petra'ka, Iris Cartecia, Iris Case, Ismarie Cintron, J H Moore, J H Sutton, J S Brown, J. Bradford Seabury, J. Christopher Walsh, J. Pepper Bryars, J. Robertson, J. T., J. Thorn, J. Welty, J.K. Pham, J.P., Jacintha Fidelis, Jack Adams, Jack Worr, Jackson Sarver, Jacquelyn Lynn, Jae McMullen, Jak Lowe, Jake Stetler, James Carlisle Holder, James Floyd Kelly, James Husum, James Johnson, James Lawton Smith, James Loscombe, James McPhillips, Jamie Maltman, Jan Gilmer, Jan Schlösser, Jane Reeves Newell, Jao Jimenez, Jared Register, Jared Shapiro, Jarkko Laine, Jarvis Taylor, Jason Coup, Jason Fuhrman, Jason Love, Jason Sharp, Jason Smith, Jay Menez, Jay Rosenkrantz, Jayden Caldarella, Jeff & Will, Jeff Couch, Jeff Fitzsimmons, Jeff Lanctot, Jeff Melvin, Jen Adams, Jen Michaels, Jenn Dize, Jenn F, Jenn Myers, Jenna Peeler, Jennifer Selzer, Jennifer Sights, Jennifer

Vail, Jenny Bowles, Jenny Lens, Jens Ívar Jóhönnuson Albertsson, Jeremiah McNichols, Jeremy Bouma, Jeremy Collier, Jeremy F Ibarra, Jeri Rivera, Jeri Smith-Ready, Jess Bertubin, Jesse T. Hart, Jessica Commins, Jessica Glendinning, Jessica Johannesen, Jessica of Gal Friday 612, Jessica Russell, Jessica Stone, Jill Goldsby, Jim Horne, Jim Lanford, Joanna Penn @thecreativepenn, Jodi Elenteny, Joe Barlow, Joe Caramanna, Joe Golden, Joel Blom, Joey Weber, Johan Dahlstrom, Johanna Rothman, John Austin, John Connelly, John Corey, John Darke, John Drinkall, John Lee Dumas of EntrepreneurOnFire, John McGuire, John Oleszkiewicz, John P, John R, John R. Bendle, John RG Young, Johnathan Blair Cox, Johnny Burke, Johnny D Starks, Jon, Jon Howard, Jonathan Adam Bailey, Jonathan Franzone, Jonathan Mundy, Jonathan Robertson, Jonny Miller, Joseph C. Farber, Joseph W. Mello, Josh Nelson, Josh S Blake, Josh Wade, Joshua Burns, Joshua Robbs, Joy Collado, JP Howle, Jude Chapman, Judith Harper, Julie M. Allen, Julie Smithey, Julie Whitley, Juliet McCormack, Justin Connolly, Justin Grit, Justin Moy, Justin Wampler, K.J. Mecklenfeld, K.L. Stevens, Kacy Kazmierczak, Kalvin Chinyere, Kamal Rai, Kara Legend, Karen Carlson, Kari Kilgore, Karla Brown, Karyn Jackson, Kate Genet, Kathryn Bryant, Kathryn Kistner, Katie Patterson, Katina Ferguson, Katrina Steen, Kay Rennie, Kayla Halleur, KB Chesnut, KC Humphries, Keith, Keith B Walters, Keith Douglas, Keith Dumble, Keith Soares, Kelly Exeter, Kelly Johns, Ken Pajala, Kendra Fleck, Kenny 'the cabbage' Norris, Keri Ruddick (Jade Belfry), Kerry Howard, Kevin D. Hendricks, Kevin Kruse, Kevin O. McLaughlin, Kevin Tumlinson, KH LeMoyne, Kim Barros, Kim Gallaway-Roberts, Kim Krug, Kim Perrine, Kimberly Black, Kimberly L. Winston-Jackson, Kimberly Shea, Kindar Ra'harashal, Kira Barker, Kortnee Bryant, Kris "MageEye" Adkinson, Kris Rippee, Krista Boivie, Kristen Healy, Kristy K. James, Kurt L. Kazmierczak, Kurt Meyers, Kyra Harrington, L M Regalla, L.B., Ladi Gbadamosi, Larry C. Herrin, Laura "V for Vixen" Roberts, Laura Hoak-Kagey, Laura Rajsic-Lanier, Lauren Hays, Lauren Loudon, Lawrence Raybon, Lee, Lee Stranahan, Lee Waverly, Leif Liberty, Leo Notenboom, Leonore Wigger, Leslie Watts, Leslye PJ Reaves, Liam Kingman, Lianne Scott, LiitTutubi, Linda Holder, Linda M. Campbell, Linda Vernon,

Lindsey Ann Fairleigh, Linton Bowers, Lisa, Lisa Buckley Hardin, Lisa Harvey, Lisa Onland, Liz Cauley, Liz Pabon, Liz Pulo, Lola Mullins, LoopyCat, Lorena Dinger, Lori R Taylor, Lorna Dounaeva, Lorna Faith, Lou Mindar, Louise, Lu and Nick Buchan, Lucas Zanenga, Lucio D'Alo, Luis Filipe Alves, Lukas Lamb, Luke Eenhoorn, Luke Lawsen Landwehr, Luke Morris, Lydia Gilman, M. E. Rehor, M.A. Brotherton, M.A. Leigh, M.E. Wynne, M.J. "Mike" Brudenell, m.r. Forbes, Maggie Harris, Malcolm Coon, Maneesh Goel, Manje Jung, Margaret Taylor, Mari Järvensivu, Maria Fiore Low, Marilyn McKay, Marion Rochelle, Mark Bottomley, Mark Dawson, Mark E Cooper Author, Mark F. Monroe, Mark G. Woodworth, Mark Hermann, Mark Leslie Lefebvre, Mark Oetjens, Mark Thompson, Mark Tucker, Mark Wrona, Marka Ormsby, Martin Greening, Martin Judd, Marty Wooten, Mary Ihla, Master Commander, Matt and Mary Bowerman, Matt Dowis, Matt Horne, Matt Leitzen, Matt Ryan, Matthew Boulay, Matthew Woodham, Maureen Tanafon, Maximilian and Dawnlyn Moline, MeiLin Miranda, Mekenzie Larsen, Mel Clark, Mel Corbett, Mel H, Melanie Saladino, Melinda Primrose, Melissa Adams, Melissa C. Banczak, Melissa Christopherson, Melissa Darnell, Melissa Lafferty, Melody Durrett, Mercy Loomis, Merlene Paynter, Mgon ♥, Michael Anonymous, Michael Cairns, Michael Coon, Michael Coorlim, Michael Day, Michael E. Sabine Jr., Michael Henry Harris, Michael Kiernan, Michael Kingswood, Michael La Ronn, Michael R. Underwood, Michael Robertson, Michael Wolek, Michael Z, Michel Baumann, Michell Prunty, Michelle Mulford, Michelle R. Osborne, Michelle Weems, Mick Gall, Mike Bergonzi, Mike Cerio, Mike Dominguez, Mike Elliott, Mike Freveletti, Mike L, Mike Nelson, Mike Sowden, Mike Stemple, Mikey Campling, Milo McLaughlin, Misha Kloet, Mitch Buchman, MK Feeney, ML Chancellor, Monica Leonelle O'Brien, Morgan Craft, mtchambers, Myka Reede, Myrna Mackenzie, Nadine Langlois, Nan Sampson, Naomi J Clark, Nathan Meunier, Nathan Sisk, Neil Mohammed, Nels Wadycki, Nicholas Brack, Nicholas Riehl, Nick Palkowski, Nicola Lane, Nicole Nally, Nicole Underhill, Nigel 'Nemesis' Hill, Nigel Sat-Nav Dad, Nik Price, Nikki Starcat Shields, Nina Morse, No, NW, Olivia Romero, Omega Orion Maverick, Oscar Arias, Owen Baillie, P Kevin Horn,

P. William Ross, P.L. Smith, P.T. Hylton, Pam Klecan, Pam Laricchia, Paris Marx, Pat Wilpenter, author, Patrice Baughman Borders, Patricia Daly Writes, Patricia Eimer, Patrick Conner, Patrick Stemp, Paul Crocker, Paul Jenny, Paul Owen, Paul S. Nowak, Paul Wolfe, Pavi Johnson, Peter, Peter B. Howell, Peter Frederick Pritchard, Peter Gray, Peter Hellerfelt, Peter Ma, Peter Monsen, Peter Trapasso, Peyam Pourbeik, Phaedra Weldon, Phat Ho, Philip Harris, Philip Yeager, Phillip Berrie, Phoebe Yerian Ezell, Pixelhead Productions, R.M. Bright, Rach, Rachael Rowe, Rachel Davis, Rachel Hore, Rafał Jacyna, Ralph Hueske, Rana K. Williamson, Ray Smith, Raye Thomas, Raymond Gardener, Rayna Cendre, Reba Lovelace, Rebecca Davis, Rebecca Ford, Rebecca Laffar-Smith, Rebecca Lavery, Reinhardt Suarez, Rena, René Tang, Renee Gordon, Rev. Deb St. Arbor, Reza Ruyan, Rhonda Lane, Ria Loader, Rich Weber, Richard Brown, Richard Grant, Richard Murray, Richard Paley, Richard Parsons, Richard Sheffield, Rick Bolton, Rick Segrest, RJ Pelton, RJ Triveri, Roanne Nagler, Rob Laman, Rob McCarthy, Rob RodenParker, Rob Steinberger, Rob Westbrook, Robbie Taylor, Robert Bucchianeri, Robert J. McCarter, Robert Scanlon, Robert W. Hegwood, Robert Williger, Roberta Loufek, Robin Gott, Rodney W. Harper, Roger "Rog42" Lawrence, Roger Blunden from Wales, Roger Emond, Roland Austin, Roland Denzel, Roland Drake, Ron Peer, Ronald Richter, Ronald Whited, Ronnie Pelletier, Roscoe Buckfucking Wild, Rosie Reast, Roy Furr, Ruby2shoes, Ryan Attard, Ryan S Phillips, Ryan Whiteside, S J Nicholson, S T Cameron, S.P. Blackmore, Sabrina & Dahlya, Saffron Bryant, Sam Reeves, Sam Witt, Samantha Hoppes, Samantha Warren, Sandra Lakin, Sandra Trbovic, Sara Meynardie, Sarah Adams, Sarah Kolb-Williams, Sarah Trumpp, Saranne Bowles, Sariah Fletcher, Scott Torrance, Sean McLellan, Sean P G, Selena Silcox, Seth H, Shana D., Shannon Clark, Shannon Quinn, Shantih, Shaquanda Dalton, Shaun M. Parker, Shaun Thomson, Shawn Hansen, Shawn Raiford, Shay Barratt, Sheenah Freitas, Sheila Ward, Shelley Buchanan, Silas P. Rafferty, Simon Boardman, Simon Cantan, Simon Donohoe, Simon Whistler, Skye Morrison, Sofia C. Otero, Sol Soloncha, SpringfieldMH, Stacey Larson, Staci Troilo, Stacy Claflin, Stefan Michael Moser, Stephanie Callahan, Stephanie Eckinger, Stephanie

Fishman, Stephanie McKibben, Stephen A. Lewis, Stephen Allan, Steve & Deborah Gomez, Steve Arensberg, Steve Becker, Steve Garriott, Steve Hanson, Steve Paulo, Steve Scott, Steve Smith, Steve Spohn, Steve Voelker, Steven Aitchison, Steven Beamish, Steven Bradley, Steven Tripp, Still Fighting, Stone Marshall, Stoneage Hermit, Stuart Brown, Stuart J Spires, Sue Black, Sue Campbell, Sue Shafer, Susan Clemens, Susan Pogorzelski, Suzanna Stinnett, Sydney Szumski, Sylvain OBEGI, Sylvie W. Farmer, T F Ehrhart, T. Paulin, T.W. Piperbrook, Tabatha Pope, Book Boost PR, Tadd Callies, Tammy Pick, Tania Dakka, Tanith Perry-Mills, Tanja Gustavsson, Tarah Benner, Taryn Hollis, Taylor A Murphy, Ted Hogeman, Ted Inver, Teresa from Bedford UK, Teri Giltner, thatraja, The Marketing & Media Monsters (Tara Jacobsen & Rebekah Welch), Thea Dee, Thea Lawson, Theodore Turner, Theresa Kay, Thomas Bennett, Thomas Dattoli, Thursday Bram, Tia Stones, Tim Gary (mindcue), Tim Lewis, Tim Moon, Tim Stout, Timothy D. Meadows, Timothy J "kboodu" Bruce, Tink Boord-Dill, Tobi Mattingly, Tom Bentley, Tom Donahue, Toni Kenyon, Tony Eddicott, Tony Hernandez, Torshi DeJarnett, Travis A Chapman, Tricia Grissom, Trina Malone, Trish Saemann, Tyler R. Parsons, Tyler Runde, Una Lin, Uncle Milky, V. Sloan, Valerie Bagwell McGreevy, Venus Newby, Vern Stevens, Vic Magary, Vito Michienzi, VPotts, W.C. Hoffman, Wade Finnegan, Waldo Wesley, Wayne Rothman, Wendy Smith, Werner, William Bushee, William J. Dennison II, William L. Wilkes III, William Salter, William Van Winkle, Wogan May, Wu-Yen Hsu, Xavier Granville, Xtopher Miller, Yes, Yuji Shimizu, Z. C. Bolger, Zac Dozier, Zachary Smith, Zack Czengöldi, Zakk @ The Mouths of Madness Podcast, Zane "True Fan" Dickens, Zella Sasnett

CPSIA information can be obtained at www.ICGtesting.com
Printed in the USA
BVOW04*1054140115

383280BV00009B/158/P

9 781629 550268